PRAISE FOR *IN T*

"Infused with . . . fresh detail . . . Between the sweetness of the relationship and the summery beach setting, romance fans will find this a warming winter read."

—*Publishers Weekly*

"Fans will love the frank honesty of her characters. [Beck's] scenery is richly detailed and the story engaging."

—*RT Book Reviews*

"[A] realistic and heartwarming story of redemption and love . . . Beck's understanding of interpersonal relationships and her flawless prose make for a believable romance and an entertaining read."

—*Booklist*

PRAISE FOR *WORTH THE WAIT*

"[A] poignant and heartwarming story of young love and redemption [that] will literally make your heart ache . . . Jamie Beck has a real talent for making the reader feel the sorrow, regret and yearning of this young character."

—*Fresh Fiction*

PRAISE FOR *WORTH THE TROUBLE*

"Beck takes readers on a journey of self-reinvention and risky investments, in love and in life . . . With strong family ties, loyalty, playful banter, and sexual tension, Beck has crafted a beautiful second-chances story."

—*Publishers Weekly* (starred review)

PRAISE FOR *SECRETLY HERS*

"In Beck's ambitious, uplifting second Sterling Canyon contemporary . . . Conflicting views and family drama lay the foundation for emotional development in this strong Colorado-set contemporary."

—*Publishers Weekly*

"Witty banter and the deepening of the characters and their relationship, along with some unexpected plot twists and a lovable supporting cast . . . will keep the reader hooked . . . A smart, fun, sexy, and very contemporary romance."

—*Kirkus Reviews*

PRAISE FOR *UNEXPECTEDLY HERS*

"Character-driven, sweet, and chock-full of interesting secondary characters."

—*Kirkus Reviews*

PRAISE FOR *WORTH THE RISK*

"An emotional read that will leave you reeling at times and hopeful at others."

—*Books & Boys Book Blog*

PRAISE FOR *BEFORE I KNEW*

"A multilayered and tightly plotted journey that's sure to tug at the heartstrings."

—*Publishers Weekly*

"A tender romance rises from the tragedy of two families—a must read!"

—Robyn Carr, #1 *New York Times* bestselling author

"Jamie Beck's deeply felt novel hits all the right notes, celebrating the power of forgiveness, the sweetness of second chances, and the heady joy of reaching for a dream. Don't miss this one!"

—Susan Wiggs, #1 *New York Times* bestselling author

"*Before I Knew* kept me totally enthralled as two compassionate, relatable characters, each in search of forgiveness and fulfillment, turn a recipe for heartache into a story of love, hope, and some really good menus!"

—Shelley Noble, *New York Times* bestselling author of *Whisper Beach*

all we knew

ALSO BY JAMIE BECK

In the Cards

The St. James Novels

Worth the Wait

Worth the Trouble

Worth the Risk

The Sterling Canyon Novels

Accidentally Hers

Secretly Hers

Unexpectedly Hers

Joyfully His

The Cabot Novels

Before I Knew

all we knew

A CABOT NOVEL

JAMIE BECK

This is a work of fiction. Names, characters, organizations, places, events, and incidents are either products of the author's imagination or are used fictitiously.

Published by Montlake Romance, Seattle

www.apub.com

ISBN-13: 9781542049030
ISBN-10: 1542049032

Cover design by Rachel Adams

Printed in the United States of America

To my husband, with love, for being a man who honors his commitments and puts his family first.

The course of true love never did run smooth.

—*William Shakespeare*

Chapter One

Certain moments in a man's life are engraved on his memory in 24-karat gold. Hunter Cabot recalled several, including his first kiss (Tina Baker) and his father's proud hug when he'd graduated from college summa cum laude. But the shiniest memory of all involved the jolt he'd felt the instant he'd laid eyes on his wife, Sara, right here in Memorial Glade on Berkeley's campus.

He'd been comparing Microeconomic Analysis notes with two classmates in the shadow of Doe—the university's massive granite neoclassical-style library—when Sara exited the building and skipped down its stairs. Unlike most harried students, her miles-wide smile had radiated something other than stress. That smile and her bouncing honey-colored hair, both warmer than the California sun, had shone like a lodestar.

Mesmerized, he'd sprung off the ground, grabbed his backpack and, without so much as a goodbye to his friends, chased her down before she could slip away. Luckily, his intensity hadn't scared her off, and she'd agreed to dinner that night. They'd been together ever since, marrying by the age of twenty-five and living that happily-ever-after dream most people see only in the movies.

Or at least he'd thought so, until recently.

Now he stood at the edge of the glade, having returned for alumni homecoming activities, hoping the faint aroma of eucalyptus and pine would trigger her memories of what they'd once been and the promise of what still could be.

"Hunter! I didn't expect to see you." Greg Maxwell approached and sat on one of the new teak benches Hunter had recently underwritten.

"I know. It's been too long since we've come to a reunion." With his finger, he traced the letters on the plaque affixed to the back of the bench that bore Sara's and his names.

Smiling, he glanced around at the other seven benches now flanking the glade. Instead of making his routine donation to his alma mater, this year he'd done something specific. Something to give Sara and him a permanent toehold on this particular ground. Not that she knew it yet. He planned to surprise her today, but Greg's unexpected presence meant he'd have to wait until later.

"Where's Sara?"

He nodded toward the library. "Pit stop."

She'd been complaining about headaches and bloating thanks to the daily course of shots and medications needed to coax her ovaries into producing more eggs.

"She still looks great." Greg crossed one loafer-clad foot over his knee and casually stretched an arm across the back of the seat. "You got lucky with that one."

"Luck's got nothing to do with it, buddy." He chuckled, although he knew he'd been damn lucky. Lucky no one else had been smart enough to scoop her up before he'd swooped in. Then again, from the start he'd known they were soul mates. No one and no thing could have come between them back then. Even with the recent tension, his faith endured.

Students were now crisscrossing the campus all around Greg and him, weighed down by backpacks and academic pressure. He wished he could tell them life got easier.

"Were we ever this young?" Greg shook his head of prematurely salt-and-pepper hair.

"Speak for yourself." Hunter patted his own trim waist in jest. Avid cycling kept him fit, and his sandy-brown hair had yet to gray. "I'm still young. Just wiser and wealthier."

Although some days he felt every second of his thirty-four years, especially lately.

"I suppose the upside of maturity is that I'm no longer invisible to women. Too bad you can't join me in playing the field." Greg glanced toward the library, raised his chin with a smile, and stood. "Here comes your wife."

Hunter turned in time to catch Sara descending the library steps. Unlike the first time he'd seen her there, her signature smile remained hidden behind a shallow grin. She'd pulled her thick hair into some kind of twist that didn't glint beneath the sun.

A cool autumn breeze tickled the back of his neck as she crossed the walkway and came to his side.

He captured her hand in his and kissed her knuckles, an intimate gesture he enjoyed. She had such soft hands, and he liked seeing his ring on her finger. "Feeling better?"

"Sure." She nodded, but he suspected she was faking it for Greg's sake. She leaned forward and pecked their old friend on the cheek. "Hey, you. Long time."

"To look at you, I'd guess no time had passed whatsoever," he replied.

Hunter knew Sara wished she were still that blithe girl, or at least that her reproductive organs were ten years younger. Still, she grinned at the compliment. "Since when did you become a flirt?"

"Better late than never. I like to practice on married women. They seem to appreciate the flattery more than others." Greg gestured toward the pathway that led to the student union, where the alumni party was taking place. "I suspect that many husbands take their wives for granted after the honeymoon."

"Savvy hypothesis," Sara teased, but didn't refute him.

"I take it back, Greg. I *did* get lucky. Luckiest guy on campus, actually." He draped his arm over Sara's shoulder as they walked along the paved pathway. He liked the feel of her against his side, her floral perfume hovering around them.

Familiar. Warm. *His.*

They entered Pauley Ballroom in the student union. Soaring ceilings and plate glass walls framed the space now crowded with alumni of all ages—a diverse group of people from around the globe. He'd been a star in high school, but amid the collective brain trust in this room, he was average. He eschewed that lame designation, but he also didn't fight battles he couldn't win.

"I need a drink. Can I get you a glass of wine?" Greg asked Sara.

"No, thanks."

"Not drinking?" Greg cocked his head, then his eyes widened, and his gaze dropped to her midsection. "Any particular reason?"

"Just my headache." Sara's nonchalance fooled Greg, but Hunter felt her tense beside him.

"Sorry." Greg then looked at him. "Beer?"

"You go ahead. We're going to make the rounds. Catch you later." He nodded goodbye to his friend before turning to Sara. "Sorry."

"At our age, it's bound to come up." She smoothed the front of her skirt, conveniently avoiding his gaze. "That's why I'd rather have gone to visit my family."

So far his plan to rekindle the spark that had thrown them together hadn't been working out as he'd hoped. Rather than concede defeat, he shifted the conversation. "Did you notice the benches outside Doe?"

"I did. A nice addition, actually."

"I'm glad you approve, because we donated them." He stared at her, hoping for her wide smile to emerge. The expansive, joyful smile that always filled him with heat and happiness.

"*We* did?" She chuckled with exasperation. "I don't recall discussing it or writing a check. Maybe I've got Alzheimer's on top of everything else."

He pulled her to him and kissed her temple, inhaling the sweet scent of her skin. "You know why I did it?"

She shook her head against his chest. He eased his hold and looked directly into those intelligent sky-blue eyes that he'd never grow tired of waking up to each day. "Because of all the good things that came from my four years at this school, *you* are the very best."

"But what's that have to do with benches . . ." Her brow furrowed. Then her face relaxed, and for the first time all day, her real smile surfaced. "You pounced on me in that glade."

"'Pounced' is an exaggeration," he defended.

She cocked a brow.

"Okay. I pounced." He tipped up her chin with two fingers and lightly kissed her mouth. "I'm not ashamed or sorry, either."

"Hunter." She hugged him, sighing deeply. "Just when I'm feeling uncertain of everything, you say something that reminds me of why I love you."

He held her tight, his own muscles relaxing upon hearing that affirmation. Things might be rocky these days, but she still loved him. He could work with that.

"Sara!" A woman's voice rang out above the din.

Hunter and Sara turned to see the gremlin, Sondra Jones, bearing down on them. He suppressed a groan, having never liked Sara's sorority sister. Sondra never said or did anything cruel or underhanded, yet he suspected her of being disingenuous and striving for one-upmanship.

Of course, Sara disagreed. She said that, even if it were true, it only meant they should take pity on her insecurities. Unlike his wife, Hunter wasn't predisposed to extending people that kind of patience.

Sara hugged Sondra, who wasn't wearing a snugly tailored outfit for a change. In fact, she looked like she'd gained a few pounds. Her big job at Google must've been cutting into her time at the gym. The only appealing thing about the woman was her rich, throaty voice—assuming one could ignore *what* she was saying.

"You're glowing, Sondra. Married life agrees with you." Sara smiled, even as Sondra held her recently bejeweled hand up to her chest, showcasing a diamond the size of a pecan.

"I'm sorry you and Hunter didn't make it to the wedding," Sondra gushed, glancing back and forth between them.

If that were true, Hunter guessed it was only because she'd wanted to show off her high-tech, high–net worth catch. He'd heard from another old friend that over four hundred guests had attended the lavish affair.

"Me too. I hear it was *quite* the event." Sara squeezed Sondra's arm. "We're happy for you both. Is Fred here? I'd love to finally meet him."

"He's running late." Sondra gazed lovingly at her sparkler before lowering both hands to her sides. "Important meetings and all that . . ."

Sara cast her friend a sympathetic look, which rubbed Hunter the wrong way. He didn't know Fred, but he *did* know that sometimes business had to take priority. It's not like he—or any other guy—*preferred* to be chained to a desk instead of being in bed with his wife. Then again, if that wife were Sondra, Hunter would regularly use work as an excuse to stay away.

"I'm sure he'll be here as soon as he can," Hunter ventured, drowning Sara's quiet sigh.

"I'll admit I don't miss the long hours now that I've cut back to part-time. Sara, I heard you left Columbia Sportswear. Can I assume we have something else in common, too?" Sondra gestured with both hands toward her abdomen. "I'm due in late March!"

No one else would've detected the stab of pain he knew had just cut through his wife or realized that the mist in her eyes wasn't happy tears for her friend.

Sara muttered something to Sondra, but Hunter didn't hear a word thanks to the angry, frustrated static in his ears. His loving, talented wife wanted a baby more than anything, and yet, for more than two years, they'd failed to make it happen.

Failed. Not a word Hunter associated with himself or her, but in this one facet of their lives, he'd been utterly powerless. He'd changed his underwear, had sex on a schedule, and thrown time and money at various treatments. Despite his efforts and the pain and suffering Sara's body had undergone, nothing had worked. The repeated disappointment had also taken its toll, particularly on his wife. This IVF was their second and, according to Sara, last chance to try.

Hunter didn't pray much, but he'd begged God to give Sara the baby she wanted. To make her the mother any kid would be lucky to have.

"So I'll be alone gaining forty pounds, getting stretch marks, and walking around with sore boobs all year?" For the first time, Sondra's throaty laugh didn't sound appealing.

He shouldn't be angry with her. Like most people, Sondra probably didn't stop to think about how a careless joke might sound to someone struggling to get pregnant. Not that she knew that about Sara and him, but shouldn't people exercise a little circumspection?

Sondra squeezed Sara's hand. "When you do get pregnant, call me, and I'll share all the tips I've learned."

Sara nodded stiffly, her composure slipping.

Hunter wrapped an arm around her waist, ready to whisk her away from this conversation. "Sondra, excuse us, but I'm actually on the hunt for Greg." Years of his mother's yammering about being polite led him to kiss Sondra on the cheek before he steered Sara out of the ballroom.

Chapter Two

Thank God Hunter had been propping her up. Sara's legs had nearly given out when Sondra announced her pregnancy. Now her knees barely supported walking.

She would not cry in the middle of the party. She would *not* be destroyed by someone else's joyful news, although deep down, jealousy howled, low and pained, like the neighbor's old malamute, Denali.

The sunlight pouring into the atrium made the space too warm, causing her already-sour stomach to curdle.

"You look a little pale, babe. Can I get you some water, or should we go outside for some fresh air?" Drawn brows framed her husband's piercing eyes, which searched her face.

Sara beat back the image of Sondra's gleeful smile. A smile that—unintentionally or not—had resembled Cersei Lannister's arrogant gloat. Closing her eyes, she chided herself for the ugly thought, having never been one to belittle others to make herself feel better. Her mom had raised her better. Boy, could she use a dose of her mom's comfort today. She should've pushed harder to visit with her family in Sacramento instead of coming to this reunion.

"No. I just need a second." She glanced over her shoulder toward the ballroom doors, thinking about how her sisters would all pat her on the shoulder and then send her back in there. "I don't want to be someone who lets another person's happy news ruin my mood. We're here. Let's go back and enjoy the party."

"There's my Sara." Hunter's face, a study in patience, grinned. She knew he'd been looking forward to this weekend. He'd even taken the day off work—something he hadn't done in almost a year.

More often than not, they'd make plans only to have him cancel because he was too busy or too tired to follow through. Rather than letting her overly hormonal body and emotions govern her mood this weekend, she'd take advantage of time together when he wasn't glued to his phone.

"Yes. Here and ready to roll." She stepped toward the doors, determined to withstand kid talk in order to laugh with her husband. She could do it. For their sake, she'd walk down memory lane with him this weekend, even if her head pounded and her needle-bruised butt hurt when seated on a folding chair for too long. "Let's go. Maybe we'll bump into Missy and Don."

"They're supposed to be here." Hunter smiled and held the door for her, but then his phone rang. He peeked at the screen and grimaced. "Bethany." He held up his hand, fingers outstretched. "I'll meet you in five minutes, I promise."

The last time Hunter kept a call with Cabot Tea Company's comptroller to five minutes was *never*.

Life with the Cabots had been very different from her childhood. Sara's parents, both schoolteachers, had been home for dinner every night. They'd spent their summers with their five kids on camping trips and coaching soccer leagues. She'd grown up in a modest home in Rocklin, outside Sacramento. They hadn't had fancy cars or clothes, and had been more than satisfied by modest dreams and ambition. If the Daly family *had* had an obsession, it was learning . . . and laughing.

She missed that slower pace and abundant warmth, especially since she'd quit her job months ago. There were lonesome afternoons, now, when she'd fantasize about what life would be like if she and Hunter lived in Sacramento instead of outside Portland. Sometimes, when she spoke with her family during their weekly calls, learning about this recital or that birthday celebration, envy would sneak up on her like a cat burglar.

When she'd moved to Portland to be with Hunter, she'd assumed they would replicate the big family she'd grown up with, but things weren't turning out that way.

Instead of two or three children, she had none. Also, she and Hunter didn't spend nearly as much time together as her parents spent with each other. And the Cabot family was a bit dysfunctional—thanks, in large part, to Hunter's hatred for his stepmother. Sara loved the Cabots, but they weren't exactly a substitute for the kind of family bond she missed.

Lately she wished Hunter didn't take so much after his dad, who'd been 1,000 percent committed to his work. Those two thought expensive gifts and surprise trips made up for the lack of day-to-day involvement. But that tired complaint wouldn't accomplish anything here in this atrium.

Sara waved Hunter off, forcing herself to smile and reenter the fray. Luckily, she ran into one of her favorite professors, Linda Wickham, a tough but fair woman with an amazing talent for distilling complex ideas into simple concepts. She'd been a young, enthusiastic educator who'd impressed and inspired Sara.

"Ms. Wickham!" Sara waved and offered a handshake. "It's me, Sara Cab—Daly. Sara Daly Cabot."

"Sara, how are you?" Ms. Wickham smiled warmly, transporting Sara back to that young college self whose future still brimmed with possibility and tantalizing unknowns.

"Great. And you? Are you still teaching?"

"Part-time. Between publishing demands and the little ones, it's been tough to juggle everything. I'm focusing on editing my upcoming book about brand building."

The professor's energy hadn't ebbed with age. Most people here would be mainly impressed by, and interested in, her publishing journey. Sara wasn't most people and would rather hear more about her personal life. "You married, then?"

"Several years ago." She glanced at Sara's left hand. "I see you did, too. It's difficult to balance work and home life, isn't it? And more than a little frustrating that it's still mostly a female problem."

Sara let the assumption pass without comment. "Of course, although currently I'm between things. I used to work for a major retailer in brand management, thanks, in part, to how much I enjoyed your class."

"You're sweet." Ms. Wickham lightly touched Sara's arm. "I'm sorry you're the victim of this tough retail economy."

Sara recoiled, horrified that her favorite professor thought she'd been let go. "Oh no. I chose to step back . . . for personal reasons."

"I hope you're not sick." A look of concern crossed the professor's pleasant face.

"Nothing like that," Sara assured her, now wishing she hadn't said anything. She couldn't remember a time when she'd had a conversation with another woman in her thirties or forties that didn't, in one way or another, lead to the topic of children.

"Well, enjoy your time off. The pressure to 'keep pace' with your peers can be high, but there's a lot more to life than one's career."

Sara knew that much. Hunter, on the other hand, didn't appear to agree. A problem he wouldn't even acknowledge. She glanced over her shoulder for some sign that he'd returned to the party. "It's so great to see you. Best of luck with your book. I'll keep an eye out for it."

"Thank you. Enjoy the weekend, Sara." Ms. Wickham nodded before strolling deeper into the crowd. The popular professor didn't get very far before another former student stopped her.

Part-time work. Perhaps that's what Sara ought to have done rather than quit. She'd been convinced that work stress had been affecting her ability to get pregnant. Six months later, she could no longer blame her former job for her childless status. Now she was bored *and* stressed.

Without thinking, her hand settled on her abdomen. *Please respond!* She pleaded with her follicles on an hourly basis. Last time she'd gone through this process, the doctor had transferred three embryos, but none had taken root in her womb. This time she prayed for a better result.

Sondra's return jarred her from her foggy thoughts. Beside Sondra stood a tall, reedy man who must have been Fred. Neither good- nor bad-looking, Fred had a kindness that shone in his warm brown eyes.

"Sara, *this* is Fred," Sondra gushed. "Fred, Sara is one of my favorite Pi Phi sisters."

"Fred, lovely to meet you. Hunter and I are sorry we weren't able to make the wedding." Sara shook his hand, smiling. She hoped her grin didn't look as sickly as she felt at that moment, as a sharp cramp wrenched her belly.

"Where's Hunter?" Sondra glanced over Sara's shoulder.

Sara had always thought Sondra had a little crush on Hunter back in school. Of course, lots of girls had. He was singularly handsome, intense, and full of energy. His confidence had made him larger-than-life and very exciting. These days his current priorities overshadowed those other traits. "Business call. He should be back soon."

"What's his business?" Fred asked.

"Cabot Tea Company. His father founded it. He's the CFO."

Fred shuddered jokingly, grimacing. "Finance."

"Fred's a tech geek, what can I say?" Sondra possessively looped her arm through his.

"And you?" Fred asked. "What's your passion?"

Passion. Something she hadn't thought about in a long time. Not with respect to a career or her marriage. For the past couple of years, she'd been on a mission, ticking off a series of boxes that included exercise, nutrition, medication, acupuncture, regulated sex, and prayers.

Before she realized what had happened, all that planning and agonizing had crowded passion right out the door. She hardly recognized herself these days. Unrealized dreams left only a weak, smoky trail where there used to be fire.

She wanted it back in the worst way, but maybe it was like toothpaste that had been squeezed out of the tube. No way to get that stuff back in there.

"I worked in marketing." The wine she couldn't drink might have made this tedious party more palatable. Another uncharitable thought. She blamed the hormone shots. One more thing standing between her and "normal."

"Sara's now a stay-at-home wife like me." Sondra smiled. "She's not pregnant. But maybe soon? Then we can go through it together!"

Fred smiled congenially. "Or maybe Sara is just happy rejuvenating the soul."

Sondra giggled, then tipped her head, brows raised in question. "Do you get bored?"

Fred's eyes widened above a grimace as he shook his head at his wife. Sara laughed aloud because that was just so, *so* Sondra.

"I'm working with my sister-in-law, Colby, at her nonprofit organization, the Maverick Foundation, while I consider my options." Sara hoped that would end the conversation. Where the hell was Hunter? Five minutes had come and gone at least fifteen minutes ago. "We're focused on issues like homelessness and battered women. It's been an eye-opener, an endless effort to fund-raise. Missy Frazer actually made a generous donation just last week."

"Fred and I would be happy to contribute," Sondra announced, as Sara had hoped she might. She recalled Sondra's competitiveness during sorority fund-raisers and suspected she wouldn't like to be outdone by Missy.

"That's wonderful, Sondra. You can donate directly through our website, if you'd like. The Maverick Foundation dot org." Judging by the rock on Sondra's finger and the way Fred seemed otherwise wrapped around it, Sara guessed Sondra would use the donation to make a statement. Hopefully, a five-figure statement.

"We'll look it up tonight." Sondra nodded and patted Fred's arm.

"Excellent. Thank you, both. Colby will be thrilled." Sara cast another glance toward the doors. "Hunter, too, whenever he returns."

"I'm sorry I missed meeting your husband. Maybe at the game tomorrow." Fred shook Sara's hand again. "Sondra, we really need to get moving. We have dinner plans in an hour, and I'd like to swing by the hotel."

"Okay." She clutched Sara in an awkward hug. "So good to see you. Hope you can make the baby shower!"

"Maybe!" Sara replied brightly, waving. *Doubtful.* Honestly, if this IVF cycle failed, she couldn't think of something she'd like to do less than attend a baby shower.

Sara had to escape before she was cornered by another person. No more questions. No more tap dancing around why she'd quit her job. No more feeling inadequate around all the other women who'd become mothers by her age.

Maybe Hunter would take her to Chez Panisse for dinner.

She strode back through the doors into the atrium and saw him in the corner, back turned, phone glued to his ear. As she drew nearer, she heard his peeved voice above the echo of her footsteps.

"I knew Jenna would pull something after I left. Thank God you're there, Bethany." As if sensing Sara's approach, he turned. "Sara and I will be back Sunday, so I'll probably stop in the office in the evening. I'll review your notes, and we can meet first thing Monday morning."

Sara cleared her throat.

"Listen, I've got to go. We'll catch up later." Hunter hit the "Off" button and stuffed his phone in his pocket. "Everything okay, babe?"

"No." Sara shook her head. "You said you'd be back in five minutes, yet there I was dealing with uncomfortable questions and speculation for twenty minutes at a party *you* wanted to attend."

"Sorry, it couldn't be helped. Jenna's pulling reports that she usually wouldn't give a shit about. Bethany overheard that Pure Foods officially opened some kind of dialogue with my dad. I can't believe this sale might really happen. It's going to take everything I've got to stop it."

Sara understood her husband's frustration. Ever since he'd been a young kid, his dad had promised Hunter that he would run Cabot Tea Company someday. He'd forgone other job opportunities and planned his career around that promise, but now his stepmother was pushing to sell the business. Still, Hunter had made a lot of money over the years, and given his stake in the company, he'd also benefit from a sale.

"If the worst thing that happens is that you get several million dollars or more from a sale, is that so terrible? You could start your own company or buy an existing one. There are lots of options that would put you in control." Unlike her, who didn't even have control of her own body. A humbling reality.

"I wish you understood how important this is to me." Disappointment edged his voice.

"And I wish *you* could look at the bigger picture. If I get pregnant, it'd be great to have you home more often." *Her* parents would've been thrilled for a payday that let them spend more time together, and with their kids. She and Hunter were young. They could take time to travel first, then he could start his own company or consult and work from home. Flexibility would enable him to be part of the day-to-day parenting. Together they'd set a foundation of love and commitment for their children and build the happy family she'd always wanted. "Doesn't the idea of spending more time with me and our child hold *any* appeal?"

He blinked, jaw slack, as if she'd spoken Farsi or some other language he didn't understand.

"I love you, and I'm happy to start a family, but I'm not about to be a stay-at-home dad." Without another word, he clasped her hand and tugged her out of the building.

"Where are we going?" She stumbled in an attempt to keep up with his long strides because he still had a tight grip on her wrist.

Hunter brought her back to the center of the glade, surrounded by the benches he'd purchased as some kind of memorial to them.

"Am I not *exactly* the same person I was the day we met?" Hunter's handsome face could look quite fierce when he got defensive. His alpine cheekbones, square jaw, and aquiline nose intimidated. Those see-through hazel eyes flashed from soft to assessing at a moment's notice. He was the only man she knew who could look that formidable while wearing glasses.

"Aside from being older?" She tugged her wrist free. On the grass, she noticed the shadows of the new benches forming a dark wall around them.

"Naturally, Sara." His arms stretched out from his sides. "I don't understand why you're so impatient with me lately. I'm the same guy who chased you down here. Who took you for pizza at Zachary's that first night and told you my dreams for the future—a plan that included growing my family's business and legacy. The same guy whose dedication to that goal has never wavered." His hands dropped. "If anyone in this relationship should be frustrated, it's me. *You're* the one who's changed. You used to have *lots* of dreams, not just one. You used to smile and laugh and want sex for something other than getting pregnant."

That last remark smarted the most. "Excuse me if I don't think ambition is the only, or most important, goal in life. If I were you, I wouldn't brag about the fact that you haven't changed at all since we graduated. Most adults evolve, Hunter."

Her husband stared at her. She'd hurt him, and she regretted it immediately. In his way, he loved her. She knew that. And yet she'd been so dazzled by him early on she hadn't seen that his first true love had been CTC. He had a connection to that company that went beyond normal ambition. Maybe because it had been where he'd bonded with his father after his parents' divorce. Or maybe it was just in his blood.

It didn't matter, really. She suspected Hunter felt most at home in his office, not with her.

He'd deny it, of course. But *she* couldn't deny the fact that she'd been growing lonelier in this marriage as the years wore on.

They stood there, sunlight fading in the late afternoon, the bells of Sather Tower playing a song, stirring up old memories. Hunter lifted his face toward the sky. He closed his eyes, listening to the music until he lowered his chin and looked at her. "You think I came here because of some Peter Pan fantasy of being twenty again?"

"Honestly, Hunter, I don't know why it was so important that we come to this homecoming."

"I did this for you." He gestured to the benches. "All of it, for you. I'd hoped being here would remind you of what we have together and get us back on track."

"I don't need grand gestures." She stepped closer, wishing her intense, beautiful man would really hear and understand her needs. She set her hands on the hard muscles of his broad chest. "I just want you to be *present*."

He stepped back and then scrubbed his hands through his hair. "I am present! I'm doing everything in my power to give you the baby you want."

"The baby *I* want?" Sara looked at the ground. He didn't even hear how that sounded, did he? He'd call it semantics, but if he wanted a family, he would've said the baby "we" want. Actually, he wouldn't have said it at all. He'd feel the same desperation she felt. He'd hurt from seeing other couples starting families, too. "And you wonder why I feel like I'm in this alone."

"I don't want to argue." Hunter closed his eyes again and breathed deeply through his nostrils. When he opened his eyes, he remained still and unsmiling. "When's your next shot due?"

"An hour."

"I'm going back to the party. I'd like you to come, but if not, I'll meet you at the hotel in time to help with your shot."

Typical Hunter, retreating when they argued. She almost wished he'd stay and fight it out, because then she'd know it mattered. Instead, he chose "space" to collect himself. Space was exactly what they didn't need, but that was *another* tired argument.

At least he'd given her the out, so she wouldn't have to suffer through more small talk or give vague answers to questions at the party.

"I'll meet you at the hotel." She turned to go, leaving him standing in the middle of the glade, knowing neither of them had won anything in that argument.

Chapter Three

Sara padded down the stairs to the kitchen, thankful for her cozy pink slippers and cashmere robe. The abundant walnut-and-limestone flooring in the house made it cool on autumn mornings, especially when fog obscured the sun. Yesterday's tense drive back from Berkeley had only enhanced the chill in their home.

Her fitful sleep left her determined to start the week off on a better note. Her mom always believed in looking at a person's intentions instead of allowing hurt feelings to fester and extend an argument. With that in mind, Sara turned on the electric teakettle, placed a few slices of bacon in the microwave, and proceeded to fix Hunter an egg sandwich. Having already returned from his morning cycling, he should be hungry after his shower.

The bacon aroma helped boost her mood. Crisp, salty, greasy goodness that went with everything from OJ to chocolate. She'd miss bacon if she got pregnant, having to eliminate nitrates from her diet for months. Maybe she should have some today just in case . . . to hold her over.

The thought prompted a smile. If she got lucky, in a few weeks she'd have to cut out all the no-no's her friends had talked about, too. Unlike them, she wouldn't complain—not even about going nine months without wine. She'd willingly give up food altogether and get nourishment through an IV if she finally got pregnant.

While sweetening Hunter's tea, she heard his footfall echoing from the hall. He hesitated in the doorway, looking much too handsome for this early hour. Although CTC was a "business casual" office, Hunter's well-tailored slacks and bespoke shirts stood out compared with everyone other than Jenna, who also took great care with her appearance. The tension in his lean body and sharp lines of his face softened when he looked at her.

"Good morning." His cautious smile signaled that he, too, wished for a truce. "What's all this?"

"A peace offering." She slid the plate along the island toward him.

He sighed and crossed to her, cupping her face. His large, warm hands made her feel delicate and protected. "I'm sorry, Sara. Barking at you hadn't been on my agenda when I'd planned the weekend. I'd hoped for us to . . . well, I'd hoped to have more fun than we did."

"I know." Her arms encircled his waist as she fitted herself against him. Although sex was not strictly prohibited at this phase, many people who'd had success with IVF discouraged it while undergoing all the procedures and tests. She and Hunter hadn't abstained the first time, and it failed, so this round she'd insisted they refrain. The lack of physical intimacy wasn't helping their relationship. "I'm sorry I've been so tense and standoffish."

He kissed her in that possessive, commanding way he did most everything. "It's okay. We're going through a lot now, and unlike you, I can't blame my moods on hormone shots."

"Let's not lay blame." She rested her head against his chest and breathed in his woodsy Azzaro Chrome cologne while he rubbed her back. "We could both be a little more patient."

"Okay." He eased away and eyed the bacon, egg, and cheese sandwich. "This looks great, thanks. I'd eat with you, but I have a meeting at eight thirty, so I'm going to have to eat it while I drive. Do you need help with a shot before I go?"

"Just the one."

"Let's get it done."

Sara retrieved a vial of progesterone oil and a pink needle from the cabinet and prepared the shot while Hunter sipped his tea and ate a bite of the breakfast she'd made. Once she'd finished preparing the shot, she handed it to him and pulled down the top of her pajama pants to reveal the grid drawn in marker on her right butt cheek.

"Babe, I hate thinking of how much these bruises must hurt." Hunter sighed while caressing her black-and-blue hip before cleaning the area with an antiseptic wipe. "Ready?"

She nodded and looked away, bracing for the prick of the needle that had to go all the way into her muscle. When it reached its target, her breath caught, and she heard Hunter mutter a curse.

"I'll be glad when this part is over." He withdrew the needle and returned it to her.

"Me too."

"I'll bet." He grinned, held up the remains of his sandwich, and kissed her cheek. "Thanks for this."

"Don't forget we have a three o'clock appointment for another ultrasound."

"I'll meet you there." He turned to go, then spun back and pulled her close, staring into her eyes. He swooped in for another kiss. "Love you."

"Love you, too." She stroked his cheek with her thumb. Something she'd probably done thousands of times since they'd met.

He kissed her palm and winked. "Have a good morning."

She watched him go, relieved that she'd extended the olive branch this morning. Now she could focus her thoughts on praying for good news from the doctor—eight or more fifteen-millimeter-size follicles on the ultrasound would be wonderful. They could celebrate if she could convince him not to return to the office after the appointment.

It'd been a long while since she'd surprised him with anything romantic. In the beginning, she'd planned many impromptu nights. They could use one now, even if it couldn't lead to sex. Emotional intimacy—reestablishing that connection—was her goal.

She'd make one of his favorite meals tonight—maybe steak kabobs with onion rings—and light candles. Perhaps she'd write out a list of her ten favorite things about him, as a gift. Adding a quick grocery run to her to-do list, Sara then went to shower and dress for the day.

◆ ◆ ◆

Sara was putting away the last of the groceries when her phone rang. "Hello?"

"Hey, Sara, sorry to bug you, but I'm wondering if you have time to check something out for the foundation," Colby said.

"Depends. I need to head up to Portland for a three o'clock appointment."

"This shouldn't take too long. If I had time, I'd do it myself. I received a grant request from the Angel House and am curious to check out one of their locations. They've got a home in Happy Valley I thought you might be able to visit."

"What's the Angel House?"

"They service homeless women and small children, many of whom are either escaping abuse or trying to overcome addiction. From what little I've read, they put them up in residential homes to give the kids a normalized environment while the moms look for work and permanent housing. Sounds much gentler than having kids end up in a large, transient shelter."

Sara glanced around her several-hundred-square-foot kitchen—outfitted in professional appliances, marble, and custom cabinetry—and beyond, to the nearly four-thousand-square-foot home she shared with Hunter. Just the two of them, rambling around this beautiful house that hugged the cliff above Lake Sandy. A privileged life—thanks to her husband—that she'd come to take for granted. One that also shielded her from seeing the plight of so many. "Of course I'll go. Text me the address."

"Thanks. And good luck with the appointment. How much longer until the retrieval?"

Sara preferred not to talk about the process, but Colby was the closest thing she had to a sister here. "Assuming things are developing on schedule, it should be any day."

"I feel very optimistic."

Sara laughed. "You've been 'very optimistic' for several weeks now, and I think it has more to do with Alec than with anything related to my fertility."

A few months ago, Colby had hired Hunter's childhood friend Alec as the head chef at her new restaurant. Not long thereafter, they'd become involved. After the difficult life Colby had had with her mentally ill first husband, who'd ultimately committed suicide, her family embraced this newfound love.

"Alec helps, no doubt." Her sister-in-law chuckled. "Trust me, though. You and Hunter will have a family. I feel it."

"I pray that you're right." Prayed every day, actually. "I'd better get moving. I'll call you later with my impressions of the Angel House."

"Great, thanks."

Within seconds, Colby sent her a text with its address and phone number. Sara called the director, Gloria Crawford, who invited her to the home for a tour. She grabbed her keys, grateful for an opportunity to be vital and productive.

Sara pulled into the driveway of an older, Dijon mustard–colored split-level home. It reminded her of the *Brady Bunch* house she'd seen on those reruns years ago. Nothing on its exterior called attention to its purpose. An outsider wouldn't think it anything more than an ordinary suburban family home. It probably had three bedrooms, maybe four if one was very tiny. She locked her car and strode up the driveway, curious to learn more.

Gloria greeted her at the door. The woman could've been her own mother—gentle eyes, silver hair, and a matronly build. She welcomed Sara with a warm smile.

"Thank you so much for coming by so soon after receiving our grant proposal. We're in such need of help these days." Gloria led Sara inside.

The home's hardwood floors extended from the tight entry into the modest kitchen and dining room. Serviceable wall-to-wall carpet covered the living room and stairs Sara assumed led to the bedrooms.

She overheard conversation coming from the upper hallway and noticed a plump woman sitting at the small desk in the living room, studying a computer screen.

Gloria must've sensed her curiosity. "That's Joan. Our residents use the computer to find jobs. Then we also prep them for the interview process. Because our facility is so small and there are so many women in need, we have a nine-month maximum residency term. Fortunately, many are able to leave before that."

"I see." When Sara had been a teen, her parents had made the family undertake service projects every summer. Working with the indigent had made her appreciate everything her family did have so that she hardly ever noticed what they lacked.

Since college, she and Hunter had never had time—or rather never made time—to give back in that same way. Hunter wrote checks. *Lots* of checks. While those were helpful, too, they didn't feed the soul.

She glanced at Joan again, who was struggling to survive each day. With winter coming, she must have been getting desperate. A place like this would offer much-needed comfort, despite the uncomfortable-looking, utilitarian furnishings. There was, however, a toy box and plastic kitchen set in the corner for kids.

The small dining room held two tables of six, and the eat-in kitchen seated another four. Although homier than a shelter, it lacked the items that make a place *home*. There were no photographs. No knickknacks. Nothing of sentimental value anywhere on the walls or tables. And probably not much laughter. Who could laugh much with such tremendous pressure bearing down?

"Let's sit in the kitchen. May I offer you coffee?" Gloria asked as Sara followed her.

"No, thank you." Sara's attention snagged at the sight of a young mother and toddler on the swing set in the backyard.

The little boy, outfitted in a too-small, ratty orange coat, must've been about two. His skin looked as rich and warm as a cup of latte, although his mother was fair enough to be of Nordic descent. She was frail—so thin and short she looked like a preteen from behind.

"Pam and Tyrell." Gloria beckoned for Sara to move away from the sliding glass doors.

"Do you strictly enforce the residency time limits with women with small children?" Sara rubbed her arms, chilled by the thought.

"We've been lucky that, in almost all cases, our residents find work or alternative placement within the stated period. I'm not sure what we'd do if a child as young as Ty were at risk for being back on the street. Let's hope we don't need to find out. A bigger question is how can women like Pam, for example, who doesn't have a family support system, get affordable, safe childcare once she finds work."

Sara blinked, her thoughts racing to how she and Hunter could be doing more to help others. How shamefully easy it was to get caught up in one's own life and turn a deaf ear to the struggles of strangers in the community.

"Well, let's see how the Maverick Foundation might be able to help." Sara took a small pad from her hobo bag, making herself a note to talk to Colby about looking into giving financial support to day-care centers for the working poor or setting up some kind of fund to underwrite those costs on an individual basis. "Tell me a little more about your needs."

"We use the bulk of donations to keep the lights and heat on, and pay for groceries and such. The local churches help out with clothing and shoe drives a few times each year. Occasionally, women from the neighborhood will drop off toys their kids have outgrown. But this year we'd like to offer a little more support for the young kids like Ty."

"How so?" Sara resisted the urge to stand and glance out the window at the beautiful little boy.

"Sadly, we're seeing more displaced single moms and kids. Many of these women have struggled with addiction, which contributes to the difficulty in keeping any kind of stable work. If we could hire extra staff to help with the kids so we could make sure these women attended support groups and got some job training, it might make a difference."

"So the funds would pay for babysitting? Can't some of the women who are staying here pitch in when they aren't on an interview or at a meeting?"

"Some of these kids born to addicts, like Ty, can be difficult or struggle with developmental delays and attachment issues. Generally, kids like him aren't easy for others to handle. Plus, the residents here have their own worries and concerns. Giving them additional responsibility isn't best."

Just then, the door slid open, and Ty toddled inside with his mother on his heels. The cold breeze had tinged his cherubic cheeks with a rosy hue. Steely-gray eyes, round as Oreos, were deeply set above a perfect button nose and pouty mouth. A living, breathing Gerber Baby.

He stopped cold when Sara smiled and waved. "Hello there. I'm Sara. What's your name?"

He stared at her, unmoved. Pam hiked him up on her hip without introducing herself or smiling, then opened the refrigerator to get some milk. "He don't talk much."

Sara chuckled. "Well, little one, that makes you like most men I know. Not big talkers, are you?"

He stared at her, eyes not blinking.

Pam wasn't nearly as interested in Sara as Sara was in Pam and Ty. In fact, Pam barely acknowledged her and didn't even say anything to Gloria. "Come on, Ty. Nap time."

Sara didn't follow them, even as something about Ty dredged up every mothering instinct she had. Once they were out of sight, she asked, "Is his lack of talking one of the developmental delays you mentioned? Can you get him help while he's here?"

"We have a contract with local social services organizations, and we call them in to evaluate whether certain kids are entitled to any state-provided disability programs."

"I see." Sara knew nothing about developmental disabilities or difficult children, and yet she couldn't stand the idea of Ty, or other children in need, going without the kind of support and intervention that could change their lives. "I'm sure the Maverick Foundation will be happy to assist you with funds earmarked for helping these children. In the meantime, I can volunteer some of my personal time to babysit or offer career counseling. Whatever you need."

That had come out of nowhere, but for the first time in a long time, Sara felt a sudden sense of purpose. A pop of the passion she'd been missing in her life.

"That's a kind offer, but we have a strict vetting process in order to protect the residents."

Sara wrote down her name, birth date, address, and phone number. "This should be enough to get a background check started. I can sign whatever waivers or other documents you might require."

"I'll be in touch, thank you." Gloria stood. "Why don't I show you the bedrooms and talk a bit more about our mission, and then you can get on with your day."

"Sure." Sara followed Gloria back to the small bedrooms, each of which had multiple beds and a crib. She barely heard Gloria's spiel because her mind kept jumping from thought to thought.

She tried to imagine having no friends or family to turn to in a crisis—frankly, imagining being in true crisis seemed impossible after spending almost fourteen years with Hunter.

How did it feel to have so few possessions that one could carry them in a bag? Would she feel safe sharing a room (and those precious few possessions) with strangers?

Distracted, she peered through the crack in the door to the bedroom where Pam and Ty were staying. Ty stood at the crib railing while his mom lay on her bed, legs dangling over the edge. Ty noticed Sara, his luminous eyes intently staring at her, almost the way Hunter's did, yet more warily. She smiled, waving a few fingers at him again.

He promptly plunked onto his little bottom and turned his head, suddenly shy or afraid. Her heart squeezed at the prospect of that little one being sent back to the streets.

"Gloria, what's the recidivism rate with the addicts? Do these women end up back here often or at other shelters? Does social services ever take the kids from them and put them into foster care?"

"We've never had anyone come back, although that doesn't mean they haven't fallen down and ended up elsewhere or on the streets. We've only called DHS if we've suspected child abuse or neglect. So far, that's been rare. Most of these women are trying to do better."

That should have comforted Sara, yet an unsettled feeling wove through her body and balled up in her stomach.

"Thank you for the tour. My offer to help out personally is sincere. In the meantime, I'll speak with our director about rushing through your grant request."

"So nice to meet you, Sara. Have a blessed day." Gloria waved her off at the front door.

Sara glanced at her watch to see how much time she had for lunch before having to drive up to Portland. On her way home, Hunter called.

"Babe." He hesitated. "I can't make the appointment this afternoon. My dad's called a meeting of the executive team to discuss whatever the hell Pure Foods proposed on Friday while we were at Berkeley."

"Can't you ask him to reschedule for tomorrow morning? If he knew why you needed the out, I'm sure he'd agree."

"That just gives Jenna more ammo and another day to work on him and others to get them on her side. She'd paint me as 'distracted' by my family obligations, which wouldn't help me convince anyone that I can take over if my dad retires."

"I really need you there, Hunter. What if I get bad news? I don't want to be alone." When he didn't immediately respond, she added, "This is our family. Isn't that at least as important as the meeting? It's not like you're voting on anything today. And even Jenna wouldn't be so insensitive to our situation as to take advantage of it."

"It's not that simple, and you know I'll never trust Jenna . . ." His sigh came through the phone. "Can't Colby or my mom go with you today?"

"Your mom isn't back from her long weekend with Rusty, and Colby's so busy she asked me to go cover a foundation meeting, so I doubt she's available."

"Gentry's always available. Maybe you could ask her."

"She's not exactly one for hand-holding." Sara thought about his baby half sister, whose favorite pastime was provoking her family. "If I get bad news, she's likely to shrug her shoulders and suggest we do shots or get a tattoo."

He chuckled, but she found no humor in the situation. He sighed. "I'm sure you won't get bad news at this stage. Every visit in this round has been very positive. I'm sorry to miss out, but it's a tricky time for me at work. Please give me a pass today."

"Fine. I'll call Gentry." She punched off the phone before he could say more. She'd give him what he wanted, but she didn't have to like it.

Her earlier determination to make this week better between them tickled her conscience, but she squashed the guilt. Why did *she* always have to bend? Why did his goals matter more than hers? She blew out a breath and refocused, then scrolled her "Favorites" for Gentry's number.

Gentry. She could be sweet and amusing when she set aside the chip on her shoulder. Chip? A boulder, really. One that kept her from getting on with her life in any meaningful or productive way. Perhaps Sara should make Gentry go with her to the Angel House so she'd appreciate her easy life more.

"Hey, Sara," Gentry answered. "What's up?"

"I need a favor."

A heartbeat passed, as if Gentry anticipated some kind of trap. "What kind of favor?"

"Hunter can't make our doctor's appointment at three, but I'd like some company in case I get bad news. Are you free?"

Another moment of silence ensued. "Let me guess. Colby and Leslie aren't available."

Although true, Sara chose to respond with a technically honest response to spare Gentry's feelings. "I didn't ask them, actually."

"Oh."

"Come on. I haven't seen you since you got back from Napa. I'll pick you up for lunch, and you can tell me all about your trip." That, at least, would be entertaining. Gentry's vacations usually involved at least one outlandish adventure.

"Okay. But we need to go someplace that serves alcohol. I'll need a drink with lunch if I'm going to be stuck with an image of your legs in stirrups for the rest of my life." While Gentry snickered, Sara wondered if this might be a mistake.

◆ ◆ ◆

"I'm so bloated and crampy. Some days I worry my ovaries will explode," Sara groaned while waiting for the doctor, lying back on the exam table.

"Fewer details, please." Gentry shuddered and wandered around the small room, fiddling with everything in reach. How she didn't topple off the stilts she called boots, Sara didn't know.

"Oh, please. I'm still trying to block out the TMI *you* shared about your exploits with 'Smith' in Napa." Sara especially wished she could unhear the specific details of Smith's *substantial* anatomy.

"What can I say? He was beautiful. I couldn't resist."

"How can you describe his 'package' in vivid detail yet not know his full name or if Smith is even any part of his real name? Hunter would kill you if he knew you spent the night with a stranger. You're almost twenty-six. Isn't it time to start using better judgment?"

"Maybe it wasn't my wisest decision, but his voice . . . his eyes." Gentry's hands flittered in the air. She made quite a picture standing there, auburn hair in wild layers, knee-high boots, and micro miniskirt with some kind of green metallic top skimming the curvy lines of her figure. "Let me have my fun before I'm too old for guys to want me."

Sara propped herself up on her elbows. "Being wanted—truly wanted—isn't about youth and beauty. Of course, there's that superficial kind of desire, but real desire sparks from who you are, what you think, and your passion for life. Those are the things that make us uniquely attractive to others, and luckily they tend to improve with age."

"Whatevs." Gentry shrugged as Dr. Barletta entered the room.

"Sara, sorry for the delay." He smiled at Gentry. "Well, hello. You're not Hunter."

"His sister, Gentry," Sara said.

Sara caught Gentry eyeing Dr. Barletta in a predatory manner as she shook his hand. Granted, the man had appealing Roman features, but Dr. Barletta was older than Sara would have thought Gentry would find appealing. Then again, maybe her sister-in-law was planning to work out her daddy issues by dating someone older. She supposed that would be preferable to the Smith situation.

Sara cleared her throat. "I'm hoping for good news."

"Me too. Blood work is perfect, so let's look at the rest." Dr. Barletta lubed up the ultrasound wand and began exploring her ovaries and uterine lining. Using a keyboard and mouse, he carefully marked off coordinates on the screen to measure each of the egg follicles.

Gentry stared at the screen with a sort of morbid fascination, which provided Sara a much-needed distraction from the significance of this appointment. Eventually, Dr. Barletta pushed back and removed his latex gloves. "Everything looks great. Eight eggs ready to go. I want to bring you back in two days for the retrieval. Schedule that on your way out."

Although grateful that Gentry had accompanied her, she wished Hunter had been here to share the moment. She felt they should experience all the little wins together and be there for these would-be children from the get-go. Warm tears filled her eyes. "Thank you, Doctor."

He smiled, probably very accustomed to teary women. "You're welcome." He then launched into detail about the preprocedure instructions. "So I'll see you on Wednesday."

Once he left them alone, Sara dabbed her eyes and sat up. Without a word, Gentry handed over Sara's clothing.

"I'm glad you got good news, Sara." Gentry's ruddy cheeks set off another wash of emotion. It wasn't often one got a peek beneath her defenses.

"Thanks for being here. It's nice to share the happy moment with someone." Sara squeezed Gentry's hands. With nine years between them, she and Gentry had never developed the sort of sisterly bond Sara shared with Colby. Hunter's poor relationship with Gentry's mother made for another easy excuse as to why they weren't closer, which wasn't fair. She would do better. Gentry deserved that from her.

"I'll step out so you can change." And then, as if needing to restore the balance of her own emotions, Gentry added, "And to avoid a second look at your human pincushion of a belly."

Sara dressed and then located her phone, which contained a text from Hunter. He'd likely be in the midst of the big meeting now, so she texted back rather than call.

Great news. Retrieval on Wednesday. Please clear your calendar.

He'd disappointed her today, but she wouldn't let it spoil her excited anticipation. The Angel House had reminded her to appreciate her blessings and the beautiful lifestyle Hunter provided. Besides, for the next few weeks, only positive karma would do.

She'd drop off Gentry and then start on dinner. A spontaneous celebration of hope that, by summer, they might finally have a child—or two or three—of their own. A grin tugged at the corners of her mouth as she imagined his delighted surprise when he came home to homemade onion rings.

Chapter Four

Hunter steeled himself for battle.

"Do you need anything else before you go in there?" Bethany asked from across his massive desk.

"No." He stood, and so did she. "I need to hear what Pure Foods is pitching before we can formulate a plan to thwart it. Thanks, though, for your diligence."

"Anything you need. I love working here, with you." Bethany slid the pro forma budget they'd been discussing into a folder. "I'd hate for CTC to be absorbed into a multinational conglomerate. What a massive cultural change that'd entail. And the downsizing . . ."

"Don't worry. I'll stop it. In the meantime, we need to keep this very quiet. There's no deal yet, so gossip in the ranks would only create problems you and I will have to deal with once I win."

"Of course." Bethany smiled. "Count on me, Hunter."

He watched her go, grateful for her loyalty. She understood him. Knew why this meant so much to him. With some chagrin, his thoughts went to Sara, who no longer had much tolerance for his ambition.

She and Gentry were probably checking in with the reproductive endocrinologist now. He was certain she'd get good news. Whether she wanted to acknowledge it, those few hours he would've lost taking her to and from the doctor had been better spent securing the future here for their kids. Still, he'd hurt his wife, and that never sat well. Quickly, he sent her a "thinking of you" text, and then he headed toward his father's office.

Unfortunately, Jenna had beaten him there, as had the head of HR, Ross Hardy, and Jim Turbot, CTC's general counsel. Hunter would have to wait until after the meeting for his father's undivided attention.

Everyone was seated at the small conference table in the corner of the large, unadorned office—a functional, unpretentious space that matched his father's personality. People liked Jed Cabot's affable air and leadership style. His friendly smile and near-folksy mannerisms had earned him loyalty and trust. He motivated his staff to work to its best ability.

Hunter didn't have that skill set. He tended toward frank, direct communication that was neither coddling nor intentionally confrontational (unless necessary, like today). He'd never needed anyone to push him to do his best. That came naturally, and he preferred to work with others who shared his drive for excellence.

That said, he'd always admired his father's rather effortless way of managing people and the business. What he didn't understand was why his father was now willing to walk away from everything they'd built.

Stomach in a rock-hard knot, Hunter nodded at everyone and then sat beside Jim and directly across from his father. He loved his dad but wouldn't make this easy for him. He didn't even feel guilty about that. As far as he was concerned, this sale idea broke every promise his father had ever made to him.

Judging from the way his dad had yet to make direct eye contact with him, *he* knew that, too. Of course, Hunter refused to look at Jenna, whom he blamed for this situation. Jenna, who'd somehow managed to get in between him and his dad throughout the years.

Looking at Jim, his dad began. "Might as well plunge ahead. I got a call from Pure Foods. It's interested in assessing the viability of acquiring CTC, assuming we're willing, and its due diligence supports its assumptions about profitability and fit."

Hunter stared at his dad without blinking, growing impatient with his refusal to look him in the eye. He'd have to force it. "Why sell?"

"Your father—" Jenna began, but Hunter held up his hand.

"I didn't ask you, Jenna." His gaze remained locked with his dad's. "I'm speaking with my father."

"It's not a done deal, son. It's just something to consider. The question isn't why sell—it's why *not* consider selling."

For a second, Hunter blanked, unable to conceive of those words coming out of his dad's mouth. Years of planning and shared dreams that had been played out in this very room flickered through his mind.

"Because this is ours. Because we can grow this company as well as any conglomerate. Better, even, because we have passion. Cabot Tea Company means something to us Cabots." Hunter paused. "Or at least it does to me, Dad."

"I appreciate your commitment." His dad gestured to the others. "The commitment of everyone here, frankly. But Pure Foods is floating a rough valuation of one point one times sales, which is one hundred forty million dollars. They'd also retain the key executives in this room."

"What about the manufacturing facilities and low-level employees?" Ross asked.

"We only had a preliminary discussion, so we haven't fleshed out all the issues and consequences. *If* we proceed, then those things will be worked out." His dad glanced at Jenna. "I can't, in good conscience, ignore this opportunity. The economy's been sluggish. I'm sixty-five and have dedicated most of my adult life to this business. I can't dismiss a chance to cash out while I'm still healthy enough to enjoy time off."

"If you want to slow down and enjoy your life, let *me* take over. You and Jenna will still receive annual dividends, so you can travel and do whatever you want. But CTC will remain a Cabot-owned business."

"You're thirty-four, Hunter," Jenna interrupted. "You're not in a position to lead this company."

Jim and Ross visibly winced, but Hunter kept his cool. Throughout the years, he'd been told of the intimidating effect of his gaze. He turned that on Jenna now and watched her shrink back in her chair. *You damn well* should *sit back.*

Decades ago, when his dad had moved out and taken up with Jenna, Hunter had worried about losing his old man to a new life. Luckily, his dad had made an extra point of reassuring Hunter that they'd remain close despite the fact that they were no longer sharing the same roof. CTC, in particular, became their "thing."

As a young kid, Hunter had trailed his dad all over this building and beyond, asking a million questions. By middle school, he'd started working here in the summer, gradually taking on more responsibility.

But once Hunter came here to work after college, things between Jenna and him had started to sour. Hunter could only assume that she'd never considered him a threat when he was young, but once he became educated and had grown up, she got jealous that she was no longer the sole person at CTC whom his dad turned to in a crisis.

"I've worked here since sixth grade. Unlike you, who's only ever worked in marketing, I know every facet of this business. I worked in manufacturing in Idaho between high school and college. Studied biology and have traveled to China, India, and Africa, and been involved with creating different blends. I run the numbers, whether we're talking payroll, capital expenditures, or marketing budgets. I know the market. I even know the employees by name. So don't *pretend* that my age prevents me from knowing how to run this business. I know the levers to pull to maximize profitable growth, and everyone at this table knows that." Hunter looked at his dad. "Don't waste Pure Foods' time or mine. If I have to start dealing with its due diligence team and answering questions, it's going to detract from my ability to do my day-to-day job."

To his credit, his dad's expression proved him to be a little bit torn. "I know you're passionate, son, but one hundred forty million dollars is a good price for this business, especially in an uncertain economy and trade environment."

"I assume they'll want a nondisclosure agreement while they investigate?" Jim Hardy interrupted, probably hoping to defuse the brewing confrontation.

"Yeah, that, and if it goes forward, they'd want some noncompetes from Hunter and me." His father met Hunter's steady gaze with a bit of trepidation.

Noncompetes? "You'd sell my birthright out from under me *and* tie my hands, too?" Hunter tossed his pencil on the table. "I can stay on at the company I helped build and take orders from some other CEO, or I get to leave but not use my expertise for however long Pure dictates?"

"Son," his dad began.

Hunter stood and rubbed one hand over his face. "Can you all excuse us? I'd like to speak with my father alone." When Jenna didn't move, he snapped, "You too, Jenna."

She looked at her husband, but at least his dad didn't argue the point. He patted his wife's hand. "I'll catch up with you later."

Once everyone filed out of the room, Hunter closed the door. He kept his back to his dad for a moment, thinking.

He drew a calming breath because he didn't want to fight, even if he was prepared to do so. "Dad, if you want to step back, step back. Stay on as chairman and keep a finger in the pot, but let me step up as CEO. You know I'm ready. No one but you knows as much about every aspect of this company as I do. Let me implement some of the ideas I've had. I *know* I can grow the business and hand it off to the next generation of Cabots. This is our legacy, Dad."

"You and Sara want to start a family. Is this the best time for you to get *more* involved in work? The price of my ambition was a broken family. Is that what you want?"

The apples-to-oranges comparison caused Hunter to sputter. "Sara and I aren't you and Mom. We're compatible."

They always had been, anyway. As soon as she had a baby, she'd stop demanding things from him that she'd never needed before. He'd have his own family that he'd provide for, love, and hand this place over to, down the road.

"Compatibility isn't the point. The more invested you are here, the less invested you are at home. No one—not even the almighty you—can be in two places at once. Think about the money. You, your sisters, and your kids would be set for life."

How could his own father not understand Hunter's motives?

"It's not about money. I've invested my heart and soul here. And even if I wanted to leave, I couldn't start my own tea or beverage company for a number of years if I'm stuck in a noncompete. Would you really expect me to be happy working for someone else at *our* company or going to work for some other company that I don't care about?"

His father laid one hand on Hunter's shoulder. "Maybe if you took a breath and looked around, you'd find some other purpose that excited you. Look at Colby. She changed careers and is happier than I've ever seen her."

"I'm happy here. I've *always been* happy here." His whole body tensed in an effort to keep his voice from booming. "This has been my dream since you promised we'd run it together. How can that mean nothing now?"

His father shook his head, voice lowering. "You're making it personal, but it's business, Hunter."

"It's not just business to me." Hunter's hands hit his chest before stretching out from his sides. "It *is* personal."

Silence settled between them. They'd probably spent thousands of hours in this room during their work together. Most of the time it had been charged with productive energy. Right now, the atmosphere seemed more like a funeral parlor.

"Let Pure Foods kick the tires and present a final offer before you get riled up. If it substantially lowers the valuation, or raises a bunch of nonsense, then this is a nonissue. If it makes a fair offer, then we all vote. Majority rules, so I can't force this, son."

"We both know Gentry will vote with you and Jenna. She doesn't have a shred of ambition, so she'll happily take the money."

His dad bristled at Hunter's criticism of his baby. "That's up to her, I suppose. I don't particularly care for your tone, though. She's your sister."

"Just because she's my sister doesn't mean I have to respect the fact that she's twenty-five and still hasn't finished college or taken anything seriously." Despite having spent his whole life proving himself to his dad, his dad had adored Gentry best since the day she drew her first breath.

"She's taken an interest in the PR work she's doing for Colby. She's coming around."

Hunter zipped his lip. He didn't dislike his sister; he just didn't understand her at all. And, he supposed if he were being totally honest, some part of him couldn't quite separate Gentry from her mother. He hated Jenna, and Hunter didn't use the word "hate" lightly. Gentry resembled Jenna physically and had a tendency toward sarcasm that matched her mother's.

"Sorry if I'm not overly impressed with Gentry's efforts. Meanwhile, I've done *everything* you've ever asked and more. I would've hoped that meant something to you. Instead, you're ready to walk away from it, and from your promise to me, just like you walked away from Mom, Colby, and me all those years ago. If you're so determined to start another new chapter in your life, I wish you'd toss Jenna, too."

His father's eyes widened, unprepared for that personal attack. Frankly, Hunter hadn't planned the barb. It had slipped out *almost* subconsciously.

"I understand your disappointment, but don't talk about my wife that way."

"Yes, let's be careful with Jenna's and Gentry's feelings. Clearly theirs take priority over mine." He shook his head. "The only thing worse than you breaking your promise to me is the fact that you don't even seem to give a shit."

Hunter turned and stormed out of the office without giving his dad a chance to respond.

Anger sparked throughout his body, seeking release. In his mind, he was tossing staplers and turning over desks as he strode down the corridor to his office. Slamming his door closed helped only a little.

He picked up the phone and called Bethany. "Hey, come to my office, please. We need to put our heads together and map out a preliminary plan to defend against a sale while I work out a plan B. It might be a late night."

◆ ◆ ◆

Hunter pulled into his driveway at eight thirty. Between missing the appointment and coming home late, he knew he'd screwed up big-time. From the passenger seat, he lifted the bouquet of yellow-and-red gerbera daisies he'd bought at the local grocer. They'd hardly be enough to assuage Sara, but he hadn't had time to plan something better. Gearing up for a dressing-down, he entered the dimly lit house through the mudroom and headed toward the kitchen.

"Sara?"

The scent of french-fried onions hung in the air, making his stomach growl. Only the light under the stove hood shone, casting a dim yellow glow across the gleaming marble counters. Everything had been cleaned and put away. He wandered down the hallway and noticed the dining room table made up. Two empty plates, burned-down candles, fancy napkins.

She'd planned a surprise with one of his favorite meals, and he'd not only no-showed but hadn't even called to warn her he'd be late. It wasn't the first time he'd gotten so caught up at work that he'd lost track of time. Suddenly, he felt about one foot tall.

He climbed the stairs two at a time and approached the master suite. Soft music emanated from within. He pictured her inside the sumptuous space she'd decorated in rich cream, blue, and gray fabrics. Maybe she'd be soaking in the tub or brushing out her hair or lying on the bed thumbing through a magazine.

When he entered the room, he found his wife curled up on the chaise beneath a blue-and-gray blanket and a circle of lamplight, reading a book. If he'd been on solid footing with her, he'd swoop in and join her or whisk her into bed. Even *he* knew neither of those options would fly at the moment.

"Sorry I missed dinner. Smells delicious." He presented her with the bouquet and kissed her cheek. "I'm happy about our good news."

"I wrapped your plate and set it in the refrigerator." Her gaze went back to her book, dismissing him.

He deserved that, he supposed. Twice today she'd gone to the effort of preparing his favorite meals, and had obviously hoped to celebrate the upcoming egg retrieval with him tonight. From her perspective—anyone's perspective—all he'd done was abandon her.

Hunter sat on the edge of the gray velvet chaise and stroked her thigh. "I'm sorry. I should've been with you today. My meeting was a waste of breath. My dad won't—"

"I'm about as interested in the ins and outs of that meeting as you were in showing up for the doctor's appointment . . . or for dinner."

Ouch. Then again, who could blame her?

He dropped his chin. "I'm sorry. Honestly, I am. I never mean to hurt you, babe. It's just horrible timing. I'm torn between two essential things right now."

Sara set her book in her lap. "I know. The problem is that it seems like when push comes to shove, CTC always takes priority."

"It doesn't. I swear."

"So you say, but your actions prove otherwise."

"Come downstairs while I reheat dinner, and tell me exactly what the doctor had to say. And I'm sure you've got at least one good Gentry story." He smiled and tugged at her hand, hoping to coax her into giving him a reprieve.

She squeezed his hand but then withdrew. "You hurt me today, but I still planned a celebration for us. I know you didn't know that part, but I'd wanted it to be a surprise. Lesson learned, especially since you didn't call to say you'd be late." She ran her finger down the spine of her book. "I'm not trying to punish you, but I don't feel like pretending everything is fine just to make *you* feel better tonight. Sorry. I'd rather relax and keep reading than force conversation."

Hunter nodded. Sara had always been calm and honest with him. He couldn't begrudge her those feelings, and maybe stilted conversation wasn't the best idea, anyway. "Okay. I'll put these in water. Maybe we can talk a little later."

"Thank you."

He cupped the back of her head and kissed her forehead. "Enjoy the book."

Hunter padded back downstairs and arranged the flowers in the crystal vase he'd bought her for their third anniversary—when life had been perfect. Sara had received a promotion that year, and they'd celebrated with a weekend trip to Seattle. Back then, they'd routinely shared ideas and office politics. Sex without a thought to procreation had been as easy as breathing, and nearly as frequent. And they'd laughed often.

Those things all happened less frequently these days. He missed it, and her, but had no idea how to get it all back.

Setting the flowers on the kitchen island, he then reheated his dinner in the microwave. He stood there watching the plate spin, each rotation strangely stirring his sense of uneasiness. He loved his wife and he loved CTC. He planned to fight for them both, but if Vegas was taking bets, odds might be against him on both fronts.

Chapter Five

Sara let out a long, deep breath as she waited twenty-five minutes in absolute stillness following the embryo transfer.

Hunter brought her hand to his lips. "Babe, the extraction went great on Wednesday, and we've just transferred three perfect embryos. Try to relax and have faith."

She wished she could be brave. Unfortunately, his kind of confidence about the future eluded her—a particular insecurity that had been reinforced every twenty-eight days (and many failed pregnancy tests) throughout the past two years. She'd stopped sharing her grief every time her period came because, instead of comforting her, he'd always made "Don't worry" remarks. Maybe he meant them to be reassuring, but to her they felt dismissive.

At the moment, it also didn't help that she'd had to endure a full bladder and catheter this morning to implant the eggs. A quick glance at the clock told her it'd be another ten minutes before she could move, get dressed, and go home.

No one but another woman in her shoes could ever comprehend what it felt like to be a human science experiment. To pop pills, take shots, insert suppositories, and closely monitor one's behavior week after week. But all of it would be worth it if, two weeks from now, she'd get the news she'd been praying for.

"Sara, look at me." Hunter waited for her to focus on his face instead of her spinning thoughts. "Whatever happens, I love you. We're in this together, and if this doesn't work out the way we want, you are enough for me. More than enough."

Lovely, loving words, yet when unmatched by his daily actions, they didn't ring quite true. Nor did they diminish her suspicion that her failure to give him biological kids would disappoint him more than he let on. After all, part of his obsession with CTC was the idea of it being a family legacy to pass down generation to generation.

His confidence might not yet allow for the possibility that he wouldn't have heirs. But if that became their reality, would she *really* be enough for him? How could that be true when she barely held his attention most days? And, aside from all that, it wouldn't lessen her own disappointment that, unlike her sisters and friends, she wouldn't be adding to the family tree.

"Let's not jinx this by talking about what happens if it fails." She rubbed her chest as if that might ease the heartburn her mental gymnastics had caused.

He grinned. "Again with the superstitions."

"Yes! Please. Only positive energy and positive thoughts for the next few weeks. When we get home, I'm going straight to bed, legs elevated, and not moving unless absolutely necessary."

Hunter's eyes darkened with desire even though she didn't feel the least bit attractive and hadn't in quite some time. "How long until we're allowed to finally have sex again?"

Not easy for a man with Hunter's sex drive. Hers used to match his, but recently it had gone into hiding. The emotional distance between them hadn't helped. She missed sex in a vague sort of way but couldn't rouse herself to do much about it.

"Can't come soon enough." He leaned in, touching his nose to hers, and closed his eyes, whispering, "I miss my wife."

He could be so adorably handsome and tender when he left the office behind. Too bad that happened so rarely. "I miss you, too."

He'd been talking about sex, though, so she doubted he got her meaning.

The doctor came in, gave them instructions, and wished them well. During the ride home, Sara panicked with each and every bump in the road. Never before had the town roads seemed like rutted backwoods byways. When Hunter took a corner too fast, she shot him a look. "Slow down! If we crash, it could ruin everything."

"Sorry." He dutifully eased off the gas pedal. "I'll get takeout for dinner. What do you want?"

"Something from A Certain Tea." Colby's restaurant had been open only a few months now, but its funky take on haute cuisine had caught on. Sara's preference for Alec's food revolved around the fact that it was locally grown and mostly organic, too.

"Those portions leave me starving within thirty minutes," Hunter grumbled.

"Then order double, or get yourself a pizza. I want healthy, organic food, but nothing on my no-go list."

"What's that?"

"The list of things I shouldn't eat if I'm pregnant." She *knew* he'd been paying only half attention when she'd talked about it the other week. "I've printed it out at home."

"I have a bad feeling that, from now on, my only good meals will be when Colby meets me for a burger at Gab-n-Eat." Hunter's phone rang, so he hit the hands-free button on his steering wheel. "Hello?"

"Hunter, it's Bethany. I've pulled those market reports you asked for."

He fell silent. Although she couldn't see his eyes because he was staring at the road, she knew he was dying to delve into a major discussion about CTC. Without glancing at Sara, he said, "E-mail them to me. I won't be returning today, so I'll take a look from home."

"Oh?" Bethany paused, probably shocked into silence. Sara was, too, but she didn't react for fear of him changing his mind. "Is there anything else I can do for you today?"

"I'll call you if I need something."

"Okay, have a good afternoon."

Sara heard disappointment in Bethany's voice. She remembered being an employee, eager to please the boss. Recalled the thrill of working on special projects, of contributing to something exciting.

But Sara had heard something else in Bethany's voice, too. A personal kind of disappointment from a woman who wanted to spend time with the man, not the boss. As far as Sara knew, Bethany had never done anything overt. Still, intuition—and Jed and Jenna's history—warned her to pay attention to that woman's "dedication" to Hunter.

As they pulled into the garage, Sara asked, "Does Bethany have a personal life?"

Hunter killed the engine, shrugging. "No idea."

After they exited the car, Sara walked into the house as if attempting to cross glass in her bare feet. She wouldn't risk moving too quickly, tripping, or doing anything else that might "jar" her uterus. "How can you have worked with her for five years and have no idea about her personal life?"

Hunter hung the keys on the key rack in the mudroom, brows drawn. "Why would I? We're not friends. She works for me. We talk about work."

Sara patted his cheek, secretly relieved by his obliviousness to Bethany, who was, in fact, quite an attractive, if slightly older, woman. "Oh, honey, you really have a one-track mind."

In this one instance, it was a good thing for their marriage.

"It gets the job done." They started toward the stairs together until he playfully scooped her into his arms and carried her up to their room. "I have a surprise for you."

"Oh?"

He gently settled her on the bed and quickly fluffed a bunch of pillows for her behind her back and under her legs. He then went to his nightstand and withdrew a jewelry box.

He sat beside her and handed her the gift. "I had this made because, no matter what happens, you'll always be my everything."

Heart melt. These sentimental moments, however fleeting, kept her fighting for their marriage instead of giving up.

"I didn't get you anything." She grimaced, turning the box over in her hands, feeling comparatively thoughtless for a change.

"Why would you? I didn't suffer everything you did to get to this point. My body is needle- and bruise-free."

Really, though, she suspected he was most concerned with the wounds to her heart. Her eyes got misty while she opened the package to find a silver heart-shaped pendant necklace engraved with the date March 3, 2004. It took her a second to register the date—the day they first met. Over the lump in her throat, she said, "It's beautiful." She leaned up to kiss him. "People would be shocked to know about your sentimental streak."

An uncharacteristically shy grin surfaced. "Turn it over."

She flipped it over in her palm to find latitude and longitude coordinates: 45.423965° N, 122.680543° W. "What are these?"

"Home." He kissed her.

"Really? Our exact coordinates?" Her eyes widened.

"So you'll never lose your way back to me."

She threw her arms around his neck and kissed his face a few times. "Sometimes you take my breath away."

"I try." He brushed some of her hair from her face and kissed her mouth before taking the necklace from her and fastening it around her neck.

She sat amid the pillows, fingering her new bauble. "Thank you for this. It's perfect."

He had no idea how badly she'd needed some sign from him that she and their life together mattered that much.

"You're welcome." When her stomach growled a reply, he laughed. "So what can I bring you for lunch?"

"Can we see what kind of soup Alec made today?"

"Sure. Where's the list of no-goes?" He smirked as he covered her with the throw from the chaise.

"On my kitchen desk. Maybe we could eat up here—a picnic in bed."

His eyes flashed with a naughty light—and, surprisingly, it sparked that long-dormant soft and fluttery feeling back to life. "I'd rather snack on you, but I guess Alec's food will have to do for a while longer. I'll order something and go pick it up. Be back soon."

He kissed the tip of her nose, handed her the remote, and then left her, whistling. He hadn't whistled in a long while, and the sound made her entire body smile. She nestled deeper into the pillows and rubbed her belly. *I'm praying all three of you make it. Your daddy and I can't wait to welcome you and start our family.*

The picnic idea reminded her of the night Hunter had proposed. He'd filled her apartment with candles, planned a picnic on the floor, and played the third movement of Rachmaninov's Symphony no. 2 during the big moment. Those early years had been filled with intimate evenings when they'd talked and kissed and laughed. When they'd found each other to be endlessly fascinating, each conversation another thrilling exploration. The good ol' days before he'd forget to close the bathroom door when he peed, she thought wryly.

A few minutes of mindless TV channel surfing later, the doorbell rang. A delivery? Girl Scout? Didn't matter. Unless the house caught fire, she had no plans to leave her bed, let alone climb the stairs again. Then it rang a second time. A stray worry threaded through her thoughts—was someone testing to see if anyone was home before attempting a break-in?

She started when the house phone rang. "Hello?"

"Sara, honey, it's me," Hunter's mom, Leslie, said. "Why aren't you answering the door?"

"I'm supposed to rest for a few days, so I'm not doing anything that isn't necessary."

"Can I let myself in? I brought you a little something. I promise I won't overstay my welcome."

"That's sweet." Sara smiled, trying to imagine what Leslie might've brought. Something unusual, no doubt. "Come on in. I'm upstairs."

Sara hung up the phone and lowered the television volume. Leslie entered the room with quick strides, carrying a lilac-colored gift bag tied with raffia. Like Hunter, his mom's bright eyes reflected intensity, although hers had a more playful energy. Sara had never seen anyone's aura, but given Leslie's radiance, she imagined it to be orange or sunny yellow. She was a naturally pretty woman whose spry step made her appear a decade younger than her sixty years.

Leslie set the bag on the nightstand and then captured Sara in a warm hug. "How do you feel?"

"Pretty good. A little sore." Sara shrugged. "Nervous."

Leslie stroked Sara's head in a mothering fashion, which Sara appreciated considering how infrequently she got to visit with her own mother. She missed her family—her sisters—and envied the fact that a few of them still lived within ten miles of one another.

"Set aside those nerves. Worrying never helps anyone with anything." Leslie stopped suddenly and glanced around, forehead creased in frustration. "Where's my son? He should be here with you."

"He went to pick up some dinner."

"Oh, good. I might've had to kill him if he went back to the office." Leslie raised a playful fist in the air, her eyes twinkling with mischief. "Now, don't you want to know what's in the bag?"

"Yes, but I also want to hear about your trip with Rusty." Sara began untying the raffia. She retrieved a small green plant from inside the bag. "Bamboo?"

"Bamboo plants bring good luck to the recipient. And, according to feng shui, if you put it in the east side of the room, it improves your chi." Leslie swiped the small plant from Sara's grasp and wandered around the room. "Which way is east?"

Sara pointed toward the bathroom door. "That way, I think."

Leslie wrinkled her nose, searching for a flat surface on which she might place the vase. Unfortunately, there weren't any because the chaise consumed most of that side of the room. "Hmmm . . . maybe I'll just put it on the floor for now."

"That's very thoughtful of you. Thanks." Sara couldn't help but smile at their shared superstitious nature. "Let's hope it helps."

Leslie sat on the edge of the mattress and patted Sara's hand. Her mother-in-law's eyes glittered with hope and yearning, even as her gaze dropped to Sara's abdomen. Of everyone in Hunter's family, only his mother shared Sara's desperate yearning for life to take root. For more family. "You're welcome, sweetie."

Determined not to focus all her thoughts or conversation on pregnancy, Sara teased, "Now, give me the scoop about your first-ever getaway with Rusty. Good, bad, or indifferent? No fibs involved, I hope?"

Some may have considered that a ridiculous question, but Leslie had fabricated a dead dog named Snickers to woo the last man she dated, so one never knew.

"No fibs. At least none that should matter." She tucked a bit of the blanket around Sara the way one might do to a small child.

"Uh-oh. What's that mean?"

"Well, you know how it is with men. Their egos are so fragile. You can't ever be *totally* honest." Leslie's eyes twinkled above a conspiratorial grin. "I might've exaggerated a bit about how much I loved the Universal Studios tour. You know. Things like that."

"So you didn't enjoy it?"

"I liked it fine, but there are other things I'd rather do in Los Angeles. Hiking in Malibu would've been more my speed." Then her eyes widened with interest as she leaned closer. "And I read about the California Institute of Abnormalarts. Sounded wild and weird, which is right up my alley."

Hunter had told childhood stories about the "field trips" he and Colby had taken with his mother. He'd acted put out, but Sara knew him well enough to know that, in some ways, he'd been as intrigued as his mother by the oddities.

"Why didn't you tell Rusty? Maybe he'd have liked that, too."

"He'd planned the whole weekend, and I didn't want to seem ungrateful or steal his thunder. Besides, we made it fun enough. Maybe next time I'll plan something . . . like a two-day yoga retreat."

Sara frowned. "He doesn't look like a guy who does yoga."

"Exactly! He needs a little exercise." She patted Sara's thigh. "He'll feel so much better once he gets into it."

Sara giggled. "How nice of you to be looking out for his health."

"I try, dear. I really try," Leslie said sincerely, totally missing that it was a joke.

"Hello, Mom." Hunter entered the room, carrying a tray loaded with their dinners.

"You don't look surprised to see me." Leslie rose from the bed.

"Your car is in my driveway." Hunter set the tray on the bench at the end of the bed and kissed his mother hello.

His mom peered at the meals and sighed. "No chocolate?"

"Not allowed, nor were half the things on the menu." Hunter chuckled.

"Really?" Sara leaned forward to see what he'd brought. *Green soup?*

"No raw, smoked, or high-mercury seafood; no custard, hollandaise, or other sauces with raw egg; no soft cheeses, pâté, or caffeine," he read from his phone. "Like I said, at least half the items on the menu were out."

"So what's that soup?" Sara eyed the vivid liquid, which was sprinkled with purple flowers and almonds.

"White gazpacho, and then there's some kind of Dijon chicken dish I can't pronounce and vegetables."

"Thank you." Sara motioned with her hands. "I'm ready."

"I'll leave you two alone." Leslie slung her purse over her shoulder. "Can I come tomorrow to help out? I can do laundry, fix your meals, whatever."

"Thanks, Mom. That'd be great," Hunter answered. "I'll feel better if Sara has some company while I'm at work."

"I'd love it, Leslie." Sara *would* like company for part of the day but hid her disappointment that Hunter wasn't planning to take another day off to be with her until she was cleared for more activity. "How about if I call you midmorning?"

"Okay. I'll see if I can find something tasty for lunch that doesn't break all those rules. Pregnancy was much easier back in my day, and you kids all turned out fine."

"Some might argue that point," Hunter muttered.

"Then some would be wrong." Leslie kissed them both goodbye and let herself out of the house.

◆ ◆ ◆

Hunter hoped Sara couldn't tell that he was a little preoccupied with his conversations with Bethany on his way to and from the restaurant. He'd need to do a little work tonight if at all possible, although Sara might kill him if he brought his laptop up here. He was banking on her being drowsy and falling asleep early. He'd work in bed so he'd be there if she woke and needed anything.

Better to wait awhile before bringing that up. "How's the soup?"

The necklace he'd given her lay against her breastbone, reflecting light. For a brief moment, his thoughts settled.

"Amazing, of course." She smiled and sipped more from her spoon. "Thanks for getting all of this. The Dijon smells fantastic."

"Will it bum you out if I order a meat lover's pizza for myself?" He grimaced.

"Just a little," she teased. "The thing that makes me most jealous is that your bad eating habits haven't caught up to you yet."

As if she didn't look more beautiful to him with each passing year. Wiser. Kinder. More a part of him than anyone else in his life. Still, given the gravity of the day's events, a little levity would help. "So you're saying I still look good?"

"You know you do. You keep getting better with age." She shook her head. "It's disgusting."

He preened, prolonging the joke. "If it's any consolation, I'm all yours."

She snorted, almost losing half the soup through her nose. "Lucky me."

"No." He handed her a napkin. "Lucky me."

Laughter felt damn good. Life had been so heavy lately he'd started to envy his sister and Alec's new relationship. Despite its rocky start, they were experiencing all those early relationship firsts and flutters. Each day allowed for the fascinating exploration of each other's likes and dislikes, passions and fears, ambitions and desires. No one had yet nagged about picking up socks or working late or missing a trip to the in-laws in California because of a production-plant crisis.

Hunter had never been particularly wise about love. In fact, the only thing he knew with certainty was that loving someone didn't always make living with them a cakewalk.

While Sara was as much a part of him as his own body, and he meant every word he'd said when he'd given her that pendant, he couldn't pretend he didn't miss the sizzle of excitement he used to feel anytime he heard her voice.

They'd forgotten how to be spontaneous. How to woo each other. He'd done some good wooing in this room, he thought wryly as his gaze wandered the peaceful space. Then he noticed a weird little plant on the floor. "Sara . . . I have a question."

"You sound odd. What is it?"

"That's the question, actually. What is that?" Hunter pointed at the branchy plant abandoned on the bedroom floor.

"Bamboo. Your mom says it brings good luck."

He nestled into the pillows beside his wife. "I'm sure I'll regret this next question, but why is it on the floor instead of on a dresser?"

"It needs to be in the eastern part of the room."

"It's only good luck if it's in that spot?" His mother's kooky ideas never ceased to amaze him.

"No, that part's not about luck. The east is the best spot for improving the room's chi." Sara chewed her chicken, shrugging. "Feng shui."

"Let me guess. Given your superstitions about the pregnancy, that plant stays there for the next nine months."

"You got it."

"Okay, then. I'll make sure not to accidentally kick it over in the middle of the night."

"*Please* be careful." Her expression turned more somber. "I meant what I said before. This is my last IVF. I can't go through the protocol and disappointment again. To come so close and lose a *third* time would break me. So I don't want anything ruining this chance at making us a happy family."

He watched her chew an enormous mouthful of food. She'd put her heart and body through so much in her quest to re-create the kind of family life she'd left in California. Not even Jenna frustrated him more than his inability to give Sara what she needed. "I'll be careful."

His mouth turned dry when he made room for the possibility of another negative pregnancy test. He'd researched surrogacy and adoption, but every single option had its own set of risks and pitfalls. To date, Sara hadn't been ready to pursue any, leaving him no surefire way to give her what she most wanted. God willing, she'd have a child to focus on soon so she'd stop nitpicking at his faults.

She pushed aside the mostly eaten plate of chicken. "Want the rest? It's tasty."

In an effort to be playful, he took a bite of chicken, moved the tray to the floor, and crawled back onto the mattress until he hovered over her. Pushing away the implications of the fact that Sara didn't seem to miss sex, he raised her shirt and kissed her belly, then started kissing his way up her torso. Before he could get excited, her fingers dug into his hair. "Hunter, we can't."

He hung his head. "Not even a little?"

"I need to be still today. No quick movements or contractions." She ruffled his hair like he was a child. "No point in getting all excited for nothing."

Hunter flopped onto his back and stared at the ceiling. He knew the "rules," but they also gave her a convenient excuse, which bothered him. He reached out to intertwine their fingers. "Promise me that, once you're pregnant, you won't find other excuses not to have sex. I've heard some women get weird about that during pregnancy. Like suddenly their bodies are all about the baby."

Or worse. He'd overheard complaints of coworkers whose lives had become overrun by kids. Whose marriages turned into coparenting jobs. Hunter liked the idea of a family . . . of a son. But the realities might be more all-consuming than he was prepared for, and he wasn't convinced he'd be good at it. That wasn't easy to admit, and *not* just because he liked being good at things.

What if instead of his son being like him and wanting to work side by side, he turned out to be more like Hunter's mom or Gentry, with their far-out ideas and crazy adventures? Hunter knew his flaws well, and rigidity was one of them. He had a hard time communicating with people he didn't understand. He didn't dislike them; he just didn't know how to relate to them.

What if he couldn't relate to his own kid? He cringed inwardly at that possibility and kept quiet.

"I know our sex life has taken a hit." Sara rolled over and kissed him, apparently misreading his silence as frustration. "We've gone through so much to get pregnant, and now we're so close. I don't want to risk anything."

He got that. He wasn't an idiot. Just frustrated, horny, and, for all the confidence he was projecting for her sake, worried about what Sara might do if she didn't get pregnant.

Before he considered his words, that thought slipped out. "You know, I meant what I said earlier . . . if that bamboo fails to live up to its reputation, you're everything I need."

Her gaze drifted to their clasped hands. She squeezed his, her voice low and somber. "I love you and know you mean well, but please . . . no negative thoughts."

He waited for a return of his sentiment. Like a black light, her silence called attention to his hidden, tender spots of self-doubt. He blinked, allowing himself a second to pivot from yet another bleak admission. "What do you want to do? TV? Cards? Scrabble?"

"Actually, I want to talk to you about something I've been considering since my meeting at the Angel House."

He didn't love the idea of her going there on a regular basis. "You said some of those women might be escaping violence. I'd rather you not spend much time there."

"I like being helpful."

"Can't you help from a distance? I don't want anything to happen to you." He stroked her hair. "And I don't want people taking advantage of your good nature, either."

"No one's taking advantage. And I don't want to live life from a distance. I *want* to be close. To make a connection. If you're so worried, come with me sometime." She set her hand on his thigh. "In fact, why don't we volunteer together? It'd be nice to share something positive like this."

"I've hardly any free time as it is. Besides, if you're pregnant, don't you want to take it easy?"

"You might feel good making a difference in the community." She withdrew her hand and pulled a pillow onto her lap. "And being pregnant won't make me an invalid. But, actually, I meant to discuss something else."

He was glad he hadn't ordered his pizza yet, because the wary look on her face made his stomach turn over. "What?"

"I told you about the little boy, Ty."

"The drug addict's kid?"

She slapped his chest. "He made me realize how many kids out there don't have enough, or any, security and support." She hesitated, looking down as if steeling herself. "I've been thinking we should be foster parents."

Whoa. Taking on kids with problems he had no idea how to handle? Brilliant idea, especially with everything going on at work and the fact that they might be having kids of their own by summer. "Sara, you might be pregnant with triplets. Now isn't the time to open up the house to strangers."

"So I get no vote?"

"That's not what I'm saying."

Her clear blue eyes reflected determination. "The approval process takes time. Let's fill out the preliminary application and get the background checks, home inspection, and classes done. If I'm pregnant with multiple kids, I'm sure we can decline taking on a foster child." When he didn't reply, she added, "If you'd see this little boy and think about how he'll never get the kind of opportunities we could provide, you wouldn't hesitate. We're so lucky, Hunter. We have so much—education, space, money. Think of how we could change lives."

When she put it that way, how could he refuse? Not that he'd refuse her much. Besides, he just knew this pregnancy would take, and then this would be a nonissue. Despite her open heart and energy, even Sara couldn't handle triplets *and* foster kids.

His ultimate goal today was to keep her calm and stress-free. "If it's that important to you, I'll support you."

When her gorgeous smile appeared, the room glowed from its warmth. "Grab your laptop. We can fill out an online application right now."

A legitimate excuse to bring his laptop into the bedroom. Maybe she was right about karma. "Be right back."

He trotted downstairs to the office, thinking about her request. Sara needed something he couldn't provide, and something she wasn't getting elsewhere.

If being a foster parent could restore their marriage to the stable patterns he'd always counted on, it'd be worth exploring. Maybe it would even alleviate the sense he was failing her in some amorphous way he couldn't grasp or change.

Chapter Six

"How are you feeling?" Colby asked while handing Sara a check to take to the Angel House.

The distracting sounds of a busy staff moving chairs and prepping for customers drifted through Colby's open office door. The same open door through which the sweet smell of whatever the pâtissier was baking wafted into the room. If Sara worked here, she'd probably gain ten pounds within two weeks.

"Better now that I can leave the house." Sara folded the check and slipped it into her wallet.

"Any signs or sense of things?" Colby's hazel eyes reflected hope and love. Although Sara wished her sisters and mother were here with her to share this process, throughout the years Colby had very much become a sister of her heart. Lately her sister-in-law's happiness shone through her skin like sunlight. Sara remembered feeling that glow herself, back in her early years with Hunter. Perhaps once they started their family, it'd return even stronger.

"My breasts are sore. My sister Mimi promises that's a good sign. Still, it's only been eight days, and it could just be the effect of the progesterone I'm still taking daily. I don't want to get my hopes up." A slight shudder ran through her, as if her insides turned cold when she made room for the possibility that she might not be pregnant.

"I'll keep my hopes high enough for both of us." Colby smiled and put the checkbook away before leaning forward. "Why do you want to hand-deliver that check?"

"I'm meeting with Gloria today to outline things I can do to help some of the women with their interview skills, and how I can also help with the childcare. I'd been hoping Hunter would get involved, too, but he's been putting me off."

"His hands are full at work. Besides, you know how intimidating he can be to strangers. Not sure that's a great fit. I wish *I* could go with you." She finger-combed her light-brown ponytail and then tossed it over her shoulder.

Sara couldn't exactly deny Colby's insight, but she'd been desperate for an activity she and Hunter could do together. "You're stretched thin enough. I've got time to kill. This makes me feel productive and keeps my mind off my own situation."

"Just don't push yourself." Colby's shrewd gaze narrowed. "And don't get too attached to the residents. Those people will be moving on, you know."

Given Colby's warning, Sara kept quiet about the possibility of becoming foster parents. Hunter had completed the paperwork, and the background checks were in process. Still, there were classes, SAFE home inspections, and certifications to complete. "Now you sound suspiciously like Hunter."

Colby mock-grimaced with a chuckle, her upward-tilting almond-shaped eyes crinkling at the corners. "On *rare* occasions, he and I do think alike."

They were more similar than either one would admit, although Colby had a softer touch and tendency toward peacekeeping. In a way, those siblings were a bit like Sara and Mimi, with Mimi resembling

Hunter's pragmatism and Sara aligning with Colby's more accommodating personality.

"I'll be fine. Better than fine. I've needed something to sink my teeth into since quitting work. It'll be nice to be useful and help others."

"That's why I'm so grateful Alec came up with the idea for the foundation. I prefer working on it to the restaurant. Thankfully, Alec is happy to oversee most of this place, so it's working out well for us," Colby said, gesturing toward the general direction of the dining room.

"I'll get out of your hair so you can get back to work, then." Sara admired Colby's drive, which resembled Hunter's. Both of them were rather sober, goal-oriented people, who moved mountains when motivated. They could be inspiring and intimidating at the same time. Sara hadn't been a slouch, but she also liked to take long walks for no reason, read books for pure pleasure, and sleep in, whenever possible.

Colby smiled with an extra twinkle in her eye. "See you Monday night at Jenna and Dad's."

"What did you get Gentry for her birthday?"

"A funky UNOde50 necklace. You?"

"A spa day at Illume." Sara slung her purse over her shoulder as she prepared to go. "I thought maybe we could make it a girls' day."

"Nice!"

"Let's hope she thinks so. Sometimes she makes me feel ancient even though I'm only eight years older than her."

"True, but we're both eons older emotionally."

"Maybe the tide is turning," Sara said with hope, before she remembered Gentry's tales from her Napa trip and realized her error. She rose from her chair, keeping that bit of info to herself. "See you Monday."

◆ ◆ ◆

Sara entered the Angel House carrying a shopping bag filled with puzzles, an Alphaberry, and My Own Leaptop: a personal donation to the limited collection of toys on hand for children who temporarily lived there. Of course, she'd had Ty in mind when she'd shopped, especially knowing that she'd be watching him today while his mother went to a support group meeting.

"The holidays have come early." Gloria helped Sara wrestle the toys out of their packaging.

"I hope this is okay," Sara said, realizing she hadn't asked Gloria for permission to supply the items. She'd also brought a small lavender-scented air freshener she planned to inconspicuously place in the corner of the living room to offset the home's depressing antiseptic odor. The homier smell would subliminally lift the residents' moods. "I assumed that these learning games would be helpful."

"It's very thoughtful. I'm sure Ty will enjoy something new."

"Are you still taking Pam and Jolinda to a meeting?"

"Yes. We'll return in about an hour. Thank you for watching Ty. These support groups are an important step toward getting the women back on track." Gloria glanced at her watch. "In fact, I'd better get them moving."

She hefted herself up and wandered back toward the bedrooms. Two minutes later, Pam, Jolinda, and Ty were in the living room. Ty stared at Sara and then looked at his little feet. Sara recalled how her niece Daisy had been at two—an exuberant chatterbox, quick to laugh. Unlike Ty, Daisy had a stable home, two affectionate parents, and plenty of stimulation.

"I'll take good care of your son, Pam," Sara ventured, hoping to form some rapport with the woman.

Without stooping to hug or kiss Ty, Pam simply said, "Be good," before following Jolinda and Gloria out the door with a brief acknowledgment of Sara.

She shouldn't judge, but Sara couldn't stop herself. If she had a child, she'd smother him with hugs and kisses and undivided attention. She'd savor every giggle, new milestone, and chance for connection.

Already she could feel her heart opening to Ty, but he wasn't hers, and she had to respect that boundary.

After a bit of research about how to support kids with speech delays, she had formulated a plan. Without pressuring Ty, she crawled across the floor to the new toys. Sitting cross-legged, she said, "I'm playing with this puzzle."

Chin tucked, Ty watched her from beneath his thick lashes. Sara separated all the wooden pieces of the fruit bowl puzzle and arranged them on the floor. Reminding herself that simplistic "self-talk" helped, she said, "I like this red apple."

She held up the piece and inspected it before putting it back into the puzzle board, then continued that routine with three more pieces.

Ty edged closer. His reluctant trust seemed a bigger victory than graduating magna cum laude. Once he was within reach, she extended a piece toward him. "Please help me, Ty."

He took the piece from her hand, turning it over in his own. After several seconds, he handed it back to her. Not exactly what she'd been hoping for, but she smiled with enthusiasm.

"Thank you. I think it goes here." She settled it into place and immediately handed Ty another piece. "This yellow banana is long. You try."

Ty crouched down this time and tried to jam the piece into an empty hole. Before he became overly frustrated, Sara suggested, "Twist it." She gently turned his hand—his soft skin warming her fingertips—until the piece slipped into place. "Good job, Ty!"

Unlike with her nieces, her praise didn't cause him to smile. He didn't say anything, either. Maybe she was foolish to think she could make a difference, but she wouldn't quit. Not when there was a chance she could help. And if nothing else, it would be practice for when she became a mom. *If* she became one, which she'd know within the next week. That thought temporarily disoriented her until Ty's rummaging in the toy box brought her back to the present.

For forty-five minutes, she played alongside him, narrating her every move as well as his. Mostly he watched her from a slightly wary distance. Finally, she read *The Very Hungry Caterpillar* book aloud with as much animation as she could muster.

Wistfully, she wished Hunter had come with her. No one would guess it, but he read aloud to children with more flair and varying character voices than she could manage. She'd learned that about him when they'd babysat her eldest niece, Caroline, two years ago for Sara's older sister, Katy, who had dropped her off for a few days on her way to Seattle.

It had been Sara's first glimpse of the kind of happy family life she and Hunter would create. Those were the halcyon days, before she'd experienced so much pain, intervention, and failure.

Ty sat quietly at some distance from her. Might he respond better to a man, or might he cower from Hunter's intense gaze? In any case, he didn't come sit beside her to look at the colorful pages, so she held them up for him to see, at which point he stared at them, wide-eyed.

He had hauntingly pretty gray eyes that, despite their innocence, conveyed the heart of an old soul.

Just then Gloria and the women returned. Pam was sucking on a lollipop when she stopped and took in the scene on the living room floor.

Maybe the drugs had destroyed or dulled her personality. Or maybe she didn't trust strangers. Or maybe the woman was petrified about her uncertain future. Sara had no sense of Pam's emotions, but she wished Ty had a mom who smiled at him and squeezed him tight.

She stood and showed Pam the book. "I think he likes this one. My nieces did at his age."

Pam paused, then simply said, "Thanks." Robotically, she waved her son over. "Let's eat lunch, Ty."

Defeated, Sara put away the toys she'd used to draw Ty out of his shell, while Gloria said something or other to Jolinda. Once Jolinda left them alone, Gloria asked, "Did everything go okay?"

"Of course. Ty didn't say anything, but I think I engaged him a little bit."

Gloria's face then shifted to the careful concern Sara had seen her exhibit before. "Don't be discouraged if you don't see progress. We only have these folks for a short while. We give them understanding and support while we can but must be ready to say goodbye when they go. I see the way you look at that little boy. Watch your heart, dear."

"Trust me, this place is good for my heart." Sara swaddled her shoulders with her lightweight wrap, feeling certain of herself and her mission. She'd been idle too long, and this was a welcome change and distraction from her own worries. "I'll see you later."

◆ ◆ ◆

"We're late, Hunter," Sara sighed as she buckled her seat belt. He could tell from her tone she wasn't pleased. "What happened?"

"I was on a conference call with a supplier in China." He checked the rearview mirror while backing out of the driveway. "Why did we plan a birthday dinner on a Monday night?"

"Colby's restaurant is closed Monday nights, that's why. Believe it or not, your schedule isn't the only one that matters."

"For most of the world, it's a work night."

That earned him a major eye roll. Sara stared straight ahead and muttered, "For most people, the work day ends by six. It's seven thirty."

"Please don't start on me. Climate change is affecting tea growth in the Yunnan province. We pay more than one hundred dollars per pound for those golden tips, and now they're going to be more expensive yet possibly yield diluted flavor. I'm sorry if that call conflicted with our social plans, but it's sort of a big deal for the company. The only upside is that it's a red flag I can wave in front of Pure Foods." He scrubbed a hand over his face. "Colby hinted that she had some announcement tonight. Any idea what it is? Are she and Alec getting engaged already?"

"No idea."

He loved Alec, but this seemed too soon for that commitment. Sure, Hunter had known Sara was the one from *their* first date, but they'd waited five years to get married. He took commitments seriously, and marriage required love that transcended lust.

Although Colby and Alec had grown up as neighbors, they'd been dating only a couple of months. After his sister's recovery from her husband, Mark's, suicide two years ago, he didn't want to see her hurt again.

Sara laid her hand on his thigh. "I know you don't deal well with change, but *whatever* they announce, please act happy. Keep your concerns to yourself until we're alone, okay?"

He couldn't argue her point. He hadn't liked change since his dad packed his bags and walked out twenty-seven years ago. Since then, his first inclination was to equate it with loss. But it went deeper, too.

Routines and structure allowed him to focus on his goals—to perfect them, whether that meant artfully steering CTC's finances or racing his bike over the streets of Clackamas County. Unanticipated changes affected his control, and he never enjoyed a loss of control.

"I'll be the picture of enthusiasm," he promised.

They pulled up to his father's house. The imposing structure reflected Jenna's tastes: formal, fancy, overblown. He didn't like it any more than he liked her. He never looked forward to spending much time with her, but tonight he wasn't even eager to visit with his dad. Since their meeting about the sale, they'd restricted their conversations to those of a need-to-know basis at work.

He hadn't told Sara about his argument with his father. She didn't need to be upset while they awaited the results of the embryo transfer. Those potential babies came before everything for her.

He also didn't dump it on Colby because he didn't want to put her in the middle. Sadly, the only person whom he could talk to lately was Bethany. He hadn't said much, given that he wasn't prone to sharing intimate family details with outsiders, but he'd needed to vent to someone. Bethany always understood what CTC meant to him.

Now that Pure Foods had started its investigation and signed a nondisclosure agreement covering the duration of the due diligence period, he and Bethany had a ticking clock hanging over their heads. He needed a solution, but pondering his options would need to wait a few hours.

He followed Sara up the front walk, past the perfectly manicured garden beds, and entered the house. The rest of the family had gathered in the massive kitchen. The one Jenna had remodeled twice even though she never cooked. Hunter glanced at his father and nodded hello, wondering if anyone noticed the awkward distance between them, or if his father even cared.

Hunter blamed Jenna, of course. Once again, she'd come between him and his dad. It hurt almost as much as it had the first time. How humbling to admit that the little boy inside was still waiting for his dad to make the first move to bridge the gap now.

"Nice of you to join us," Jenna quipped, her chin slightly raised. She'd been sexy when younger, and Hunter couldn't deny she looked good for fifty-four. Tonight she wore a fitted dress and high heels. She'd pulled her red hair into a tight bun, which enhanced her harsh appearance. In truth, though, nothing about her appealed to him. "Dinner is likely ruined."

"Chill, Mom. It's not like you slaved all day cooking. Take-out enchiladas can't be ruined by a warming drawer." Gentry handed Hunter a beer with a slice of lime and winked.

"Sorry, Jenna," Sara said, smoothing things over like always. She set a small gift bag on the marble-topped island, making him realize he'd never even asked what they'd bought his sister. He should remember to thank his wife later. "Can I help get things to the table?"

While Sara helped Jenna, Hunter kissed Gentry on the forehead. "Happy birthday."

“Go ahead, say it. I know you’re thinking something about my being a year closer to thirty and still being a drifter.” She raised her own beer to her lips, revealing the vine tattoo scrolled around her left forearm.

“Actually, I’m told you’re taking to your part-time position with Colby. Maybe you’ve found your calling.” He aimed for compliments because he didn’t like the idea that he hadn’t been as good of a brother to her as he’d always been to Colby. While some reasons for the disparity weren’t his fault, others were. He could do better. He *would* do better.

Gentry blinked, possibly surprised by his lack of sarcasm. She responded with some of her own. “Well, it’d be impossible not to be better with social media than you and Colby.”

Recognizing her deflection for what it was, he pressed his point, hoping to encourage her.

“Maybe you could start a social media consulting business,” he suggested, the idea immediately making him excited. As predictably as a Swiss watch, he constructed a mental outline—identify target clients, research fees, estimate overhead, set a budget. “I could help you with a business plan, if you’d like.”

She looked stunned, but then covered with more sarcasm. “Hunter, this is a party, not a business meeting. You do know what a party is, right?”

He couldn’t help but laugh at her astute barb. “It’s been a while.”

Gentry smiled. She could look quite cute and sweet when she smiled, so he hugged her and kissed her forehead again before wandering over to Colby and Alec. A quick glance at his sister’s left hand indicated she wasn’t yet engaged, leaving him to wonder what they might be announcing.

When he leaned in to kiss her cheek, Colby murmured, “Things are tense with you and Dad?”

“You could say that.” He swigged more of his beer. “But don’t get involved. Just enjoy the party and all the good stuff going on in your life.”

"It sucks to be on the outs with your dad." Alec patted Hunter's shoulder, referring to his own tortured relationship with his father.

Hunter would never have imagined being at an impasse with his, but if CTC did end up in someone else's hands, he also couldn't promise there wouldn't be an irreparable breach. That truth caused a pang of disillusionment to strike his chest.

"I still think he's not looking good lately, either, Hunter." His sister's brows knitted together. "He's been complaining about joint pain. Is he sick and not telling us? That might explain the sale."

She'd mentioned that about a month ago, too. Hunter had noticed a creeping lethargy that had never before been part of his dad's persona, but the man was sixty-five. Wouldn't they all be slowing down and be hit with a bit of arthritis in another thirty years? "Dad wouldn't hide an illness from us."

"I wouldn't think so, but maybe he's being tested and is waiting for confirmation or something." Her hushed tone sounded ominous, and for a second, he worried. An illness would explain the otherwise inexplicable decision to consider a sale.

Hunter cast a sidelong glance toward his dad, who was smiling in conversation with Gentry. Of course he was. Then, ashamed of his petty mental snipe, Hunter looked away from the aggravating scene.

No. If his dad was sick, he'd tell them. And Jenna wouldn't be able to keep it quiet, either.

"I think he's fine, Colby. Let's change the subject." He pivoted back to Alec. "Tell me why we're having Mexican instead of something you made?"

"Alec needs a day off now and then," Colby interjected.

"I didn't know Alec couldn't speak for himself," Hunter teased.

"Let's not pretend either of you would prefer my dishes to high-carb, oversized, cheese-stuffed platters. You and she"—he nodded to Colby—"have terrible palates."

"To each his own," Hunter chuckled.

"Let's finally get seated." Jenna snapped her fingers.

Hunter stifled a groan and took a silk-covered seat beside his wife at the massive burled-wood dining table. He covered a smirk at the fact that Jenna had transferred the take-out food to fine china platters. Moving a crystal wineglass aside, he set his beer bottle on a coaster.

Because dinner had been delayed, folks dug in without too much conversation at first. Or maybe it was easier to focus on eating than tap-dancing around uneasy topics—like the business or the possible pregnancy.

His dad raised his wineglass. "A toast to my little girl on her twenty-sixth birthday. I hope this year brings good surprises for you and for all."

Hunter felt his wife's hand stroking his thigh the way one might comfort a child—a subtle plea not to ruin the dinner. He joined the rest of the family in raising a glass and wishing Gentry well.

"Any special wishes for the year?" Sara asked, digging in to an enchilada.

"Not really." Gentry fell uncharacteristically quiet for a second. Then a sly smile crossed her face, and she cocked a brow while staring at Sara. "Maybe another trip to Napa."

Sara's eyes bugged before she dropped her chin, hiding something from everyone. Hunter made a mental note to find out what Gentry had shared with Sara about that vacation. Then he wondered what other things his wife didn't tell him, and why.

"How are things at A CertainTea?" their father asked Colby and Alec.

"Great. Business is strong." Colby brightened and looked at Alec. "And Alec and I actually made another big decision."

Sara leaned forward, appearing eager to be let in to their confidence. "Do we have another reason to celebrate?"

"Alec and I are moving in together." Colby beamed, although Alec flushed a bit.

Hunter was happy for his friend's and sister's newfound love, however unexpected and slightly awkward. Still, he smiled. "Congrats. Will you be moving to Colby's in the city, or is she coming this way?"

"I'm putting my condo on the market, and then we're going to look for something small around here. Closer to work and all of you is the right move for me now." Colby's voice wavered only slightly, and he knew she'd given a brief thought to Mark.

Hunter still hadn't quite processed what he'd only recently learned about the full truth of her first marriage—of the manic-depressive swings Colby had lived through with Mark before he violently ended his life in front of her.

"I'm thrilled that you'll be closer. Makes spontaneous outings much easier." Sara clapped.

"Absolutely. And I'll also be a very involved aunt." Colby's smile filled Hunter with deep gratitude that his sister and wife were also dear friends.

He knew Colby meant well with that comment, but Sara tensed beside him, almost as if the mention of that happy future would somehow make it disappear. He leaned to his left and kissed his wife's temple, whispering, "It's all good, babe."

Naturally Jenna had to probe. "When's the big test date?"

Sara cleared her throat. "Thursday."

Hunter studied Jenna. Did she care about the pregnancy, or was she fishing to learn which day Hunter would be out of the office so she could try to dig into what he and Bethany were up to? Sara would call him paranoid. Yet with Jenna, it was always best to be on guard.

"Do you feel any different?" Jenna continued, her gaze fixed on Sara. "I swear, I knew exactly when I got pregnant with Gentry. My breasts were so sore, and my sleep cycles were off. I told Jed, but he only laughed."

"She likes to tell this story because I have to admit she was right." Their dad chuckled. He had a kind face, which turned even warmer when he laughed. Hunter hated to think of a future in which he and his father didn't work together each day, let alone one where he harbored this kind of anger and resentment toward the man.

Meanwhile, Gentry's expression turned odd—almost stricken. Maybe she didn't like thinking about her parents having sex. Who did? Not him, that's for sure.

"I'm sure everyone's different," Colby jumped in, seeming to pick up on a subtle downshift in Sara's mood. "My friend Kathleen had no idea she was pregnant for weeks. She just figured work stress made her late."

Jenna's gaze then turned toward Hunter. She sipped her wine before saying, "Speaking of work stress, I hope you're not going to increase your father's by playing games with the due diligence requests."

"Jenna." His father shook his head. "Not tonight."

"Why not?" Jenna set her glass down and crossed her arms. "Everyone here is affected by the outcome of this situation. We deserve to know that no one else is trying to sabotage the opportunity to walk away with millions, especially considering that we"—she then gestured between herself and her husband—"worked for decades to build the company."

Hunter might regret ruining Gentry's party, but he couldn't let Jenna's remark go unchecked.

"As someone who's also worked at CTC for two decades, I know we already all have a lot of money. There's no reason to hand over the upside of all our work to someone else." He leaned forward, determined to persuade the others. "The fact they want it proves they see untapped value. We should keep that for ourselves."

Hunter then stuffed a large bite of enchilada in his mouth to keep himself from saying more.

"Colby, just think what you could do with the foundation if you had a multimillion-dollar payday *this year*." Jenna's seductive taunt caused his sister's eyes to temporarily glaze over.

He cleared his throat, feeling a flush rise up his neck. Surely Colby wouldn't turn her back on her promise to stand with him against a sale.

"While that's tempting, I have faith in Hunter and his vision for the future of the business and our family. CTC's a legacy that can be passed down to our children." Colby looked across the table at Hunter, wearing a confident grin. "I don't need a windfall. Alec and I are doing fine on our own."

"Thank you," Hunter replied.

"What about you, Gentry?" Jenna asked.

Gentry darted a quick glance at Colby and avoided Hunter's gaze. "I don't know."

"How can you not know?" Jenna scoffed. "Of everyone at this table, you should be the one most eager for that payday, considering the fact that you don't have a career."

Hunter covered a smug grin. Jenna might sink her own boat if she continued to insult her daughter. Like Alec's father, the woman seemed to think that bullying one's child might somehow motivate her to change. To date, he'd never seen that approach work well.

"Hunter said he'd help me start my own consulting business." Gentry chugged her beer while everyone else at the table stared at him with surprise.

Jenna chuckled. "What kind of business could you start?"

"Social media promotion," Hunter interjected. "She's doing a great job for Colby. Maybe she can market this skill to other small businesses who don't have the time or interest in properly running those platforms."

Gentry shot her mom a smug look, prompting Jenna to glare at Hunter before looking at her daughter. "You won't need Hunter's help if you have seed money from the sale."

"How typical of you to overlook the importance of budgets, strategic planning, smart growth, and everything else except branding," Hunter snapped and then glanced at Gentry. "Gentry, if you start a business without a good plan, you'll end up losing your investment. I'd also help you revise that plan as the landscape changes so you don't waste a lot of time and resources."

"None of which will be necessary if she can live off the proceeds from the sale." Jenna set her chin on top of her steepled hands.

"Some of us work for reasons that have little to do with money and everything to do with purpose," he replied.

"Enough," their dad said, looking at Gentry. "As I told your brother, nothing is decided. We're only exploring our options. If—*if*—the final offer's something I feel is a good deal, I'll bring it to you all for a vote. Until then, this isn't to be discussed outside of these four walls. I don't need our employees to panic and jump ship, or for the local paper to get wind of this possibility."

Hunter felt Sara's stare, as if she was wondering how far he'd go to sabotage the sale. He wasn't stupid. He didn't want to destroy the company—just Jenna. He wouldn't need to sabotage it, anyway. He'd simply use all the improvements and expansions his dad and Jenna had never let him implement against them now. There were dozens of legitimate investments he could argue were needed to update CTC's infrastructure, which would make for a hefty capex line item on the books. Once Pure Foods got the full picture, they might reevaluate the deal or decrease the purchase price.

"Why is everyone looking at me?" Hunter eyed the group and let his gaze linger on his dad.

"Because everyone knows that you have the power and motivation to mess this up." His dad stared back. "I hope I can count on you to do as I've asked."

His father's distrust dealt another blow. "Ironic, considering I can't count on you to do what you promised."

"I thought we were celebrating my birthday?" Gentry interrupted.

"Of course we are." His father squeezed her hand and smiled, but tension kept its grip on the room.

Hunter could not sit through another forty-five minutes of Jenna's baiting comments and his dad's refusal to acknowledge Hunter's position. Without thinking, he stood, sending his chair screeching back. "Sorry, Gentry, but I'm suddenly feeling a little ill. I'll make it up to you. Happy birthday." He looked at his wife. "Babe, let's go."

He sensed her disappointment, but she made apologetic goodbyes to his family. "Sorry, everyone. Gentry, I hope you like our gift. Call me tomorrow."

"Hunter," his dad said, "your attitude isn't helpful or persuasive."

"I'd say the same to you, but why bother? It's pretty clear that Jenna's opinion is the only one that means anything to you." He kept bitterness from his voice despite his insides churning acid.

Once in the car, Sara huffed. "I can't believe you ruined your sister's birthday dinner. Honestly, Hunter, in the bigger scheme of things, doesn't family matter more than CTC? You're so fixated."

"I'm fighting for what's mine, and I'll be damned if I let Jenna win." He stared at her for a second. "Mark my words. CTC will remain in the Cabot family. I'm not giving up my dreams for the company and my kids."

"What if our kids want to be doctors or artists instead of working by your side?" Sara frowned and stared out the window.

He'd always envisioned the next generation of Cabots creating new products and new jobs. Celebrating their accomplishments. What could be better? And unlike his own dad, he wouldn't break the promises he made to *his* kids.

"I'm not a dictator. I wouldn't force them to do something they hated." When he realized Sara was actually talking about the future and kids, he frowned. She hadn't been willing to do that with him before because of superstitions. "By the way, why am I barred from voicing any kind of daydreams about our future kids, but it's okay for you to project about them when you want to attack me?"

"I'm not attacking you. I just disagree with you."

"Disagree? You think we should sell the business?" He stared at the road, pulse pounding.

"I think you should be willing to consider a good offer, that's all."

"That's *all*?" If the sunroof had been open, his head might've shot right through it and up to the moon. "My father has betrayed me."

"Your dad has a right to change his mind without it being labeled a betrayal. Don't take this so personally, Hunter. It's unlike you to be this dramatic."

Dramatic? Since when does stating the truth translate to drama?

Maybe his dad's about-face shouldn't be a shock, given the way the man broke his vows to his first wife. Hunter had always admired his dad's intelligence and work ethic while privately demeaning his mom's flighty lifestyle. In truth, he'd never taken a hard look at his parents' integrity. In retrospect, his mother—not his father—had been the more loyal, committed partner and parent.

Sara broke the silence consuming the car. "If you want to spend all your energy fighting the sale, I can't stop you. But do *not* cause a rift in the family, Hunter. It's small enough as it is, and with mine so far away and you always at work, yours is all I've got most days."

His thoughts turned gloomier. "Let's drop it. There won't be a rift because I'm going to find a solution that benefits everyone."

Chapter Seven

"My team's getting pressure to provide reports faster." Bethany closed her laptop and pressed her lips together. Her expression exhibited the kind of shared focus and concern Hunter wished his wife would give him. "Jenna's been unusually critical of the details of the marketing department budgets and projections, too."

"Of course she has," Hunter grunted, ignoring the call on his direct line. "Every year she makes our job ten times harder by being uncooperative during strategic planning. Now suddenly she's going to pressure us to set sky-high projections to make the company look like it's poised for rapid growth. She'll be getting *this* in response," he said, flashing his middle finger.

When Bethany's eyes widened, he regretted making her uncomfortable. Like the professional he counted on, she brushed it off. "She won't make it easy. And I suspect even your dad will gripe about the capex estimate you're floating."

"You and I both know that the Idaho plant has been held together by rubber bands and bubble gum these past two years. It's *past* time we invested serious capital there to bring it up to code. Don't let Jenna bully you." When Bethany's obvious discomfort didn't subside, Hunter added, "I'll handle her and my dad."

Alec's warning from the other night drifted through his thoughts. He didn't enjoy opposing his dad, but it couldn't be helped. For the first time since the early months following his parents' divorce, he felt cast aside—adrift. Like then, he buried his unease beneath determination and a good plan. It had worked for him in the past, but now he and his dad no longer shared the same goal.

"What else can we do to stop the sale?" Bethany was smart enough to know it would take more than aggressive accounting to put Pure Foods off if it truly wanted CTC.

Every time he thought about how he'd handle losing, his body flushed with heat. He glanced around his large office. The saltwater tank bubbling in the corner, which housed a handful of colorful fish, had a soothing effect on him, reminding him of one of his and Sara's first-ever vacations, when they'd gone to the Cayman Islands. His diploma and CPA certification hung on one wall, and the fine art Sara had bought him for their fifth anniversary—an abstract in the tradition of Jackson Pollack—hung over the small conference table in the corner. Handsome navy leather chairs, worn from use, flanked his desk.

This single, spacious room—one that contained decades of memories and hopes—was as much his home as the one he shared with Sara. He wouldn't give it up without a fight.

"I've got an idea, but sussing it out will be tricky," he said. "I want to bring my ready-made bottled tea idea to fruition. If we can produce our most popular flavored teas as ready-mades and take advantage of a national bottler's expertise and distribution channels, revenues will soar, and the value of the company will significantly increase. If I can get a major bottler to agree to a joint venture *and* convince my family of that potential for growth, they might not sell."

"I can't believe that idea hasn't been pursued sooner."

"My dad's wedded to our core business, and Jenna hates anything that I propose. Or maybe she wasn't up to the challenge of marketing a new product line."

“Really?” Bethany wrinkled her nose. “I know you two don’t get along, but she’s got a vested interest in making the company profitable. She’s never come across as lazy, either. Would she honestly block your idea just for the sake of getting one over on you?”

“Who the hell knows?” Hunter raised his hand in question. “Maybe she’s not as smart as she pretends to be and didn’t see the merits. She’s never taken the time to understand the growth levers from a financial perspective.”

A knock at his door interrupted them.

“Come in,” Hunter called.

His reed-thin assistant, Haru, came in. She’d worked for him for only seven months, but she’d made herself indispensable. Like him, she didn’t socialize much at work or smile. Of course, there wasn’t much to smile about around here these days. Still, it couldn’t hurt to try.

Haru met his gaze. “Your father wants to see you in his office right away.”

“Thanks. Tell him I’ll be there in a minute.” Hunter forced an awkward smile, which only appeared to fluster her. He’d be better off sticking to what he knew.

Once she closed the door behind her, he returned his attention to Bethany. “I’ll catch up with you later, and we’ll figure out which reports we can send over to Pure Foods and which we should ‘double-check’ for a while longer.”

Bethany grinned. “Sounds good.”

Hunter followed her out and then ambled down the hall to his dad’s corner office. Given the update from Bethany, he anticipated backlash from Jenna and his dad. If they were wise, they’d back off. He had enough pressure bearing down on him. Sara had scheduled the SAFE home inspection with the foster care people for tomorrow morning, and then they had the doctor’s appointment after lunch to determine whether the IVF had resulted in a viable pregnancy.

Unlike last time, Sara refused to take a home pregnancy test first. She wanted the blood test with all the numbers. Hunter didn't know if that was the best course, but things between them were frayed enough without adding another argument. If things went well, by this time tomorrow, he might be a father of triplets.

That thought literally stopped him in his tracks, which drew a raised eyebrow from his dad's assistant.

"They're waiting for you," she said.

Hunter nodded, closing the curtain on his personal life for the moment, and then entered the office. His father was seated at his desk, and Jenna had taken one of the seats opposite him. Hunter casually made his way to the other chair, sat down, and crossed one foot over his knee. "You summoned?"

"I want to talk about some of these numbers I'm seeing go out the door." His father's typically genial expression had hardened into something Hunter might describe as stern disapproval.

"Fire away." Hunter slouched back, linking his hands behind his head.

"Twelve million in capex improvements?" His dad leaned forward.

Hunter counted to five in his head to prolong the pause in conversation. Finally, he asked, "Is there a question?"

Jenna rolled her eyes and groaned. "We're not stupid, Hunter. There's no way Idaho needs all those improvements to function."

"Oh, really?" Hunter twisted in his seat to face her. "And when, exactly, is the last time you went there, or spoke with the environmental compliance manager, or bothered to read the footnotes in any of the reports Bethany generates?" He raised his index finger. "Wait, I know. Never."

Jenna's nostrils flared, but his dad jumped into the fray before she replied.

"Hunter, don't tell me that every single one of the upgrades you're noting is an emergency or priority. You're running up the expense estimates in order to make the business less attractive."

"I'm still the CFO, aren't I?" Hunter made a show of glancing around the room, then stretching his arms out and looking at them before patting himself down. "I'm the one who has to sign off on all the financial information and attest to the accuracy of all the data. Make warranties as to completeness. Any responsible CFO would err on the side of being conservative so we don't end up in a lawsuit for misrepresentation after a sale." Hunter felt pretty damn good about himself at that moment, so he decided to make one last nick with the scalpel. "What, Jenna? No snappy comeback?"

"If it makes you feel better to play your little games, be my guest. You can't stop the inevitable." She crossed her ankles and straightened her spine.

"Inevitable?" Hunter felt the flush rising up his neck. He settled a narrowed gaze on his dad. "You said we'd wait on a final offer before you'd bring it to the shareholders."

"I did, and we will. But you've got to cooperate and not purposely screw it up." His father rubbed his shoulder and winced.

Colby's concern about their dad's health tickled Hunter's conscience. *Was* there more to this sale than his father was letting on?

"Are you sick?" he blurted out.

"What?" His father shook his head.

"Colby's concerned about your aches and lethargy. If you're sick, at least that would explain why you'd trash our plans and sell out now."

Jenna mocked him. "I never realized how whiny you can be when you don't get your way."

"Jenna." His dad raised a hand to cut her off. Hunter fantasized about dragging her—chair and all—out of the office, then noticed his dad staring at him. "No, son. I'm not sick. Just getting older. I've already told you I didn't go looking for this deal, but I can't, in good conscience, ignore it. You know what's happening with climate change and global competition. Pure Foods has more money, more distribution—especially internationally—and more personnel than us. They can weather these problems better than we can."

"Guess this is one of those 'agree to disagree' things." Hunter had no interest in a sales pitch, so he stood. "If there's nothing else, I've got lots of work on my desk."

He and his dad engaged in a sixty-second stare-down. Hunter had never lost that kind of contest in his life, and he wouldn't now. His father finally blinked, but the victory didn't fill Hunter with his typical sense of triumph. "We'll talk tomorrow."

Tomorrow. Another showdown—this time between him and science.

"I'll be with Sara at the doctor's office tomorrow." His stomach tightened, and he avoided eye contact with anyone. He'd been busy enough that he hadn't had much time to worry about the results. But as the hours ticked by, his anxiety about how Sara would react to bad news increased.

She'd purposely scheduled that foster care home inspection ahead of the doctor's appointment so she wouldn't get caught in a state of despondency if the test came back negative. He hated the fact that he couldn't control the outcome. He dreaded those final minutes when the doctor would walk in and Hunter would try to read his expression before the results were announced.

The only thing he knew for sure was that if Sara wasn't pregnant, he'd have to comfort her first and deal with his own feelings of loss at some later time . . . on his own.

His father's expression transformed to concern. "How's Sara?"

"Anxious," Hunter admitted, needing to borrow a bit of his dad's strength in that moment. "Quiet."

"I know how tough this has been on her. And you."

Hunter wished things between him and his father weren't so strained—and that Jenna wasn't in the room. He could use his old man's advice but couldn't form the words. He'd never felt this much uncertainty in his life. One kind—how he'd manage three kids at once—he could handle, and in a way, excited him. The other—how he'd help Sara recover from bad news—only terrified him.

"Give her our love." His dad tapped his fingers on his desk. "Call me either way."

"I will." On that note, Hunter took his leave.

On his way back to his office, his stomach turned over from considering the worst-case scenario at tomorrow's appointment. From imagining Sara's disappointed face, her broken heart, and his own desperation to find the words to soothe her.

He stopped at Haru's desk and gave himself a mental shake. It was way easier to focus on stopping this sale. At least he had *some* control over the outcome of the CTC negotiations. "Haru, call Bethany back to my office, please."

Once inside his office, he closed the door and exhaled. The damselfishes, dartfishes, and clown fish swam calmly around the tank. He envied the pristine, controlled environment. No predators. Regulated temperature. Constant food. Beauty and peace. Everything that real life was not.

Abruptly, he picked up the phone and dialed his fraternity brother's father, Rich Cortland, who sat on the board of King Cola. Time to kick off his discreet inquiries.

◆ ◆ ◆

"Babe?" Hunter's voice sounded uncharacteristically small and anxious, even within the small space of the car—the ridiculously expensive car that could drive itself. Scientists and engineers had made amazing breakthroughs this past decade, yet they couldn't get her pregnant.

Sara squinted at the sunlight pouring in through the windshield, hot tears blurring her vision. She wound the long purse strap in her hands until the skin on her fingers ached. The quiet rage building inside had no voice because her throat had constricted so much that even breathing hurt.

She wasn't pregnant. None of their perfect embryos had survived or attached or whatever the hell they were supposed to do and didn't . . . again. Despite enduring another round of drugs and shots and hope, she was going home today empty and bruised, inside and out.

She searched her memory for some terrible wrong she must've committed to warrant this punishment. For some mistake she'd made during the cycle that might've hurt their chances. Nothing. She could think of nothing. And no reason why she and Hunter had been denied this blessing.

"Sara." His hand brushed her thigh. "Talk to me, please. What can I do?"

She couldn't look at him. Couldn't answer, either. The truth was there was nothing her husband could do. No words or deed that would reverse the result or ease the loss. Hunter wanted to help, but he couldn't. Fair or not, the mere fact that he wasn't falling apart like she was only fueled her sense of isolation and pain.

Sniffling, she wiped her damp cheeks, wishing there was an escape hatch from reality. Her parents were waiting for a call, as was Hunter's family. He'd have to make them for her because she couldn't say the words, much less listen to hushed apologies laden with pity. She just wanted to close her eyes and block out the world.

Lost in her thoughts, she hadn't realized they'd arrived at home until Hunter opened her door.

He crouched to look at her face, his warm hand caressing her cheek. "Help me out, babe. How can I make this better for you?"

Her fixer. He'd always been that way—identify a problem, generate options, execute a solution. That wouldn't work in this situation. They both had to feel their way out of this tunnel. She was buried more deeply than him, so it would take her longer to see any light.

Her voice sounded tinny and distant when it finally emerged. "You can't make it better."

He backed up as she moved to get out of the passenger seat, then he followed her into the mudroom, trailing closely behind her as if he feared she might collapse. The mudroom, where she'd envisioned teaching her children to tie their laces, undressing their muddy clothes after a day spent at the lake, and organizing sports equipment and uniforms. Now it would continue to be little more than a fancy breezeway between Hunter's high-tech car and the kitchen.

After months of eating healthy food, of avoiding alcohol and other vices, she headed straight into the kitchen to find some wine. Of course, her always-confident husband had bought champagne to celebrate. He didn't know she'd found it stashed in the basement refrigerator yesterday. Ridiculous as it was, she almost wanted to blame that for jinxing them. In any case, they had no cause to celebrate. Just as well, because today called for something dark and heavy.

Without a word, Hunter stood at the island while she pulled the cork from a bottle of Niepoort Redoma Tinto, poured a large glass, and chugged it.

"Sara!" He reached for the bottle, but she withheld it.

"I need this." Staring straight at him, she poured herself another glass. Her entire body vibrated as if she'd been plugged in to the wall and turned on. "I'm not like you. I can't separate my feelings into boxes and keep moving forward. My dream *died* today, and if I need this bottle and six others to get me through the night, then that's what I'm going to do."

He snatched the bottle from her hand on his second attempt. Some of it sloshed over the side and splattered on the counters. He set the bottle in the sink and wiped up the spatter with a paper towel. "You'll regret it tomorrow and feel even worse than you do now. Trust me. Let's find another way."

"Another way? Exactly what way does one make peace with this?" The finality of her situation struck. She wanted to scream and hit him or smash plates or kick the island, but instead her knees weakened from a surge of pain-fueled adrenaline. Hunter must've seen the signs, because he wrapped his arms around her. As soon as he'd swaddled her in his embrace, sobs erupted from some bleak corner of her soul.

"Sh, sh, sh," he cooed, stroking her head and back while gently swaying from side to side.

Her crying wouldn't be contained, turning into messy, throaty wails before settling into sporadic hiccups.

Without a word, Hunter lifted her, cradling her in his arms and carrying her up the stairs. Exactly like he had the day they'd transferred the embryos, a memory that triggered more tears.

Hunter laid her on the bed and spooned her, holding her close without saying a word. The pendant around her neck and warmth of his body suffocated her, but she didn't have the energy to complain. He tucked her hair behind her ear and kissed that side of her head. Minutes passed, the sedative effects of the large glass of wine she'd chugged taking hold. Her body grew heavier with each breath.

"We need to call our parents," she said, voice cracking. Today, not even her mom's loving words and sympathy would help.

"No, we don't." He stroked her head again. "They'll know what happened when we don't call with good news. I'll make the calls in the morning."

She knew he thought that would make her feel better, but the ache in her heart only throbbed harder. When she shuddered, he cocooned her more fiercely.

"Sara, don't shut me out." He paused, kissing her head, then her neck. "I'm sad, too. I need you. We need each other."

When she didn't answer, he moved her hair aside and kissed the back of her neck. "I miss you. Come back to me."

She'd always envied the way he could use physical intimacy to make himself feel better, no matter how upset he might be. It reminded her of how her sister Lisa would overcome sadness with a little window-shopping, because looking at pretty things made her happy. It seemed that some people were equipped to cope with loss by using any kind of distraction.

Unfortunately for Sara, she didn't rebound quite so well. And yet her husband needed her. He was hurting, too, even if she suspected the depth of his pain didn't quite match her own.

She turned toward him, giving in to his plea, hoping that accepting his love and comfort might help her, too. He caressed her face and looked into her eyes, as if seeking permission to kiss her.

It'd been more than two months since they'd made love, thanks in part to her paranoia during the treatments. In the scheme of fourteen years, that shouldn't have mattered much, except now their rhythm felt stilted.

Hunter's eyes darkened with need and want. Set deeply in his striking face, they pressed her for proof that all had not been lost. That this marriage—this love—would withstand its latest test.

She kissed him and raised the hem of his shirt so that her hands stroked the corded muscles of his abdomen and chest. Despite the emotional distance, the familiarity of his body and scent drew her into the moment. "For better or worse," they'd promised. This day would be remembered as one of the worst, but maybe this act might make it slightly better.

Hunter did nothing in half measures, whether it was exercise, work, or lovemaking. At the first sign of her willingness, he'd deftly begun his passionate assault. He knew her well. Knew where to kiss, stroke, or blow heated breath. Knew when to be rough, then tender, when to murmur her name and "I love yous," and when to be silent.

Until recent months, sex had not been a problem for Hunter and her. It had never become too predictable. But they'd never before undertaken it at a moment of such profound sadness. Even in his capable arms, today she couldn't find joy or passion or the bond that had tied them together.

As Hunter spilled himself inside her, her eyes began to burn with tears again at the reminder that they would never need a condom, or any other aid, to avoid getting pregnant.

She knew she should be grateful for this amazing, proud man who loved her regardless of her fertility. For the freedom he'd given her to quit her job, and the patience he'd shown in the face of her inability to cope with disappointments. For his family, who'd treated her like one of their own since the beginning.

She didn't want to be distant or to lose these people or her marriage, yet she felt herself slipping away little by little, powerless to stop it.

As Hunter's breathing settled, he propped himself up on his elbows, his expression turning distraught. "Are you crying?"

She turned her face, ashamed.

He withdrew, sitting back on his calves, hands on the mattress. "I thought we were connecting, Sara. That we were helping each other. But it looks like you felt forced. Or you took pity on me. Neither is very flattering."

"I'm sorry." Even to her ears, those words sounded weak. Her leaden limbs wouldn't budge. Absently, she wondered if this was how Colby's dead husband, Mark, had felt during his depressions.

"So am I. I'm sorry you're hurting. I'm sorry the IVF failed. I'm sorry I don't know how to make you happy anymore. But sorry isn't helping either of us, is it?" He shook his head, and though she'd rarely seen him cry, he looked as if he was fighting back his own tears. "I'm at a loss here. You've got to help me. Help me help you . . . help *us*. Regardless of what happened today, we still have each other."

"I don't know what to say. Obviously, you didn't want the babies as much as I did, or you wouldn't be so quick to turn the page."

"That's unfair. Of course I want a family with you, but I don't *need* it. I love you, and I loved our life before baby making became the number one goal. I can still be happy in this marriage without children because I've got you. *Obviously*, you don't feel the same."

He slid out of bed.

"Hunter." She reached for him, but he waved her off.

"I need a minute." He padded to the bathroom, pausing by the bamboo plant from his mother, and closed the door. Seconds later she heard the shower running.

The setting sun cast a peach glow over the room. It glinted off the mirror and glass surfaces, highlighting the sheen of the silk-satin drapes. The bedroom looked like heaven even though, at the moment, it felt a lot more like hell.

Sara stared at the plant that hadn't brought them luck or good chi. Closing her eyes, she prayed, even though she didn't even know what she was praying for. Ultimately, she guessed she was praying that she'd get out of her funk before she destroyed her marriage.

The bathroom door opened. Hunter returned, towel wrapped around his waist. He picked up his discarded clothing and took them to the walk-in closet, presumably to dump them in the hamper. When he reemerged, he was wearing thin sweatpants and a long-sleeve T-shirt.

Sara sat up and reached out again. "Hunter, wait."

He approached but sat at the end of the bed. "I'm going to make something to eat. Grilled cheese or whatever."

Greasy, high-carb meals had always been his go-to for comfort. Comfort she ought to be providing. "I'm sorry I've been acting like this has all been about me and my disappointment. I'm sorry you've had to spend all your time comforting me and I haven't reciprocated. I don't want to be this way, to feel like this. I don't want to hurt you, either. I love you."

He clasped her calf. "I know this is hard, but we need to be able to turn to each other. If we lose that, we've got nothing left."

She nodded, reaching both arms toward him. He edged closer and hugged her, resting his cheek against the top of her head. They sat together in bed for a minute or two, cuddling.

Sara suspected he, like her, wished for some kind of miracle to come fix whatever had broken in their relationship. But miracle fixes were for kids' dreams, not grown-ups'. Only she and Hunter could knit the cracks back together, but neither seemed to know how.

Chapter Eight

Hunter strolled down the hall toward his father's office, head bowed, filled with thoughts of his wife. For two days, he'd been holding his breath, wary of doing or saying the wrong thing. If he could go back in time and not have had sex with Sara that day, he would. That was saying a lot, because never before had he wished for such a thing.

He hated the fact that, after many weeks of abstinence, their first time together had ended on a sour note—another unpleasant first for them. So he'd refrained from making more overtures, instead choosing to make the calls to their family members, all of whom had offered heartfelt condolences. Each time he'd passed along their love, Sara's face had turned splotchy, and her eyes filled with tears.

He'd brought her flowers and her favorite chocolates, and remained holed up with her while she got herself together, all the while stuffing his own feelings of loss down deep, to be dealt with later.

This morning, when he'd returned from a vigorous bike ride that hadn't quite lowered his stress, she'd announced she wanted to go to the Angel House for a couple of hours. He resented that that place comforted her when he could not. But when his attempt to discourage her from going failed, he'd come to the office.

Now, strolling the halls of this business where he'd worked side by side with his dad for so long, he had to face a reality he hadn't before allowed himself to imagine. He might never be working in that corner office with his own son. He might never have any progeny to take over the legacy that had meant so much to him.

His sisters might have children, but those kids would take their fathers' last names. The idea that he might be the last male Cabot in this family—the end of the line—seemed incomprehensible and vast, like the sadness swelling inside.

Things looked bleak today, but as long as he didn't quit, there'd be hope for the future he'd always believed in. If he was to be the last Cabot, then he'd make damn sure the legacy of the name endured. He looked up as he approached his father's office, shaking off all sense of defeat.

"Was that Gentry?" Hunter asked his dad's assistant, Cindy, while staring at the closing elevator doors. His sister's auburn hair and vibrant clothing were hard to miss, but she rarely visited CTC.

"Yes," Cindy replied, as if it was perfectly normal for Gentry to be in the building.

"Why was she here?" He suspected Jenna had been courting Gentry's vote. Bitterness festered, but he refrained from growling. Although Cindy had always liked him, she remained loyal to his dad. Hunter wouldn't allow her to see him as anything less than calm and collected.

"I don't know, but it got a little loud. She just whipped out of there and stormed off." Cindy returned her gaze to the computer screen, unfazed by (or perhaps just accustomed to) Gentry's antics.

Interesting tidbit, though, about the argument. Perhaps Gentry was giving Jenna a hard time, as Colby had predicted. For a split second, he thought maybe all was not lost. He couldn't do anything about the failed pregnancy, but he could still save CTC.

"Can I go in?" he asked.

Cindy smiled. "Enter at your own risk."

With his hand on the knob, he could hear Jenna through the closed door. Her brittle voice sounded even shriller than usual. "How could she do this? So foolish! What do we do now?"

Admittedly, Hunter savored a smug sense of satisfaction, guessing that Gentry had told them that she couldn't be bought. He opened the door and waltzed into his dad's office with a spring in his step, but almost immediately he lost his composure.

Whatever had transpired must have been something bigger than he'd guessed, because he'd never seen his father or Jenna look so pale. He almost joked but sensed it wouldn't be appropriate.

His father's expression turned even graver when their gazes met. "Hunter."

Oddly, something sounding a lot like compassion laced his father's voice in spite of his obvious angst. Not at all what Hunter expected in that moment. That tone reminded him of all the reasons he'd loved his dad. Of why he'd spent his childhood in these offices, trying to impress and please the man.

"Why do you two look like you just lost your best friend?" He paused, then ventured his original guess. "Did Gentry threaten not to vote for the sale?"

"You have a one-track mind. Not everything revolves around CTC. I'd think you'd realize that by now," Jenna barked, her brows drawn. Hunter opened his mouth to snipe back, but she rubbed her forehead and looked at his dad. "This will ruin her life."

Jenna thought *every* decision Gentry made would ruin her life, whether it was dropping a class or dating a street vendor. With everything going on in *his* life these days, Hunter didn't have much patience for her histrionics. But considering the deepening lines of his father's expression, he decided to keep quiet.

In fact, he started to worry about what kind of trouble his sister might be in, and if he could help. He would feel better if he could fix at least one thing in his family now.

"Jenna," his dad said in a way that indicated he didn't want to discuss the matter in front of Hunter.

Of course, that only piqued Hunter's interest.

"What?" she snapped. "He's going to find out, anyway."

"Find out what?" Hunter rested his hands on the back of a chair in front of him. The tension in the room worked its way under his skin, locking him in place, muscles tight with anticipation. His mind was ruled by logic, so it couldn't begin to predict what someone as impulsive as Gentry might've done.

Following a heavy sigh, his father rested his chin on his fist.

"I'm sorry, son. I wish the timing were better, given what you and Sara are coping with, but your sister's gotten herself pregnant." His father held his breath, his eyes a study in both disappointment and empathy.

It took a minute for the words to sink in, though. Hunter had heard about out-of-body experiences before but never experienced one until that moment. When the room came back into focus, he noticed that his fingertips had dug into the chair.

Gentry was pregnant? By whom? And for how long? The injustice of the fact that someone so careless became pregnant by accident, when, *despite* medical intervention, his wife could not, prompted a sudden wave of nausea.

"Son?" Hunter only vaguely registered his father rounding his desk, so he flinched when his father's hand landed on his shoulder. "Are you feeling okay?"

"No." He shook his head, wishing Jenna wasn't there to witness any sign of his weakness. "No, I'm not. This news couldn't have come at a worse time for Sara."

"Or you," his father quietly added.

He'd been suppressing his own feelings for so long it hadn't occurred to him to consider how he felt about it. Gentry was having a baby. He'd be an uncle in several months. Uncle, not father. Jealousy reared, making him twitch. Would this same hostility crop up if Colby were pregnant? Did that even matter? My God, nothing made sense.

"Sara doesn't have to know—not if Gentry quietly terminates the pregnancy." Jenna kept her eyes on her husband. "She's not ready to be a mother. She can't even take care of herself."

"Jenna." His dad waved, trying to cut her off, but it was too late.

"What?" Hunter turned on her. "Did you actually just say that in front of me?"

She looked perplexed by his snappish tone, so he clued her in.

"Sara's been curled in a ball for almost three days because her last hope of pregnancy went up in flames, yet here you are, *cavalierly* suggesting my sister get rid of her baby? Are you kidding me?" He pressed his palms to his temples in order to keep his head from exploding. "I don't know what Gentry's planning to do, and she's your daughter, so I get you having opinions about this situation, but do *not* encourage abortion in front of Sara."

He heard his voice rising, but he didn't care. He imagined that when Sara heard about Gentry's pregnancy, she might literally lose her mind. And if Gentry terminated it, Sara might never forgive her. He understood that it was Gentry's choice. Under other circumstances he'd have less judgment about that, but the timing made it impossible for him to feel anything other than disdain and rage for that option now.

He needed to get away from his dad and Jenna before he said something unforgivable, so he turned to go.

"Where are you going?" his dad asked. "Take a seat and let's talk more until you calm down."

"No time. Gentry's on the loose, which means I need to find Sara before she hears about this from someone else." Hunter almost broke into a sprint to get to his car while simultaneously shooting Bethany a text to postpone their meeting. Sara would be shocked to see him home in the middle of the afternoon, but this conversation needed to take place in person.

◆ ◆ ◆

Sara smiled at Ty, who sat so close to her today that their legs touched. She wanted to give him a little hug while she read to him but thought at best it would make him uncomfortable and at worst could be crossing a line. She closed *Sheep in a Jeep* and went to pick out another book.

"Seep!" Ty exclaimed, reaching for the book.

Another word. Hunter had worried that her spending time with Ty would be depressing. When she'd first seen his tiny face that morning, it had shot an ache straight to her heart. But then Ty spoke to her—not once, but three times—and her heart had expanded and floated up like a luminary lantern in a Thai festival. Granted, the sum total of words he'd used had been six, but that was a 600 percent increase over her prior visit. She'd felt proud of herself, and of him. For the first time in days, she gained a little perspective on her broken dreams.

She opened the book again. "Okay, Ty. One more time."

Sadly, Pam breezed through the front door, chewing gum. Sara admired her for going to meetings and seeking to improve her circumstances, but she had yet to establish any connection with the younger woman.

Pam wandered into the living room, head tilted to the right. "Why are you so into hanging out with my son?"

The unexpected question startled Sara and, like an open window in January, sucked all the warmth out of the room. She handed the book to Ty and stood to avoid giving Pam the advantage of looking down, literally, on her.

"Aside from the fact that he's adorable?" When Pam didn't smile, Sara said, "I'm only here to help so that you and your son, and others, can get back on your feet."

Pam's eyes roamed Sara's body, checking out her clothing. Unlike Gentry, Sara never wore couture, but the price tag of her simple slacks and sweater could probably feed Pam and Ty for a month or more. The soft cashmere suddenly seemed as itchy as coarse wool.

"Don't you got your own kids and family to worry about?" Pam cracked her gum, one hand on her hip.

"Not yet." Sara paused, surprised by the hopefulness of that answer.

"Ain't you old not to have no kids?" Absurdly, the forthright observation was less painful than silence or pity would've been.

"I'm thirty-four," Sara countered, but one look in Pam's heavily made-up eyes proved that had only confirmed Pam's suspicions. The young woman might be Gentry's age at most. What kind of life could Pam—a homeless, uneducated recovering addict—realistically build for herself and her son? A renewed sense of despair filled Sara.

"Well . . ." Pam paused, hoisting Ty onto her hip. "Good luck."

Pam sashayed out of the living room, disappearing up the stairs that led to the bedrooms. One of these weeks, Pam would disappear with Ty altogether. That acknowledgment turned over in Sara's stomach like sour milk.

Maybe Hunter's concern about her time here at the Angel House wasn't completely misplaced. Still, nothing would make her give up another chance to experience the joy she'd felt when Ty spoke or sat so close it had almost constituted a snuggle. He wouldn't remember her in the future, but if she helped make a few of his days just a little more interesting and bright, it would be enough. That made her smile, inside and out.

Instead of returning home to her empty house, she decided to pop in on Colby to persuade her to share a quick lunch. She'd been ignoring her calls for days, preferring not to have her bruises poked by well-intentioned sympathy. Now that she knew she wouldn't be having a baby, let alone three, Sara would get more involved with the foundation. She could help dozens or hundreds of kids like Ty that way. *That* would be a legacy worth leaving.

A CertainTea was nestled on a wooded lakeside lot at the end of a long driveway. The renovations gave the old stone-and-glass building a modern facelift. In the distance, a gazebo sat near the water's edge, where one could gaze upon the homes and activity on the lake.

Inside, the soothing cream-and-gray palette provided a sophisticated environment for fine dining with a twist. The floor-to-ceiling glass wall also afforded patrons year-round views of Lake Sandy.

Sara crossed through the dining room, listening to sounds from the kitchen as she headed toward the back office. She rapped on Colby's door and then peeked inside, pasting a smile on her face and bracing for Colby's pity. To her left, Gentry's yellow tights, red boots, and Moschino dress caught Sara's attention. "Oh, Gentry! I didn't expect to see you today, too."

Gentry's sober demeanor offered the first hint that something that had nothing to do with her and Hunter was way off. Sara glanced at Colby, whose jaw had gone slack beneath wide eyes.

"Sara!" Colby stood, smoothing her long, straight hair; then she froze, her fingertips pressed to the desktop. Hint number two . . .

The odd reception and subsequent silence waved a red flag in Sara's subconscious. Questions about what they were hiding—and why—arose, heedless of all warnings.

"I was on my way home from the Angel House and thought I'd see if you were free for lunch. It's perfect that Gentry's here, too." Sensing their hesitation, Sara added, "I'm sorry for hiding out from everyone, but I needed a few days to regroup. I'm feeling better after a wonderful morning with little Ty and am not ready to go sit alone all afternoon. So how about it? Let's have lunch."

Colby and Gentry exchanged an inscrutable glance that ended with Gentry's apprehensive shrug.

"Something's wrong," Sara said, disappointed by their lack of enthusiasm. "Are you mad at me for avoiding your calls?"

"No! We're not upset with you," Colby promised, casting another fretful look at her sister. "Not at all."

Colby's forced smile and stiff body suggested otherwise.

Sara tossed her purse on an empty chair. "Spill it, then. Something's obviously going on. I've never seen you both so tongue-tied, especially you." Sara nudged Gentry's foot. "Is it Hunter? Is he bullying you about your shares or something? No matter what, you're entitled to vote how you see fit."

If either sister thought Sara's remark was disloyal to Hunter, neither one said anything. In her own mind, stating the truth wasn't disloyal or wrong. "Wrong" was a female body denied the basic ability to reproduce.

"No." Colby gestured to the chair where Sara's purse rested. "Maybe you should sit for a minute."

Sara lowered herself onto the chair, trying and failing to read the wordless messages being passed between the two sisters, which were exactly like the kind she and Mimi might telegraph in some silent choreography of a dreaded conversation. A flush rose up her body. "This weirdness is scaring me now. Please just tell me what's going on."

Colby sank back onto her chair and exchanged another look—the resigned "We've got no choice" kind—with her sister.

Gentry sighed, then tucked her chin. She stared at her clasped hands as if fascinated by the way her thumbs were rolling over each other. Without realizing it, Sara had begun tapping her foot. That seemed to spur Gentry to talk. "Remember my escapade with 'Smith'?"

Sara frowned, leg stilled, thinking back. "The Napa fling?"

Sara had kept Gentry's secret fling to herself, partly because she worried about how the family would react. Colby didn't appear to be taking the news well.

"Bingo." Gentry shifted in her chair, her gaze still falling everywhere except on Sara's face.

Sara leaned forward, looking at Colby. "I wasn't any happier than you when I learned about it. It wasn't a safe choice, but it isn't the end of the world. Nothing bad happened, thank God."

Gentry cleared her throat, her legs now crossed, one foot twitching. "Actually, something bad did happen."

"Oh?" Sara sat upright, curiosity piqued. If Smith did something to hurt Gentry, Hunter would go ballistic. He'd be unhappy about Sara keeping it a secret, too. "Did he contact you? Please tell me he didn't post photos!" When Gentry shook her head, Sara timidly asked, "An STD?"

"No STD! Jeez, chill. And he can't contact me, remember? We never exchanged names or phone numbers. I don't remember him taking any photos, but even if he had them, he couldn't tag me." She grimaced then, wrinkling her nose. "Guess I'll never know about that one."

Colby let loose an exasperated sigh, causing Gentry to lift her chin. That was the only sign of "normal" Gentry behavior Sara had witnessed so far.

"So what happened?" Sara asked, her body now strung tight in anticipation.

Mixed emotions washed over Gentry's face while her boot-clad foot continued its spastic wiggling. Her sister-in-law still wouldn't meet her gaze. As scenarios started running through Sara's mind, one in particular finally dawned. She shook her head to clear the waking nightmare. The words wouldn't come, either, as if her silence could make it untrue. The tense moment stretched out, ending with her whisper. "You're pregnant."

Gentry nodded and reached for Sara's hand. Without thinking, Sara flinched, bolting from her chair and bending at the waist. The shock of this news—so unexpected and unfair—struck her system like the sharp nerve pain of biting down on a bad tooth. Her sanity might very well be whisked away, too.

Colby approached her and rubbed her back. "Sit before you pass out, Sara."

Mutely, she obeyed, closing her eyes, hoping for darkness to hide her ugly thoughts. Jealousy washed over her in bitter-cold waves, drowning her until her mother's voice cut through the noise in her head, telling her to find the grace to be a good sport. She managed to choke out "Congratulations."

"Whoa! Let's not pretend this is something to celebrate." Gentry stretched out in her chair, one hand on her abdomen. "I don't want to be anyone's mother. Not now, maybe not ever."

Colby bugged her eyes at her sister for the insensitive remark. Sara bit her tongue. She would not cause a rift today. Gentry had never learned to think before speaking, but she also never meant to hurt most people. *Breathe.*

Gentry then dropped another whopper. "My mom wants me to terminate the pregnancy."

"What?" Sara blinked rapidly. The windowless room seemed impossibly bright, like a spotlight had been pointed in her direction. "Gentry, please don't do that. Not when so many women would trade places with you in an instant. If you don't want to raise the baby, there are other options. I know I have no right to tell you what to do, but please. Please think about that before you make any decisions."

"I have thought about it, actually. That's why I came to talk to Colby." Gentry finally looked Sara in the eye. "I wanted her opinion about the idea I got after leaving my dad's office. That's what we were discussing when you walked in."

Suddenly Sara wanted to be any place else. At home alone now sounded perfect. "I'll leave so you two can finish that discussion."

"No, don't. This involves you." Gentry took a deep breath.

"Me?" Sara glanced at Colby, who'd never looked less certain about anything in her life.

"Yep. I'd planned to come see you and Hunter together, but since you're here, I'll just ask you. Would you and Hunter want to adopt this baby?"

Sara didn't know what she'd expected Gentry to say, but that wasn't it. She felt the weight of their gazes but couldn't speak. Adoption wasn't something she and Hunter had discussed in great detail, because he'd always been convinced they'd get pregnant. He'd reluctantly gone along with the foster care certification, but only to satisfy her. She'd no doubt he'd believed, all along, that they'd have their own kids, and then she'd be too busy to take on others.

Now that he'd been proven wrong, would he agree to this? If so, was Gentry's offer worth considering?

She stood and paced, her body warm and sticky from the stagnant air. "What about the father? Can you give up the baby without him signing away his rights?"

Gentry snickered. "Trust me, Smith isn't looking to become a daddy. And I told you I have no idea where to find him."

That still shocked Sara. So much so she stopped moving. What if Gentry was wrong? What if Smith resurfaced and objected? Sara couldn't take another loss. Yet the idea of being handed a baby in several months made her heart heat with hope. Was she crazy to think it might work?

"You're very quiet," Sara said to Colby. "You have reservations?"

Colby calmly repositioned the crystal vase on her desk and straightened her pile of mail, carefully avoiding eye contact. "It's not my decision."

Typical Colby. Like her brother, she could detach and rely on logic when most others slogged around an emotional tidal pool. Unlike her brother, however, she didn't bombard others with her judgments or try to control the outcome.

"I'd still like to hear your opinion," Sara said.

"Like I told Gentry, this is something you, Hunter, and she need to discuss. My opinions, whatever they may be, aren't relevant." She leaned forward. "Whatever you all decide, I'll support you. If you three choose to proceed, I'll call my old firm and find the right lawyer to paper this."

"Lawyer?" Gentry rolled her eyes. "We're family. We don't need lawyers."

"Gentry . . ." Colby began, then clamped her mouth shut. "Actually, this conversation can wait. Before anything happens, Hunter and Sara have to agree."

Colby's suggestion reinforced the ramifications of this decision. Sara did need to speak with Hunter and consider all the potential pitfalls. Even so, the mere idea of having a newborn to mother in only two hundred or so days glittered like the lake on a sunny day. After years of trying and failing, that wait would pass like no time at all.

She envisioned turning the guest room closest to the master into a nursery, imagining the two a.m. feedings, where she'd cradle the infant in her lap and stare through the window in wondrous silence at the stars. Then she reminded herself that Gentry hadn't always been reliable, Smith was a wild card, and Hunter would have concerns. Many concerns.

Sara's phone rang.

"Speak of the devil." She held it up. "Hi, Hunter."

"Babe, are you still at the Angel House?" Trepidation colored his voice.

"No. Why?" Both of her sisters-in-law were staring at her, making her self-conscious.

He paused before answering. "I'd like to have lunch with you and talk. I'm at the house. Can you come home?"

Sara frowned. He was home in the middle of the day? She must've seriously worried him with her behavior these past several days.

She looked at Gentry for a long moment and made an impulsive decision. "Actually, that's perfect. I want to talk about something, too. I'll be there soon."

Sara stuffed the phone in her purse. "Gentry, if you don't have other plans, maybe the three of us could discuss this now."

"I might not ambush him this way," Colby cautioned.

"It's not an ambush," Sara insisted. "It's a discussion. Nothing is decided, but it makes sense for the three of us to talk about it together. What's the point of delaying? Let's start the discussion. Unless, of course, you have someplace to be."

"I don't want to go back to CTC today. One go-round with my parents is enough for now."

Gentry backing down from confrontation? The pregnancy had clearly rocked her.

"Hunter's actually at home. He must've come by to check on me. You won't have to see your dad or Jenna until you go home later."

"I really don't need a lecture from Hunter, either." Gentry actually looked a tad green sitting there gripping her stomach like she might barf. Sara supposed the prospect of Hunter's disapproval could be daunting. "Why don't you break it to him?"

"It'll be better if we all hash it out together. He'll be too floored to lecture. That might come later, or not at all." Not knowing where the conversation would lead seemed to intensify the sense of urgency building inside. "Come with me, please."

"Fine." Gentry stood and crossed to Colby. "Give me a hug in case I don't survive Hunter's death stare."

Colby snickered. "It can be quite lethal."

They were right, but Sara was willing to brave it for a chance to be a mother instead of an aunt. Her limbs hummed with energy as the idea of adopting Gentry's child blossomed like a field of sunflowers.

Before she realized it, tears had filled her eyes. She gathered Gentry into a tight hug. "Thank you. Thank you for this generous, beautiful gift you're willing to give to your brother and me. Whatever happens, know that I'm honored."

Gentry, who'd never embraced shows of affection, eased away, hiding her face. "You're welcome."

"Sara," Colby said.

"Hmm?"

Colby pressed her lips together for a second, as if taking measure of her words before speaking. "You sound decided, but remember, this decision isn't yours alone."

Chapter Nine

Hunter sat on the sofa, head bowed, hiding his expression from his sister and wife. Of all the ill-conceived ideas Gentry had suggested throughout the years, surely this was the biggest whopper of all.

He would've dismissed it outright had it not been for the hopeful look on Sara's face. Even now, she sat poised at the edge of the sofa, looking like a kid waiting for her turn on Santa's lap. As usual, he'd have to play the grinch, shoveling a dose of reality on this naive plan.

"Gentry, I appreciate the love and trust behind this offer. It means so much to Sara and me that you'd choose us as your baby's parents." He cleared his throat, loosening the tightness caused by the sentiment. Beautiful gestures aside, he needed time to adjust to his sister's pregnancy, let alone consider this crazy adoption proposal. "But I'm not sure you've considered the problems with this arrangement."

"What problems?" Gentry asked.

"For starters, what about the baby's father? He might want some say." Hunter kept his focus on his sister, although peripherally he became aware of Sara's gaze boring into him.

Gentry laughed. "Not in a million years."

How she found humor in *that*, he surely had no idea.

Sara set her hand on Gentry's arm. "Of course that's a worry. Maybe we could hire an investigator to find him?"

"No way!" Gentry protested. "Aside from being a monumental waste of time, it'd be humiliating."

"You really don't know anything about him other than a nickname and what he looks like?" Hunter scowled. Could the guy assert rights when he didn't even know Gentry's name? And what of the child? Didn't he or she have the right to know his or her father? The facts leading to this present circumstance raised so many questions he didn't know where to begin. "Setting 'Smith' aside, this idea is loaded with other complexities we wouldn't face in a typical adoption."

"Complexities?" Gentry teasingly mocked him with a snobby pronunciation, then turned her palms out in question. "How so? It'll be easier, faster, and cheaper. Usually you *like* efficiency."

He couldn't help but chuckle, despite the gravity of this discussion. He did prefer efficiency, but he also needed logic and good judgment to be part of the equation. Control over the possible outcomes and a known—or at least highly predictable—result. This idea lacked those important foundations.

He stalled for time by rubbing his forehead and looking at the ground. The weight of Sara's disappointment in his reluctance settled on his shoulders like a yoke. "Gentry, how long have you known of your . . . situation?"

"I had a light bulb moment at my birthday dinner, then took a couple of at-home pregnancy tests. I didn't want to announce it the same day that you and Sara got bad news. Plus I needed time to figure out how to tell Dad."

"So you've known for less than a week." He shot Sara a wide-eyed look before returning his attention to his sister. "Not much time to sort through your feelings and consider *all* your options. Are you ready to carry this baby to term and then give it up?"

"Unless you and your genius friends know of a way to shorten gestation," she joked.

He ignored her sassy attitude, determined to make her get real about what she was offering. The toll it would take on her body. The changes it would force in her lifestyle. "Nine months without drinking or smoking or sex with strangers like Smith, who could be dangerous or a disease carrier, by the way. Sara has a whole list of dietary restrictions written out somewhere, and so much more. Not exactly the kind of lifestyle you're used to. And that doesn't even get into the maternal attachment that will form during the pregnancy."

Sara's expression turned gloomy. Although he was relieved to see her brain finally kicking in, he was sorry to see the light in her eyes dim. "Hunter's right. You might get attached and change your mind."

"I'll hardly get attached to something that's making me fat and keeping me from all my favorite vices. Trust me, nine months will be my limit. I've no interest in years of sleepless nights and diapers, potty training, and helping with homework. You and Sara can take over the minute this baby pops out, and I can go back to my debauchery." Gentry's irreverent remark reinforced her immaturity—yet another reason this was a terrible idea.

"This isn't funny. Stop the act and be serious," Hunter commanded. Both Sara and Gentry winced at his tone. He sighed and blew out a breath. This was coming out all wrong. He loved his sister for her willingness to do this for them, but it wasn't the kind of thing people decided on a whim. Certainly not people like him. "Have you talked to your mom and dad about this idea? I can't imagine Jenna wants me raising her grandchild."

Hell, would he like raising Jenna's grandchild? The kid would have that woman's DNA. She'd likely feel possessive of him or her, too, and probably butt her nose into Hunter and Sara's parenting choices over and over and over.

"I don't need to talk to them. This is *my* child and *my* choice. Unlike my mom, I won't keep a child that I'm not interested in raising. Better to give this baby a mother like Sara."

His wife's grateful smile came into view as she reached for Gentry's hands. Then, as if steeling herself to battle, she turned to him with grave solemnity.

"Hunter, I know we've only talked about adoption in a generalized way, and I hear all of your concerns, but at the same time, this feels like a miracle." Sara's cheeks and eyes glowed with hope, making him feel like an ogre for being unenthusiastic. "What if this is the way we're supposed to start our family?"

Sara liked adventure. She'd always been able to handle chaos, a by-product of being raised in a large, loud family, he supposed. He wanted to embrace this for her sake, but warning bells rang everywhere.

"Won't it be confusing for the kid to have his biological mom as his aunt? And what if Gentry doesn't like the way we do things? How much say does she get? And those are just a couple of concerns off the top of my head. This is a huge decision." He stood and paced in a circle. "It's not like giving someone a car."

"Here's the deal." Gentry stood, too, and began ticking off her fingers. "I feel bad about the results of your last IVF, and I really, *really* don't want to be a single mom. I won't interfere with your decisions in the future. I don't need this baby to know that I gave him or her up, either. I'll simply be Aunt Gentry, the *fun* one in the family."

"We can't keep that secret!" Hunter looked at Sara to make sure on *that* point they were in agreement.

"I agree. If we do this, we'd need to set some ground rules, honesty being at the top of the list," Sara said. "We'd have to figure out the right age to talk about it, but I wouldn't want to keep secrets from my child."

On some level, he understood his wife's willingness to skim over the pitfalls of this arrangement. But how had his sister cut herself off from any emotions about this baby?

Gentry shrugged. "Fine."

"Sis, if you give your child to strangers, I suspect, in time, it will become less of a thought in your life. It'll be easier to move on. But if we raise this child—which would be *ours*—you'd see it every week. A constant reminder of what you gave up. Are you sure that won't hurt?" Hunter would never hand off his own flesh and blood, which was why he couldn't believe anything coming out of Gentry's mouth today.

"On the other hand, giving the baby to strangers could be harder," Sara interjected. "She'd never know, with certainty, that the baby had a loving, safe home. Whereas if we do this together, she can have a close relationship with her child without the responsibility."

Clearly, Sara was well on her way to making up her mind. To her, it was almost as easy as reciting the alphabet.

He glanced at his sister again, willing her to step back and give this more thought, even though he knew that could mean serious trouble between him and his wife. They didn't need more trouble, but he much preferred to face problems right away than deal with unexpected turmoil later.

"My mom wants me to terminate the pregnancy. Honestly, I'm not fundamentally against that idea. I'm only considering carrying this baby to term for you two. I wouldn't make all those sacrifices for strangers." Gentry shrugged unapologetically. "Maybe that makes me a bad person, but at least I'm honest."

Now he had the weight of Sara's happiness *and* this baby's life in his hands. Given the fact that Gentry was about eight or nine weeks into her pregnancy, he didn't have much time to decide, either.

He raked his hands through his hair, stalling again. He'd never resorted to such tactics before, but he'd also never been forced into such a monumentally life-changing choice, either.

"You really want this, Sara?" His stomach burned from being forced to make this decision in too short a time frame, but after watching Sara suffer, he couldn't outright deny her this chance. Maybe she was right.

Maybe this miracle was a sign. Good God, now he sounded like his mother.

"I know it's complicated, and there will probably be speed bumps we don't see, but a few days ago I had no hope, and now we could have a baby in seven months. Better yet, I could go to all the appointments with Gentry and be part of the pregnancy, which I wouldn't get to do with a normal adoption. It's like the next best thing." His wife brightened visibly at this latest realization. If she hadn't already been fully on board, now she'd torn up the ticket and boarded the one-way train to motherhood.

"Payback! Now you'll have to see *me* in stirrups," Gentry joked, elbowing Sara.

When Hunter detected Gentry's joy in making Sara—and him—happy, his eyes watered, which rarely happened. Who would've ever thought Gentry would be so selfless for his sake?

"I'm touched by your magnanimous show of love, which I'll never be able to repay. But you know me. I can't make a snap decision about something this big. Can you, Sara, and I take a day to really think through this huge commitment we'd all be making to each other? It requires more than a single conversation, although I also understand that we need to decide very soon."

Gentry sighed. "You worry too much. Life's much better when you go with the flow. Call me tomorrow or the next day. In the meantime, I'll prepare my mom for the possibility."

"Maybe you should wait, Gentry," Sara interrupted. "No reason to get into a fight with her if this isn't going to happen. And if we decide to go forward, then it might be better if we all make that announcement together."

"Fine. I'll wait. I'll figure out some way to avoid her tonight." Gentry hugged Sara. Hunter gave her a hug, too, and when he did, she grinned. "Honestly, Hunter, there's no need to drag this out longer than the morning. We all know you won't say no to Sara."

He kept quiet, because as much as he didn't want to deny Sara anything, he couldn't quite wrap his head around this plan.

◆ ◆ ◆

Sara waited until Gentry had pulled out of the driveway before resuming the conversation with her husband. She found him standing at the family room window, staring so intently at the lake she could probably dance around naked without gaining his attention.

His reaction hadn't surprised her. Despite her own enthusiasm, she understood his reservations. Rather than launch back into the discussion, she gave him a break. "Are you hungry? I can fix us some lunch."

"I'm hardly hungry now." He twirled around and grabbed her hands before she could busy herself in the kitchen. "Slow down, babe."

She pressed her lips together and inhaled through her nose. Selfishly, she didn't want to give him a chance to talk her out of this. He had logic on his side, after all. But for her, hope always proved more intoxicating than logic.

"I know Gentry's offer feels like a miracle to you, but when something seems too good to be true, it usually is." His owlish gaze was filled with compassion and concern.

Sara didn't want pity. Concern didn't help much right then, either. She wanted him to trust that his sister knew what she wanted.

"In an ideal world, we could analyze every detail and make perfect decisions, but sometimes you just need to go with your gut." Even as she said the words, she knew that she might as well have been asking him to move to Mars.

"*My* gut is telling me that this could be a disaster. Are you honestly without any concerns?" Hunter asked. "Let's set aside issues about Gentry's reliability. We know *nothing* about 'Smith.' What if he or his family finds out about the child later? What if he's a psycho or has some illness that's important to know about?" His runaway thoughts were written all over his expression.

"If we adopt *any* child, we'll be facing some of those same questions. Why not adopt one related to you? Gentry really wants to do this for us. That's huge, Hunter. Huge *of* her and *for* her."

He released Sara's hands and resumed his pacing. Then he stopped. "Assume the pregnancy goes well, and we bring the baby home. You know Jenna will think of it as *Gentry's* child, because it is. We'll be forced to suffer through that woman's intrusive advice for the rest of our lives."

Her husband's face reflected his horror at that thought.

"With your dad's help, we can draw boundaries."

"You think so, do you? She's talking him into selling CTC, so I wouldn't bet on it. Who knows what she'll convince him to do or say when it comes to their grandchild."

"Can we *please* have one discussion that doesn't mention the business, Hunter?"

"Oh, for God's sake." He rested his hands on his hips after pushing his glasses up the bridge of his nose.

"And don't use Jenna as a scapegoat for your hang-ups."

"That's not what I'm doing. But don't *you* deny the obvious downsides."

"Like I already said, no matter what option we choose to have a family, there will be drawbacks. So tell me the truth. Are you jealous . . . wishing it were your Cabot DNA instead of your sister's?" Typically, Sara did anything to avoid the blistering cold spot in her subconscious that wondered if her husband resented her infertility. Today it had to be addressed.

Hunter paused, considering his answer, and his hesitation opened up a pit in her stomach.

"In all honesty," he said, "of course I wish we were able to have children together. But that doesn't mean that I have any ill feelings about it, or you, just because we haven't succeeded yet."

"Yet?" Had he forgotten her promise? "I told you I can't go through another IVF. We won't be having children together."

He removed his glasses, tossed them on the table, and rubbed his eyes. "Both IVFs only failed at the last step, but we've always ended up with multiple grade-one embryos. With surrogacy, it would be *our* child—our DNA. You refused that option because of *its* complications. With Gentry, we have all those complications plus a Gentry-'Smith'-Jenna gene pool. That might be more than we can handle."

Sara thought of Ty and how attached she'd already become despite his parentage and speech problems. "DNA isn't important. Besides, surrogacy would take months to plan, and I'd be subjected to more poking and prodding. I'm tired of being a science experiment. Why go through all that when Gentry's baby is already on the way?"

Hunter's shoulders slumped.

Was she being selfish to deny him another chance at a biological child, or was he being too demanding to expect her to undergo the hormones and shots and ups and downs a third time with no guarantee of success?

Everything in the house fell deadly quiet except for the whoosh of heat clicking on. Hunter eventually collapsed on the sofa and sighed. "You really need this to be happy, don't you? Our life together—our history, our home—isn't enough."

"Don't say it like that. It's not a fair characterization of my feelings or needs."

"Not surprising, considering I haven't been able to get a grip on either in some time. Why are the only things that make you happy lately so risky?"

"Risky?"

"Yes, Sara. Risky. This thing Gentry's proposing is loaded with risk. So are foster kids who are wounded from difficult backgrounds. And working with indigent strangers at the Angel House opens you up to trouble. All these years I've tried to build us a secure life, and now you want to shake it all up."

Sara's throat ached with emotion as she sat beside her husband. "I want what my sisters have. What I grew up with—a big, sloppy, happy family. To me, the risks are worth it, so I'll take Gentry's child and some foster kids, too. I want to be a mom, surrounded by children and teaching them how to make the world a better place. To grow old with grandkids of our own."

Hunter pulled her close. With her ear to his chest, she could hear his heart beating steadily and prayed that it would move him from fear to optimism. She couldn't see his expression, but the tautness of his body suggested his face was pinched with indecision and stress. After a moment, he spoke, his words sounding thick. "I want you to have what you need, babe."

"Does that mean we can adopt Gentry's baby?" Sara held her breath.

He eased her off his chest and touched his forehead to hers. "Let's give her and ourselves the night to think about it, Sara. This is too big of a decision *not* to take at least twenty-four hours to consider."

In Hunterspeak, that was a yes, and she knew it even if he didn't.

"Okay." She kissed him, feeling down-to-her-toes optimistic for the first time in days. "I know you have reservations, but I've got enough faith for both of us."

He would thank her in the summer, when they were doting on a bundle of love. For now, she'd find another way to persuade him. How lucky for her that he'd come home in the middle of a workday. She wanted to make it memorable so he'd be incentivized to do it more often.

She unbuttoned the top two buttons of his shirt and pressed a kiss to his chest. "I know this is really hard for you. Let me prove how satisfying and wonderful risks and spontaneity can be."

He grinned, but his eyes flickered with desire. "Really?"

"Really." She kissed him again, pressing against him as his hands cupped her butt. The last time they'd had sex, she'd cried and ruined it. Today would be different.

"Go fill the tub. I have a surprise." He gave her a quick tap on the hip and went down to the basement. She guessed he might be getting that hidden bottle of champagne. Although she still mourned those would-be children who hadn't survived the desert of her womb, now she *almost* had something to celebrate.

Her parents had always promised that all her dreams could come true as long as she never gave up. It hadn't been easy to believe in that lately, but Gentry's offer had proved their point.

She padded up the stairs to draw a bath. Hunter arrived as she began to disrobe, carrying the bottle of champagne and two crystal flutes.

He filled the glasses and set them on the vanity. "Allow me."

She couldn't say who liked his ritual of undressing her more, him or her. Throughout the years, he'd bought her countless sets of lacy underwear, which he liked her to model for him. Watching his pupils expand, hearing his low whistle, feeling his fingertips trace the lines of her body as her clothing slithered to the ground—these reactions always stirred something in her chest that then slid down to her core.

"Miami?" he asked, tugging at the blue satin bra strap.

"Good memory."

"Who could forget that dressing room?" He chuckled against her neck before planting a warm kiss there. Then he raised her arm and twirled her around. "That may have been five years ago, but you look every bit as beautiful now as you did back then."

A falsehood, to be sure, but she appreciated that he saw her that way. It helped her get in the mood, which was something of a feat in recent months. "Flattery will get you everywhere."

"A man can hope." He unceremoniously shucked his shirt and pants, then tugged her to him so they were skin to skin. His arousal pressed against her abdomen as he unfastened her bra and let it fall. He cupped her breasts before slipping his fingers beneath her panties and removing them. "Into the tub with you."

He brought the champagne flutes to the ledge of the soaking tub and then joined her in the warm water, which she'd infused with lavender bath oil. After handing her a glass, he twisted her around until she was sitting in his lap, her back against his chest. "I love you, Sara. Here's to us and our growing family."

The most perfect eleven words he could've said. "I love you, too, and promise you won't regret this." For an instant, she sensed his apprehension. Bone-deep desire for motherhood eclipsed her guilt.

He recovered, then, and stroked the silky, wet skin of her thigh. Within minutes, Gentry's baby was no longer on their minds.

Chapter Ten

"This is insanity," Jenna snapped.

For the first time in the past decade, Hunter didn't completely disagree with his stepmother. She sat on the couch, her hands balled into white-knuckled fists on her thighs, looking like a snake poised to strike. The karmic maelstrom that led them all to this tense moment in his living room—one of maybe two dozen times Jenna had ever been there—still left him a little dazed.

"Of course you'd say that." Gentry rolled her eyes. "Anything I do that doesn't perfectly conform to your opinions is 'insane' in your mind."

Jenna held her head with both hands, then turned toward her husband. When he didn't immediately speak, she bugged her eyes. "Jed! Please jump in."

Sara clasped Hunter's hand while they awaited his dad's reaction. Her serene expression projected a certainty he now faked. He wished he felt certain, because then it would be easier to defend Gentry and their plan. Easier to share in Sara's bliss instead of pushing down the periodic resentment of being manipulated whenever it surfaced. Right now, the best he could muster was to lean forward, hold his wife's hand, and try to decipher the turmoil in his dad's eyes.

His dad and Gentry stared at each other, and then his father's gaze flicked to him and Sara. Hunter had witnessed that conflicted look in his dad's eyes throughout the years. Like when he'd announced his intention to divorce his mom, or when he'd told Hunter and Colby that they'd soon have a baby sibling. The last time he'd seen it was years ago, when Colby had eloped with Mark after knowing him for only three months.

Typically, Hunter would be upset by not having his father's full support. In this case, he couldn't blame the man for having doubts.

"Jed, tell me you're not seriously okay with this idea?" Jenna's cheeks were flushed, her voice high and thready. If she were anyone else, Hunter might feel sorry for her. "This is *our* baby girl. Don't you care about her future?"

His dad patted Jenna's thigh before waving a hand toward Gentry, Sara, and Hunter. "These are three adults, Jenna. Our daughter got herself in a pickle, but I'm proud of her for coming up with an idea to turn it into something positive. She's young and healthy. There's no reason to think this pregnancy will bring her any harm. By this time next year, she'll have moved on, and Hunter and Sara will have the family they've wanted for so long."

Jenna's face transformed into something inhuman . . . like the creatures in *Predators*. Hunter couldn't remember having ever seen her ready to rip his dad's head off. Fortunately, she settled for whipping a throw pillow at his chest before turning a narrowed gaze upon Hunter. "You're awfully quiet. Was this your idea?"

He shook his head, dumbfounded that she'd think that *he* thought this was a good idea. She must not know him at all, which he found oddly disturbing.

"I told you, Mom. This was my idea." Gentry glanced at Sara, heaving a "told you so" sigh. "Honestly, why did we need a family discussion? The three of us have agreed to do this. I don't need permission."

Sara's grip on his hand tightened like a vise, belying her calm voice. "No, you don't, but given how this affects the whole family, it's best to get everyone's support. And we want to make sure that whatever ground rules you, Hunter, and I set will be respected."

Deep down—buried beneath all the obvious problems he'd raised with this adoption—Hunter began to suspect that part of his fear was about how *he* might be destroyed if he allowed himself to fall in love with his sister's baby and then it all went sideways. And things often went sideways when he couldn't control the outcome.

"Jenna, I still have some doubts. Once the baby is here, the lines could get blurry fast. I can't do it unless I know that everyone will let Sara and me raise this child as we see fit, without interference."

He'd just voluntarily put himself in a position of asking Jenna for something and of sharing her concerns. If that wasn't proof of his love for his wife, nothing was.

Jenna's green eyes turned flinty. "I expected your spite when I wanted to sell the business, but stooping to stealing my grandchild is beneath even you, Hunter."

"Jenna, cut it out," his dad interrupted. "That's not what's happening. He's just saying we need to respect boundaries."

Jenna threw her hands up, looking heavenward. "It's no secret that he and I don't get along. Now my daughter is handing her child over to him, and you expect me to accept his limitations on my future relationship with *my* grandchild?" She shot off the couch and strode to the window, rubbing her shoulders as if she'd been tossed onto a tundra in a swimsuit. "Someone please tell me I'm on some horrid hidden camera show."

Hunter let her insults glance off him, conserving his energy for bigger battles. He hadn't expected her support, but he wanted his dad's. "Dad, what's your honest opinion?"

Jenna didn't face them, but Hunter noticed her spine straighten. His father stalled for time, possibly to give his wife a chance to return to the sofa. She didn't. Stubborn as usual, as if her tantrum might change the outcome. Perhaps that's how she always got her way. Hunter had never paid that much attention until recently.

He returned his attention to his father, praying that his dad wouldn't disappoint him.

"We all want you and Sara to become parents." His father's sad smile foretold of a "but" on the way. "But having the perspective of *being* a parent, I'd be remiss not to point out that Gentry has no idea of what she's giving up or how she'll feel after the fact. I worry she'll have regrets down the road."

"Dad!" Gentry scowled, even though Hunter agreed with their father.

"Hold up, girl." Their dad raised one hand. "I'm entitled to answer my son and to be worried about you. That said, this isn't up to me. It's up to you three. I'll support whatever you do and hope for the best."

"Jed!" Jenna whirled around so fast Hunter checked the hardwood for a divot from her heel.

"Jenna, it's not our decision. Besides, Gentry's twenty-six. If we want our kids' respect, we need to give them ours. And you can't argue that Hunter and Sara won't be loving, thoughtful parents." That compliment sent much-needed warmth flowing through Hunter's heart. "Let's not turn this into a fight. We've got enough of that at the office. I'm too old and tired to keep arguing with the people I love."

"Thanks, Dad." Hunter cleared his throat. This man—that speech—was the father he'd loved and admired his entire life. The kind of dad he'd want to be to his own children in the future. He needed to remember that, instead of viewing him as the enemy at the office. "I know it's rough at work lately, but I appreciate your support on this."

"You and Sara will be tremendous parents." His dad then rubbed his knee, wincing. He did look old lately. When had that happened? He'd denied being sick when Hunter had asked the other week, but he definitely wasn't well.

"Can I get you an ice bag, or some ibuprofen?" Sara asked, staring at his knee.

"No, honey. I'm okay. But enjoy your youth. An aging body can be a real pain in the ass." His dad smiled at Sara, whose eyes looked suspiciously watery. He then rose from the sofa and pulled Gentry up into a hug. "Baby, don't take this the wrong way, but I didn't know you could be so selfless. I'm glad for it, though. And proud."

Hunter braced for one of Gentry's smart-aleck remarks, but she surprised him by hugging their dad and mumbling a thank-you.

Sara and Hunter both stood to offer him a hug, too. For a moment, Hunter had his dad, wife, and sister all joined together, with Jenna on the outside. This kind of moment should have shot off a tiny thrill. But given everything that was going on, he couldn't quite muster a sense of victory. Nor could he clear the vague, ominous fog taking up space in his head and chest.

"Jenna, let's go home." His dad started toward the hallway.

"Jenna," Sara called, crossing to her and giving her a stiff hug, which was pretty much the only kind Jenna could manage. "Try not to worry. As far as I'm concerned, there can never be too many people loving a child. No one will box you out. In fact, once the shock wears off, I hope you and I can share Gentry's pregnancy journey together."

Jenna forced a small smile and then looked over Sara's shoulder to Hunter. "She's the best decision you ever made."

"I know." Hunter grinned at Sara, reminding himself of why he was willing to take such a monumental leap of faith. She would be a fabulous mother and build a happy home for him and their children. Of *that* he had no doubt.

"I'm off, too," Gentry announced. "Guess I'd better start searching out fashionable maternity clothes."

"I think you have some time." Sara chuckled and hugged Gentry for the hundredth time in two days.

While Sara walked everyone out, Hunter scrubbed his face with both hands and then shook them out. The stress had messed with his circulation, making his arms and feet tingly and cold.

"You're upset?" Sara said when she returned to the kitchen and poured herself a cup of tea. "I thought your dad handled it well."

He laid his hands on the island and hung his head. He'd just put his future in Gentry's hands, of all people. Every day for the next several months, he'd be relying on her and her body. He'd be worrying about all the things that could go wrong and whether all three of them could be on the same page with each bump along the way. Oh, Christ, he felt like he might be sick.

Unable to give voice to those fears, he deflected. "If I thought Jenna was gunning for me with this CTC sale before, she's going to be twice as bad now."

Sara set down her cup, her face stricken as if he'd slapped her. "Are you seriously thinking about how this amazing gift—this beginning of our family—might affect the business?"

Why did she think these were somehow mutually exclusive events . . . as if he could separate one part of his life from the other?

"We both know that today's conversation will make Jenna more determined than ever to stick it to me."

Her expression pinched as if she'd swallowed bleach. "Is that why you've been so hesitant to get on board?"

"No. It didn't cross my mind until today." He saw her chest puffing up as she prepared to lay into him, so he raised a hand. "Before you start, remember that I'm going along with this adoption for you, so maybe you could stop chewing me out for trying to protect what I want, too."

Sara pressed her lips together, clearly biting back whatever remark had zipped through her head. "Don't you hear how it sounds when you talk about this adoption that way—like you're doing this for me instead of for *us*?"

For the love of God, he didn't understand her nitpicking his words. "Of course it's for us. We're married. This is our family."

"If you know that—if you feel that way—why do you say things like 'going along with this for you'? That makes me feel like you don't really want a family. It makes me feel like I'm alone."

He held his breath even though, in that moment, he wanted to stomp his foot or shout or hit the wall. Nothing he did or said came out right these days. Was this slow erosion of communication inevitable in marriage? Did anything good lie on the other side of this hideous downward slide, or were the "Hunter and Sara" of yesteryear forever gone?

"Let's not get tripped up on semantics, Sara. You're my wife. I love you, I want to make you happy, and I'd love a family. We're in this together, like we've been for years. When I said going along with *this* adoption, I meant that it has peculiar problems that give me pause, *not* that I don't want kids." He decided to withdraw from this conversation before it turned into an argument. "Now, if you don't mind, I need to make a call."

"Right now?" She crossed her arms. "What's so urgent?"

"The future, that's what. Especially if I'm going to have a growing family to take care of." Hunter tried to cut through the tension with a quick kiss to her forehead and then went directly to his office and closed the door.

She thought *she* felt alone? He'd never felt more alone in his life. His father had turned his back on their long-held plans. His wife was always disappointed in his priorities. And now he'd agreed to undertake an adoption he sensed would lead to trouble.

He scrolled through his contacts until he located Rich Cortland's number. Last they spoke, he'd expressed some interest in Hunter's bottling idea. Now Hunter had to proceed with caution because he couldn't talk about the Pure Foods deal thanks to the nondisclosure he'd signed, and he didn't want Rich reaching out to his father, either.

Hopefully, his personal relationship might allow him a little latitude. He just needed to secure solid letter-of-intent terms for a bottling joint venture to present to the shareholders. If he could hammer that out before Pure Foods floated its own LOI, he'd have his best shot at saving CTC and taking it to new heights.

◆ ◆ ◆

The next morning, Sara took her frustration out on her hair, brushing it as if plowing through thousands of tiny knots. After Hunter took off for CTC, she'd called her parents—by herself—to share their big news.

"Gentry's sweet, but isn't she a little flaky?" her mom asked.

"Incredibly generous is more like it."

"Won't it be hard to raise the baby with her looking over your shoulder and bonding with her child?" her mother's halting voice replied.

Sara's throat burned. "Why are you casting doubts instead of being happy for me?"

"We're happy for you, honey. Just get everything in writing," her dad cautioned.

The lack of unequivocal support had caused her to end the call more abruptly than planned. Even an hour later, their doubts left her a bit shaken. Her sisters hadn't been much more enthusiastic, although Mimi had rallied toward the end of their conversation.

So far, only Sara and Gentry thought this plan was the perfect solution. Limitless gratitude overwhelmed Sara, so she decided to go pick up a little thank-you gift for her sister-in-law and then stop by the Angel House. Ty and her volunteer work there always made her feel better. Just as she was thumbing through her wallet and getting her keys, the doorbell rang.

"Gentry?" Sara's gaze fell to the suitcases in Gentry's hands, her stomach then following that downward turn. "Where are you going?"

"I can't stay at home anymore. My mom's being a nightmare about the adoption plan." Gentry cracked her gum, staring at her expectantly. "Can I live here for a while?"

"Of course." Sara uttered the words, envisioning Hunter's reaction to this development. It hadn't even been twenty-four hours and already an unexpected wrinkle had surfaced. She took one of the suitcases and waved Gentry inside. "I hate to see you become estranged from your parents."

"*Become* estranged? You know my mom and I never had a good relationship. I should've moved out a while ago." Gentry set the bag down and sighed, quickly scratching the section of stomach revealed by her crop top. "I won't be here forever, so don't panic. I just need a place to crash while I look around for something I like."

While Hunter might not be glad about this news, Sara didn't mind the idea of company. Gentry's attitude could exasperate others at times, but generally speaking, she'd spared Sara the worst of her moods throughout the years. Given Gentry's current condition, Sara would be happy to make things easy for her for a while.

"I'm happy to have you here." Sara tried to imagine Gentry's flat belly getting round but couldn't. She suspected Gentry would be one of those pregnant women who wore midriff-baring clothes until the very end. Maybe she *should* show off her body as it nourished and grew a child. Sara's body hadn't been able to pull it off, after all. She tore her gaze away from Gentry's navel, blinking back the melancholy tears that had started to form. "Like I said, I'd love to participate in this pregnancy as much as you'll allow. But I know you'll want your own place and space, too. I'll even help you house hunt." Palling around with Gentry could prove fun. If nothing else, it would keep Sara busy and feeling younger. "In the meantime, maybe you can join me when I volunteer at the Angel House. They can always use more help."

"You think I should counsel women?" Gentry made a wonky face and shook her head. "I'm not exactly a role model of responsibility,

Sara. Besides, I'll be busy setting up my own place and dealing with being pregnant. If we sell the company, I'll have beaucoup bucks and can afford an awesome house."

That remark burst the bubble of confidence that had been rising in Sara. Losing CTC would devastate Hunter. Lately, she'd been thinking a sale would be a gift to her marriage and future family. That once Hunter got over the loss, he'd see how much more enjoyment he'd get out of life if he were more present. But she wanted him to slow down by choice, not force. "Sounds like you're in favor of selling."

Gentry shrugged. "I'd never have to work again. I could travel the world in high style. Do whatever I want, whenever I want. How can I be against that?"

"That's all true." Sarah bit her lip, weighing her words and thoughts. Her dream of motherhood had been revived, thanks to Hunter's cooperation, so maybe she should stay neutral in this debate.

"What?"

She shrugged. "Hunter says he can expand the business and make it worth even more down the road."

"Down the road I could be dead or God knows where. Honestly, I just don't understand why everyone always puts off the good parts of life until later. What if later never comes? I plan to live in the here and now. Forcing Hunter to do the same wouldn't be the worst thing for him, you know." She emphasized that statement with raised brows and a sharp nod.

"It's complicated. I don't want him to suffer, which he will if it's forced on him before he reaches that conclusion on his own." Surely, though, when the baby came, Hunter would fall in love and realize that he needed more balance. That people, not paperwork, would most enrich his life.

Speaking of Hunter, she had to warn him about their houseguest, but this news called for a face-to-face meeting. "I was on my way out to run errands. Pick a bedroom and make yourself comfortable. I'll be home in a while. Maybe the three of us can have dinner at A CertainTea later."

"Cool." Gentry hefted her luggage and started up the stairs. Staring up at the landing, she said to no one in particular, "I always liked the lake view from the yellow guest room."

The nursery, Sara thought, but didn't say. It did have a beautiful view of the lake below. Its window barely cleared two lovely dogwood trees. For several weeks each spring, that sight line included pretty pink flowers. Perfect for a baby, especially if Gentry had a girl. *A girl!* Sara's entire body grew warm in anticipation of those quiet moments when she'd share that view with her baby.

"See you later," Sara called out, and then dashed over to CTC's offices to find her husband.

As she strolled down the executive hallway, she saw that his door was closed, as always. Haru sat at her desk just outside his office, her face awash in the unflattering glow of her computer screen. A quick glance around proved that all of the assistants were similarly transfixed.

Sara didn't miss being tied to a desk, poring over e-mails and spreadsheets and reports. Had she grown lazy, or had she simply pointed herself in a direction that she knew she'd find most rewarding?

"Hi, Haru. Is Hunter in there?"

Haru stood, her expression officious. "Yes, but he's with Bethany and asked not to be disturbed."

Discomfort slid through Sara. Why would Haru think Sara wouldn't be welcome to interrupt her husband? A montage of Bethany's admiring glances at Hunter played in her mind. She'd never thought Hunter lacked integrity, but could she be wrong? Was *Bethany* the reason for all the long hours? "I'm sure that doesn't apply to me."

Before Haru could stop her, she swung open Hunter's door, stomach clenched, bracing for an awful revelation.

Hunter and Bethany were working at the small table in the corner beneath the painting she'd bought him in Carmel. Hunter's focus remained aimed at the papers splayed before him. Bethany's body canted toward his, her gaze lingering on his face as he spoke, even though he was still looking at the figures. The blouse under Bethany's tailored pantsuit revealed more cleavage than necessary, in Sara's opinion, but otherwise nothing untoward was happening. Her heart, which had been pounding against her ribs, settled.

Her husband looked up at her and Haru and smiled.

"Hey, babe." Hunter rose to greet her with a kiss. "This is a surprise. What brings you by? Is something wrong?"

"That depends on your perspective." She grimaced, thinking of Gentry's overstuffed suitcases.

He scowled in confusion. "Bethany, can you take these estimates to your office and look through them? I'll catch up with you in a bit."

"Of course." Bethany gathered her things and smiled at Sara. "Nice to see you again, Sara."

"Thanks. You too," Sara said but didn't mean. Not after, once again, seeing a hint of Bethany's interest in her husband. Did Hunter notice? Did he care? She didn't think so, but how many wives had been duped by husbands who had affairs at the office? Might Bethany eventually capture *his* interest? She'd seen it happen to friends, and with Hunter's own dad, more or less.

Wives nagged about sharing the housework and kids and in-laws, while women in the office looked up to and shared the goals of men like Hunter, making those men feel smart, desirable, and successful. Reminding them of what life was like before the obligations and sacrifices required by marriage.

Once she'd closed the door, Hunter tipped his head. "What's wrong?"

If she hit him with her suspicions, he'd take it as an accusation, which it wasn't. She needed to keep her eye on Bethany, but for now she had a more immediate issue to address. "It's Gentry."

"Did she flake already?" Hunter's eyes gazed upward before reaching out for Sara. "I knew she hadn't thought this through. Are you okay?"

"Relax. She hasn't changed her mind." Sara stared up into his perplexed expression and faked a big smile to sell this living arrangement as something positive. "She's temporarily moving in with us."

His brows rose above the rims of his glasses as he released her. "What?"

"She plans to find her own place soon but wants to get out from under Jenna's thumb for a while."

He squinted. "Days?"

Sara shrugged. "Probably weeks or maybe even more. I can't say."

He shook his head and rested his hands on his hips. "So much for privacy."

"This is a good thing, Hunter. I'll be able to keep an eye on her during these early months of the pregnancy." Sara looped her arms around his waist and hugged him. It had always bothered her that he wasn't as close to Gentry as he was with Colby, even if his reasons had some merit. Family should knit together, not remain separated by invisible lines of loyalty and mistrust. "And you should take advantage of the opportunity to get closer to your sister."

She looked up and recognized the dawning light in his eyes that typically preceded his ideas. "The chance to court her vote is a silver lining, but you know Gentry's going to disrupt our lives."

Sara eased out of his arms. "I meant get closer for *personal* reasons, not business ones." When he tensed, she decided a joke might work better than a lecture. "As for disruption, it'll be good practice for when the baby comes."

Sara laughed at Hunter's startled expression, as if he hadn't ever thought about the realities of children. Of course, perhaps he hadn't. She went up on her toes to kiss him, but then a knock at the door stopped her.

"Come in," Hunter called.

Jed stuck his head in the door and smiled when his gaze landed on Sara. "Hey, Sara." He entered the room and closed the door. "I'm glad you're here, actually. Jenna's in a tizzy over Gentry, and I haven't had a chance to play peacemaker yet."

"I'm sorry you're bearing the brunt of their problems. Hopefully, it'll be temporary. But Gentry's safe. She asked to stay with us until she finds her own place," Sara said.

"I've heard." Jed scratched his jaw. "And that's okay with you?"

"Sure," Hunter interjected.

"I've always wanted all my kids to be closer, but I can't lie. This isn't exactly how I foresaw my wish coming true." Jed crossed his arms.

"We certainly understand something about not getting your wishes exactly the way you planned," Sara added quietly.

Jed softened. "I know you do."

"Gentry will be fine with us until she finds her own place," Hunter said in the definitive tone that usually ended a discussion. But Jed was worried about his baby girl and wasn't intimidated by it today.

"Jenna's already on the edge, and now this." Jed shook his head. "Hunter, promise me you won't put your sister in the middle of our disagreements or your piss-poor relationship with my wife."

Hunter clenched his jaw. "I'm not going to censor myself in my own house, Dad. If Gentry asks for my opinions about the sale, I'm not going to lie. But I won't manipulate her or try to get between her and Jenna, if that's what you're worried about."

"Why do you hate Jenna?" Jed's flat voice landed with a thud.

"Hate's a little strong." Hunter shrugged. "Dislike. Distrust."

Sara bit her lip to keep from disagreeing. She knew Hunter, and he pretty much hated his stepmom.

"In the beginning, you two got along. Colby was the one who kept her distance. I don't understand why everything flipped." Jed looked past her and Hunter now, as if he were watching a movie of their lives and trying to figure out where it went wrong.

"When I was young, Jenna acted like she liked me. Now I see she was pretending until she felt more secure with you. Colby and I are constant reminders of your life before her. She hates sharing you with us. If Jenna hadn't treated Colby and me like second-class citizens after Gentry came along, maybe we'd all be closer. But the final tipping point was when I came here to work side by side with you. Since college, Jenna's worked against my rise here every step of the way. If this didn't exist"—Hunter gestured around the office—"we might've gotten along okay."

"Another reason why selling might be best for our family." Jed shrugged.

"If you two retired, we'd reach the same result without you going back on your word."

Sara saw a rosy flush creeping up Hunter's neck. She rubbed his back to calm him down, realizing her hope of convincing him to see any bright side to the sale of CTC was no more likely to happen than her getting pregnant.

"Okay, let's not start this again." Jed waved his hands. "I just came in to find out about Gentry."

"Jed, she'll be fine. I'm actually looking forward to her company and being more involved in the pregnancy." Sara crossed to hug him because he looked depressed. One day neither she nor Hunter would have the chance to hug him, so she wouldn't take this for granted. "I'll make sure that Jenna isn't excluded."

"Thanks, Sara." He looked at his son. "I'll talk to you later."

Sara felt torn. That spat about Jenna had made Hunter accept Gentry moving in, but it had also exacerbated the deteriorating relationship between him and his father.

For all of his intelligence, commitment, and loyalty, her husband couldn't see how his obsession was slowly destroying his family. "Try not to fight with your dad. I know you're upset with him, but at the end of the day, he's your father. He's loved you your whole life. Isn't love more important than these bricks and mortar?"

"Please, Sara. Not now. I'm about at the limit of how much change I can be expected to handle at once." He closed his eyes and drew a deep breath.

"Okay." Unlike her, he'd never enjoyed change. He hadn't even much liked real adventure. He preferred plans and process, and at the moment, he had little of that to cling to. She set her hands on his chest. "I'll make something special for dinner. Will you be home by seven?"

He stiffened. Clasping her hands, he said, "I'll try."

"I think it would be nice, for Gentry's sake."

"I said I'll try. I *am* up against a ticking clock, and these interruptions don't help."

She turned to go, then stopped and whirled back on him. "Assuming you win this war for the company, can I count on you to keep reasonable hours once the baby comes, or will there just be some other excuse for you to spend most of your time in this room instead of our home?"

His eyes flashed white-hot. He stretched his arms wide and pivoted. "This isn't some kind of whim or ego trip. Hundreds of families count on these jobs, and not all will survive a merger. I've got a responsibility to them *and* to our growing family. It's not just about me and my own ambitions."

"I get that, but aren't our marriage and I your most important priorities? My parents raised five kids and still managed to eat dinner together most nights."

His jaw clenched as his gaze drifted somewhere above her head for three seconds. An unnerving calm settled over him, and in a distant voice he replied, "I won't ever be home by five and have my summers free, and I never promised you that." He turned from her and went around to his desk, knocking on it. Finally, he looked right at her. "If that's the kind of husband and life you wanted, why the hell did you marry me?"

The force of his words struck her chest like a punch. He was angry and hurt, but so was she.

"Trust me, I don't have any illusions that we will be like my parents, which is too bad, since they've been happily married for thirty-seven years, unlike *your* parents. There's something to be said for spending time together, whether you want to acknowledge it or not." Before he replied, she turned on her heel and stalked toward the door. "See you later."

◆ ◆ ◆

Hunter made sure to get home for dinner, although his mind buzzed with a ten-foot-long to-do list while he poured himself some wine. Any hope for a peaceful meal vanished when his mom rang the bell. In all the hubbub, he'd forgotten to tell her the news. Or maybe he hadn't yet fully accepted it and had subconsciously chosen not to spread the word.

"Mom."

She blew past him and started down the hallway to the kitchen, full of animation, talking to him over her shoulder. "I heard the big news from Colby. I can't believe neither you nor Sara called me to tell me about Gentry's pregnancy or this adoption—"

"Sorry. It just happened. I planned to call you tonight," he lied. He followed her, trying to catch hold of her to warn her that Gentry was in the house, but she kept talking.

"I bet Jenna is none too pleased that her daughter got knocked up by a stranger. My goodness, Gentry's a wild one. My hair would've been gray by thirty if she'd been my daughter. Thank goodness you and your sister were such good kids." His mom clucked just before entering the kitchen.

"Well, hello to you, too, Leslie." Gentry sat, water glass raised in the air, in front of a bunch of magazines she'd strewed across the island.

Sara busily stirred something that smelled like her vegetable-lentil soup, offering his mother a quick smile.

"Oh my word. I didn't expect to see you here." His mom avoided Gentry's gaze and set her purse down, doing her best to cover her embarrassment from being caught gossiping.

"I'm living here now. Guess they didn't tell you *that*, either." Gentry tapped her lips with a questioning finger. "Gee, why do they like to keep you in the dark?"

"Gentry, no picking on my mom while you're in my house." His mom could be kooky and intrusive, but she was essentially a harmless, lonely woman.

"But it's okay for her to rag on me even though I'm handing you my baby?" Gentry pulled a puss.

Well, *there* was something he hadn't considered—did his sister plan to throw her offer in his face all the time, or use it to manipulate him? He hated that those thoughts crossed his mind, but he couldn't quite separate Gentry from Jenna, and Jenna *would* do that, no doubt.

"Let's be honest, sis." He slung his arm around her shoulder. "She didn't say anything that you wouldn't normally boast about, so don't pretend to be offended now."

Gentry shrugged him off. "I guess I can't argue with that. Still, you go at *my* mom way worse."

"Your mom and I have worked together for half your life. It's different. But if I were living under your roof, I wouldn't take shots at Jenna in front of you."

"Fair enough." Gentry lazily turned the page of some oversize fashion magazine while tossing his mom a sidelong glance. "Sorry, Leslie."

His mom was stunned into silence, something rare. "I'm sorry, too. I'm just shocked at this whole situation, except for the pregnancy part."

"Mom!" Hunter ground out. "Enough."

"What? You said if it was true, it was okay." His mom went to give Sara a kiss hello. "Gentry's never made a secret of her fast lifestyle. It's part of her whole persona."

"Everyone stop." Sara circled one hand in the space between them all. "This is a truce zone. Everyone who enters my house will put down their weapons and be kind. Only positive energy now. There's a life growing, and we want to surround it with love."

Gentry leaned forward and touched her forehead to the island. "Oh boy."

"Tell me about it," Hunter commiserated, and when she lifted her head, he winked at her. A bubble of affection rose in his chest. No matter how different they were, he'd never be able to express his gratitude for her tremendous sacrifice. Maybe she'd earned the right to throw it in his face a time or two.

His mom's gaze drifted from him to Gentry and back again. Her expression shifted to something he could only describe as oddly emotional. She stepped close to Gentry—close as she'd ever been—and touched her hand.

Gentry nearly flinched, unaccustomed to his mom being anything other than caustic with her.

"Gentry." His mom cleared her throat. "I know what you're doing has nothing at all to do with me, but I still want to thank you for doing this for Hunter and Sara. For the good of the family, motley crew that we are. It's very brave."

Gentry surprised Hunter by refraining from a joke or a barb. Instead, she smiled at his mom. "You're welcome."

The energy in the room—something he'd rarely notice or discuss, which meant his mom was having more influence on him than he enjoyed—turned nearly solemn. He stood there, with three of the four most important women in his life, feeling exposed and awkward.

Living through Sara's IVF hormones had been tough. Now he'd have his pregnant sister, obsessed wife, and doting mother underfoot all the time. He and Sara were in the middle of a serious rough patch in their marriage, and now they'd have no privacy. And yet, Sara hadn't looked this hopeful and excited in so long. If anything was worth the total loss of control over his life, that should be it.

In a lame-ass attempt to reassert himself somewhat, he turned to Sara. "I'm starving. Let's eat."

"Aren't you glad you made it home in time?" Sara smiled at him while handing him a basket of freshly baked rolls with melted butter.

"Oh? Lots of late nights?" his mom chimed in, her gaze narrowing.

"Busy times." Hunter set the rolls on the kitchen table, then snatched one and took a big bite.

"I remember *that* excuse all too well." His mom wagged her finger.

He noticed Gentry grow still and suspected she was now only pretending to read that magazine. "It's not an excuse, just the truth. There's a lot happening at the office. Bethany and I are up to our ears in reports."

Sara washed the cookie sheet that she'd used to cook the rolls, clearly avoiding eye contact with him or his mother.

"Bethany." His mom clucked for the second time in ten minutes. "She never married, did she?"

"Not yet." What the hell did that have to do with anything? He popped the rest of the roll in his mouth and chewed while frowning.

His mother cast a surreptitious glance at Gentry and then muttered through her teeth, "Reminds me of another ambitious upstart. Don't you forget where your bread is buttered, Hunter."

Gentry snickered, then covered her mouth. "Sorry."

"Oh, for God's sake, Mom, I'd never be unfaithful to Sara." He scowled at his mom and then at Sara. He doubted his wife put his mom up to that remark, but she also hadn't scoffed or otherwise made fun of it. He saw her toy with her pendant and felt marginally better. They might not have been in sync lately, but she had to know he loved her.

"I'm sure most husbands say the same thing, but something happens in those offices. Late nights working together to solve problems, celebrating wins. Pretty soon you have more in common with the people there than you do with the other people in your life, like your wife and kids . . ." His mother shook her head.

Gentry fell suspiciously quiet, gazing at his mother like she was seeing something new. She then turned on him. "Hunter, I don't want my baby raised like me, with work-obsessed parents and nannies and everything. I also don't want it with parents who end up divorced. I want it to have a home. A place. To belong. Promise me you won't be like my mom and dad and give everything to your career."

Instead of the defensiveness he'd gotten used to wearing like a coat of armor, Hunter felt an unexpected stab of sympathy for his sister. For years he'd judged her to be quite spoiled, but he'd never really considered that, all along, she'd been lonely. That all her loud clothes and louder sarcasm might actually be her crazy way of calling attention to her need to feel like part of this family.

But that feeling didn't last, because all three women were basically accusing him of being neglectful at best and disloyal at worst. If this kind of ambush was what he got for coming home early, he wouldn't be overly eager to repeat it. Right now, Gentry stared at him, awaiting his response.

"Sara and I haven't discussed all this yet, but I doubt she plans on going back to work anytime soon. Maybe never. Maybe she'll just want to keep adopting children. But whatever we decide, we'll love our children, and they'll have a sense of family. I'm sorry that you never felt that way, and that Colby and I didn't do more—or even realize—that you felt left out. I was in college before you hit middle school, but that's no excuse now." He'd let his negative feelings about Jenna become more important than his sister, an admission that fueled a little self-loathing.

Still, he couldn't lie or pretend that he didn't want both a flourishing career and family. "I love my family, but I also love my work. Sustaining our family legacy matters to me. I doubt I'd be a good father or husband if I didn't have that sense of purpose."

"Well, if my mom has anything to say about it, you might have to find some other purpose soon." Gentry lifted her chin, challenging him.

She clearly didn't like his answer. He didn't know what she expected from him now, but he wasn't going to play games or give her any information that she could feed back to her mother.

"Let's eat before the soup turns cold," Sara interjected instead of supporting him. If he didn't know better, he'd guess she'd aired some of their dirty laundry with his mother and sister. "I promise, Gentry, CTC's fate will *not* affect our love for this child."

Hunter took a seat, although his appetite had waned. He picked up another roll, but even that didn't taste good to him now that his stomach had turned over. All around him, the women chatted, though he didn't pay much attention to what they were saying. Halfway through the meal, he glanced up to find his mother staring at him with a solemn expression.

His skin itched from her scrutiny. In that moment, he had the oddest sensation that his whole life—his job, his marriage, his family—was built of glass and that, somewhere along the way, he'd inadvertently kicked a stone into some corner, causing a fracture that would eventually make the whole thing crumble.

Hours later, after his mom had left and his sister and Sara had watched some nighttime drama, then gone to bed, Hunter turned off the lamp on his desk and wandered upstairs in the dark.

Quietly, he stripped down to his boxers while staring at his wife, who slept peacefully on her side. He wouldn't wake her, but he wanted to scream. Scream about how no one appreciated his way of showing love and support. About why she and everyone else kept subtly pressuring him to choose, when he believed he could have it all: the company, the wife, the child . . . happiness.

He slipped between the covers, and for the first time ever, he didn't spoon her. He rolled on his other side and stared at the closet, trying to quiet the storm building in his head.

Chapter Eleven

"You have an extra spring in your step," Gloria remarked with an approving smile when Sara arrived at the Angel House. She waved Sara back toward the kitchen, where the aroma of fresh coffee lingered.

"Must be because my husband and I are adopting a baby." Sara bit her lip then, deciding not to share the details of the situation. She and Gloria had become friendly but weren't quite friends.

"Congratulations! What a lucky baby." Gloria handed Sara a steaming cup of coffee. She supposed one perk of not being pregnant was that, unlike Gentry, she could drink as much of it as she wanted. "When will it be final?"

"The baby is due in May." Sara sipped the hearty brew while vivid images arose on a swell of emotion: swaddling an infant and taking long summer strolls amid leafy trees and flower beds, stretching a blanket out by the lake on a sunny day, and blowing raspberry kisses on her baby's belly while birds flew about overhead. These visions and more had bombarded her thoughts for the past few days, filling her heart with love for a child she couldn't wait to meet. "I'm counting the days."

The creases around Gloria's eyes deepened as her maternal face conveyed friendly compassion. "I hope everything goes smoothly."

Her cautionary tone sounded too familiar. Hunter, her family, and even Colby had reacted with the same hesitant optimism. No one but Gentry and her took this adoption at face value. "I'm sure it will. The birth mother is young, healthy, and committed to giving us her child."

Gloria fiddled with the silver cross dangling around her neck. "I'm sure that's true, dear. Ignore me. I've been working in the system too long not to become a little cynical."

"Oh?" Sara finished her coffee and set the mug in the dishwasher. "I didn't know you dealt with adoption here."

"Only indirectly. Sometimes we're privy to situations affecting the women here at the center. Once, we were working with an indigent who knew her infant would be better off with another family. We met the foster couple that we assumed was a shoo-in for the adoption, but the paternal grandmother surfaced in the eleventh hour, and ultimately the court sided with her. Devastating for the couple."

The coffee Sara had been enjoying now burned in her gut. What if Smith resurfaced? Maybe she should revisit the idea of Hunter tracking him down. But how do you track someone down without a full name . . . or even a real name? Then again, seeking him out would be inviting trouble. Sara breathed a sigh of relief that Gentry didn't know Smith, then shuddered from admitting that ugly, selfish truth. "That's very sad, but I don't think I'll face anything like that."

"Of course not!" Gloria said, glancing at her watch.

"In fact, I've been so moved by this place I convinced my husband to consider being foster parents. We're working through the requirements, so it's possible I'll be taking care of two kids by summer."

Hunter had grumbled about taking on more responsibility before they mastered life with one child. Sara knew that, when it came to having kids, the best way to go about it was to dive in the deep end. Families and love and all the fun chaos that came from those bonds couldn't be planned or scheduled or controlled.

Gloria's proud smile filled Sara with contentment. "The system can always use more special people like you, Sara."

"I'm not so special." She'd never been particularly comfortable accepting compliments.

"I beg to differ," Gloria said, her index finger raised high.

"Well, thank you." She stood there steeped in an awkward silence, then remembered what she'd brought for Ty. She dug into her purse to pull out a box of straws. "On another note, I read that these help kids with speech difficulties to strengthen the tongue and other muscles. It'd be great if Ty would start drinking at the table from a cup with a straw instead of the sippy."

Gloria took the box with a funny look in her eye. "That's very enterprising. I'll find a way to gently encourage Pam to try. And speaking of Pam, I'd better get her and Jolinda moving. Also, we have a brand-new resident, Meg, but she's likely to stay in her room this morning. She's been through a bit of domestic abuse and isn't comfortable mixing with strangers yet."

"I'm sorry. I'll do my best to keep Ty quiet and out of the bedroom area." Sara couldn't help the tiny grin that came from knowing that, in minutes, she'd have Ty to herself. An hour or more with him would distract her from concerns about Hunter's recent quietude.

At first, she'd been glad that Leslie and Gentry had reiterated some of her own concerns about Bethany the other night, but she'd come to regret their interference. Hunter had withdrawn in the nicest, politest way a man could withdraw from his wife. So subtle that no one else would notice. No one but her, and she couldn't even point to any one thing he did or didn't do, or did or didn't say. She simply felt the rupture in her bones. Now, a new thread of worry stitched through her thoughts: could all her attempts to pull Hunter close end up pushing him away?

Her musings were interrupted by Gloria, Jolinda, and Pam, who were putting on jackets and saying goodbye.

"Oh, Sara, I almost forgot. My son, Ian, just returned from Guatemala and is planning to stop by today." Gloria's face beamed. "Don't be alarmed if he shows up. We should be back in about an hour. If he comes before then, maybe he can wait on the patio with an iced tea or something."

"I hope I get the chance to meet him." Sara waved them off.

Once the women left, Ty stood in his footie pajamas, staring at the front door. She'd yet to see his tiny face erupt with emotion, but she suspected his mom's periodic absences confused and troubled him. To brighten his mood, Sara started humming the old *Sesame Street* theme song she remembered and went about the routine she'd established when watching him.

She'd worn comfortable slacks and shoes so she could settle herself on the floor with ease. Still humming, she piled a couple of books on her left and brought two puzzles out of the toy box. Ty toddled closer. His placid eyes and pouty little mouth remained enigmatic. He didn't smile or clap or trot around, showing off like some toddlers. She wondered if he had feelings about her at all, or if, like her husband, he kept his emotions tightly guarded.

Determined to get him talking, she announced, "I'm going to read now. If you want to see the pictures, come sit by me."

She opened the *First 100 Words* board book and began pointing at the images on every page, saying each aloud. Within seconds, Ty had plopped down on her right. When he wriggled, his diaper crinkled beneath his pj's. Such a cute little sound.

She wanted to shower him with affection and giggles to see if that would provoke any laughter, but he was not hers, nor did he give any sign that he'd welcome that kind of attention.

He pointed at the image near the bottom of the page. "Duck."

"Yes, yellow duck. Very good, Ty. You are smart." She risked patting his hair. His eyes widened, but he didn't flinch. She turned the page. "Red tomato."

They continued reading the pages until a knock at the door interrupted them. She made a happy face at Ty, assuming that Ian had arrived. "A visitor!"

Ty didn't seem to care. Sara lugged herself up and headed for the door, not quite reaching it before a heavier knock sounded.

"Sorry!" she called as she swung the door open.

She sensed trouble immediately. A rail-thin man with a receding hairline stood before her, pulsing with frenetic energy. She had to tip her head to meet his gaze, which was so penetrating it made her step back. "Ian?"

He frowned. "Who's Ian?"

"I'm sorry. I was expecting someone." Damn, she'd assumed it was Ian instead of following protocol before opening the door. Little Ty was only several yards from her. She tried to pull the door tight behind her as she stepped forward. "May I help you?"

"Yeah. I'm here for Meg."

The name didn't register for a second until she remembered Gloria telling her about the new resident. The one with an abusive partner. This guy's face twitched, and he clenched his fists. *Think, Sara. Think.*

She forced a bright smile.

"Sure. Please wait here while I get her." She turned her back on him, hoping to step inside and lock the door. Unfortunately, he threw his hand out to prevent the door from closing.

"No need to close the door." His voice was thick with suspicion.

"Sorry. It's a rule." She held her most winning smile in place and tried, again, to close the door. This time he jammed his foot in its way.

"Hey, lady, fuck your rules." He cocked his head.

The edge in his voice and confidence of his stance set her back. "Please move your foot or I'll call the cops."

Sara reached into her back pocket for her phone and realized, too late, it was still in her purse on the coffee table in the living room. The man must've noticed the moment of panic in her expression, because he pushed the door open, calling out, "Meg! Get your ass down here now."

He stuck out his arm, effectively pushing Sara against the wall, and in two quick strides, he'd come inside. He headed back toward the stairs. "Meg, goddamn it. Where are you?"

Sara's attention was split between protecting Ty from this man and worrying for Meg. "You must leave!" She tried to grasp for his arm, but he shrugged her off and glared.

Upstairs, a door closed. His head snapped toward it just before he took the steps two at a time.

Sara dashed to the living room to call 9-1-1 and scooped up Ty, hearing the man banging on the bedroom door and snarling at Meg. She whisked Ty downstairs to Gloria's room while telling the emergency operator about the break-in. Although she was advised to stay with Ty in the basement behind a locked door, the nonstop banging and yelling upstairs tugged at her. Meg must be terrified. What kind of coward did it make Sara if she sat by and let this go on?

"Ty, time for hide-and-seek. You stay here. Don't move. Don't open the door. No sounds, okay." She backed out of the room, staring into his eyes, pleading with him to listen. He didn't move from his spot on the chair, so she closed Gloria's door and ran up to the living room.

At the top of the stairs, she saw the man yanking Meg, a petite, middle-aged brunette with spiky hair, by the arm. His grip was so tight his fingertips were red. Meg struggled to get free, but her feet found no purchase on the carpet. The wiry man had the strength of someone twice his size.

"The cops are on their way. Let her go and leave before you add aggravated assault and kidnapping to the trespassing charge," Sara pleaded.

"I'm not kidnapping," he spat. "I'm bringing my wife home."

"She obviously doesn't want to go home."

He pulled Meg up against his side. "Yeah, she does." He turned and spoke right into Meg's ear. "Tell her, babe. Tell her how you want to come home."

Sara snapped when he uttered the same endearment Hunter called her. She launched herself up the steps without a plan and didn't see his backhand coming.

It struck her face with enough force to twist her neck and send her sideways against the wall. She collapsed, partly in shock and partly from pain, cradling her jaw and the spot on her temple that had connected with the doorjamb. No blood . . . no gash or split lip. Thank God for small miracles.

Meg started crying, adopting a submissive posture now, but fortunately, approaching sirens pierced the air. The man released Meg and growled, "I'll be back," before he turned and spat at Sara. "Bitch, you better mind your own business next time."

He bolted out the door before the cops arrived. Sara went to Meg, who was visibly shaken. "Did he hurt you?"

Meg shook her head, mumbling apologies, unable to make eye contact with Sara.

"It's not your fault. We're okay. We're both okay." Sara awkwardly patted Meg's back, unsure of what to say. She wished Gloria were there, or that she'd had any training on how to handle this situation. "The cops will be here any second. It's going to be fine."

Would it, though? She doubted this was the first domestic abuse report on file for this couple. How could Meg get a fresh start? And how many women suffered this kind of treatment at the hands of men who'd once vowed to love and respect them? Maybe if she pressed charges, too, he'd back down from Meg . . . or would that make it worse?

When the cops arrived, they came in through the open door. Sara relayed her account and then left Meg to give them her husband's name and address. She took advantage of that free moment to rush downstairs to find Ty.

The cops and lights and squawking walkie-talkies might give him nightmares, or flashbacks to his life on and off the streets. Hard to tell. She needed to go back upstairs and sign off on whatever paperwork the cops might need. She'd have to make it seem like an adventure so he wouldn't be traumatized.

"Ty, guess what? Some nice policemen are here to make sure we are safe and happy. Let's go see their fancy cars and lights." She held out her hand, needing to hold on to him even if he didn't need her.

He took it without any fanfare and followed her upstairs. Only two cops remained, and as Sara finalized things with them and Meg, Ian showed up. She guessed him to be about thirty years old. Tall and lean with striking green eyes. His mop of wavy, chocolate-colored hair curled around his ears and jaw. That jaw hadn't seen a razor for two or three days, and his blue jeans were so worn they were nearly white in the knees.

He stopped in the entry and stared at her, his curious gaze taking in the scene before dipping to Ty. "Is everything all right here?"

Sara waved off the officers. "Ian, I presume?"

Meg quickly ducked back upstairs to her room.

"Yeah. I'm just here to see my mom." His gaze then landed on Ty, whose lovely saucer eyes stared at the strange man.

Sara doubted the tyke had many male influences in his life, a thought that sank in her heart like a stone to the bottom of a lake.

"I just got back from Guatemala." Ian scratched his neck, eyes assessing her. "You don't look like the typical resident."

"I'm a volunteer." She felt Ty's hand clasp her pants. Her heart clenched from the realization that he must trust her.

Ian stepped just close enough to get a better look at her face. "You've been hurt."

"It's fine." Everything was fine now, she thought, glancing at the little boy by her side.

"I'm an EMT. Why don't you let me make that call?" He had an easy smile. In fact, now that she could let her guard down, she could see that he was quite nice-looking beneath his scruff and unkempt clothing. "It looks like you got hit or hit your head?"

"Both." She gently brushed her fingers against the goose egg on her forehead.

"Any vision problems or loss of consciousness?"

"No."

"Dizziness, nausea, ringing in your ears?"

"No. Honestly, it wasn't pleasant, but I'm okay. I'm just glad Meg and Ty are safe."

"Understood. But ice and ibuprofen are your friends today." He then crouched to Ty's level. "Hey, buddy. Is this nice lady taking care of you?"

Ty stared at him in silence and barely nodded. Sara cleared her throat to spare him Ian's questioning gaze. "Sara. My name is Sara Cabot."

Ian stood and shook her hand. "Nice to meet you."

Determined to normalize things quickly for Ty, she changed the subject. "So, Guatemala? What were you doing there?"

"I volunteer with Relief Corps, helping with disaster preparedness and other activities."

"How interesting." She'd read about those organizations but had never met someone who'd been willing to upend his own life in order to serve others in disaster areas. Talk about rewarding. It made her little attempts at helping others seem wimpy.

"It can be."

Sara looked at him, trying to picture him cleaned up. He wasn't much older than Gentry. He had an affable demeanor, a caring heart, and piercingly beautiful eyes. This was the kind of person that might give Gentry a broader perspective on life. Unlike "Smith," *this* was a guy to admire.

"Are you single?" she blurted before she thought better of it.

His eyes widened. Then a quick glance at her left hand made him frown. "You're not. Maybe that bump on your head is more serious than you think."

"Oh no, not for me." She waved her hands in embarrassment. "My sister-in-law. She's twenty-six, and—"

He held up a hand to stop her. "Thanks, but I have a girlfriend . . . at least I do for now." He rubbed his cheek in a shy manner, shrugging. "I'm gone for stretches of time, and it's hard for her."

"I can imagine." Sara thought about how she struggled to deal with Hunter's work commitments. At least he came home every night. Then again, Ian was saving lives, whereas Hunter was just saving pennies. "Maybe when the *right* girl comes along, you'll stick closer to home."

A generous smile stretched across his face. "Funny, that's kinda what she's been hinting."

"Ah," Sara replied, feeling lighter despite her bruised face. "We women are strange that way. We like our men to be close by."

"I guess we guys should be more grateful." He grinned while rubbing the back of his neck. "Well, if you're feeling okay, perhaps I should also go check on Meg."

"Yes. That's a good idea. She's pretty shaken."

Ian nodded and directed his gaze to Ty. "Be good, buddy." Then he wandered upstairs in search of Meg.

Sara acted as if nothing had happened, for Ty's sake. She settled back on the floor and picked up another book, but her thoughts strayed to Meg's life, then to Ian. Maybe Sara could arrange an accidental meeting between him and Gentry. Unlike Ian's current girlfriend, her sister-in-law might enjoy traveling with him come summer.

She frowned, wondering if she was looking for a way to remove Gentry from the scene until she and Hunter had time to bond with the baby. That didn't sit well, but honestly, adventure and intrigue with a hot humanitarian might be exactly what Gentry needed. And right now, playing matchmaker held more appeal than thinking about Meg's husband, or how she'd explain her bruises to Hunter.

◆ ◆ ◆

"I don't want you going back there again, Sara." Hunter's big hands cupped her face. "Dammit, I want to kill that man."

She laid her hands over his. "I'm fine. I get to come home to you and this house and all of the beautiful things in our life. But Meg and the women like her . . . they're the ones we should be thinking of. The ones who need our help."

"So let's help in ways that don't put you in danger."

"I'm not in danger." She knew he'd overreact. He always did when it came to things he couldn't control. "Not really."

"He could've pulled a gun or a knife. Anything could've happened." He crushed her against his chest, hugging her like she might disappear if he let go. Speaking over her head, he said, "I sympathize with those women, but we can't save them all or solve all of their problems. And we certainly can't risk your safety to do so. Promise me, Sara. Promise me you won't go back there."

"Hunter, I have to go back. They need my help. Ty needs me."

"*I* need you." He eased her away far enough to look in her eyes. "I need you, Sara. That man you described doesn't sound like he'll give up and go away. Next time he comes back, he'll be locked and loaded. If something worse were to happen—God, I can't even think of it. Don't my feelings count here? What if the roles were reversed?"

Seeing Hunter so unsettled didn't happen often. Maybe never. He made a good point, too. But she couldn't turn her back on the Angel House or on Ty. Not when she was finally making progress with him. "I'm sorry you're so upset, but I honestly think he won't come back. There's a restraining order now, in addition to the charges. The cops will drive by more often. Call Gloria and ask her. Historically, it's been a peaceful house."

"And yet here you sit with a lump on your head and a bruise on your cheek."

"Exactly. What are the chances it would happen again?" She grinned, hoping the childish logic might persuade him.

"Zero, if you don't return. I mean it, Sara. Find another way to help the community." And then, as if realizing his dictatorial tone was out of line, he added, "Please."

She sucked her lips inward, thinking. His concern clawed at her conscience. She didn't want to torment him, yet she couldn't walk away from those women or Ty.

Hunter tugged her against his chest again. "I love you, Sara. Don't scare me this way again."

He kissed her head, and the guilt rippled all the way to her toes. How could he not see that he was asking her to give up something that made her feel like she was making a difference in the world?

"Please don't ask me to stop volunteering there. I'm improving lives. I've taken control over something in my life for a change, and that matters to me. You, of all people, should understand the importance of that."

He released her and sat back, head tipped, and tapped her breastbone right near her heart. "Or maybe you're getting too fixated on that little boy."

"That's insulting. I'm not *fixated.*"

"Aren't you? You're putting his welfare above your own. Above ours." He shrugged. "Does that sound healthy?"

"This isn't just about helping Ty. Pam, Joan, Jolinda, and now Meg rely on me to help with job applications and interview skills. They're getting their lives together. I'm giving them confidence." She crossed her arms, unhappy at having to defend herself like a child. "I've bent for you and your family a lot, Hunter. For years. But not on this. *I* get to decide how I spend my time while you're at work."

She didn't add "which is often," even though she thought it.

"I see." He stared at the carpet for a moment. Finally, he stood and started walking away.

"Hunter . . ."

He stopped, glancing over his shoulder, eyes narrowed. "Before you complain about me and my 'obsession' again, remember that CTC doesn't put me in danger, and it benefits us both. You can't say the same about the Angel House."

He left the room before she could reply, and she heard him call out, "Put some ice on your forehead," before his office door clicked shut.

She threw herself back against the sofa cushions. No matter how good their intentions, they kept hurting each other. If Gentry had been home to witness this argument, she might think twice about her offer. Sara would have to tread lightly while proving to Hunter that he wasn't the only person in this marriage whose personal goals mattered.

Chapter Twelve

Normally, Hunter could walk into his house at any time of day or night and find it in orderly condition. Ever since Gentry moved in, he risked breaking his neck whenever he didn't keep his eyes on the floor.

Her shoes—with those expensive-looking red soles—were kicked off willy-nilly in the mudroom, turning it into an obstacle course. The kitchen sink now held at least one or more rinsed dishes, cups, or glasses because, apparently, his sister hadn't ever learned how to open the dishwasher.

Like a warped version of Hansel and Gretel, he could literally follow the trail of opened magazines, stray socks, and tea bag wrappers to find his sister wherever she lazed about in his home. Today she was lying on the family room sofa with her laptop on her stomach and earphones in. Her head bobbed from side to side to the beat of some song as she swayed one foot to that same beat.

"Gentry." When she didn't answer, he moved closer and tapped her head. "Gentry."

She started. "Oh, hey."

A quick glance at the screen showed A CertainTea's Facebook page. At least she was working on something for Colby instead of lounging around while Sara waited on her. "Don't we have to leave for the doctor soon?"

"Yep."

He waved around at the mess she'd made. "How about you clean all this stuff up before we hit the road. I don't want Sara to be your maid."

"Me neither. I was hoping to make *you* my maid." She snickered.

"Ha-ha." He wondered how often he'd be telling his child or children to clean up, do their homework, respect their mother, and on and on and on. The mere thought made him a little exhausted.

He'd be a dad soon. Not for the first time, he wondered if he'd be any good at it. The confidence that fueled his competence at most things remained elusive in this realm.

"What's wrong?" Gentry closed her laptop and lugged herself off the sofa.

"Nothing. Please fold that blanket before you tackle the kitchen. I'll go get Sara." He kissed Gentry's head and then trotted up the steps.

He hadn't quite decided how he felt about Sara standing her ground about the Angel House, but he was sick of fighting. He'd let it go for both their sakes and because he didn't want Gentry to see them bicker. For now, he'd bite his tongue even though he knew Sara would get hurt—physically or emotionally—by being so invested in those people's lives.

He strolled down the hallway toward the master suite. "Babe, you back here?"

He entered the room at the same time she was exiting the master bathroom. She finished fastening her earring and then gave him a warm kiss hello. Her mood had been better since he'd backed down from the argument. "Just about ready."

Her smile—an unwitting weapon—melted him, just like it always did. In the days since they'd informally agreed to this adoption, Sara had been humming and smiling and more like her old self than she had in ages. He owed Gentry a lot for this gift. If only the overall positive mood in the house would help him forget about his trouble at work.

"Uh-oh, you just thought about the office." Sara sighed while she slipped on her shoes. "What's wrong?"

He didn't want to complain that he was running out of legitimate reasons to delay the due diligence documents Pure Foods had requested, or lament that his hopes were all pinned on his ready-made bottled tea idea, which might require a trip to New York. If that option died, he might truly need to prepare to kiss Cabot Tea Company goodbye. "Just stuff on my mind."

He knew *she* knew what he was thinking about. Instead of inviting him to share his troubles, she said, "This appointment should cheer you up. Today we'll hear the heartbeat and see some kind of ultrasound."

Perhaps it was best for her to keep him moving forward. To remind him that his life had other meaning, too.

"According to the book you gave me, we won't see too much today. At this early stage, the fetus is only about as big as a kidney bean."

She brightened. "Oh, Hunter, you've been reading up! Thank you. I know this is a busy time for you. I really appreciate the effort."

"Exactly how appreciative are you?" He kissed her again, letting his hands run down her waist and over her hips. He knew her body so well and still wanted it every bit as much as he ever had. He tugged her closer, suddenly wishing they had a little extra time.

She pushed away. "Gentry's right downstairs."

"So?"

"She's awake and waiting for us."

"I think she knows we have sex, Sara."

Sara blushed. "We don't have time right now, and besides, she's walking around. What if she bursts in on us?"

"She wouldn't burst in without knocking." As he said the words, he remembered that she'd almost done that two nights ago. She'd knocked first as a warning but then wandered into their room with a bowl of popcorn, plopped herself at the bottom of their mattress while they watched TV, and asked if she could hang out for a while. "Okay, she might do that. I can lock the door."

"She's lonely and displaced. I don't want her to feel unwelcome." Sara briefly kissed his neck.

"She is unwelcome in our room, for God's sake."

"She's only here for a short while, and she's giving us so much. Surely we can keep her company at night." Sara eased out of his arms. "I think she's scared."

"Scared?"

"Of course. Her body is undergoing massive changes. Her relationship with her parents is worse than ever. Her future is still so uncertain."

He hadn't stopped to consider all that. He'd been consumed with his own concerns about the adoption, the Angel House, and fending off Pure Foods. It *would* be scary to grow a person in your body. Then again, how freakin' amazing? But the upcoming months would leave Gentry feeling a bit at odds, no doubt. "I'll talk to her more about trying to set up some consulting business."

Sara rolled her eyes and chuckled. "Only you think the answer to every problem is a career."

"That's not true or fair, but her future is important. At least it's something I'm qualified to help her with. It's not like she wants my fashion advice."

"Why not use this time to get to know her better? There doesn't always have to be a bigger purpose. Talk about music or travel or books."

"She reads?" His joke fell flat. Rather than argue, he asked, "How long do you think she'll be here?"

"I don't know, and I'm not asking. As far as I'm concerned, she's welcome for as long as she needs us." She plucked her purse off the chaise.

Hunter let his head fall back and sighed. He didn't want to be ungrateful, but if they had only a few months before they'd be parents, he'd like to spend that time alone with his wife. "Has she set up any Realtor appointments?"

"Not yet." She stroked his arm. "I admit I'm surprised you aren't taking advantage of an opportunity to persuade her to see things your way when it comes to CTC."

That was the closest she'd come to opening the door to a conversation about work in days.

Hunter shook his head. "I won't make things awkward here by bringing that up or give her any ammo to take back to her mom. The less Gentry knows about what I'm doing, the better."

Sara stilled. "Is that why you've been so tight-lipped with me, too?"

"I know how you feel about CTC, so I'm not bothering you with it."

She frowned. "Just because I don't always agree with everything you think doesn't mean I don't want you to talk to me."

She said that now, but he knew better. Things at home had improved a bit since he'd stopped dumping all his worries in his wife's lap. He'd resolve those things without Sara's help. He had Bethany to talk through strategies and such, anyway. "We'd better hit the road if we don't want to be late."

"I'm so excited." Sara's eyes gleamed. "Let's go!"

An hour later, he and Sara were sitting near Gentry's head, staring at a monitor, looking at the tiny blob that would be their baby. Although he was glad Jenna wasn't at this first appointment, he felt torn about his dad missing out.

His wife's watery eyes glistened. She kept squeezing Gentry's hand and kissing her forehead. Hunter had never been effusive or overly demonstrative with anyone but Sara, but even his throat ached from the significance of what they were seeing.

"The black space is amniotic fluid, and this here is the baby's head." Dr. Sutton moved the cursor around the monitor and clicked things to measure the length of the embryo. "These here are little leg buds, and these are arm buds. That flickering is the baby's heart beating."

When the blob actually wriggled, they collectively gasped.

"Oh my God," Sara whispered, her gaze transfixed on the screen, cheeks flushed.

"Do you want to hear the heartbeat?" the doctor asked.

"Yes," Hunter said, eager to a degree that he hadn't predicted. He looked at his sister with a new kind of awe. Her body was busy creating this life. He would put up with her messy habits for weeks or months if needed. He was as close to tears as he could remember being about anything since his wedding.

For the first time in history, Gentry didn't make any wisecracks. She didn't appear blasé or disinterested. If anything, she seemed transfixed and distant from Sara and him.

Dr. Sutton did something to the equipment, and soon a rapid, hushed *whaw whaw whaw* emanated from the speakers.

"He sounds like he's in distress." Hunter felt his face frown. That heartbeat matched the rate of his own whenever he biked up Hilltop Road.

"It's actually quite normal. We'd expect anything between one hundred sixty to one hundred eighty beats per minute at this stage." Dr. Sutton turned off the equipment, which made the room fall eerily silent.

"See, it's already perfect." Sara squeezed his arm and then patted Gentry's head. "Just perfect."

Hunter stole another look at his sister. Something about her expression—not quite haunted, but filled with an uneasy tension—turned his stomach. How must she feel now, looking at this monitor and seeing her baby growing inside her? Had it prompted doubts about her decision to give them the child?

Sara wouldn't recover from another loss. He needed assurance that Gentry wouldn't rescind her offer, and yet how could he pressure his own sister to give up her child?

Maybe he was reading into things. He leaned close to her. "How're you doing?"

She started, not paying nearly as much attention to him as he had to her. "Glad to have that wand removed," she quipped, defaulting to sarcasm as usual.

Under other circumstances, he would've been put off by the joke—by anything that called attention to that wand, really. Right now, he merely breathed a sigh of relief—and surprisingly not just for Sara's sake—that she hadn't changed her mind.

The doctor made one last note, then printed a photo and turned off the equipment. She handed it to Gentry, who looked down at her fingernails like she hated her turquoise nail polish. "Give it to Sara, please."

Sara's shaky hands cradled that photo as if it were the most fragile, beautiful thing on the planet.

"If you're going to be like waterworks at every appointment, I might have to come alone," Gentry warned as she scooted herself into an upright position.

Dr. Sutton patted Sara's arm, then excused herself from the room.

"I'll step out and let you get dressed." Hunter hugged Gentry and realized it had probably been a long time since he'd really hugged her. His mind drifted to Colby's recent talking-to about how the two of them needed to make Gentry feel less like a "half" sibling. "Thanks for letting us be part of this. For everything."

She wouldn't meet his gaze. In fact, she didn't say anything, which brought that queasiness back.

Hours later, Hunter slipped out of bed, restless. He padded downstairs to the kitchen to grab a yogurt and brew a cup of CTC's Sleepy Tea. When he entered the dark kitchen, he found Gentry staring at the ultrasound picture Sara had put on the refrigerator. While her pointer finger stroked the image, Hunter's stomach hit the floor.

He didn't want to frighten her. "Psst."

She recoiled, then turned around. "Can't sleep?"

"No. Big day." He crossed his arms, trying to decide how to quell his concerns.

She nodded, averting her gaze.

"You okay?" he asked.

"I suppose that depends on your perspective." She wrinkled her nose. "I wish I were meeting up with friends at a club now, not sitting in a dark kitchen with a glass of milk."

He could joke or he could try to get to know her better. "Do you really miss it, or are you secretly enjoying the excuse to slow down?"

She shrugged. Noncommittal as ever. "What I'm going to miss most is men. Don't you have any friends besides Alec that you could bring home to keep me company?" She folded her hands in prayer and grinned.

"Don't expect me to play matchmaker. You want to get serious about starting your own consulting business, I'm your go-to guy. You want boyfriend advice, ask Sara and Colby." He crossed to the pantry to fish out a tea bag. After filling a cup with water, he set it in the microwave, remembering the EMT Sara had mentioned. He repressed the sick feeling he got anytime he remembered that brush with violence and said, "The other day, Sara met someone who sounded like a good guy."

"The humanitarian? He has a girlfriend, and besides, Sara and I don't have the same taste in men." As an afterthought, Gentry grimaced. "No offense."

"None taken." He grinned. And then, because he couldn't get the worry out of his head, and he'd always been one to favor the cold, hard truth over all else, he asked, "If you start having second thoughts about all this, you'd tell me right away, wouldn't you? Because the longer you let Sara believe she's going to be this child's mother, the harder it will be for her to accept a different outcome."

"You love her." Gentry tipped her head. "It's pretty sweet, Hunter. You're usually a scary guy, but when it comes to Sara, you're one big pile of mush."

He let the "scary guy" comment pass because he didn't want her deflecting the conversation. "I love her completely, which is why I worry."

"I love her, too." The kitchen was dim, so he couldn't be sure, but he thought his sister's eyes looked dewy. "Good night."

She left him alone with his thoughts, which is when he realized that she'd never directly answered his question.

Chapter Thirteen

Sara unpacked their suitcase while Hunter stepped onto the deck to make a call, his shoulders hunched against a brisk wind. Autumn could be chilly, but gorgeous nonetheless. Bright sunlight streamed through the glass doors, casting him in shadow. Beyond him she saw Haystack Rock just off the coast of Cannon Beach, jutting out from the glittering, dark-blue water. He'd planned this weekend getaway for their anniversary, yet he was on the phone with Bethany . . . again.

Leslie's warnings resurfaced. Hunter had always admired his father and strove to emulate him in business. She couldn't imagine he'd disrespect their marriage, but she suspected Jed had never foreseen himself falling out of love with Leslie, either.

She turned away from that thought. Hunter had agreed to the adoption and surprised her with this trip, which meant that she and this marriage still mattered despite their conflicting priorities.

They'd brought their bikes, fleece jackets, and hats. He'd even booked them a couple's massage. The fireplace in their suite made it cozy and romantic. If she could get him to relax for the weekend, maybe he'd open up to her like he used to.

In her memories, she could still see the way his face had lit up with every thought he'd shared about books, workplace dramas, dreams, and whims. More recently he'd turned those thoughts inward. Not that he agreed with her assessment. If she prodded him, he'd brush it off as more of her complaining about his obsession with work. He didn't see how those complaints were related yet distinct.

Hunter connected through physical contact, but she needed more and didn't know how to make him understand, especially when he never wanted to discuss the changes in their relationship. She'd had to work hard to get him to show up for the foster care classes. He hadn't even seemed all that interested in talking about *A Man Called Ove* with her the other night, but he used to love discussing books.

Through the glass door she saw her husband, his back still turned, head bowed, and, if she had to guess, brows pinched into a tight knot of concentration.

Once she closed the last drawer, she nestled among the pillows of the sumptuously made bed and called to check on Gentry.

"Is something wrong?" Gentry asked.

"No, I'm just checking on you."

A long sigh preceded Gentry's reply. "You're celebrating your anniversary, right? Don't think about me. I can take care of myself, Sara."

She bristled. Knowing how Gentry had always felt neglected, she'd thought her attentions would've been welcomed, not scorned. "I know that house can feel empty when you're alone."

"Not to me. A little break from each other isn't a bad thing. In fact, I'm going condo shopping today. It's time I get out of your and my brother's hair."

"There's no rush. I like your company." Their idle chitchat had helped pass the time and reminded her of when she'd lived with her sisters. She also liked ensuring that Gentry stayed hydrated, ate well, slept well, and took those vitamins. "Is your mom going with you?"

"No. She's still giving me the cold shoulder. Colby said she'd spare me a couple of hours."

She shouldn't be jealous of the sisters, yet she was. Her own sisters were hundreds of miles away, living their lives and raising their families together. She glanced out the sliding glass doors again and caught Hunter's stern profile. "Well, good luck finding something."

"Thanks. No more calls, Sara. Have a nice weekend." Gentry clicked off before Sara could reply.

She sighed, gazing around the spacious room, with its beige-and-green decor. Home for the next two days. She shimmied off the bed and was plugging her phone into the charger when Hunter came into the room, letting a cold breeze follow him inside.

He closed the door, shivering. "It's nippy." After inspecting the fireplace, he flipped the gas switch. In an instant, golden-orange flames flickered behind the screen. "That's better."

He tossed his phone and glasses on the chair and steadily approached her, a lazy smile softening the hard planes of his face. "Cozy."

"Very." She reached for him, her hands twining through his hair, when he caught her by the waist and kissed her.

"You smell good," he murmured against her neck.

"You're easy to please." Goose bumps trickled down to her shoulders, like they used to whenever he touched her.

"Most people wouldn't agree." He chuckled and began unbuttoning her shirt. It skimmed over her shoulders until it fell away, and then he looped his fingers beneath her bra straps. "I always loved this set."

The pale-blue satin and cream-colored lace lingerie had been a Valentine's Day gift one year. "I know."

"But as much as I like it, I think I prefer you in nothing at all." He unhooked her bra and removed it, cupping the weight of her breasts in his warm hands.

She arched into him and kissed him, making him moan. That sound in his throat boosted her confidence. It'd been too long since they'd had really great sex. Since she'd felt eager and free and hopeful and desirous. Playfully, she pushed him onto the bed and straddled his hips. His eyes lit with appreciation and surprise.

Her skin warmed as he ran his hands up her thighs and back.

"Come closer." He tugged her down until his mouth found her neck, shoulders, and breasts.

Her blood heated, and a pleasant, urgent ache pulsed in her abdomen and between her legs.

The firelight danced around the room as they kissed, fondled, and murmured dirty words. His hot mouth trailed down her neck, his hands cupped her bottom. "Sara," he moaned, squeezing.

Desire shot through her like it hadn't in a long time. She closed her eyes, wrapping a leg around his hip and stroking his thigh and back. "Yes."

His powerful body took control, muscles flexing as he worshiped her with each touch. He kissed her jaw, tongued her ear, and then crushed her mouth with his in a hungry kiss.

She opened her eyes to find his intent gaze on her as he slid inside her, filling her with his essence. Skin to sweat-soaked skin, tongue to tongue, fingers tangled in each other's hair, until they cried out in exaltation. Exhausted, they lay in each other's arms until their breathing settled.

She pillowed her head in the crook of his shoulder as he stroked her hair.

"It's nice to be alone without fear of interruption." He kissed the crown of her head.

"It is." And then, hoping to convince him to leave the office behind for two days, she added, "Until the phone rings."

He tensed. "I have to take calls this weekend. I'm working on something, and I can't risk letting anything go unanswered."

So, he'd come up with a plan. She should feel happy for him, but a growing part of her believed they'd be better off if CTC were sold. "What's this super-secret solution?"

"Nothing you'd find interesting." He continued to rhythmically stroke her hair and shoulder.

She stared at the ceiling, considering his meaning. "Don't you trust me?"

A measure of silence passed between them.

"Why risk an accidental slip in front of Gentry?" He toyed with the pendant he'd bought her weeks ago. "Besides, you hate talking about CTC."

She couldn't deny having given him that impression. But the truth was she hated competing with CTC for his attention, which was a little different. "Bethany knows, though, right?"

"Of course."

"Of course." She recalled the way Bethany had leered at Hunter at his conference table and felt a frown form.

As if sensing her mood, Hunter rolled her onto her back and lay on top of her. "Sara, we're here to celebrate our anniversary. To spend time together *away* from work and my family. To walk on the beach, laze around, indulge in good food."

"I know. I just don't like the idea that you confide in her instead of me." Her petulance might not be fair, but her misgivings were sincere and deep-rooted.

"Don't let my mom's paranoia get in your head, babe." He twirled her hair in his fingers, then used it like a paintbrush against her jaw. "You've been happy and busy with Gentry and the Angel House." He paused for a fraction of a second there, but let it go. "Why do you care if I'm busy at work? You know what's going on."

"No, I don't."

"Yes, you do. I'm in the fight of my life. A fight you've made it clear that you're sick of. I purposely planned to leave it behind and be with you, and *now* you want to talk about it?"

"I'm sorry. You're right. This is a beautiful surprise, and I don't mean to ruin it." She trailed her fingers along his back. His gaze softened and spurred a well of tenderness to rise in her chest. "I just want us to share everything like we used to. No secrets or silences." Now she could no longer blame only him for that widening gap. "Lately we're shying away from tough conversations, while hardly discussing fun stuff, either."

"I'm not shutting you out of anything that matters to us and our marriage." He kissed her.

She didn't agree, but then again, she wasn't exactly giving him the blow-by-blows of her work at the Angel House.

"Let's get dressed for dinner." He kissed her shoulder. "I promise I'll talk about anything else you want . . . politics, that book you just borrowed from Colby, even family gossip. What's your crazy sister Lisa doing these days, anyway? Still having trouble with that composting toilet?"

Laughter bubbled up in her chest. Lisa, her baby sister, had recently bought a tiny house and parked it on Mimi's farm. The whole contraption was less than two hundred square feet and didn't even have a real stove. A tight space, especially when one factored in Lucas, her sister's eighty-pound black Lab.

Hunter dragged her out of bed and into the shower. Forty minutes later, they dressed for the dinner show at EVOO and turned off the fireplace.

On a whim, she asked, "Can we leave our phones here during dinner? It would be rude to step out in the middle of their cooking lesson to take a call."

He paused, nostrils slightly flared as he thought. "Sure." He tossed it on the bed and reached for her hands, the corners of his eyes crinkling above a soft grin. "I love you in this red dress."

"You're not too shabby yourself." She tugged at his freshly pressed collar. "Let's go so we're not late."

◆ ◆ ◆

"Tell the truth. Do you want to grab a pizza?" Sara's face filled with good humor as they left EVOO and crossed the parking lot to their car. If he could somehow capture this moment and keep her locked in it, he would.

"Nope." He hadn't expected to like the food so well, given that EVOO was a foodie place Alec had recommended. But the chefs, Bob and Lenore, had been entertaining and educational, and the portions hadn't left him hungry. "That chicken was amazing. I hope you were paying attention and can make that at home."

"I was. Tonight was fun. If we come back to this town, let's eat here again." She kissed his cheek as he held her door open for her, then slipped into her seat.

Her buoyant mood boded well for the evening and tomorrow's bike trip. And they'd made it through dinner without bringing up CTC or babies—a welcome change.

"Should we go out for a drink?" Her bright eyes glittered.

He started the engine. "I packed two of our favorite bottles of wine. Why don't we go enjoy one on the deck? We can pull a blanket off the bed and watch the ocean for a bit. Talk without crowds."

"It's chilly."

"I'll keep you warm." He glanced at her in time to see her blush.

"I bet."

"Is that a yes?"

"Sure. Take me home, then take me to bed." Sara stroked his thigh, and he thanked God he'd been struck with the inspiration for this getaway.

This was what they'd needed—an escape from the mundane. From the family and work and the future. A couple of days to unwind before they went back to reality.

She brushed her hair away from her face, her tone turning wistful. "Did I tell you Gentry was going to look at condos this afternoon?"

This night kept getting better. “Great. We’ll have a few months alone before the baby arrives.”

“True.” Sara turned and stared out her window, not nearly as enthused.

The car remained quiet for a minute or two. “You don’t sound as excited as I am about having time alone together.”

“I’ve enjoyed Gentry’s company. Like a surrogate for my own sisters, who I miss. Plus, with her right there, I could be part of the pregnancy. It’s been fun to eat with her and take walks and stuff. I’m sure it sounds silly, but it’s given me a little taste of what it would be like to be pregnant. Once she moves out, it’ll feel like I’m imposing if I ask to tag along.”

He stared at the road, absorbing the wistful sadness in her voice when she spoke about how she would never experience pregnancy. Her sorrow physically hurt his heart—he couldn’t stand being powerless to help. The best that he could do was redirect her thoughts.

“Babe, you’ll still be involved. And besides, we should probably do some more things like this before the baby comes.” He squeezed her hand, wanting her good mood to continue. Truthfully, Gentry’s moving out would be healthier for everyone, and his sister deserved to experience this pregnancy with some degree of freedom and privacy, too. “Let’s try to squeeze in that trip to visit your family soon, too.”

Sara perked up. “I’d love that. You’d come?”

“Yes.” He needed to go with her, no matter how poor the timing. “You’re always with my family. It’s been too long since I’ve made it down to see yours.”

She kissed his hand. “I’ll check with them for potential dates.”

They finally arrived at their room. He switched on the fire while Sara uncorked the wine. In the middle of the bed, he noticed his phone. His fingers itched to pick it up, but he’d been doing so well he didn’t want to blow it. Just as he was about to turn away, it lit up with an incoming text.

Sara noticed, too. She poured two glasses of wine and conceded. "Go ahead."

"Thanks, babe." He snatched the phone and scrolled to his texts, then frowned. A total of eighteen text messages from both sisters and Jenna, plus some voice mails. *Dad. Coma. Hunter? Hospital. Tests. Where are you?* "Jesus!"

"What?"

He sank onto the edge of the bed rather than stumbling on shaky legs. "I don't know. I think my dad's in a coma. I . . . I can't tell."

Sara's face drained of color. He, meanwhile, froze. Just froze.

Sara set down the wineglasses, pried the phone from his hand, scrolled through the texts, and then called Colby. She stood beside him, stroking his hair while waiting for an answer. "Colby? What's happening? Hunter and I just got these messages."

Hunter willed himself to move, stretching his fingers while watching his wife's face pinch with concern. Abruptly, he held out his hand and gestured for the phone.

"Here's your brother." Sara handed him the phone and immediately began packing their things.

"Sis?"

"Dad's in the hospital." Her voice cracked. "They've kept him from slipping into a coma, thank God, but they're running all kinds of tests. They don't know the extent of damage or have a real prognosis yet."

"What the hell happened?" His wife winced at the volume of his voice.

"His brain is swollen. They think he has some rogue virus or something. They're trying to control it. Can you guys come back tonight?"

"We're leaving now. How'd this happen, and where the hell was Jenna?"

"You know he hasn't been right for a while. He really felt sick yesterday evening and through the night—groggy, headache, feverish—so he stayed home today thinking he had the flu. By the time Jenna came home from work, he was sprawled out on the sofa totally out of it."

Hunter shook that image away. "So we don't really know how long he was in that state?"

"Not exactly, no. Look, the nurse is coming back. Just get home. We'll be at the hospital until they kick us out."

"Okay. Take notes." He hit "End," closed his eyes, and pinched the inside corners with his fingers to stop the burning.

An image of his dad prostrate on his sofa, mouth open, eyes wide and dazed, returned. His proud father had been alone and probably afraid—had recognized oncoming danger yet been unable to call anyone. Helpless. Nothing was more terrifying than helplessness.

"Hunter?" Sara crouched in front of him, placing her hands on his thighs. "Stay strong, honey. Your dad will be okay. The doctors are on it now."

His swollen throat choked off any response. *Stay strong,* she said. How many times did he tell himself those very words, and how often had his strength failed to affect the outcome of things like this?

"Honey, hand me the keys." She stood and rolled the suitcase toward him. "I'll drive so you can make calls or research stuff on the ride home."

He nodded toward the table, where he'd tossed the keys after they'd returned to the room. Mutely, he followed her to the lobby, dragging their suitcase along. No matter the ups and downs in his relationship with his father, he'd never stopped to consider life without him. They were both too young to have those thoughts, weren't they? How did they end up here, with his dad getting this sick right under his nose?

"Go load the car." She kissed his cheek and handed him the keys. "I'll check us out and catch up in a minute."

Her soft, confident tone settled him, although he didn't register much else going on. Everything seemed darker now than it had twenty minutes earlier. Were people nearby, listening and watching? Had the weather changed?

He kept his head down during the first thirty minutes of the drive. He'd read at least six websites, including the Mayo Clinic's page, to learn more about encephalitis. At this point, he still understood little to nothing, especially because he had no idea what had brought it on in his dad.

His dad had struggled with a series of colds this past spring and summer. Colby had raised bigger concerns about his health—the lethargy and aches—for months, but everyone, including their dad, had ignored her. Blamed it on stress and age. Not only had Hunter dismissed the warning signs, but he'd increased that stress by playing spiteful games at work.

Anger had clouded his observations and judgment, causing him to miss the truth. Regret bunched up in his chest as he watched the road signs blur as they passed, the low hum of the tires on the pavement playing like an ominous soundtrack.

"Is this my fault?" His voice—raw and cracked—sprang from a sore spot in his chest.

"No." Sara firmly shook her head. "You're not responsible for this."

"We've been arguing." He bent over in the seat, head in his hands. "There's been so much tension at the office. That can't have helped matters."

She reached across the console and tugged on his forearm, forcing him upright. "Honey, you just read all about encephalitis. You know it's not caused by workplace tension. He's been lethargic for weeks and rubbing that knee all the time. He must've picked up a virus somewhere."

"I feel sick." He rocked forward, rubbing his pecs, but it didn't help. It seemed as if the vents were sucking all the air out of the car. "My chest hurts."

"Should I pull over? Do you need some fresh air?"

"No, keep going. I won't throw up. No more delays." Delays. His sisters had been calling for two hours. Guilt squeezed his chest, turning him hot with fear and bitterness. He played with the air vents. Were the fuckers even working? "If I'd had my phone with me at the restaurant, we'd be home already."

Sara stared at the road in silence, possibly holding her breath. He knew this wasn't her fault any more than it was his, but his anger needed a target, and she was the only one available at the moment.

His body betrayed him more with each minute, queasiness and heat spreading like a rash. Sara remained quiet, allowing his anger to consume the car without telling him how to feel or asking for an apology. Her stoicism enraged him. He wanted to scream or hit something to release the anxiety that had hijacked his sympathetic nervous system.

Miles later, Sara finally uttered, "I'm sorry. About the phone."

Her dejected voice flooded his overwrought system with shame. Something inside snapped. He rolled down the window and puked over the side of the car.

Chapter Fourteen

The funky odor of industrial cleaning products mingling with alarm pheromones gave Hunter a headache whenever he entered a hospital. Tonight was no different, nor did it help settle his queasy stomach. He strode through the hallway, dodging anxious strangers who strolled aimlessly, with their overly caffeinated eyes and down-turned mouths, while awaiting news of their own loved ones.

Harried nurses bustled around, managing sick patients, worried family members, and exhausted doctors. Machines beeped. Carts creaked as they wheeled past. Hospital workers shouted instructions at one another to be heard above the din.

Chaos.

He hated chaos, and no amount of plate glass windows and new construction made it any better. He wanted to oil those creaky wheels, tell people to sit and wait calmly, invent some sound for those machines to replace that sterile beep, and open all those windows to make the whole place feel less claustrophobic.

His sisters and stepmother sat clustered together in the corner of a waiting room. Colby saw him first and jumped from her chair, hugging him so hard he could barely breathe.

"Where's Alec?"

"At the restaurant. Friday nights are busy, so I told him to stay because I knew I'd have everyone else here." She eased away, wiping her eyes and then acknowledging Sara. "I'm glad you made it back."

"We're sorry we missed your calls earlier." Sara's bright eyes glistened, her smile faltered.

"*Don't* apologize. You were celebrating. I'm really sorry that got cut short, but I'm also glad we're all together now." Colby hugged her.

Hunter kissed Gentry hello before addressing Jenna. Their habitual antagonism didn't make stressful family times easier for anyone. Tonight, neither her emerald-green designer dress nor those sparkling diamond earrings could disguise her uncommonly pasty complexion.

Setting aside his animosity, he attempted the world's most awkward embrace. "Any news?"

She quickly broke free and shook her head. "Not really. They're testing for a bunch of stuff that can cause encephalitis."

"Like what? Meningitis?"

"A lot of things, Hunter. I'm not a nurse." Her blistering attitude didn't shock him, but the deep worry lines on her face helped him remain polite. "I couldn't understand half the names, except for simple ones like Lyme."

"Lyme?" A rare affliction in Oregon.

"When we visited my sister in April, we spent time helping her with yard work and mulching."

"Doesn't Lyme have a distinctive rash?"

"Twenty percent of the time there isn't a rash. If he got it, maybe it was on his scalp, and we missed it under all that thick Cabot hair." Her strident voice broke apart. Although he disliked her, he knew she did love his father, and in that, they were united.

"That trip was months ago," he mused. "Wouldn't we have seen other signs sooner?"

"Most of the other symptoms present like a mild flu. How would we tell the difference? And, anyway, they haven't confirmed the Lyme. It could be something else." Her eyes, ordinarily filled with self-assurance, conveyed a sort of vulnerability that underscored the gravity of the situation. "Nothing they rattled off sounded good, so I don't know what to pray for."

"Whatever it is, we'll fight it." Hunter patted her shoulder, unsure that his attempt at comfort was welcomed, or that he'd been able to fake the confidence he did not feel. He turned back to Colby. "Did the doctor mention next steps if it is Lyme? Catching it this late . . . what's the treatment?"

"I've no idea. We're just waiting, waiting, waiting." Colby raked both hands through her hair. "The tests are being rushed, but we won't know anything tonight."

"Is he awake?" He leaned closer to her and lowered his voice. "Can I see him?"

Colby shot a quick glance toward Jenna, then replied, "They don't want too many in his room at one time. We were kicked out a while ago so they could take him for more tests. I'm not sure if they've brought him back yet."

Hunter closed his eyes before forcing himself to ask Jenna for a favor. "Can I go see if he's awake?"

He doubted he'd respect her wishes if she said no, but this situation called for diplomacy he seldom extended to her.

She hesitated before nodding. "Don't stay long."

Sara had quietly greeted Gentry and Jenna while he'd been speaking with Colby. Now she stood uncertainly off to the side, worrying her lip and staring at the floor. The tense drive back from Cannon Beach hadn't exactly brought them closer.

"Babe." He reached for her hand. She clasped it, and together they searched the hall for his room.

Sara's concern showed in the creases in her forehead. She'd loved his father right from the start, nearly fourteen years ago. Her silence proved she doubted Hunter would welcome her support. His fault, of course. Fear had turned him into an ass in the car. "I'm sorry I snapped at you earlier."

"I know." She kept her eyes downcast.

He stopped and lifted her chin so she had to look at him. "I mean it. I'm sorry I took out my fear on you. We were having a nice evening, and then this happened. Every time we take a step forward, something yanks us back six steps."

"Hunter, let's focus on your dad. Everything else can wait, okay? His well-being is the priority."

"We're okay, though, right?"

"Yes."

He clutched her to his chest and kissed her head. "I can't lose my dad or you, Sara."

She rubbed his back. "How about we stop talking about losing everything. Let's stay positive and keep our thoughts on healing."

"Okay." They found his father's room, then stopped outside the door. Hunter inhaled deeply and said, "Let's go."

Through the window, the city lights below twinkled in the distance. It would have been peaceful if not for the incessant beeping from the heart monitor. The machinery cast a sickly greenish light across the dim room, which enhanced the sallowness of his dad's skin. An IV line ran along his dad's arm as he lay there, eyes closed, in the hospital bed.

"We should come back later," Sara whispered.

His father stirred and opened his eyes. The man's drawn, distorted face crinkled slightly as he tried to talk, but no sound came out. At least he was awake. Hunter couldn't tell if his dad recognized him or his surroundings.

"Don't talk, Dad. Just rest." He sat on the edge of the bed, wanting to collapse against his dad's chest like a child and beg him to get better. Yet grown-ups couldn't fall apart, so he gently settled one hand over his father's heart.

Sara went around to the other side, smiling reassuringly. "You gave us a scare, Jed. Now you need to listen to the doctors and get well so you can have fun with your grandchild."

His father's facial muscles twitched like he was trying again to communicate, but nothing comprehensible came out.

"We're all here, and everything will be okay." Hunter fought the stinging in his eyes. He wouldn't let his father see his fear or hear his doubt. "Once we know what's going on, I'll get the best experts involved. Count on me, Dad. Okay? I won't let you down."

His father's hand flexed, so Hunter clasped it and squeezed. More time. They needed more time. Hunter's throat had grown sore from emotion and bile. "I love you. I'm sorry I've been so preoccupied . . . I'm just sorry."

Something that sounded like "all right" finally emerged from his father's lips. Then his dad's eyes closed. Hunter's heart banged against his ribs, but a quick check of the monitors indicated that his father's heart hadn't changed its pace. None of the other lines on the screen zigged or zagged or set off any kind of alarms, either.

He looked down at their clasped hands. When he'd been about eight, his dad had taken him to a Seahawks game after announcing that Jenna was pregnant. Hunter had been so mesmerized by the crowds and the vendors that he'd forgotten to stick close to his dad. He'd been lost for only a few minutes, but for the rest of that day, his father had held his hand. Hunter remembered the security instilled by that firm grip. The absolute trust he'd had in his father's ability to take care of him. To do anything, really.

Now he compared their hands. Although roughly the same size, his father's veins were more pronounced, his skin thinner and marked with a few dark spots. Now it was Hunter who had to provide that secure, assured grip to pull his dad through.

Hunter had never been a caretaker. How would he manage that, the company, and revive his marriage? His body tensed when he remembered to add a baby to his list of future responsibilities.

"He's exhausted. We should let him rest." Sara waved him away from the bedside.

"We'll be down the hall, Dad." He kissed his father's temple and tucked the thin covers up around him.

Reluctantly, he followed Sara out of the room, at which point she wrapped her arms around him and stroked his hair. "It's okay if you need to cry."

He did need to cry, but not here, surrounded by strangers. "I'm not prepared for this, babe. I can't stand seeing him so frail."

Everything inside loosened and weakened, making it a feat to remain upright. Honestly, if she weren't holding him up, he might collapse.

"Just be you. Strong. Steady. Calm. Rational." Her soft hand cupped his jaw. "You do what you do best—stay in control now, okay. Your sisters and Jenna will be looking to you for guidance."

He nodded, clinging to her like a baby. His family might depend upon him, but he'd fall apart without Sara—a humbling realization. He should confess so many things to her, but all that came out was "Thank you."

When they returned to the waiting room, he couldn't believe his eyes. "Mom? Why are *you* here?"

"Your sister called to tell me what happened." She rushed forward to hug him. Her petite frame scarcely came up to his chest.

He patted her back, still shocked. "I don't think she expected you to drive up here for Dad."

"I didn't do it for him. I'm here for you and your sister." She smoothed her hair, keeping her back to Gentry and Jenna. "But I *was* married to the man. He gave me you two, so I owe him at least a little concern, don't I?"

The hint of mist in her blue eyes betrayed her otherwise-cool demeanor. Despite the hurt and pain of their divorce and the many,

many digs she'd taken at him throughout the years, a part of her still loved her ex. That left Hunter thunderstruck.

He'd spent years misjudging his mother as flighty and untethered to anything normal. He'd even blamed her, in some ways, for the breakup of the family because she'd nagged at his dad so often in the early days of CTC.

Now he understood how much inner strength it took to overcome that loss with dignity. To hold her head high in the face of the man who broke her heart, especially after he started a new family with another woman in the same small town where their friends lived. Hunter doubted he could gracefully accept Sara leaving him, especially if she quickly took up with someone new, as his father had done.

Another truth dawned then, too. If Sara left him, he'd end up like his mom. Alone. Endlessly searching to replace the irreplaceable. Never finding anyone to live up to the great love of his life.

He shuddered.

"It's okay, honey. Your father's a tough old bull. No little virus will be his undoing," she teased, as she often did to break up tension. He absorbed the comfort of her nurturing smile like a paper towel sopping up water.

"I hope you're right."

She patted his cheek. "Contrary to your opinion, you're not the only one in the family who knows things."

He chuckled, which eased some of the tightness in his chest. "I don't tell you this near enough, but I love you, Mom."

Her eyes grew dewy, and she touched his face. "I love you, too, sweetheart."

He didn't share near enough tender moments with his mom, so he hugged her again before glancing at the others. Sara had suggested he needed to take charge. Because that role always made him feel better, he dug in. "It doesn't make sense for all of us to sit here all night.

Gentry, you probably need rest, anyway. Why don't we take shifts? I'll stay tonight."

"He's my husband, Hunter." Jenna stared at him, carefully avoiding his mother's gaze. "I'll stay the night. You can come back in the morning."

He was debating whether to challenge Jenna when Sara cleared her throat.

"Of course, Jenna," his wife conceded. "We'll take Gentry home with us."

"Actually, I think I'll stay at home this week with my mom." Gentry's gaze flitted away from Sara.

"Oh, okay." Sara covered her disappointment. "That makes sense. We'll drop you there, then."

He didn't like giving in, but he supposed Jenna had the right to stay, and she'd probably be whom his dad preferred to see when he woke up. "You'll call us if anything changes or if you learn anything new?"

"Naturally," Jenna said.

"Fine. I'll be back at eight in the morning to spell you."

"Actually," Colby interrupted, "I'd like to come in the morning. That way I can also go to the restaurant by the time we open in the afternoon."

He sighed. With his dad unable to work, his own schedule would become even more grueling. But he'd accommodate the others' schedules for now. "Then I'll come at noon."

"I'll come back with my mom later, then," Gentry said.

He realized that Gentry had been unusually quiet this entire time. Given everything going on with her, it didn't surprise him. As much as she pretended to be independent, and angry with her parents, he suspected what she really wanted was their undivided attention. Now, with this crisis, she might be experiencing regrets, just as he was.

When did life get so complicated? Or did people like Gentry and him just make it harder than it had to be?

◆ ◆ ◆

"You've been an absolute star all week. I couldn't have handled getting Jed back and settled without your help. I hope Hunter appreciates the way you treat his family." Jenna took the tray of lasagna from Sara and put it in the refrigerator. "Thank you for the food and daily visits."

"It's my pleasure, Jenna. However I can help, just ask." She clasped Jenna's hand. "I'm sure you're thrilled to finally have Jed at home again."

"Yes and no. He's out of immediate danger, but at the same time, there are no promises or guarantees. I'm no nurse, so that makes me nervous." Jenna withdrew from Sara and rubbed the back of her neck as if working out a kink. "Apparently, Lyme isn't very well understood. He might experience intermittent neurological and other symptoms for some time. He's still shaky and feeling lousy."

"I'm so sorry." Sara glanced around, noting signs of Gentry, like the boots kicked in the corner of the kitchen and a dirty dish in the sink. "How's Gentry coping? She acts tough, but seeing her dad so sick has to be stressful."

"Honestly, I'm not sure. Things between us have been strained for so long, and this pregnancy hasn't helped." Jenna flattened her palms on the island. She stared right at Sara, wearing a rueful grimace. "You know my feelings about this adoption have nothing to do with you. *You* will be an excellent mother. I just don't think my daughter has a clue about what will happen to her in the coming months and how difficult it'll be to hand over her child."

Sara swallowed hard, unable to dismiss that characterization. Jenna wasn't the first to raise it, but Sara didn't want to make room for that truth.

When Gentry had been living with her and Hunter, Sara had been able to bond with Gentry and remind her sister-in-law that she'd still have a relationship with her child after the adoption. Now that Gentry was back at home, her mother's disapproval could slowly chip away at Gentry's confidence.

But with Jed so sick, Sara knew she shouldn't be thinking of herself now, so she nodded thoughtfully and then changed the subject. "Is the nurse coming today?"

"Yes. She'll change the antibiotic IV line."

"And how are Jed's spirits?"

"Hard to say. We were warned that things could get worse before they get better. I'm told Lyme bacteria gives off a toxic chemical when dying, which can cause insomnia, short-term memory loss, numbness or pain, fatigue, headaches, heart palpitations, and on and on." Jenna tapped her fingers on the counter. "Jed doesn't like to lose control."

"Like father, like son."

"Maybe in *that* way." Jenna's gaze hardened. "I'm sure Hunter's taking advantage of my and Jed's absence at the office."

"That's unfair, Jenna. I know you two have your issues, but Hunter's distraught about his dad." She frowned. "He's idolized the man his entire life."

"That doesn't mean he'll take his eye off the ball. He's determined, and you know as well as I do that CTC is Hunter's *top* priority."

Sara bristled inside but kept her cool. "I know things are stressful, but don't use that as an excuse to insult my husband."

Jenna raised her chin. "Sorry."

"Boy, it's chilly in here." Gentry waltzed into the room in the middle of the standoff. "What's up?"

"Nothing. I just dropped off a lasagna." Sara forced a smile and refrained from dipping her gaze to Gentry's belly. She wouldn't be showing this early, but Sara couldn't help wondering what miracles were happening in there every hour. Miracles Gentry seemed to take for granted. "You know, my house feels empty now that you've gone."

"I'm sure you don't miss the mess," Jenna snorted.

"We all have our flaws, Mom." Gentry flashed a smirking grin.

The energy these two wasted trading sarcastic remarks could light the city of Portland for a week, but listening to it could be equally as draining. "Are you feeling well?"

Gentry's auburn hair hung unkempt, but the real shocker was her outfit. No labels, no frills, no eye-damaging colors. Simple black leggings made her stick-thin legs look even longer. An oversize gray merino sweater hung just past her hips. The absence of necklaces and bangles completed her new look.

"I'm fine." Gentry poured herself some orange juice and then sat at the island. "Hungry. Thanks for bringing us something *good* to eat."

"I can't believe you've never had any queasiness yet." Sara's sisters had lived in the bathroom during the early weeks of pregnancy. She supposed one upside to not getting pregnant was avoiding that discomfort.

"She's too busy sleeping day and night to be queasy." Jenna made a show of picking Gentry's boots up and then walking them out to the mudroom.

Gentry rolled her eyes. "You'd think she'd have bigger concerns than picking on me."

"She's not picking on you." Sara patted Gentry's hand. "She's mothering you, trying to make sure you're mature and responsible. I'm sure Jed's illness has her on edge, too. Be nice to your mom."

"Her mothering skills suck. I'm not an underling or employee." Gentry gulped more juice. "When I'm a mom, I won't force a bunch of bullshit rules on my kids."

Sara's breath stuck in her lungs. Was that a subtle message? Second thoughts? "From what I've read, rules actually make children feel safe. It's psychologically better for them to know and test boundaries than to live with the uncertainty of no boundaries at all."

"People raised kids for centuries without modern psychology, Sara." Gentry's green eyes sparkled with challenge.

"People also thought germs didn't exist because you couldn't see them. Progress is called progress for a reason." Sara noted the way

Gentry seemed to be withdrawing and thought better of having an argument about parenting styles with the woman whose child she wanted. "But let's not argue. How are you coping with your dad's illness? Can I do anything to help?"

"If you want to help, convince Hunter to stop fighting the sale of CTC. Our dad needs to be at home getting better, not worrying about the price of tea in China." Gentry's shrewd gaze didn't waver as she leaned closer. "Wouldn't you like it if Hunter were around more? If he cashed out, you could take a proper anniversary trip instead of a simple overnight stay here in Oregon. If he's serious about being a father, then he should prove that family matters."

That sounded like a test or a threat, or both.

"I don't need fancy vacations to be happy. And Hunter will be a devoted father, no matter which way this CTC deal breaks." The tension in the kitchen knitted around them. She told herself the uncertainty of Jed's condition had these two on edge, but it wasn't easy to not take their moods personally. Gentry seemed to be looking for reasons to reconsider her decision, and Sara didn't want to give her any. "Hate to run, but I need to head out. Please tell your dad I stopped in. I'll come back tomorrow to visit."

"Didn't you just get here?"

"Just to drop off dinner, but I've got other errands before I'm due at the Angel House." A genuine smile bubbled to the surface at the thought of spending an hour or more with little Ty.

With each visit, he'd grown more comfortable around her. Every stray word or smile boosted her confidence and fueled her enthusiasm for motherhood.

Gentry slid off the stool and put the dirty cup in the sink. "Okay. See you tomorrow."

Under other circumstances, Sara might've tried to coax Gentry to reconsider her stance on volunteering. She pulled her jacket over her shoulders, her mind replaying that subtle threat from minutes earlier.

She paused before asking the question she'd been withholding. "Want some company at your next OB appointment?"

"Maybe." Gentry looked away. "I'll let you know."

"Think about it. We could grab lunch or go shopping after." She fought to keep her smile from turning upside down.

"I said I'd let you know." Gentry raised a brow, her tone dripping with annoyance.

O-kay. Time to go. Sara's smile pulled into a tight line. "See you later."

Gentry's fickle mood wouldn't have been particularly remarkable except that Sara had almost never been on the receiving end of her contempt. Rather than give in to the kernel of fear in her gut, she chose to blame Gentry's mood on Jed's illness and her mother's badgering.

On her way to the Angel House, she called Hunter.

"Hey, babe. What's up?"

"I just dropped off a lasagna at your dad's."

"Thank you. You're the best, and my dad loves your homemade meals. How's he doing today?"

"I didn't see him, but according to Jenna, he's not improving much."

"Sitting around waiting is driving me crazy."

"I know. So I was thinking we should distract ourselves. Let's have an early dinner and go look at cribs and baby furniture."

A brief hesitation passed before he replied. "Isn't it a little early for that?"

"We don't have to buy anything. But it'll be fun to check out all the cute things and daydream about if it's a boy or girl. Maybe even think about names." She waited a second, then added, "Come on. It's been a stressful week. We need to relax together, don't you think?"

"I can't get out of here early tonight, babe. I'm busier than ever with my dad gone and Jenna working less."

Exactly the kind of thing she did not want Gentry to hear him say. "Of course."

"What's that mean?"

"It means that I wish you were as excited as I am, and as invested. I don't want to be a de facto single parent."

"I promise you won't be. But unlike the months we have to prepare for the baby, it's only a matter of weeks before this Pure thing comes to a head."

If she brought up Gentry's veiled threat, chances were good that he'd confront his sister and make things worse. A different tack would be better. "Given your dad's condition and the stress in the family, maybe selling the company is in his best interest."

Silence.

"Hunter?"

"I'm here."

"And?"

"And I'm not surprised when Jenna uses his illness as leverage to sell the company, but you? Let's set aside how that makes me feel and address the stupid argument. I can run this company if my dad wants to bow out. When he's better, he can come back or not. Selling the company won't improve his health."

"It might improve yours."

"What?"

"You've been under tremendous stress, Hunter. For what? You act like this sale is a death, when in fact it could be a blessing for *everyone*. We could do so much with that money. We could even start our own business, like Colby and Alec. Invest our money and time in something that brings us closer instead of pushing us apart." She nearly ran the red light, thanks to her preoccupation.

"It's a bit hypocritical to say you're worried about my health when you spend your time at the Angel House, where you got smacked around. Frame it how you want, but the truth is that you're thinking about what you want *from* me, not what's best *for* me."

"What if what I want and what's best are the same, Hunter? Maybe I see what you can't. Not to mention that I worry that you'll regret spending this time fighting your dad and Jenna instead of visiting and caring for him. At the end of the day, aren't his health and family unity more important than the business?"

"I don't need to give one up for the other. I can manage both."

"Not as far as I can see. And if you and Gentry oppose each other, it could affect our adoption plans. Is CTC worth losing the baby?" The raised pitch of her voice filled her car. Her heart zoomed along with the traffic. He might be pissed off at her, but she was furious with him for never taking a minute to consider anyone else's point of view.

A long sigh preceded his reply. "I warned you from the outset that relying on Gentry was a gamble. I can't control her or what she'll do, but I'm not going to let her control me, either. As far as I'm concerned, CTC's future is a separate issue from the adoption and from my dad's recovery."

"You know it's not that simple."

"But it *is* that simple."

She shook her head, even though she knew he couldn't see her. "For you. Only for you."

He didn't see the truth, or he was willfully ignoring it. Either way, Jenna's ugly prediction echoed in her thoughts.

"Why can't you be on *my* side for a change?" His deflated tone blunted her anger.

"What's that mean?"

"It means that ever since we've had trouble starting a family, nothing's been the same. Nothing I do is right. You drum up problems that never existed before. You get mad about stuff that didn't used to bother you, like my work. Then you wonder why I don't share everything with you." He sounded utterly exasperated. "I don't know what you want from me."

His words hammered into her heart like nails. She paused, thinking about how far apart they were in how they viewed their life together.

"Sara?"

"I'm sorry you think we're on opposite sides, but that's unfair. *Everything* I do is for us, including asking you to consider a new perspective on the future. I'm fighting for us, for 'our' side. For our life, our future, not just yours. Not just *your* job." She passed the Angel House and circled the block, needing an extra minute to finish her thoughts. "Think about the big picture. About what's best for both of us in the long run. Family connection. Children. Harmony. *Those* are the things that make life good. Not a job title. Not a business model. What I can't fathom is why you're willing to risk destroying your whole family to hold on to a business."

"God, I'm tired of this argument."

"Me too." She pulled up to the curb in front of the Angel House. "But you never get it. Everything takes a back seat to your priorities, whether it's a movie or lunch plans or whatever. I guess the offer to visit my family in California soon is just another thing that won't happen because you're too busy."

"Is that really how you see me? A selfish dick with no heart? Like I'm not committed to our life and future? From where I stand, I manage all this responsibility, *and* I'm still there to move mountains for you and everyone in my family."

He *was* always there for the big things—the guy who figured out the difficult puzzles or did the undoable. But being there in a crisis wasn't exactly a good measure of a healthy relationship. Or of balance.

She was the one quietly keeping things together day to day. She was the one who could be counted on to make peace, to hold hands, to be patient. With Jed sick, she was the one cooking meals and doing laundry to help Jenna. At the end of the day, she believed those smaller, consistent acts of love meant more than the grand gestures. How did he never get that point?

"I shouldn't have started this conversation while you're at work and I'm in the car. Let's drop it for now. Your dad needs our full attention until he's feeling better."

The charged silence went on forever. She would've thought he'd hung up on her except she could hear his breath on the other end of the line.

"I'm planning to stop over there on my way home from work. I'll make nice with Jenna and Gentry, okay? Relax."

She hated being told to relax, like she could flip a switch and instantly change her feelings. Or worse, like she had no right to be upset. Sometimes being upset was the appropriate response. "I'll see you at home tonight."

"Love you."

He said those words, but lately she wondered if he remembered what they meant . . . or what they should mean. Love required more than platitudes, nice words, and sex. It required compromise. Sacrifice. Everyday sharing. Making decisions that benefited both people, not just one.

They'd begun their life together holding equal cards, but somewhere along the way he began hoarding all the aces.

Chapter Fifteen

"Eat." His dad gestured toward the tray of Sara's lasagna on the island. A gray velour robe hung over his slackened shoulders. The exhausted grooves on his face aged him considerably.

Hunter forced an assured grin. "I'll eat with Sara when I go home."

"It's good." His dad took another bite, then glanced around surreptitiously. "Don't tell Jenna, but I'm a little jealous that your wife cooks."

"Mum's the word." Until this year, he would have said Sara's cooking was the least of the reasons his dad should be jealous. She'd been a perfect wife; they'd enjoyed a carefree relationship. Lately, he couldn't make that claim. No matter what he thought to do about it, he either thought wrong or eroded any progress with his next misstep. "I'm glad she's feeding you well. You need your strength for our annual trip to Jackson Hole in January."

His father's weak smile indicated that their father-son sojourn looked doubtful. As the seconds passed in silence, Hunter thought about his earlier argument with Sara. About how easily he, and most people, took the future for granted. What if last year turned out to be the last father-son trip they'd ever take? The look in his dad's eyes suggested he'd just had the same thought.

A damn awful thought that he didn't want to dwell on.

"In the meantime, I brought you this." Hunter slid a Snickers bar across the table. His dad slipped it into his robe pocket with a sneaky smile, but then he winced.

"How's the headache?" Hunter asked.

"Relentless. My left arm tingles. I lose words. My short-term memory is shit." He shook his head. "Today's better than yesterday, but who knows about tomorrow."

"I'm sorry, Dad. It's only been a week, and they warned it would get worse before it improved. I guess that's cold comfort, but don't lose faith." He almost laughed at himself. Faith. He'd never put much stock in that, preferring to take matters into his own hands. "I wish I could do more to help."

"Me too," his dad said. "It's my fight, though. I'll beat it."

"You will." Hunter leaned forward, resting his elbows on his knees to help steady himself against rising apprehension. "We need you too much for you to stay this sick."

"The only good thing about this is that it's made your sister less rebellious. Jenna's happy to have her back under our roof. I'm sure you aren't sorry for your privacy, either."

Hunter didn't exactly miss Gentry's messes, but her absence had Sara even more on edge. He, too, had become uneasy about what Gentry was thinking these days. "Sara enjoyed her company. Did Gentry show you the outline I'd given her to help her draft a business plan? I think if she took a few more classes and finished college, she might be able to do something with this PR interest."

"Maybe I ought to send her back to live with you and Sara for a while longer. Your work ethic might be the influence she needs." His dad wiped his mouth and then set the napkin down. "Speaking of work, update me. Have you heard from Pure this week? Jenna's been tight-lipped."

Hunter paused because he'd updated his father just last night on the phone. The doctors wouldn't make any promises about when, or if, his dad's memory would improve, but he couldn't come back as CEO until it did.

Hunter wanted that job, but not this way. And he'd always assumed his father would still maintain an emeritus role for another decade or more. Their shared passion for the company had always been their biggest connection. Without it, Hunter had a hard time envisioning their future relationship.

"Pure has everything it requested. I expect we'll hear back from them in another couple of weeks." Hunter could only hope King Cola expressed interest in his proposition before Pure made a firm offer. Contrary to Sara's beliefs, Hunter knew he was doing the right thing by everyone, including his dad, in trying to save CTC. They'd all thank him one day when the company's value doubled and provided careers for the next generation of Cabots. "Dad, can I ask something without upsetting you or arguing?"

"I don't know. Can you?" He grinned, then winced and rubbed his forehead.

The timing wasn't ideal, but Hunter couldn't stop himself. The question had been nagging him for weeks. "Why don't you trust me to take CTC into the future?"

"It's not about trust, son. I know you can run it, probably in your sleep. Right now it's about an opportunity to get a more than fair price for the business."

Hunter didn't believe that for a second. Neither his mother nor father had ever been particularly materialistic. In their different ways, they'd taught Colby and him to prize contribution, to explore the depths of one's talents and passions, and to leave a mark on the world. None of those values could be bought.

"But we had plans, you and me. Plans to build CTC into an international powerhouse. I'd always assumed it'd be you, me, and my own son or daughter one day up on the third floor. A dynasty. How can you throw that all away for money?"

His dad stared at the empty plate for a few seconds. When he lifted his gaze, his eyes held a note of sad resignation. "I'm older. And tired. And to top it off, now I'm sick. That's all given me a different . . . view . . . on how I want to spend whatever time I've got left. Fretting over trade laws, taxes, climate change, minimum wage—not that interested anymore. I spent so much time building that company I missed out on some other things in life, like travel. I want to do some of that before it's too late. Maybe you should think about that for yourself, too. But, also, if you're committed to building a legacy, you're talented enough to do it from scratch."

"I don't want a new legacy. I've poured everything into ours. So step down, travel with Jenna, find a new hobby, but give me the chance to prove myself." Sensing he might be making headway, he added, "We can set some targets, and if I don't meet them in two or three years, then we can talk about selling."

"But if you don't meet them, or if the market declines, the sales price will reflect whatever problems have cropped up, which means we'll lose money." His head tipped to one side, and Hunter saw some regret reflected in his expression. "I didn't go looking for this, but you know what they say about striking while the iron's hot."

His father's answer proved, despite his words, he lacked confidence in Hunter's leadership. Worse, that his father wouldn't miss the day-to-day relationship and camaraderie they'd developed over the years. He'd walk away from it and Hunter as easily as he'd walked away from his first wife.

Hunter's voice roughened slightly from having to overcome the lump in his throat. "If you step down and let me run things, let me put in place some of my ideas—"

"Hunter!" Jenna said from the kitchen door before she rushed over and set her hand on her husband's shoulder.

His dad patted it. "Jenna, we're not arguing. Just discussing options."

She stared at her husband. "I'm sick of his guilt trips. You started the company, not him. The biggest mistake you made was listening to that tax adviser and giving away most of the stock years ago. Now you can't control its future."

Hunter snorted. "How shocking that you don't understand money and value. Naturally, you wanted him to ignore that advice so you would end up with everything, or we would've had to sell the company to pay inheritance taxes on the stock bequest." God, he despised her. Truth be told, maybe he'd even started to lose some respect for his dad for being so devoted to a woman with so few redeeming qualities. The only thing Hunter had ever admired about Jenna was her work ethic. Now even she was ready to ditch that for a fat paycheck. "You've never respected money, as proven by the way you spend it on things you don't even know how to use, like these high-end appliances."

"Enough." His dad coughed, as if the energy to shut down the argument had totally drained him.

"Honey, drink some water." Jenna handed his dad a glass before glowering at Hunter.

Hunter shut up. He didn't come here to upset his father or argue with Jenna. He'd come hoping for things he didn't get—good news about his dad's recovery, assurance of his father's faith in him.

"Sorry. I didn't come here to fight. I'll go." He stood, then belatedly thought of checking in on Gentry. "Is Gentry around?"

"Now that she's giving you her child, you suddenly care." Jenna pressed her hand to her chest and mocked him. "How touching."

He knew he hadn't been the best brother to Gentry. She'd been hard to know, being almost nine years younger than he was and growing up across town with a mom who didn't exactly try to knit together the blended family.

"I'll take that as a no." Ignoring her bait would irk Jenna more than anything else, and despite his guilty conscience regarding Gentry, he had no love lost for his stepmom. He smiled at his dad. "I'll stop in tomorrow."

"Gee, can't wait!" Jenna quipped.

"Jenna, for chrissakes! Stop it." His dad shook his head. "If we sell, I sure won't miss you two going at it every single day."

Hunter hadn't been particularly sensitive to putting his dad in the middle throughout the years. Then again, neither had Jenna—not that he liked the idea that he wasn't any better than she was. "I'll see myself out."

The five-minute drive home passed in a blur: he'd been so consumed by his thoughts. He didn't even look forward to seeing Sara because he couldn't really talk to her about all these feelings. She was basically on their side when it came to CTC, and now worried that his personal goals would affect the adoption.

He should call Colby. She'd understand without judging him. She'd been there all along, watching him connect with his dad through work. Knowing what that bond had meant to him, and how seeing his dad toss it away like it never mattered was a kick in the balls.

Hunter entered the mudroom, surprised to find a dark, quiet house. He switched on the kitchen light and, in the shadows of the family room, saw Sara sitting on the couch, knees curled up to her chin.

Not a good sign.

"Hey, babe. Whatcha doing in the dark?" He approached her with some caution and sat beside her. What had he done now? As his eyes adjusted to the dark, he noticed her puffy face. Just like that, his heart squeezed. "What happened?"

She shook her head and rested her forehead on her knees. "Nothing."

He wrapped an arm around her shoulder and kissed her head. "It's not nothing. You're crying in the dark by yourself. Did you have a fight with Mimi?"

"No." She raised her head. "I'd tell you, but I don't want to fight."

"I promise I won't argue."

"You'll be furious."

Well, shit. Now what could he say? "Now you have to tell me. I swear I won't be furious."

She peered at him like a child terrified of being punished. "It's Ty."

"Ty?" He searched his memory.

Her expression proved he'd hurt her feelings somehow. "The little boy at the Angel House that I've talked about for weeks."

"Oh, yeah. Sorry. I blanked on his name." He grimaced. "A lot is happening these days."

"Yes, I know."

When she said nothing more, he asked, "What happened to Ty?"

She eyed him as if judging whether or not it'd be worth telling him the story. "Their time at the house expired, so Gloria helped his mom find 'affordable' housing in Lents near that Eastport Plaza. Pam got a waitressing job, but makes nothing. I went by today to bring some books and toys to Ty. They're in this tiny section-eight place. It smells, and you know that neighborhood is a higher-crime area than most." Her face crumpled again.

His first thought was to jump up and yell about her going alone to that neighborhood, but, with effort, he remained seated and calm. "If the whole point of the Angel House is to help these women get their own places and jobs, isn't this a *good* thing, even if the housing isn't the best? It's a solid first step."

"At the shelter, Pam had help. Ty had healthy meals. They had a clean, safe place to sleep. Now they're out there in a crime-riddled area, and everything's all on her shoulders. I'm not sure she's ready. Who will watch Ty? What if she turns back to drugs to cope?"

"You're projecting a worst-case scenario. Surely Pam is in better shape now than months ago when she first arrived. She must have friends or family to help her."

"If she had friends or family, she wouldn't have ended up at the Angel House." Sara's voice sharpened. He needed to tiptoe through the minefield of her emotions, or he risked making everything worse.

"She has a job and a roof over her head, which is more than she had before." He reached for her hand. "Try not to worry about things you can't control. You did what you could."

"I would've offered for them to stay here for a while so she could save some money, and I could watch Ty, but I knew you'd object." She peered up at him with guarded hope in her eyes.

He reeled back a bit, unprepared for that kind of request. "You'd invite a drug addict to live in our home?"

He stopped short of pointing out the faded yellow bruise on her cheek.

"A *recovering* addict. Pam isn't friendly, but she isn't threatening. I'd risk it for Ty. That sweet baby is so vulnerable."

"Babe." He hugged her hard. His heart felt like it was wedged beneath someone's boot. "This is exactly what I've been worried about. You're putting yourself out there this way and taking on all their responsibilities. It's not rational."

"You think I'm stupid for getting attached." She tried to pull away, but he held her tight.

"I *never* think you're stupid. Just tenderhearted." He stroked her hair. "I'm sorry you're worried."

Those brilliant blue eyes dimmed. "I know you're right. But he's so . . . special. I think I could've really helped him if I'd have had longer. He'd finally started talking to me, and I know he likes when I read to him. His mother never reads to him. She hardly talks to him. How can a kid like that have a chance in this world?" New tears leaked from the corners of her eyes.

He didn't have an answer to her question, so he pulled her onto his lap and rocked her, murmuring endearments and wondering what it must be like to have her heart. One that opened up to everyone so easily. One that gave everything without asking for much in return. One so easily broken.

He'd never been that way. Most days it felt like a blessing, but recently a little part of him worried that maybe he was missing out on something.

"Sara, I can't welcome a strange woman into our house, but if I rent them a safer place for a short time, will that make you feel better?"

He heard her breath catch. She looked up and cupped his face in her hands. "You'd do that?"

"I'd do anything to see you smile again." He kissed her, and for a little while, some of their troubles vanished.

◆ ◆ ◆

When Gloria learned about Hunter's offer, her eyes had gone round as buttons before she'd clucked a warning about setting precedents and getting too personally involved. Sara ended that lecture by saying she'd be spending less time with the residents and more time working directly for the foundation.

After Hunter's magnanimous gesture, she'd thought it only fair to make a compromise for him. She could do plenty of good in the community with Colby, and she really ought to be getting ready for the baby, too.

The real disappointment had been Pam, who'd initially acted as if the offer had insulted her, although ultimately, she accepted the help. Now Sara and Hunter were on their way to pick up Pam and Ty and take them to their new temporary apartment. Hunter had rented a two-bedroom unit for three months in a safer neighborhood with an easy commute to her new job by bus.

"Thank you, again." She leaned across the console to kiss Hunter's cheek, feeling indebted even though she'd given something up, too.

This was helping Ty, so it was worth it. "I'm so touched that you did this for them, and me."

He glanced at her. "What's mine is yours. If this is what you want, then it's done."

"You really don't understand how much this means to me, Hunter." Mostly because it proved that the man she'd loved was still in there, even if he was harder to reach these days. And although this was yet another grand gesture, she couldn't deny that, in a crunch, being able to count on him this way meant a lot. "When you meet Ty, you'll understand why I want him to have a fighting chance at a good life."

Like most neighborhoods in the Greater Portland area, even this more impoverished one had lush old-growth trees and relatively clean streets. Upon closer inspection, the rusted cars, barred windows, and graffiti hinted at its seedier side.

Hunter pulled up to the curb of the three-story, gray, cement-block building where Pam and Ty currently lived. A gang of teenage boys stood huddled on the nearby corner, eyeing his high-tech car with interest.

Hunter looked around and shook his head. "I hate that you came to this neighborhood by yourself."

"Think of all the women and children who live here and walk around, defenseless, all the time. Even those boys . . . what chance do they have when the schools aren't good and they've got no hope?"

"I don't disagree, but there are safer ways to make a difference."

"I have mace in my purse, and it's not particularly dangerous here in the daytime."

He tipped his head. "I thought we agreed you'd be more cautious."

"I know."

"Good." He squeezed her thigh. "Now let's get Pam and go."

She gripped his hand. "Thank you. A million times, thank you."

"You're welcome." He leaned over and kissed her. "Let's just hope this woman doesn't cause any trouble, since it's my name on the lease."

"She's not a troublemaker."

He cocked a brow. "She's an addict, Sara."

"A recovering addict with a job. Hopefully, she'll use this chance you're giving her to save a little extra. If so, maybe she'll be able to afford to stay in the new place on her own." Gratitude prompted another smile.

He tapped her nose. "I hope knowing Ty is safe will make it a little easier to let go of seeing him again."

Nothing would make that easier. She'd purposely avoided thinking about it because it made her heart sore. "Actually, I thought maybe I could babysit during some of Pam's shifts. You can't complain, because they'll be in a safer neighborhood."

His eyes widened. "Is it wise to get *more* invested?"

No one else thought so, but she couldn't change her heart any more than she could change her height. "It can't hurt to offer, maybe just for a couple of months. If I help with childcare, those savings can go toward food and rent down the road."

"I thought the foundation was setting up childcare subsidies? Besides, you know you can't get this involved with every case." He squeezed her hand.

"I know."

He sighed in resignation, his eyes darting back to the gang of boys, who hadn't moved. "Let's talk about this later. Right now I just want to get this done and then visit my dad."

Jed's recovery hadn't progressed much, which increased her husband's stress levels. "Yesterday I took him soup, but he didn't even get out of bed."

"I don't think the antibiotics are helping." His brows pinched together.

She stroked his forearm. "Jenna was planning to speak with the doctor. Maybe they'll have answers today."

"Let's hope."

When they exited the car, Sara noticed Hunter don a tough, confident expression before giving the gang of boys a pointed look. He then put his arm around her shoulders and escorted her up the front steps.

Fall breezes whipped dead leaves along the sidewalk. Each week that passed brought her closer to Gentry's due date, and closer to being a mom. That cheerful thought temporarily distracted her from the troubles of the people living in this neighborhood.

They stepped past some trash left in the hallway and knocked on Pam's door. She answered without much of a smile. Beside her sat one standard-size suitcase. Sara couldn't imagine having so little, or lacking the education and wherewithal to land a decent job with benefits. The world must feel frightening and cold to those in Pam's shoes. No wonder the woman kept her defenses on high alert.

Sara crouched to Ty's height. "Ty, this is my husband, Hunter. Isn't he tall?"

Ty ducked behind Pam's leg while peering up at her imposing husband.

Hunter waved at him, grinning, and then looked at Pam. "May I carry your bag?"

"I got it." She cracked her gum, chin raised.

He slid Sara an inscrutable look. "Okay, then we might as well leave."

Once they were loaded in, Pam buckled Ty into the toddler seat Sara had borrowed from the Angel House. Ty strained to see the gigantic computerized monitor on the dash, while Pam's hands brushed the supple leather seats. Hunter's car cost as much as some small condos. That realization—or rather her concerns about Pam's judgment of them—made her uneasy.

An awkward silence descended as Hunter pulled from the curb. Fortunately, they had to go only a few miles to arrive at the two-story apartment complex Hunter had found. The shingled building, in a graffiti-free neighborhood, was painted in shades of light and dark gray. Dormant flower beds that would probably look quite pretty in the spring surrounded the parking lot. In the common area on the left, there was a small playground.

Sara waited for Ty's reaction.

"Swing!" he said, pointing at the swing set and slide. The fact that he spoke made Sara want to lift him into a hug. Her smile nearly split her cheeks.

"Won't that be fun?" Sara wanted to lift Ty onto her hip and play with him, but Pam's hand was on his shoulder.

Hunter removed the suitcase from the trunk, and then they followed him to unit 117. After he unlocked the door, he handed Pam the key without crossing the threshold. "It's furnished, and I'm told this is a safe neighborhood." He hitched his thumb over his shoulder. "There's a bus stop one block east of here, so commuting should be pretty easy."

"Thanks." Pam, who'd never been effusive, stared at them, appearing impatient for them to leave.

"You're welcome." He handed her his business card. "Keep this handy. If you have any trouble, you can call my private line at work."

Pam flicked the card with her finger, then tucked it in her jeans.

"If you ever need help with Ty, please let us know," Sara added, sensing their imminent farewells. Her stomach tightened into a hard pebble as she prepared to say goodbye to Ty. "I'm happy to watch him a few days a week if it will help you get on your feet."

Pam's eyes narrowed. "We're good."

"It's no problem," Sara began, but Hunter squeezed her waist to signal her to stop. A lump formed in her throat as she stared at Ty, desperate to memorize the curve of his cheek, the color of his eyes, the shape of his tiny ears. She wanted to hear his voice one last time, too, but that was a long shot. She bent over and poked him in his belly, holding back tears. "You be good, Ty. Keep reading."

Her eyes stung, but she made a mental note to drop off a box of books and toys on this doorstep in a couple of weeks as a surprise. Right now she'd give anything for two minutes alone with Ty, just to ruffle his hair and give him a hug. To tell him that he was the most special little boy.

"Good luck." Hunter nodded at Pam and then tugged Sara away.

They walked to the car in silence. She dabbed at a tear once she was seated in the passenger seat.

"Babe?"

She shook her head. "I'm fine. I hope it works out for them."

"We've done everything we can—now it's up to Pam. You can't live other people's lives for them."

"I know." She inhaled deeply and tried to quiet her thoughts. "Let's go see your dad. I want to hear about Gentry's appointment this week. She didn't invite me to go with her."

Hunter's gaze remained on the road, but tension flowed off him in waves. Had something happened that she didn't know about? Had his ongoing battle with Jenna angered Gentry?

"Has she said anything to you?" Sara asked.

He shook his head.

"Do you know why she blew me off? I've been so grateful. I couldn't have offended her, could I?"

"When have I ever understood what motivates Gentry to do anything? Like I've said, you can't control what people will do. Gentry is more unpredictable than most, Sara. You know that."

His tone sounded like a warning, which did nothing to ease the knot that leaving Ty behind had tightened in her chest. To make matters worse, Sara saw Bethany's name pop up on the monitor when the phone rang. On a Saturday.

"Hey, Bethany. I'm in the car with Sara." Hunter drove on, eyes fixed on the road.

Was that a warning, too? What didn't he want Bethany saying in front of her?

"Hi, Sara" came Bethany's smooth reply, although Sara would bet the woman was disappointed by her presence.

"Hello." She wanted to make a smart-aleck crack about working overtime but kept quiet. If she became a shrew, it would only make it easier for Bethany to lure Hunter away.

"What's up?" Hunter asked.

"I finished revising those projections for Ki—er, that you wanted. They should be well received."

Hunter brightened, his spine straightening a bit in his seat. "Great. Go ahead and send them along. Hopefully, it'll open a door."

"Okay. Anything else?"

"No. That's it. Thanks. Bye." Hunter punched off the phone.

"What projections?" She stared at him, trying to decipher the truth.

He had that killer look in his eyes she'd seen whenever he felt confident. "Let's just say I'm not dead in the water yet. My Hail Mary may succeed."

She knew she should be happier for him, but success meant he'd be working more often, not less. "What's the plan?"

He didn't look at her. "I'd rather not jinx it."

She pressed her lips together. "But Bethany knows."

"I *work* with her. I share work-related things with her, period." More quietly, he added, "Besides, I know you're hoping I fail."

It sounded awful when he put it that way.

"Hunter, trying to get you to see how the sale could be a win for everyone and prevent a family rift is *not* the same thing as wanting to see you fail." She laid her head back against the seat. "I really wish you understood."

"You want me to roll over and make it easy." He glanced at her. "A sale isn't a win for everyone, because I lose my dream. *My* plan is the *real* win for everyone."

His gaze returned to the road, but she saw that smug grin tug at his lips. She wanted to be thrilled for him. He'd built his career around CTC, and he wouldn't pretend confidence he didn't feel. She had a sinking feeling, however, that his secret plan could have unintended consequences. "Well, I guess I'll have to wait and see."

The car fell silent, then in a soft voice he said, "I hear that you're hurt, but you've hurt me, too, you know. Yet despite the fact that you don't have my back, I just signed a lease for a woman I've never met in order to make you happy. So how about you cut me a little slack today."

She swallowed hard. She'd *hurt* him? Hunter had always been a force of nature, and rather impenetrable. Most of the time he commanded everything and everyone to bend to his will, and she could count on one hand the number of times she'd seen him cry in fourteen years. "I'm sorry."

"Thank you." He pulled into his father's driveway and turned off the engine. Instead of opening the door, he closed his eyes and put his forehead on the steering wheel.

"What are you doing?"

He sat back and opened his eyes. "Trying to find some Zen before having to deal with Jenna."

Sara wrinkled her nose. "Come on. Time to rip off the Band-Aid."

Chapter Sixteen

"He's still in bed?" Hunter glanced at the kitchen clock above Jenna's head.

"That's what I said." Jenna poured two containers of soup from A CertainTea into a pot and turned on the stove.

Colby must've visited earlier this morning. He wished she were still here to act as a buffer. Sara's focus would remain on Gentry and the baby—not that his wife should have to be his referee.

"What are the doctors saying?" He leaned forward, flattening his hands on the island, trying his best to make nice with his stepmom for Sara's sake. "Shouldn't he be improving by now? Perhaps his medication needs to be adjusted."

"Do you think I haven't asked those questions?" Jenna stirred the soup, then clanked the ladle onto the spoon rest. "I've explained this already. This isn't an uncommon reaction to the antibiotics."

He mentally repeated "She loves my dad" a few times to keep from sniping at her caustic tone. Given his dad's lack of progress, Hunter thought it was time to seek other opinions. If he wanted to persuade Jenna to consider that, he couldn't alienate her. Taking a page from Sara's playbook, he softened his voice.

"There's so much controversy about Lyme diagnosis and treatment. Maybe we should take Dad east to a specialist or investigate other avenues." He'd already started that research—lately having read pages and pages of papers online. "Things like MS, lupus, and Epstein-Barr can be misdiagnosed as Lyme and vice versa. Or there could be a coinfection that complicates the diagnosis. His doctors could be wrong, and these treatments could be hurting him or masking something else."

Jenna closed her eyes like she needed patience to deal with him instead of it being the other way around. "Smart as you are, I don't see a medical degree hanging on your wall. Besides, your dad's in no condition to travel, Hunter. His whole body hurts, and he's exhausted."

He dragged his hands through his hair. Helplessness clawed at him, making him twitchy. When he noticed his hands had balled into fists, he shook them loose.

"Chill out before you burst a blood vessel." Gentry stuffed a grape into her mouth. "Mom and I are taking care of Dad. The nurse comes here almost every day. No one but you is freaking out. Dad will be fine in time, just maybe not on *your* schedule."

He faced his sister. Sara made a little sound, like she was clearing her throat. He ignored her unsubtle cue, but he measured his words and tone to make his point. "It's proven that doctors make misdiagnoses every year. Patients need to be their own best advocates. What can it hurt to get another opinion?"

"I'm not putting your dad on a plane." Jenna retrieved a few bowls from the cabinet and set them near the stove. "He has great doctors right here in Portland. I won't interrupt this treatment based on your Google degree and your vague feeling that his doctors have screwed up."

"Let me help, Jenna." Sara jumped up to get silverware and set the table, while Gentry continued eating grapes like a princess.

Hunter remained on edge, as he'd been for days. So much so, he'd even thought about calling his mom to discuss homeopathic remedies. He was getting nowhere with Jenna or Gentry, so he would go over their heads. "Sara said she didn't see Dad yesterday. I haven't seen him in two days. I want to talk to him."

"Why? So you can upset him with these theories that his current doctors aren't helping, or do you want to badger him about the business?" Jenna bit out. "He doesn't need more stress. That will only hurt his immune system."

"Are you accusing me of something?" He narrowed his eyes, giving up the pretense of getting along or sparing her feelings. Jenna never let up on him, but if she was wise, she wouldn't push him today.

According to the company bylaws, if the CEO can't fulfill his duties, the CFO becomes the acting CEO in charge until a new one is appointed. He'd refrained from enforcing that clause because he didn't want to cause more tension or upset his dad, but if the doctors couldn't clear his dad for work soon, he'd have to invoke it. CTC needed a leader.

In the periphery, he noticed Sara approaching him. She and his family would pitch a fit if he put that clause in play, but he might not have a choice.

"Hunter, Jenna's a worried wife looking out for her husband's best interests. If he needs rest, let's not push." She rubbed his back like he was a baby in need of soothing. He shrugged her off. She stiffened, eyebrows raised. If Jenna and Gentry noticed their wordless argument, they didn't react.

Fortunately, it ended abruptly because his dad shuffled into the kitchen. His ashen face did nothing to ease Hunter's concern. "Stop the commotion. I'm here and I'm hungry."

Gentry sprang off her seat and pulled out a chair. "Sit here, Daddy. Mom made soup."

Daddy? Since when had Gentry reverted to that endearment? And "Mom" hadn't made anything—Alec had.

Gentry had used a light hand on her makeup application, thrown her hair in a simple ponytail, and worn casual clothing. At first, he figured she was doing so for comfort's sake, but now he wondered if she wasn't somehow regressing, seeking some kind of do-over of her childhood now that her parents were finally spending time at home with her.

God, this house made him crazy, but not as crazy as seeing his dad so ill.

"Dad, how are you?" Hunter crossed the kitchen to get a closer look at his dad's appearance. His pasty face needed a shave, and he remained dressed in that drab old robe. Every painfully slow movement appeared to sap a huge amount of his energy. "Maybe it's time we see a specialist?"

His dad waved him off before Jenna could rant. "No, son. There's so much inconsistency when it comes to Lyme. No one knows anything. Let's stay the course and hope for the best."

The illogical conclusion only confirmed Hunter's suspicion about his neurological deterioration.

"Dad—" he started, but Sara cut him off when she squeezed his shoulder.

"Jed, are you enjoying anything about your time off?" She smiled as she deftly steered the conversation into more pleasant territory. "Have you caught any good daytime television or read any good books?"

Hunter had always admired Sara's desire to keep peace in his family, but today he felt managed. It might be tolerable if he didn't suspect her motives were personal and self-serving. She'd do anything, including shut down a discussion about his dad's health care, in order to keep her relationship with Gentry on track. That didn't sit right. Of course, she'd say *he* was being selfish by ignoring his dad's and Jenna's wishes, which would be bullshit.

Anyone could look at the man and see he hadn't improved one bit. He might even be worse off than when they released him from the hospital.

"Gentry turned me on to *Judge Judy*. What a hoot." His dad chuckled and picked up a spoon as Jenna set a bowl of soup in front of him. He stared at the lumpy golden broth sprinkled with green-and-red oil and topped with some blue-toned ribbons of whatever weird food Alec had selected, then scowled. "What's this?"

"Some fancy Mexican corn chowder." Jenna crossed her arms. "Don't judge it by its appearance. It smells divine."

His dad poked at the blue stuff with his spoon, then he looked at Sara. "Don't tell Alec, but I prefer your chicken noodle soup."

"I can bring more." She covered his hand with hers, grinning.

Gentry eyed Sara in an oddly assessing manner, then must've sensed Hunter staring at her. She raised one brow, challenging him to speak his mind. He flicked his gaze to his wife, who'd been feeling slighted by Gentry, but he kept his mouth shut . . . for about ten seconds. Unlike all the women in the room, he preferred a direct route from A to B, and a straightforward conversation to one that never got to the point. If he didn't say something, he'd explode.

"How was your doctor visit, sis?" He turned from Sara and caught Gentry's eye again. "Sara was sorry to miss it."

"Everything's normal. No worries. I've been following all the rules."

"Of course you are," Sara quickly replied. Hunter guessed she was wearing a look that begged him to back off. "Did you get another sonogram picture or learn anything new?"

"Nope. Just a checkup." Gentry stood and went to the refrigerator, lingering behind its open door, where neither Hunter nor Sara could see her face.

"When's the next one?" Sara asked, her voice sweet and hopeful.

Gentry closed the refrigerator door, her expression turning bitter. "Sara, I can manage to keep my own appointment schedule. If there's something to report, I'll share it."

"Sorry." Sara clasped her hands together on the table and chewed the inside of her cheek.

That's it! Hunter shot from his chair, propelled by his pent-up frustration with the entirety of their family situation. "Don't snap at Sara. She's been nothing but kind to this whole family from the first time I brought her home from college. You owe her more respect than that, Gentry."

"Hunter, it's fine." Sara frantically waved her hands to stop an argument from erupting. "She didn't mean anything by it. It's just hormones."

"You've been *loaded* with hormones—literally injected with them—and never snapped at my family."

"Sorry, Sara," Gentry said.

Hunter slid a glance to Jenna, who'd been suspiciously quiet. He noticed mother and daughter exchange some kind of wordless glance that spoke volumes, stoking his fears about how Jenna might be interfering with the planned adoption.

That would devastate his wife.

He needed to nail down the plan sooner than later. "While we're on the topic of the baby, let's talk about formalizing our arrangement. I'll pay for your lawyer so it doesn't cost you anything."

"Hunter, this can wait." Sara's panicked response didn't help his case.

"Why? We might as well get the ball rolling. Who knows what kinds of things might come up in the next few months? It's best to have everyone's rights and obligations spelled out in advance." He should've insisted on this from the start, *before* they'd started counting on Gentry.

"Don't feel pressured by Hunter." Jenna brushed some of Gentry's stray hair back behind her ear. Possibly the first time he'd ever witnessed a gentle moment between those two. "He can't force you to do anything."

Force her? "That's not what I'm doing. *She* came to us with this proposal, not the other way around. I'm just trying to finalize the details." His dad had been the one who taught him to always paper every transaction, so he turned to him for support. "You agree with me, right?"

"If Gentry is absolutely certain of her plans, then yes, I agree." His dad looked at his youngest child, a bit of sorrow in his eyes.

What was with "if"? She'd promised weeks ago. No one but him probably noticed the way Sara had gone still, her breath caught in her chest. He pinned Gentry with his gaze and swallowed hard. "Has something changed?"

"For God's sake, Hunter, can't we ever have one family gathering that doesn't have an agenda?" Jenna dismissed the topic out of hand, effectively allowing Gentry to avoid the conversation. "I thought you came to visit your father."

"Gentry—" he began, until Sara interjected.

"Hunter, please. As you yourself said the other day, we have months to prepare for the baby." She flashed the phony smile she used to mask her anger. Why she was mad at *him*, he had no clue. He was only trying to secure the thing she most wanted.

His father jumped in, possibly sensing trouble. "Sara, Colby mentioned that you've gotten really involved in a local charity supported by her foundation, but I forget what it's called."

"The Angel House. I was very involved helping those women and kids get on their feet, but I'm redirecting my time now. Colby could use more support at the foundation." She squeezed his dad's hand again. "But did Hunter mention how he helped one of its residents?"

"No." His dad eyed him with interest. "How so?"

"The shelter home can only accommodate people for about nine months because they want to make sure that other people get help, too. This week, a woman and toddler I'd become attached to had been moved into a miserable section-eight housing apartment. When Hunter saw how upset I was, he signed a short-term lease for them in a better neighborhood. Now, hopefully, they can save some money and get a fresh start without being in a high-crime area."

"That's mighty kind." Jed smiled and leaned closer to Sara. "Something tells me this was your idea."

"No! It was all his idea."

For a moment, Hunter saw a glimmer of love in her eyes. Well, at least that was something.

He suspected she mentioned it to make him look like less of a bully in front of Jenna and Gentry. He was damn tired of being viewed as a bully. Bullies did things to make other people feel bad. That was never his motive—at least not with anyone other than Jenna.

He wasn't a bully. He was a guy who solved problems—who got shit done without letting chaos and emotions overshadow reason and logic. How come no one got that about him? When had he become the bad guy who needed his wife's brand of PR?

"No big deal." A wave of emotional exhaustion pushed him onto a seat.

"Like I told you, all mush inside." Gentry grinned, referring back to the time when she'd called him out on his soft spot for Sara. Wasn't it ironic that, of all the people in the room, *she* was the only one who saw that?

"What can I say? I love my wife." He drummed his hands on the table, uncomfortable being the subject of everyone's scrutiny. "Have you made any decisions about the consulting idea we discussed?"

"Uh, *no*. Been kind of preoccupied." Back to sarcasm, just like her mom.

Thank God Sara and Colby weren't like those two, who falsely equated posturing with real strength.

"Okay, then." He turned to his father. "I know you've been tired, but how about you let me get you out of here for a bit? We can take a drive down to the lake. Get some ice cream or something?"

"You two go on," his dad said. "I'm not up to it."

Defeated, Hunter stood, having been in Jenna's presence for about as long as he could tolerate. Hugging his dad, he said, "We'll let you rest, then. Let me know if you need anything, okay?"

"Go enjoy some time with your wife today. I've got plenty of people taking care of me." He smiled at his wife and Gentry.

Hunter detested the envy that slid through him then. If his parents had stayed married, his dad would never have been in Connecticut and gotten bitten by a tick. Jenna wouldn't have so much influence at CTC or on his dad. She'd ruined *everything*. Without her around, his dad would've been a bigger part of Hunter's formative years and beyond. Life would've been simpler—better—in so many ways.

At least for him and Colby, anyway. Of course, then Gentry wouldn't be in their lives, and even though she could drive him crazy, he did love her and appreciate the unique perspective she brought to the family dinner table.

"I'll check in tomorrow." He reached for Sara.

Normally, when they joined hands, a sense of contentment rippled through him. Today her cool touch did not soothe.

◆ ◆ ◆

Once at home, Sara followed Hunter into his office. A large picture window afforded a pretty view of the surrounding forest. The massive desk and sleek walnut built-ins, with plenty of shelves, drawers, and nooks, enabled him to maintain a perfectly neat and orderly desk. His laptop sat in the center of the credenza behind that desk.

His space, where order and logic—and an absence of emotion—prevailed. But not for long if she had her way.

The frustration she'd been sitting on in the car bubbled inside like boiling water turning to steam. Right now she didn't care if it blew and burned them both. "I asked you *not* to rock the boat with Gentry, then you brought up every uncomfortable topic you could think of."

Wearing a blasé expression, he pulled out the refrigerator drawer and retrieved a bottle of water. He held it toward her like a damn butler. When she shook her head, he closed the door and cracked the bottle open for himself. "There's no point in pussyfooting around those issues."

"No. Better to try to control everyone by running them over like a bulldozer, right?"

"That's not what I did. For God's sake, I'm worried that my dad's been misdiagnosed." He tossed the cap in the trash and guzzled water. His long frame remained as taut as the tension between them. She watched him swallow; then he peered down his nose at her with those penetrating hazel eyes.

"It's not *what* you say, Hunter. It's *how* you say it." She crossed her arms. "You're not the boss of everyone and everything."

"Don't I know it!" He finished the water in another long gulp, then crushed the plastic in his hand. "I'm sick and tired of having to defend myself over and over. All I did today was look out for the people I love—you, my dad, Gentry."

Honestly? "How exactly did you look out for me?"

"You mean aside from signing a lease for a woman I don't know and shelling out a few thousand dollars?" He narrowed his gaze, which set her back a step.

She took a breath. He had done that, and she didn't mean to be ungrateful. Yet once again, he'd used a grand gesture to compensate for the little ways in which he constantly edged her out and neglected—or blatantly ignored—her wishes. Still, it was quite a gesture. Besides, he'd only keep his defenses up if she argued. She relaxed her stance and continued. "You know I appreciate that with all my heart, Hunter, but it's beside the point."

"I want my dad to get second and third opinions. That's for his sake, not mine. I want Gentry to sign some documents so she doesn't flake out on this adoption. That's to protect you."

"I don't need your protection, just your love and support. We should make decisions together instead of you always taking charge." Her arms flailed from her sides until she reined them in.

He shook his head, his face tight with frustration. "What. Are. You. Talking. About."

"I'm talking about how you ignored my wish to have a *pleasant* visit with your family. How you don't trust me with your work secrets. How you keep distancing yourself and making me feel like you're doing this adoption for me instead of *with* me."

"Us. You. Me. *Why* do you always get hung up on the pronoun? Isn't it all the same thing? We're married. I see 'us' as one, no matter which word I use."

"Easy to say, but it doesn't make it true."

"Stop second-guessing me."

"I'm not. Look at your actions. If we disagree, you either manage me to go along or you 'give in' to shut me up. But we rarely make decisions *together* anymore."

He blinked, staring at her in silence, then turned his back and went to the window—fists on his hips—leaving her standing in the middle of the room, waiting.

The moment stretched until she sensed, suddenly, that she'd run to the middle of a frozen pond only to realize that the ice was too thin. As her adrenaline ebbed, she steadied herself by holding on to the edge of his desk.

"Do you still love me?" He'd asked so quietly she almost hadn't heard him.

"What?"

He turned around, arms now crossed, face a study in agony. "Do you still love me?"

His pain stole her breath. She went to him and placed her hands on his chest. "Of course. Why else would I fight so hard for us?"

He tipped his head and threw her own words back at her. "It doesn't feel like it."

"Hunter." She ran her hands up to his shoulders. "All I *ever* ask for is more of a partnership. And more of your time."

He didn't soften or wrap his arms around her waist or do anything that he typically did when she touched him. "You harp on how I'm too focused on work, as if your focus these past two years hasn't been almost exclusively on having babies, and now on Gentry's baby."

"*Our* baby."

He shook his head. "Like it or not, Sara, it's her baby until she signs off on the adoption. And even then, I'm pretty sure there are laws that give a mom some kind of right of rescission after the birth, just to make sure."

She pushed away. Sara expected Gentry to have moments of doubt but ultimately believed she knew weeks ago that she'd made a good decision. "When you talk like that, so cold and detached, it makes me feel like you hope Gentry changes her mind."

"No, but if she's going to, let's find out now. I'd rather not get invested—rather *you* not get more invested—until it's certain. That's all I was trying to do today at my dad's. Hardly sabotage."

She closed her eyes, unwilling to discuss the possibility that Gentry would renege on her promise. "To the extent I am focused on the baby, it's for us, for our family. How can you use that as evidence that I don't love you?"

He threw his arms wide open, but not to seek an embrace. "Maybe you love the idea of us, of a family. Maybe you're too comfortable or too afraid to change the circumstances, so you're clinging to the idea of a family like it will fulfill you in some way I don't. I'm not sure. I just know that you don't look at me like you used to. You don't like the way I 'manage' things, even though it never used to bother you. You see me as some kind of bully. Nothing I do is right anymore, yet I'm not the one who has changed, Sara."

His nostrils flared and his breathing had grown heavy, but those eyes never lost focus. He'd trapped her in a smug, self-righteous gaze, daring her to prove him right. To tell him that she didn't love him. That she'd been too weak to leave.

He was wrong about all of it, though, but too arrogant or guarded to see the truth.

Her own frustration brimmed to the tipping point, and she launched forward and shoved at him with a grunt.

He captured her hands, and they wrestled for a second or two until, somehow, they were face-to-face, his one hand cupping her neck, the other clasping her wrist. Heartbeat to heartbeat, sharing each other's breath, they were locked together in a tangle of limbs and emotion. Then, shockingly, he kissed her.

Not a gentle kiss. Not even a loving kiss. A fierce, harsh, possessive kiss. His way of reestablishing some kind of control, because God forbid he ever not be in control.

And yet, she didn't push him away. She didn't fight that angry kiss. She met it with equal force. Right there in the office that so often took him away from her. She wanted to have sex on every surface, like a brand, so he could never again come in here to hide from her. Everywhere he looked, she wanted him to have a memory of her.

She kissed him, ripping at his shirt. If it surprised him, he didn't show it. He growled and lifted her onto his desk, yanking her shirt loose, pushing her skirt up, and tossing her panties. He'd barely shoved his own pants down his hips when he entered her, swift and hard.

She cried out as she wrapped her legs around his waist and anchored her arms around his neck, coming in bursts she couldn't control. He thrust again and again, her name rough on his lips, his fingers marking her ribs. She bit his earlobe and sucked on the curve of his neck beneath, dragging her fingers through his hair.

Anger, love, betrayal, frustration—the cyclone slammed them together and ripped them apart until he cried out and began to shudder, laying her back on the desk as he spent himself.

They lay there, chests heaving. No tender kisses or words. No eye contact.

In fourteen years, they'd never done hate sex, angry sex, or makeup sex, and she didn't like it. From the way he refused to meet her eyes, she doubted he did, either.

When he stood, his face was flushed. He glanced at her before gently helping her sit upright. "Are you okay?"

She paused. Her heart—her chest—ached, but that wasn't what he meant. "Yes."

He nodded and scrubbed a hand over his face. "I'm sorry, anyway."

"Me too."

He started to bend down to retrieve his pants, but she caught his hand and kept him there. "Hunter, are *you* okay?"

"Sure."

An abrupt and insincere reply, running inward for cover like always. She released his hand. He put his pants on without saying anything, so she found her panties and straightened her own clothes, too.

The discomfort persisted. How had they gotten even further apart than before the argument started? Moments ago she'd been determined to create memories, but not these negative ones.

"Hunter, despite this rough patch—or whatever it is that we're going through—I do love you. I just miss you."

He held his hands out, face drained from exhaustion and defeat. "I'm right here, just like I've always been."

Chapter Seventeen

"I'm kind of in a rush, Mom." Hunter checked his watch, patience frayed by a restless, unpleasant weekend. He couldn't remember a time when he'd felt more isolated and misunderstood. At least at work he was respected and productive.

Cortland was scheduled to call him about the projections for the bottling partnership today. Hunter didn't want to miss the call or give Jenna a chance to snoop through his messages.

"Oh, settle down. It's Monday. You've got all week to conquer the world. Have some coffee and give your mom another minute." She shoved the coffee mug at him with a smile. "Now hang tight. I have something for you."

She patted his shoulder and then disappeared into her room, walking on her heels so that her YogaToes didn't fall off. Her ancient tabby cat, Stitch, seemed to share Hunter's skepticism about those things as he stared after her, meowing.

God love her, but his mom made him antsy. Ever since he was young, her odd habits and disorganized thoughts had embarrassed him. Yet at the same time, he now appreciated her unconditional love and loyalty, two things he hadn't been able to count on with his dad.

While he waited, he glanced around the house where he'd grown up. The modest Craftsman had always been homey, and each room held memories of his childhood here with Colby. His mom hadn't been a neatnik, preferring to spend time outdoors and embroiled in activities with him and his sister. This formerly warm, noisy home was now empty (aside from Stitch), quiet, and clean.

He guessed his mom must get lonely with no kids and no job. Now that he had an inkling of how awful loneliness felt, he realized he should spend more time with her—just not this morning.

She returned with a tiny amber spray bottle labeled Lyme Nosode. "I swear I don't understand Jenna any better than you, so for your dad's sake, let's ignore her. Slip this to him. Two to three sprays under the tongue three times per day."

Hunter turned the bottle over in his hand. "What the hell is it?"

"Watch your mouth." She tapped his cheek. "I read about this when researching homeopathic sites and recommendations for Lyme."

"I can't just throw this down his throat. It could react badly with his other medication." He twirled the bottle in his hands, squinting to read the tiny print. "What kind of weird medicine gets sprayed under the tongue?"

"I thought you wanted to explore all options." She frowned. "Don't dismiss it just because it doesn't immediately make sense to you. You don't know everything about everything. Something unconventional might work. There's an entire movement behind homeopathic remedies."

"Come down off that high horse, Mom. All I'm saying is that I won't blindly dispense this without knowing what it is and whether it's dangerous if combined with Dad's other meds."

"Fine. If you can pry him away from Jenna, take him to Lelah Fekke." She flashed a conspiratorial grin. "She's a homeopath up in Portland."

Hunter tried not to cringe when imagining his dad's response to that suggestion.

"I'll see." He kissed her cheek and thrust the coffee mug at her. "Gotta run."

"Wait!" She refused to take the cup. "What's up with Gentry and the baby? And how's Sara?"

"Why do you ask?" The weekend had been excruciating. His memory of the bleak moments following the desk sex still made him sick.

"Do I need a reason?"

"No, but you look like you've got one." He set the cup down on the small foyer table.

"Fine. You're right. I'm glad this thing with Gentry has revived Sara's hope for a child, but I'm worried that she's lonely and maybe a little scared."

"In other words, you think I'm a lousy husband." *Just great.*

"Not 'lousy.'"

He raised a brow. "Gee, thanks."

"Anyone can see that Sara isn't herself lately. She's going through the motions, but she's lost the sparkle in her eyes."

His mom regarded him as if she'd delivered sage advice. He had eyes. He knew Sara better than anyone, so the fact that she'd changed hadn't escaped his attention.

His mother sighed. "I don't think she's grieved enough."

That was unexpected. "Grieved?"

"Yes. But more than just the failed IVF. She's got to grieve the loss of the future she'd probably envisioned—even taken for granted—for most of her life. She's from a big family. Her sisters have kids. Now she's at the mercy of your sister and other women who are giving kids up for adoption. She won't pass on her bloodline. She won't experience pregnancy. You may only get one kid, not three or four. It's not what she expected. Not what she wanted.

"Instead of coming to terms with all that, she's distracting herself with the foundation and Gentry." His mom set her hand on his forearm. "And, not to upset you, but I suspect you haven't been as sensitive to all that as you should be. In fact, I doubt you've processed what *you've* lost, either. You keep on burying yourself in your work to fill those holes."

Reflexively, he shirked her off.

"We grieved. She cried a lot, and believe it or not, I *was* sensitive." Then he remembered Sara crying during sex right after the last failed IVF. Maybe he hadn't comforted her the right way, but not because he didn't care. He just didn't know how to handle these, or her, emotions. "I 'bury myself' because I like what I do, and I have hundreds of workers' livelihoods in my hands."

"I see." She waved dismissively. "Your whole life you've ignored me and my opinions in favor of your father and his. You're so much like him now it worries me. As smart as you two are, you don't know everything. And something *I* know a little about is loss—and loneliness. So, you can blow me off, but I see Sara's loneliness because I've been there. Trust me, choosing to ignore it, or letting her fill the void with other activities, won't end well."

"We're not getting divorced, if that's what you're implying." He hoped that sounded more assured than he felt.

"I hope not. Sara's like another daughter to me." She squeezed his arm. "If you start turning to other women instead of sitting down with your wife and working through your problems, you'll be sorry in the end."

"For Pete's sake, I go to work and I go home. There are no other women."

She looked him dead in the eyes. "There's Bethany."

His head went back as if she'd slapped his face. "Why would you think I'd be interested in Bethany?"

"You think your dad fell for Jenna like lightning?" She shook her head, the hurt in her eyes erasing all the years between then and now. "No. But she was there, working at his side, sharing his dream. I was at home, raising two babies, feeling abandoned. The slow erosion happens before you notice. I know you're battling for CTC, and no one wants to see you stick it to Jenna more than I, but not at the expense of your marriage. Be careful, dear."

She picked up the abandoned coffee mug and kissed his cheek, then sent him on his way, YogaToes still in place.

He left her house, the weight of her warning dragging at him. Instead of striding in command down the hallway at work like normal, he didn't say good morning to a soul.

Haru handed him his messages. "How's your dad?"

"Hanging in there." He shuffled through the notes, distracted.

"Good. Everyone misses him around here."

"Me too." Hunter forced a grin before going into his office. A short while later, someone knocked at the door. "Come in."

Bethany walked in, coffee in hand, and closed the door. "Just checking in. I sent the projections to King Cola on Saturday like you asked. Have you heard anything yet?"

Between his wife's and mother's assumptions, he had a hard time meeting her eye. He shook his head. "They should be enough to get a meeting, but who knows."

"You sound defeated. Did something happen? Is your dad okay?" After taking a seat opposite his desk, she crossed her legs and tugged at the hem of her skirt.

He'd never noticed her legs or her skirts before. He shifted his gaze away and frowned. "He's not bouncing back as quickly as I'd hoped. Jenna and I disagree about his doctors—big surprise."

"That's tough, but you'll figure it out. You always do." She smiled, and for a second her confidence made him feel better. She'd been an exceptional employee and dependable cheerleader. Now his mom and

Sara had warped this working relationship into something it wasn't. "I'm sure Sara helps keep the peace."

"Of course she does." Most days his wife kept in better touch with his family than he did. And she'd done it all despite her own disappointments.

His mom was right: they hadn't grieved together. In fact, they hadn't done much of anything in recent months. Even the anniversary trip he'd planned had been cut short. And he hadn't even tried to set up the trip to visit her family that he'd promised.

"Well, I'm here to help, too. Whatever you need." She crossed her legs in the other direction, a feline smile on her face.

He tugged at his collar, then stuck his hands beneath his armpits. Was she playing some long game of seduction? He couldn't imagine it. They'd worked together without any trouble or misunderstandings for five years.

More likely his mom's and Sara's paranoia was affecting him. Still, he sat farther back on his chair to put more distance between them.

"Thanks, Bethany. I'll let you know the minute I hear back from Cortland. In the meantime, let's go about business as usual. Don't want to tip off Jenna."

"You got it." She stood, sipping her coffee, leaving a red lipstick mark on the rim.

He nodded and purposely dropped his eyes back to his screen, dismissing her. After she left, he put his forehead to his desk and clasped his hands behind his head. He couldn't start losing it around here, too.

Stuff like this didn't happen to him. He'd always planned every move to make sure he wouldn't be blindsided by life's ups and downs. Took charge of his problems instead of reacting to them, because passivity never helped one damn thing.

Yet he'd been passive at home. Both he and Sara felt like shit, but talking about their problems wasn't working. He'd have to try something else.

He called Bon Fleur and sent a bouquet of fall lilies to Sara that read "Dress up for dinner tonight."

◆ ◆ ◆

Sara pushed the backings onto the aquamarine earrings Hunter had bought her for her thirtieth birthday. The ones he'd said matched the color and twinkle of her eyes. That memory made her smile as she adjusted her hair one last time.

Swaying back and forth, she checked out the rear view of her sheath dress in the mirror before turning off the bathroom light and heading downstairs.

The vibrant flower arrangement greeted her in the kitchen. She stuck her nose into the elegant petals and inhaled their perfume. Like a sunburst, the orange-and-yellow bouquet marked a hopeful turn away from the unpleasant weekend. They'd more or less lived around each other since Saturday, neither one bringing up the argument or the hostile office sex.

He'd made this effort, so she needed to reach across the gulf. She loved him. She didn't want to hurt him or add to the growing distance. She just wanted her husband back.

When the garage door rumbled open, she set her hand against her stomach.

He came into the kitchen smiling and kissed her, fingering one of the earrings. "You look gorgeous."

She teased, "I do my best to keep up with you."

He brushed his nose against hers. "I'm pretty sure you surpass me, even when you've got hives and a runny nose."

She lifted the wire-rim glasses off his face and peered through them. "Maybe you need a new prescription."

"I see clearly." He snatched them back, then lowered his voice and tugged her against his chest. "Especially when it involves you."

"Okeydokey, Mr. Magoo."

He chuckled. "Are you all set?"

"Sure. Where are we going?"

"I hope you don't mind, but I asked Colby and Alec to join us since they have Mondays off. We haven't hung out with them in a while, so I thought it would be fun."

A little part of her might've liked to have had him to herself, but she was never against hanging out with family, especially Colby. Hopefully, he didn't invite them because he needed a buffer. "Sounds lovely."

"Great." He kissed her hand. "I really love this dress, although you might be slightly overdressed for Gab-n-Eat."

Her mouth fell open, then he laughed.

"Kidding. Colby and I know better than to drag you and Alec to our favorite diner. We're meeting at Headwaters."

"Ooh-la-la. Very nice." She took his hand and followed him to the car. "Alec picked it, didn't he?"

"Maybe."

As she slid into the passenger seat, she said, "So you'll want to stop for a burger on the way home."

He laughed. "Maybe."

An hour later, she nestled against the pea-green leather banquette seat and sipped a rich chardonnay with tangerine and peach undertones. Colby and Hunter opted for Ex Novo's IPA, while Alec settled for flat water, keeping his palate clean.

Sara savored the lemony last bite of her shaved brussels sprout salad. "I'm glad these two let you choose the restaurant, Alec."

"Me too." He feigned pain when Colby slapped his arm. "One of these days we'll get them to appreciate truly good food."

"I'm learning to appreciate it." Colby then leaned toward Hunter, snickering. "But nothing beats the onion rings at Gab-n-Eat."

"Hear, hear!" Hunter raised his beer mug.

"It's nice to see you smiling." Colby rested her chin on her hands and grinned at her brother.

Sara concurred, but kept quiet.

Hunter grabbed her hand, sighing. "Well, we haven't had much to smile about recently, with the IVF and now Dad's health."

That was the first time he'd acknowledged any sense of loss about the IVF without her prompting. A minor point but a marked change. His distant gaze suggested that he'd gotten lost in his thoughts.

She squeezed his hand. "Let's celebrate the *good* news, like A CertainTea's success, the difference the foundation is making in our community, and the adoption."

Hunter released her hand, nodding while averting his eyes. "Yes, the restaurant is exceeding CTC's expectations."

"We've been booked for several holiday parties in December and just got a big wedding gig for early spring. If this keeps up, I might be able to buy CTC out in less time than I originally thought." Colby's proud smile stretched across her face.

"What happens if Pure buys CTC? Does it *want* the restaurant, or will it let us buy it back?" Alec asked. This time Colby elbowed him hard.

"No need for violence, sis. I'm a big boy. We all know what's happening at work. I doubt Pure has any interest in the restaurant, but Colby's the general partner, anyway. You'll be fine. And it may not come to that, so don't count me out just yet." Hunter grinned and finished his beer with a gleam in his eye.

"Something happened. Something good?" Colby asked, leaning close.

"Nothing certain. But I'm heading out of town on Thursday for a day or two."

"Where to?" Sara couldn't hide the surprise in her voice but stopped short of questioning whether Bethany would be going with him.

"I've said too much." His expression sobered. He pointed his index finger at everyone. "Don't breathe a word. I don't want Jenna sniffing around and screwing it up. As far as anyone knows, I'm making a routine trip to our Idaho plant."

"You don't trust us?" Colby asked.

"So, how 'bout them Seahawks?" Hunter leaned back and stretched his long legs.

Colby wouldn't be put off. "Hunter, whatever you're doing, promise me it won't hurt Dad or his recovery."

Sara bit her lip, knowing Hunter would get defensive.

"When have I ever done anything to hurt Dad, or *anyone* in the family? If I'm successful, it benefits us all—even Jenna. I just hope I can nail it down before Pure comes back with an offer." He cast a furtive glance at Sara. "Let's not talk shop, though. What have you two been up to outside of the restaurant?"

Sara intertwined her fingers with his.

"Well, yesterday after we closed the brunch service, we went to Powell's for coffee and books." Colby grinned softly at the memory, and Sara felt a twinge of envy, wishing she and Hunter could spend a lazy afternoon together. "Today we actually took the Shanghai tunnels tour."

"You did not." Hunter pulled a face.

"We did." She nodded. "It was fun."

Hunter shot a cockeyed stare at Alec, who shrugged and confessed, "It was kind of fascinating to imagine all of the smuggling and activity that happened beneath the city. The ghost stories are a bit ridiculous, but the labyrinth down there is wild."

"I haven't done any touristy things since my early visits to Portland with Hunter." Sara tugged at his shirtsleeve. "We need to be more creative."

"You want to scurry around underground?" Hunter asked her, his face filled with amusement.

"Why not? Besides, we should take advantage of our freedom before the baby arrives."

Hunter nodded weakly. "True."

"I expected Gentry to be climbing the walls with boredom at this point, not happily back at home with Dad and Jenna, acting like a perfect family." Colby's tone sounded much like Hunter's did when grousing about his dad's "other" family. "What's the due date again?"

"May eleventh," Sara said, the date stamped on her brain and circled in red.

"Excited much?" Colby's warm smile didn't fully hide her lingering doubts about the adoption. Again, just like her brother.

"Thrilled." Sara's resounding smile didn't wobble, not even a little.

The waitress interrupted them to serve the main course. Fortunately, the menu not only catered to Alec's palate but also included a New York strip to satisfy Hunter, and a funky burger that Colby decided to test.

Alec cut into his duck. "Sara, how's the Angel House?"

"It's a wonderful organization. Your brother and Mark would be happy to have their names associated with supporting it." Sara smiled, recalling that Colby and Alec had started the Maverick Foundation to honor Alec's dead brother and Colby's former husband, Mark.

"And you enjoy volunteering there, Colby says," he said.

"I did . . . do." Sara didn't look at Hunter but felt him shift in his seat.

"Must be rewarding." Alec sampled his food, his eyes closing briefly, as if he were savoring the bite.

"I miss Ty." It was an honest answer that avoided directly discussing her reduced role at the Angel House. Also, anytime she thought of Ty, a little pang pinched her chest. On a daily basis, she wondered how Pam and he were faring. "I dropped a box of books and toys off at the place Hunter rented for them, but no one was home. For all I know, they're sitting unopened in a corner of the apartment."

Hunter patted her hand, softly adding, "Babe, you need to let him go."

"Hunter's right." Colby downed the rest of her IPA. "And while leasing that apartment was really nice, I worry that other residents might target us, expecting the same level of help from you or the foundation. How will you say no?"

"No one will ask. The women aren't entitled. They're hurting. They're eager for a second chance to prove that they can stand on their own." Too late. She heard the defensiveness in her voice.

"I didn't mean to insult them, or you, Sara." Colby reached across the table.

"Sara has a big heart. She really wants to give those women a fresh start. If we have to shell out extra money to help, I'm okay with that." Hunter kissed her cheek while stroking her thigh under the table. His big hand warmed her leg, and she wished he hadn't needed to remove it to cut his steak. "She's always had a soft spot for underdogs."

"Must be how you ended up with her," Alec laughed, lightening the mood.

"Thank God."

Hunter grinned, and a little part of Sara's heart melted. Hunter made a lot of mistakes, but so did she, and he still loved her, anyway. That admission slightly thinned the fog that had been hovering over their relationship. Suddenly, she wanted to race through dinner so she could be alone with him and replace the memory of their recent angry sex with something much better.

Chapter Eighteen

"Do you know why we've been summoned?" Hunter pulled into his dad's driveway, the thumping wipers' sound nearly drowned out by the rain hammering the car's roof. "Did my dad take a turn for the worse?"

"I don't know. When I dropped off the chicken curry casserole earlier, we chatted. He's still struggling with memory issues and achiness, but he didn't seem worse." Sara wrinkled her nose. "Gentry and Jenna were a little standoffish, but everyone's on edge these days. Let's look on the bright side. Maybe they have *good* news from his doctor."

He doubted it. Good news would be trumpeted quickly and wouldn't require a face-to-face meeting. Jenna didn't relish having Hunter to the house any more than he enjoyed being there, so he sensed a sober purpose—or trap—underfoot.

"Did you accidentally mention something about my trip tomorrow?" It'd be just like Jenna to call him out in front of his dad. He didn't need that, especially not in front of Sara.

"No." She held her breath, her blue eyes filled with unease. "What could I say, anyway? I don't even know if you're going alone."

"Sara." He leaned across the seat and kissed her. "I'm going alone. I keep telling you, you have no reason to be jealous of Bethany."

She released a relieved sigh. "Well, I'm glad you'll be back Friday afternoon. I hoped we might go hiking or something on Saturday morning."

"Maybe." He killed the engine, eyeing the sky. An umbrella would be useless in this downpour. "Let's see what this is about before we make any plans."

Sara nodded, then looked over his shoulder at the empty side of the driveway. "We're late, but I don't see Colby's car, either."

"She and Alec are at work."

"But it's a family meeting. Why would Colby skip out?"

"Hell if I know." He feigned confidence, but his instincts whispered warnings. Had his dad heard directly from Pure Foods? Glancing at the McMansion that often made the short hairs on his neck stand on end, he said, "Let's get this over with. Make a run for it."

Sara squealed as she raced for the door, unable to avoid becoming soaked. When they reached the cover of the portico, they laughed. Her hair was pasted to her skin; her eyes, alight with humor. He cradled her wet face and kissed her, the heavy pummel of rain on the portico drumming along with his heart. "My beauty."

"Your glasses must be dirty again." She smiled. He loved that smile. When she shivered, he remembered why they were standing there and rang the bell.

Gentry answered the door, looking like a pale imitation of herself. Pale purple circles beneath her eyes, yoga pants and an old Berkeley sweatshirt he'd bought her years ago, head somewhat lowered instead of shoulders thrown back. No trace of haughtiness or humor. "Hey, guys."

Sara kissed her cheek as they entered the house. "Hey yourself."

He couldn't remember ever seeing his sister wear that sweatshirt. It lacked the designer label or glitz that she preferred. He threw an arm around her shoulders and kissed her head. "Nice outfit."

Following a weak smile, she eased away. "You're soaked. Hang on a sec. Let me get you guys some towels."

She avoided eye contact as she ducked around the corner to fetch them.

"This is all very cloak-and-dagger." He grimaced at Sara.

She shrugged, not nearly as concerned. Of course, she'd wanted him to sell the company, so it made sense that her stress level didn't match his.

Gentry returned with towels. While they quickly dried off, she asked, "Do you want anything to drink?"

Her mottled cheeks and downcast eyes signaled trouble. As usual, the energy in this house sucked up his intuition like a black hole, leaving him on edge.

"No." He strengthened his grip on Sara's hand as they followed Gentry to the family room.

A hearty fire crackled in the stacked-stone fireplace. His father rested in the recliner, with a quilt thrown over his legs. The tightness in his face belied his lingering pain, even as he grinned upon seeing them. Hunter made a mental note to persuade his dad to go see that homeopath in Portland next week, even if it meant another fight with Jenna.

"Sara, thank you for the casserole. Why don't you quit the foundation and go work with Alec at A CertainTea?" His dad's eyes crinkled. Neither the joke nor his smile hid an unexpected sympathy in his gaze, or the fact that he didn't look at Hunter.

"I'm on a mission to help you regain some of the weight you've lost." Sara hugged his father.

"Jenna." Hunter acknowledged her with a polite glance before leaning down to kiss his dad hello. "Hey, Dad. How are you?"

"The same," he mumbled. "Why don't you two have a seat?"

Hunter braced for an argument. Jenna's spies must've discovered his plans to fly to New York. Any other time, he'd enjoy going toe-to-toe with her, but not here and now, with his father's health being so fragile.

He and Sara moved aside a handful of fringed decorative pillows and sank onto the chenille sofa. Gentry sat, cross-legged, on the floor beside their dad, toying with the hem of the sweatshirt. Jenna remained in the swivel bucket chair beside his father, suspiciously low-key.

Their positioning enhanced his sense of some kind of face-off. A moment of uncomfortable silence passed, broken only by the pop of hot embers.

"Are we waiting for Colby?" Sara asked, her voice forcibly bright.

"No," Jenna replied, her gaze flitting away from Hunter's.

"Well, don't keep us in suspense." He kept his voice steady and his gaze squarely on his father. "Why'd you call us here?"

He refused to be ashamed of his backroom negotiations. His father knew he didn't want to sell CTC and that he'd do anything to prevent it. If they'd found out about his inquiries with King Cola, so be it. Maybe Hunter's projections would make his dad question Jenna's impatience and give Hunter more time to negotiate before making a final decision about Pure Foods.

But when his dad nudged Gentry, whose head remained bowed, other alarms went off. She finally looked up, eyes wary and glistening, shoulders rounded. Hunter reached for Sara's hand as he looked at his sister, understanding why Colby's presence wasn't required.

"Did something happen to the baby? Did you miscarry?" The words left his mouth before he considered their insensitivity. Beside him, Sara inhaled sharply, and she squeezed his hand.

"Oh no. Please, no." Sara's voice wobbled, her grip tensing.

"No. The baby is fine." Gentry had now pulled her knees up against her chest. She slid a pleading look at Jenna, who merely pressed her lips together and raised her brows at her daughter.

Hunter's stomach sank because he knew what was coming before Gentry said another word. He wound an arm around Sara's waist, staring at his sister, who'd had the gall to wear his college sweatshirt *today*. The edge in his voice carried only a fraction of his anger. "Spit it out, sis."

Beside him, Sara had turned to stone. He massaged her side—a feeble attempt at comfort.

"I think I want to keep my baby." Gentry closed her eyes and set her forehead on her knees, as if she thought blocking out his and Sara's reaction would somehow lessen her culpability for the pain she would cause.

Sara trembled, folding in on herself while muffling a muted cry. Tingles fanned through him until his body went numb.

A thousand insults raced through his mind. He imagined himself towering over Gentry, screaming about how he'd known better than to trust her to keep her word. How she'd never kept a commitment in her life. How she was exactly as selfish as her mother.

But what good would that do Sara? He fastened his wife to his side in a futile attempt to keep her from falling apart. How much loss could she bear? The IVF, little Ty, now this baby, too? What had Sara ever done to deserve so much disappointment? To deserve such a betrayal?

His fingers ached to wrap themselves around Gentry's skinny arms and shake sense into her. How could she be a mother when she was still such a fucking child?

"Hunter, Sara, we know this is hard to hear," his dad began. "But in the end, this is Gentry's baby, so it has to be her choice."

Hunter had lost all patience with the way his father and Jenna always made excuses for his sister. He knew it was her baby. That's why he'd never been enthusiastic about this plan from the start. Yet *she'd* come to them. *She'd* made a promise. What happened to all the times his dad had told him that a man is only as good as his word? Apparently, that didn't apply to his coddled baby girl.

"Don't even—" He glared at Jenna to preempt any defense she might raise. Turning to his sister, who hadn't yet made eye contact with him or Sara, he sneered. "Don't you even have the guts to look at us?"

Gentry raised her chin. "I'm sorry. I never meant to hurt you. But when Dad got sick and I moved back in . . . well, I started to think maybe I made a mistake. Maybe I'm supposed to keep my baby."

Maybe? Even now she didn't know what she wanted. How could they be related? He'd always known what he wanted, and he'd never shirked a commitment or broken a promise.

Hunter thought about the night, weeks ago, when he'd caught Gentry staring at the sonogram picture. He'd begged her not to let Sara get more invested if she had any doubts. What kind of monster breaks the heart of someone as kind as his wife, especially in light of what Sara had already lost?

Sara whimpered against his shoulder, reminding him that now was not the time to indulge his anger. He needed to get his wife out of this ice palace. "Come on, babe. Let's go."

"Hold on, son." His father coughed. "Let's talk this through so there aren't hurt feelings and a family breach."

He sat on the ugly, loathsome thoughts stacking up in his head. The kinds of words that could never be taken back. For the second time in a matter of months, his father had sided with someone other than him on a critical decision that hurt him. Ever since his dad had gotten sick, Hunter had been trying to rationalize the thing with CTC, but he couldn't accept the way his father immediately defended Gentry's choice and expected Sara and him to just get over it.

Hunter had pretty much dedicated himself to his dad for years, giving everything he had to keep and foster their father-son bond. He'd yearned for the man's approval and assurance of love. All for nothing, it seemed.

Acid burned his stomach, but he couldn't wallow in this realization now. Nor could he mask his disgust. "What's left to discuss? When push comes to shove, you always stand with these two over Colby and me."

He turned his back on the room and helped Sara to her feet.

"I'm sorry," Gentry croaked from behind him. "Sara, I'm really sorry."

"Stop talking," he barked, aching for his wife. His sister's tears were cold comfort, and probably an act. Escalating fury provoked him to hurl an insult with the full intention of destroying her. "I'm sorry, too. Sorry for that child you're carrying who had a chance to have Sara for a mother but now will be stuck with you."

"Hunter, stop," Sara moaned. "Please, let's just go."

"Son," his dad implored, but he ignored him, fixated instead on his wife's pain-stricken face.

For once Jenna knew to keep quiet. A small mercy, because if she'd said one thing, he wouldn't have been able to hold back the full force of his animosity. Without another word—without giving his father the closure he sought—Hunter ushered Sara out of the house.

His body felt supercharged, muscles taut, jaw clenched. It took concentration to force air in and out of his lungs as he held Sara's waist. Her unsteady legs kept them from running through the rain.

While walking around to the driver's side, he stopped and picked up a sizable rock from the flower bed. He stood, showered by rain, staring at the house, seriously considering tossing the thing through one of the Palladian windows. Why not? He'd probably never return. Never forgive his sister. Never.

With great restraint, he let the rock fall to the ground. He got into the car and sat behind the wheel, water sluicing off his body and drenching his seats.

"Babe," he said, but Sara's head rested against the window, eyes closed tight, face crumpled.

Away from his family's watchful eyes, Sara's agony poured out of her for the duration of the drive home. She was crying just as she had when the last IVF failed. The sound of lost hope consumed the car. His knuckles whitened on the steering wheel as he sped up, his hazy thoughts obscuring the road.

None of his strength or intellect could stop her tears or fix what had broken. He hated nothing more than listening to his wife's pain gush in sobs and hiccups. Well, maybe he hated Gentry more.

His father's loyalties fueled Hunter's rage. Time to flip the switch. He'd invoke the bylaws and take over as interim CEO. His fiduciary duty to the shareholders meant he couldn't exactly stop the Pure Foods deal, but he could exert greater control over the negotiations and terms, if it came to that. Meanwhile, he'd now have more authority in his meeting with King Cola.

If he could nail down that deal, he'd borrow money to buy his father, Jenna, and Gentry out of CTC. That coup would be his *new* legacy. His father had let him down in so many ways that he felt almost nothing at the thought of total estrangement.

When they got home, Hunter tried to hold Sara, but she wouldn't be consoled. "What can I do?"

She looked at him, swiping at her puffy face. Her eyes were full of agony and betrayal. "Look at you. Not a single tear. It's like you don't even care."

"What are you talking about? Of course I care. I can't stand to see you this upset." He reached for her, but she shook him off.

"You care that I'm upset, but you don't care about losing the baby or the fact that, once again, our dreams of a family were snatched away. You're just angry because Gentry changed her mind, and you can't do anything about it."

He didn't know how to respond to that accusation. He *did* feel angry. Angry as hell. Did she expect him to cry? That was never his MO. He acted. He made—or forced—change. He fixed problems. What he didn't do was cry. "Just because I don't react like you doesn't mean I don't care, Sara. Please don't push me away right now."

She sank to the ground and leaned against the side of the island. "I should've listened to you and your warnings. I should've known you'd be right. You're always right. Sometimes I hate that about you."

Her brows furrowed before she closed her eyes. He crouched to embrace her, but she batted him away in favor of hugging herself. He sat beside her, hands clasped on his lap, waiting for her to fall against his chest and let him hold her. It took longer than usual, but eventually she leaned against him, hugging him like he was the only thing keeping her alive.

Her last words echoed in his mind. For the first time in his life, he also hated being right.

◆ ◆ ◆

A muffled noise in the bedroom woke Sara. Not that it mattered. She'd slept in fits and starts all night. No light filtered through the blinds, so she glanced at the clock: 4:38 a.m. A shadow moved in the distance, causing her to start. She felt across the mattress for Hunter, but his side of the bed was empty.

A drawer opened, and as her eyes adjusted to the dark, she saw him on the chaise, putting on socks.

"Where are you going?" she whispered, even though no one was sleeping.

He looked up, his expression shifting from surprised to apologetic as he tied his shoelaces. "Sorry I woke you. I have to catch my flight."

She pushed herself up onto her elbows. "Can't you reschedule?"

"No." He stood and raised the handle on his overnight bag. "I've got to jump on this. It's my only shot."

Yesterday they'd basically lost another child, yet today he was right back to business—his true love. Never mind that she'd be alone, not even able to turn to *his* family for comfort. "I can't believe you're leaving after what just happened."

He sat on the bed and stroked her hair, his intent gaze cutting through the dimness. "Sara, if I could avoid it, I would, but I've got to take this meeting. I need to nail down this option. I'm going to win this fight and then force Jenna, Gentry, *and* Dad out of the company."

"Revenge?" She shook her head. "Since when has that been a goal?"

"Since yesterday." The sharp planes of his cheekbones looked harsh in the shadows. He pulled her head toward him and kissed her forehead.

"Vengeance won't give us back what we lost. I need you to stay with me today." She reached for his hand and held it to her cheek. "Please, Hunter. Please don't go."

He looked away. "The timing sucks, but I called in a personal favor to get this meeting, so I can't cancel at the last minute."

"You can. You *can* realize what really matters and get some perspective about CTC." She dropped his hand and slumped against the pillows. When he shook his head, what remained of her heart went cold in her chest. "Just leave, then."

"Sara . . ." he started, but she rolled away, pulling the covers up over her head.

He sighed before she felt his weight lift off the mattress. "I love you. I'll be home tomorrow. I'll clear my calendar for the whole weekend so we can get away. We'll go on that hike, okay?"

She didn't respond. He was using her pain as twisted justification for some form of retaliation. Did he think a hike would make her feel better now? She lay under the blanket, listening to his footsteps fade as he made his way down the steps.

Frustrated, she tossed the covers off but remained curled in a ball. The headlights from his stupid, silent car slipped light through the slats of the blinds as he backed out of their driveway.

A tear trickled down her cheek. She was tired of feeling alone. Of being kind and good and hopeful only to lose out to fate and fickle whims. Of trying to be understood by her husband only to be met with his frustration. Of coming in second place to CTC.

Maybe she was growing tired of being Mrs. Hunter Cabot, and the only way she could be happy now would be to return to being Sara Daly.

When dawn's first rays finally peeked through the window, she roused herself from bed despite the pounding headache and aching muscles.

Listlessly, she went to the bathroom and splashed cool water on her face, hoping it would revive her. Patting her skin dry, she stared into the mirror. Sara Daly Cabot. Thirty-four and counting. Faint wrinkles fanned out from the corners of her eyes. Fainter ones showed around her lips. A few rogue gray hairs could be found if one looked hard enough. Her body still looked young and strong. No stretch marks on her belly, of course. She hadn't been that lucky.

Who might she be today had Hunter not chased her down in the Glade? Would she be living close to her mother and sisters? Would she have married someone less ambitious? Would she be happier?

She stared at herself, as if her image could give her the strength to do what she'd been considering. *Leave.* Forever? The sudden thought shocked her, yet maybe sudden was the only way this kind of notion ever struck.

The word "separation" tasted like a mouthful of vinegar, but she needed to regroup. To get distance from Hunter so she could think about her future.

At the back of the cavernous closet, she found a large suitcase. She set it on the bench and opened it. Her breath came in shallow gulps as the walls closed in around her. With effort, she forced herself to thumb through her clothes. A lifetime of items accumulated, one by one. The dress she'd worn to Colby's first wedding. The jeans she'd bought when she'd gone with Hunter to New York last year. The funky belt Gentry had bought her for Christmas two years ago. Sara closed her eyes, as if she could unsee that silver-and-turquoise buckle.

She couldn't stand it, so she spun around to another corner of the closet. For now, she'd take enough to get her through a couple of weeks. She wouldn't think about Hunter or his family, or how they'd feel about her decision. Only herself. Her family. Her heart. She needed a sense of family and love she seemed to have lost here, no matter how terrifying it felt to leave.

She folded four pairs of jeans, some wool slacks, and several shirts and sweaters. At the bottom of the suitcase, she layered her favorite boots and a couple of pairs of shoes first, then added the clothing. She had to sit on the suitcase to zip it.

Choosing her favorite lululemon pants and cozy hoodie, she dressed and then tied her hair back, brushed her teeth, and applied a stroke of mascara. She stared in the mirror again, this time feeling somewhat stronger and more determined than earlier. The vanity was full of her stuff, so she retrieved a smaller bag and tossed in her makeup, facial creams, brushes, and hair gizmos.

Her bravery faltered when she took a final sweep around the bedroom. Years of memories—so many of them happy—replayed. The warmth of her comfy bedding after she and Hunter made love. That first Christmas as husband and wife, when Hunter had surprised her by setting up an extra Christmas tree in the room simply because she loved tree lights. His face had beamed with pride from pleasing her.

If she closed her eyes, she could smell the lingering scent of his cologne that wafted through the room every morning when he dressed for work. Hear his humming while he shaved.

They'd begun their marriage with so much love and no comprehension of how life might blindside them. No concerns about the limits of what they or their bodies could do. No doubts that their values and goals would remain in sync.

Somewhere along the way, they'd grown in different directions, and no amount of talking had bridged the gap. She didn't know why their communication had faltered, but continuing to torment and frustrate each other wasn't making it better. They both deserved *better*.

Her gaze landed on the bamboo plant from Leslie. It hadn't lived up to its promise any better than anyone or anything else had.

Right now, Hunter believed the most important thing he had to do was save CTC. That left it to her to save herself. The drive to Sacramento would take nine hours, but the pull toward home had never beckoned more than it did this morning.

She passed by the pictures hanging on the wall along the stairwell, refraining from looking at them, especially the candid black and white she'd taken of Hunter. He'd been lounging in his pajama pants and an old T-shirt, reading a book, his feet propped up on the leather ottoman. She'd captured him in a rare relaxed moment. The beauty of his face in repose always took her breath away, so she could not let herself see it now.

She got as far as the kitchen before she hesitated. Before the enormity of this act hit her. Everything inside these walls—from the paint they'd selected to the knickknacks they'd collected—owned a piece of her heart, and if she left, those pieces would be ripped away, leaving even more raw, exposed wounds. That scared her, but fear wasn't a good reason to stay.

Before she left the house, she sat at her kitchen desk. The early-morning quietude mirrored the solemnity of her mood. Pulling out a sheet of paper, she chewed on a pencil, thinking.

Her throat ached from the lump wedged in there like a too-big bite of bread. Her heart beat out an irregular and heavy pace. She pushed away the image of how Hunter's face would droop when he read her note. When he discovered the missing bags and realized that everything had changed.

Sadly, she welcomed the guilt of hurting him because at least it made her feel something other than numb. Despite it all, she couldn't continue living in limbo, hoping for change.

> Hunter,
> I'll always love the life we had and the love we shared, but it's not the same anymore. We've reached a place where our wants and needs no longer match, and we both deserve better than feeling misunderstood or

> unappreciated. I know you love me, as I love you, but love is only part of this equation. You want CTC to be your legacy, while I wanted love and a family to be our legacy. I'm accepting that I won't get my wish. Knowing you, you won't stop until you get yours. I hope it's worth it.
>
> Love, Sara

Her hands trembled slightly, but she set the note on the island. She twisted her wedding band around and around, staring out the window at the lake far below, remembering the thrill of buying this house. A home. Their home.

But mementos and pretty views didn't make a home. A home was founded on love, constructed by shared values, commitment, and compromise, and decorated with laughter. The foundation of her home had been strong, but somewhere along the way, the construction had grown shoddy, the decor neglected. Now the roof couldn't keep out the rain.

She dragged her suitcases to the garage and loaded them into her trunk, nose tingling from the urge to cry. Adrenaline surged through her heart as the engine roared to life.

For a moment, she sat in the car, garage door opened. Her fingers were wrapped tightly around the steering wheel, eyes staring at the back wall, throat swollen from unshed tears. The low hum of the engine muddled her thoughts. For all the drama in her head, she'd be leaving without fanfare. No teary goodbye. Nothing but her memories and disappointments.

She backed out of the driveway and, as she drove away, couldn't stop herself from watching the home get smaller in her rearview mirror. She swallowed hard.

Once on the main road that led out of town, she put her foot on the gas and headed south, praying for relief.

Chapter Nineteen

Hunter removed his glasses and rubbed his eye with the palm of his hand, waiting for his garage door to open. Hellish day. Cortland had brought two board members to lunch, but despite their interest, the board members' approval, which was needed to green-light this undertaking, would take time. More time than it would take Pure Foods to finalize its offer.

More troubling than that, however, was the fact that Sara hadn't taken his calls all day.

In the doghouse—again.

Despite exhaustion, he'd taken advantage of the time difference and rescheduled his return flight for today. That effort should mitigate his offenses. He'd hoped she'd still be awake, but the dark house suggested otherwise. Only after he'd pulled into the garage did he notice her missing car.

He lugged his unused overnight bag out of the trunk and speed-dialed Colby to see if Sara went to A CertainTea for a drink and some company.

He stood in the garage, staring at the empty space. "Hey, sis. Is Sara down there with you?"

"No. Why would she be here?"

"I just got back from my trip, and she's not home." He sighed, too exhausted to come up with a white lie. "She's not answering my calls."

"You took that trip after what happened?"

So she knew about Gentry. It shouldn't surprise him, but right now he didn't need her judgment or a debate. "Have you spoken with her today?"

"No. I left a message, but she didn't call me back. I assumed she wasn't ready to talk. I'm really sorry, Hunter. I worried about something like this happening. Now I'm torn between hurting for you and Sara and understanding how Gentry's feelings changed."

"Stop there. I'm not near ready to empathize with Gentry."

"I'm sorry. I get it. As for Sara, maybe Mom coaxed her into coming over for dinner. If they opened a bottle of wine, they could've lost track of time. You know how Mom loves to keep people talking, especially if she's worried about Sara being alone."

"Maybe." He couldn't picture that, though. Sara wouldn't want to talk about everything yet. She'd want to do something or go someplace that made her feel better. "I think I might know where she went. I'll talk to you tomorrow."

He set his suitcase just inside the mudroom and got back in his car. A total long shot, but he couldn't think of anything else, and she'd mentioned something about hearing that Pam got that waitressing job. Ten minutes later, he drove by the apartment he'd rented for Ty and his mother. Strike one.

He then took a spin past the Angel House. Strike two. A quick drive by his mom's turned up empty, too. Only one place left, and his stomach soured just thinking about it. He slowed as he approached his dad's house, not sure what to hope for. He didn't want to see Gentry yet, but he wanted to find Sara. It was possible she'd gone there hoping to persuade Gentry to reconsider.

No luck, and now it was after eleven.

On his way home, he dialed Sara again, but it went straight to voice mail. Where the hell had she gone? Panic flitted around like a hummingbird in his chest.

He returned home to a still-empty garage and stormed inside, leaving his bag in the mudroom. When he flipped on the kitchen lights, he saw a letter on the island. Thank God—an explanation. Relief whooshed through him, making him a little light-headed.

He blew out a long breath to settle himself, then picked up her note and its familiar cursive script. Line by line, the room around him dimmed until his peripheral vision turned nearly black. He focused on each loopy letter, convinced that his brain was misunderstanding her. That she hadn't actually left town. Left him.

She'd left him.

Sara was gone.

He set the note down and stared into space, aware of the heated air pushing in and out of his lungs as he struggled for each breath. *Sara.* Aside from the low hum of the refrigerator, the house was silent and still. He'd been alone in their house before, but it had never felt this lonely.

It wouldn't be a home without her. Just an assortment of furnishings and carpets, dishes, and artwork. Her leaving might as well be a match tossed in the living room for how it would burn the place to the ground.

He'd been happy here with her, with their friends and family. Of course, Sara had always projected ahead to when the spare bedrooms would be nurseries. To when they'd host first birthday parties and leave cookies for Santa. Her enthusiasm had always made him smile, although, in truth, he'd never needed that in the same way she did. He'd just needed her. He'd been satisfied—no, grateful—for her, and their marriage would've been enough.

Obviously, she didn't feel the same.

His phone buzzed, causing his heart to jump. "Hello?"

"Did you find Sara?" Concern edged Colby's voice.

"Not exactly." Although she hadn't mentioned where she'd gone, he knew she'd run back to the comfort of her loving family. The kind she'd tried and failed to re-create in Portland. Her sisters and their kids would help her regroup. "She went to Sacramento."

"That makes sense." His sister sounded relieved, but only because she didn't understand that Sara had gone for more than a visit. "Her mom will help her get over this latest setback."

"Or maybe she's not planning on coming back."

"Of course she will, Hunter. She's upset, but she loves you. She just needs a little time away from Gentry to get perspective."

"I'm not so sure." He then read the note to his sister.

For a short while, Colby said nothing. "I'll call her tomorrow."

"No. Don't pester her. She obviously wants space." He closed his eyes. "Listen, I'm exhausted. I'll talk to you later, okay?"

"I'm here for you."

"I know." A grateful yet bleak smile flickered. "Thanks."

After he hung up, he glanced at the note again, staring at it for minutes, memorizing each word.

His wife had left him.

What now?

His body jerked to attention, and he ran up the steps, through their room, and into the closet. A trickle of hope soothed him when he found a majority of her clothes, shoes, and other personal items left behind.

Burying his nose in one of her sweaters, he inhaled, searching for her scent. He tried three more before realizing nothing clean would smell like her. On the top of the pile of discarded things in the hamper, he found the sleep shirt she'd worn last night.

He slung it over his shoulder and went to the sink to brush his teeth. His reflection wasn't pretty. Pale. Hair disheveled from raking his hands through it a few too many times. A hint of panic in his weary eyes. He looked away, spit out the toothpaste, wiped his mouth, and headed to bed.

Once under the covers, he looked at the empty side of the bed where his wife should have been. The bed—the whole room—was cold. He clutched her pajamas to his chest like a kid with a stuffed animal, hoping to keep the monsters away.

◆ ◆ ◆

The sheer white curtains of her childhood bedroom billowed from the breeze coming through the window Sara had cracked open last night. The room might as well have been a furnace, despite the fall weather. Or maybe it was simply her body temperature burning hotter than a summer sun in Phoenix.

Restless. Distraught. Benumbed. In the span of twenty-four hours, she'd experienced pretty much every emotion on the spectrum of human reaction.

Her old twin mattress hadn't helped matters. If she tried to stretch her limbs wide, like she could on the king-size mattress at home—or former home—she'd have banged into the wall or fallen off the edge. In truth, a part of her was grateful that the narrow bed didn't leave room for a blank space where Hunter should be.

She couldn't remember the last time she'd awakened alone. Curling into a ball, she pulled the rosebud-print quilt up to her chin and gently brushed her wedding ring against her lips.

Hunter's original plan was to fly home this afternoon, so his worried messages last night had caught her off guard and unprepared. They'd stopped at eleven, so he must've finally found her note. She'd texted him around midnight, after she'd cried to her mom and settled down, saying she wasn't ready to talk yet.

He hadn't replied or tried to reach her again since then.

Tap, tap, tap.

"Yes?" She sat up with some effort, looking toward the door.

Her mom peeked into the room and smiled. She was a little on the short and stout side, and her round face and sandy hair lent a bit of youthfulness despite her sixty-one years. Although decades had passed, Sara was reminded of all the mornings of her childhood when her mom's pleasant smile had been the first thing she'd seen each day. "I made some coffee."

"Okay. I'll be out in a minute." Her stomach clenched at the thought of digesting the acidic drink. In fact, her whole body ached and begged to lie down again.

Still standing in the doorway, her mom tilted her head to the left, face glowing with compassion. That look, coupled with her naturally sweet voice, had always comforted Sara. "You don't look like you got much sleep."

Sara shook her head and pinched her nose to stop it from tingling.

A sad, lopsided grin appeared. "I'll make French toast with almond extract. That was your favorite, right?"

"Mimi's, actually. But I like it fine, too."

"Oh, sorry. I'll go to my grave getting all of you girls' preferences jumbled up." Her mom closed the door, and Sara sank back into the pillow.

The memory remark made her think of Jed's neurological issues. For most of her adult life, he'd been like another father to her. Of course, over the past couple of months, Jed's choices and health had wrought unwelcome changes on the man who'd otherwise always been loving and kind and fair.

Those changes had conspired to send her husband even further into a tailspin.

Losing another baby hurt. Losing her marriage and her other family hurt more. Would they care? Would her leaving turn them against one another, or would they rally around Hunter? Worse, had her absence only jacked up Hunter's anger toward his dad and Gentry?

Hunter would be awake now, if he'd slept at all. Maybe he had. Maybe, after the shock wore off, he was relieved to have her and her complaints out of his life.

She hadn't thought ahead yesterday, so she wasn't exactly sure what to do next. Separation, divorce, conscious uncoupling—concepts she'd never planned to consider. Didn't know where to begin to do so, either.

One day at a time, she supposed.

Looking around her cluttered room, she marveled at the assortment of crap her mother had kept. Each memento represented old dreams—some fulfilled, others not yet realized. Triumph on the soccer field had yielded a couple of trophies. Her high school diploma and National Honor Society certificate were pinned to the large bulletin board hanging over her old desk. There were pictures of her high school friends along with her dried-out senior prom corsage. There were also a few college photos, including one of her and Hunter from a Pi Phi formal.

He'd bowled her over with his enthusiasm and drive—his commitment and their immediate connection. She'd never met a guy like him before, or since. Hunter Cabot was a force of nature, and she'd been more than content to be swept along for the ride, until it felt like she was grasping at loose ends, just trying to hang on.

Now what?

She swung her legs over the side of the bed and dug out her old robe from the tiny closet. By the time she reached the kitchen, her mother had already fixed her a plate and poured some coffee.

"Any other day I would've called in sick, but the kids have been working on this history project for weeks, and today is the big presentation. They're so excited. I can't let them down." Her mom snapped a slice of bacon in two and chomped on one half.

"It's okay. I know you and Dad have to work." Her mother still taught fourth grade, but her dad had moved into administration over the years and was now a high school principal a few districts south of town.

"He's sorry he had to leave before you woke, but his commute is longer than mine. As it is, I need to leave within ten minutes." She sipped her coffee. "I hate leaving you alone today. What will you do?"

"Go see Mimi and the kids. We've traded messages but haven't had a real conversation in weeks. Is Lisa around, too?"

Her mom rolled her eyes. "Lisa is definitely around, still parked at the rear of Mimi's property. Maybe you can encourage her to supplement her massage therapy income with another job. Lord knows anytime I try to talk some sense to her, she treats me like the enemy."

Lisa had never liked advice. In fact, suggesting something was the surefire way to make certain she absolutely never did it. She was a free-spirited girl with a tendency toward moodiness, similar to Gentry. That thought made Sara frown.

Her mother must've read her thoughts. "When I get home today, we'll talk about what's happened and how you're going to move forward and fix your marriage."

"You think I haven't tried fixing it? I think it's beyond saving." She poured extra sugar in her coffee.

"Did he lie? Cheat? Hit you?"

"Of course not." Hunter was honest, loyal, and had never really raised his voice to her, let alone his hand.

"Do you still love him?" Her mother's tone held no judgment but reminded Sara of the anguish in Hunter's face when he'd asked her that same thing not long ago.

Layers of anger and disappointment sat on her heart, but beneath all that beat the frustrating truth. He'd been her one and only for nearly fourteen years, and that wouldn't fade easily, even if she wished it would. "Yes."

"Then it can be saved." Her mom stood and set her cup in the sink. "You take a few days here to hit 'Pause,' but you can't just walk out on your life because you don't like the way it's going. That won't solve anything."

Sara realized her mom would be one of many people who might think her crazy or ungrateful to have left Hunter. Who didn't understand that sometimes love and good intentions weren't enough. Who couldn't see how his ambition and need for control had taken over their lives. How he'd grown more invested in things outside their marriage than within.

She admired him but deep down wished it could be like the beginning, when he couldn't wait to *leave* the office so he could spend time with her, whether reading by a fire or cooking on the grill or simply sharing jokes while walking around the lake. When he never forgot to show up for dinner. When the idea of skipping doctors' appointments for business meetings would've appalled him. When volunteering with her would have been something he'd have asked to do rather than refused.

If other couples were happy making it work Hunter's way, hooray for them. It didn't work for her, and she wouldn't feel guilty about it . . . or at least she hoped she wouldn't for long. He'd taken for granted that she'd be there for him and his family despite how little time he spent talking to her, exploring the world with her.

Sara buried her head in her hands. "No lectures, Mom. I already have a headache."

Her mom came over to hug her from behind and kissed her head. "I'll see you later. Tell your sisters hi from me. Let's plan a family dinner for tomorrow since you're home. I don't see them enough these days."

"Okay." That surprised Sara, who'd always been a little bit homesick. If she'd lived within a thirty-minute drive of her parents or siblings, she'd visit all the time. As it stood, she'd seen them all only once or, if she was lucky, twice each year, mostly at holidays or other milestone celebrations.

She missed the day-to-day kind of relationship with her own family that she'd somewhat re-created with Hunter's.

Colby already knew about her leaving from Hunter. She couldn't return that call yet because she had no idea what she'd say. Poor Colby would be smack in the middle of Hunter and Gentry's fight, too. And when Jed and Gentry got word of what she'd done, they might feel responsible.

Hunter would blame them, but Gentry's reversal was the tipping point, not the root cause. Unless he grasped that, she didn't see any hope for them, no matter what her mother thought.

Chapter Twenty

Haru stared wide-eyed at Hunter. He looked like hell, and he knew it. That's what three minutes of sleep all night did to a guy. He'd tried to quiet his dark thoughts about Gentry, his dad, Sara, and Pure Foods, but they'd slid through his brain, burning like hot oil, until his head was so messed up he couldn't do anything but stare at the ceiling and pray for relief.

By morning, he'd decided he'd be better off taking control of CTC than trashing his house or telling off his family.

"Do it," he instructed Haru, whose shell-shocked expression didn't stop him from forcing her to hit "Send" on a company-wide memo invoking his power as interim CEO. Jenna would come screeching into his office sooner than later, so he strolled on in and shut the door, welcoming the showdown.

Sunlight poured through the massive window behind his credenza, flooding the office—or command central, as he'd jokingly referred to it from time to time—with light. He scowled. Nothing about this day matched that kind of brightness, nor did command central inspire the confidence it typically instilled. Even the bubbling of his massive fish tank didn't soothe him today.

He sat in his chair and turned on his computer, his gaze falling on the wedding photo on the corner of his desk. The loving image mocked him. Nearly a decade old—that time made obvious by the fact that their faces were no longer so young and innocent. Sara had been a breathtaking bride in her lacy gown and organza veil.

People had told him twenty-five was too young to marry, but he'd known at twenty that he wanted her for his wife. Waiting five years had shown remarkable restraint as far as he'd been concerned.

In the photo, her adoration shone in her eyes. Admittedly, he hadn't seen that look for months, maybe longer. She'd become disenchanted, nitpicking the minutiae of their lives instead of looking at the bigger picture.

Her note had been a sharp, unexpected slap to the face. Last night, he'd planned to jump in his car this morning and drive down to Sacramento. But by dawn his heartache had hardened to anger.

She'd betrayed him and their love. Sneaked away and refused his calls. A bit hypocritical, too, after the way she'd complained that he'd left *her* when she needed him most. Not that she'd agree.

His office door slammed open, bringing an abrupt end to his musing. He didn't need to look up to know Jenna now stood in the middle of his office, fuming. Ignoring her would be a fun but unrealistic option.

He flicked a bored gaze her way. "Can I help you?"

She held a printout of the one-paragraph memo with two fingers, the same way she used to handle Gentry's dirty diapers. "What's this?"

With almost nothing but misery in his life, he couldn't pass up the pleasure of making her squirm. Wednesday night he'd held back for Sara's sake, but he would make Jenna pay for her role in Gentry's change of heart and its ramifications. As CEO, he could fire her now, and he might if she pushed too hard. "Sorry. I presumed you could read."

"Don't be a wiseass, Hunter." She strode forward and slammed the page on his desk. "You can't do this, you know."

"I can, actually. And I did. Haru can send you a copy of the bylaws if you don't have your own. Since you've never bothered to pay attention to the details, let me summarize. Given my father's memory issues and the fact that he's been advised not to work for at least another month, I, as CFO, am entitled—most might argue I'm required—to act as interim CEO until it is determined whether he can and will return. If, after one hundred eighty days, he cannot return to his role, then the board must appoint a permanent CEO. So, now that I've cleared that up for you, please leave. I have work to do." He returned his gaze to his screen, wearing a bit of a shit-eating grin. In the midst of a hellish week, this little win was long overdue.

"Are you trying to break your father's heart?" She crossed her arms. The desolate tone of her voice almost made him feel guilty, until she added, "Is this your way of punishing us because Gentry decided not to hand you her baby?"

Gentry decided, as if Jenna hadn't persuaded her to reconsider. Did she think he'd forgotten her initial, strong objections? He'd bet his 401(k) that Jenna had been planting doubts in Gentry's mind every day since she'd moved back home.

"No, Jenna. I'd never toy with CTC just to punish you, no matter how much fun that would be. I want CTC to survive and flourish. It needs leadership to do so, and without my dad here, I have to step up. I'm merely following the rules in place for the smooth transition of power when the CEO is incapacitated or otherwise unable to uphold his obligations."

Seeing her squirm might make others uncomfortable. Not him. He relished exerting this power over her, *finally*. His dad had always given her more say than her position should warrant. Now she'd be restricted to weighing in solely on marketing matters. Nothing more.

"Let me know when the doctors think he can come back to work. Until then, if there isn't anything else you need from me, please see yourself out."

Jenna opened her mouth, but his mother's surprise appearance stunned them both. "You two might want to lower your voices. I could hear you from Haru's desk."

"Leslie, perhaps you could wait with her until your son and I are finished." Jenna gestured dismissively.

His mom held her ground. "I need to speak to Hunter about something important, so perhaps *you* could step out until *I'm* finished."

"Something important?" Jenna mocked. "I didn't realize you did anything important."

Hunter shot from his chair, but his mother held up her hand. She approached Jenna, head shaking, eyes sober. "You never did. You've always thought that the only things that matter are careers and power and money and possessions. No one denies you've succeeded on those fronts. But while you were investing all your energy here with my former husband, I was investing mine in my children.

"You know my kids, right—the accomplished CFO and the former lawyer turned restaurateur? The ones who love each other and me? The ones who've proven they know how to love and commit to another? So let's compare my 'unimportant' work with yours. How's Gentry these days? Oh, wait, I know. Undereducated, pregnant by a man she doesn't even know, still living at home, and breaking her brother's and sister-in-law's hearts." She playfully punched Jenna's shoulder. "Nice job."

His mother lifted her chin just a touch when she finished her put-down—her beautiful put-down. Normally, he wouldn't want her to insult Gentry, but he was out of charity for that sister at the moment. He couldn't tame his smile, which only made Jenna's red cheeks more flushed.

With no ready comeback, Jenna turned on him, grabbed the memo, and crushed it in her hands. "I know Sara and you are disappointed right now, but you'll recover and find other options. Your father is sick, Hunter. Instead of supporting him, you refuse to make peace with Gentry, and now you're stealing his job. It's cold and heartless. If this stunt causes any setbacks in his recovery, you'll answer to me."

"If I'm cold and heartless, it's a side effect of being forced to work with you all these years. As for betrayals, he and Gentry cornered the market on those before I got in the game."

"You can't unilaterally stop the sale. Even with Colby in your corner, you don't have a majority of the shareholders," Jenna spat.

"I can't stop it, but I can slow it down. Don't count me out so fast, Jenna. You have no idea what might be up my sleeve."

He savored the moment of doubt in her eyes right before she grunted and stormed out of his office. He beamed at his mom, but her face didn't reflect the victory she should've felt after their go-round with the enemy.

She closed the door and then sat across from him. Such a diminutive little thing yet surprisingly tough at times. "What are you doing?"

"Working," he teased, folding his hands on his desk, temporarily buoyed by his fight with Jenna. "What are *you* doing?"

She shook her head. Instead of pride, her eyes filled with pity and disappointment. "Colby called me. Why aren't you on your way to Sacramento, Hunter? Do you want to lose your wife?"

He sat back. Of course Colby had told her. Openness was her "new thing" these days. His muscles twitched. "Sara left me, not the other way around."

"Does that matter? Is your pride so valuable?" Her cobalt-blue gaze lit with challenge.

The temporary high of his spar with Jenna ebbed. "Thanks for the concern, Mom, but I don't want to discuss my marriage."

"Look at me." An authoritarian tone she rarely used lent steel to her words as she tapped her index finger on his desk. "Do *not* let this pile of bricks and those spreadsheets become more important than your family or the future you were planning. Be a better man than your father. Go be a husband to your wife."

"I've been a good husband. I've loved Sara since the day we met and have done everything I know how to do to prove it. I've helped her family when they needed it. I didn't complain when she quit working. I've agreed to be a foster parent, given housing to strangers, and gone against my instincts when it came to Gentry's baby, and look where it all got me. Nowhere. I can't make Sara happy. If she doesn't love me for who I am, maybe I should let her go."

Those last words emerged as a raw rasp, as if they'd scraped his throat on their way out of his mouth.

"Honey, I know you don't mean that."

He didn't like being as transparent as the window at his back. Maybe he didn't mean it yet, but he knew, on some level, it was the truth. "Mom, seriously, I don't want to discuss this. And please don't interfere. Leave Sara alone, and let me deal with my own relationship."

She heaved a sigh and gripped her purse, which had been resting on her lap. "I could strangle your sister."

"Get in line."

His mom stared at him, waiting for him to engage. When he didn't, she stood. "If you need anything, you call. I can bring you dinner—and don't even start making fun of my cooking like Colby does—or I'll help with laundry, or whatever, until you get your head on straight and bring Sara home."

He walked around his desk and hugged her. "I'm a big boy, thanks. Besides, a little alone time might be exactly what I need."

Time to reflect.

She didn't look convinced. "You're going to learn the hard way that being alone is just plain lonely. Don't be like me, Hunter. Don't give up on the person you love too soon or you'll live to regret it."

"What are you talking about? You didn't give up on the marriage—Dad left."

"I *did* give up. Instead of swallowing my pride and trying to work through things, I let him go. I believed he was wrong and I was right.

I thought he'd miss you kids and me so much that he'd come running back once he realized his mistake." She shrugged while wearing a wry grin. "You see how well that worked out for us all."

"Mom," he said, a little shaken.

"I love you. And you know I've always preached that real love means being honest. You're a good man. You're reliable, you have integrity, and you get things done. But you aren't the most considerate son on the planet, and I suspect I'm not the only woman you take for granted. You might want to rethink your priorities." She patted his cheek and then left him standing there as she waltzed out of his office.

For a second, he considered snatching his keys and jumping in his car. Then Haru buzzed his office. "Richard Cortland is on hold."

◆ ◆ ◆

Sara pushed her niece Daisy on the swing in Mimi's backyard. Daisy's giggle rang out like jingle bells. It was almost as adorable as the polka-dot ribbons tying her ponytail and her sunflower sweatshirt.

Her sister's yard—actually, more of a tiny farm—would be any kid's idea of paradise. A grassy area within the four-acre parcel contained a built-in sandbox and swing set. The other three acres consisted of gardens: multiple berry bushes, an orchard, rows of vegetables and herbs, and a chicken coop to boot.

Their California ranch–style house was small and a bit rundown, but Mimi and her husband Tom didn't care about picture windows and quartz countertops. Their loud, gas-guzzling, rusty pickup truck had miles of love on it.

Her sister Katy, who lived in Reno with her husband and her daughter, Caroline, also led a relatively simple life like Mimi. Their baby sister, Kelly, was working at a public school an hour south of Sacramento, in Stockton, and dating a gym teacher—broke, but happy.

Everyone in her family defined success differently from Hunter. He needed to prove something to himself, his dad, and maybe even the world. And, apparently, he didn't need Sara to do it.

Mimi came back outside with six-month-old Betsy on her hip, jeans stained with some kind of baby food.

Betsy's angelic face, surrounded by golden curls, had ruby-red lips that broke into a wide, gum-filled smile. Sara's heart could hardly handle the cuteness.

Mimi smiled at Daisy. "You having fun with Aunt Sara?"

Daisy nodded and kicked her little legs, leaning back for another push.

"We're going to Grammy's for dinner tomorrow," Mimi said. "How 'bout we pick the last of the apples and make a pie?"

"Okay." Daisy hopped off the swing and ran to the shed to get a pail.

"Gimme the little bundle of love." Sara reached for Betsy with grabby hands and then smothered her face with kisses. Nothing in the whole world smelled as sweet as a baby. "They're precious, Mimi. You're so incredibly lucky."

A small wave of envy threatened to ruin the moment, but she rode it out and let it wash away.

"I know." Her face crinkled a little. "I'm really sorry about Gentry's change of heart."

"Me too." Sara blinked twice to stop the tears from welling. "But it could be for the best. Hunter was never really on board."

"Why do you say that?" Her sister leaned against one of the swing set posts. Her shoulder-length light-brown hair blew around her face. They were barely a year apart, and although Sara had been a high achiever compared with Mimi's laid-back approach to life, they'd always enjoyed a good relationship.

"He went along for my sake, but he always thought it was too complicated, given the family dynamic. Looks like he was right."

"That's never easy to admit, is it?" Mimi stared off for a minute. "Then again, it's been a while since I've had that problem."

"Oh?" Her sister's disgruntled tone surprised Sara.

"Well, you know. Tom's laid off *again*. My part-time job at the yarn shop isn't exactly keeping us flush. Thank God for all this food we grow, because things are tight. I keep telling him that he won't find a new job by watching TV and moping."

"I'm sorry, Mimi. I had no idea . . ." Sara felt ashamed for the excesses of her life with Hunter. "I wish you'd have told me sooner. I'm happy to help."

Her sister waved her off. "I still owe you from the first time I borrowed money from you."

"You don't need to repay me. You're family."

"Thanks, but I don't like owing you, or Hunter."

Sara didn't want to be beholden to Hunter on that score, either, but she kept quiet. "Now that I'm back home, I can help. I'll watch the kids while you and Tom figure things out. Maybe I can help him find a job."

"You can't solve your problems by trying to fix mine." Mimi raised her brows.

"That's not what I'm doing." She hugged Betsy a little tighter.

"If you say so." Mimi glanced toward the tiny mobile home one hundred yards away. "So, what's your plan?"

"I'm not sure. Leaving was impulsive, but I'd run out of solutions. Maybe I can find some consulting work in Sacramento so I can be closer to *my* family. Lease a small place in the area." Sara stared off in the distance while kissing Betsy's head. "See how it feels to be single."

Mimi kicked her toe in the dirt and let a moment or two pass. "That can't be what you really want."

"Why not?"

"Because it's too sudden. You haven't given yourself or Hunter time to talk through the options. And it's pretty clear you've idealized what happens here in Sacramento when you're not around. Let me clue you in. Everyone, including Mom and Dad, is busy with their own lives and problems. We aren't still taking family camping trips all summer or doing the Sunday-dinner thing every week. Sometimes we go a month or more without getting together.

"If you move back here, you'll be just as lonely as you say you are up there with Hunter and his family. Maybe even more so, because you'll be sleeping alone." She crossed her arms, her tone softening from lecture mode to something pleading. "Besides, I've seen the way Hunter looks at you. He might not get it right every time, but he'd do anything for you. How can you leave someone who loves you that much?"

How indeed? "Grand gestures can't make up for the fact that I'm alone ninety percent of the time. When he is home, he's barely present. He thinks he hasn't changed, but he has in a million little ways that add up to a lot. And his animosity with Jenna is beyond unbearable." Sara stroked Betsy's hair and kissed her again. "The truth is, I'm not so sure he wants the kind of family I do. He's perfectly happy with his busy life and no kids. Biking, work, and sex are his three needs."

"Don't knock the sex part." Mimi wrinkled her nose. "Tom and I have stumbled on that one a bit lately, which sucks."

So had Sara and Hunter, truthfully. The baby-making efforts had taken a toll, and even since the last IVF, they'd had their ups and downs in the bedroom—and his home office. "Bottom line, our priorities aren't aligned. I want a real partner. A real family."

Mimi reached for Betsy, whom Sara reluctantly released. "I bet he wants those things, too."

"Maybe in some vague way. But CTC is his big passion—the center of all his decisions."

"That's nothing new. It's always been his baby."

Sara gaze drifted downward. CTC *was* Hunter's baby. A living, breathing thing that he'd nurtured for years. A family legacy he meant to leave behind. His dad's change of heart about its future had destroyed a part of Hunter just as sure as Gentry's change of heart had destroyed a part of Sara.

Daisy careered back to the group, white-knuckled grip on her pail, and captured Sara's hand. The exertion stained her chubby cheeks with a deep-pink hue. "Let's go, Aunt Sara. If you lift me, I can pull them."

"You two go ahead. I'll take Betsy in and put her down for a nap." Mimi moved Betsy's hand to make her wave. "Bye-bye!"

"Bye, my angel." Sara blew Betsy a kiss, then turned to Daisy. "You're such a good helper."

They strolled to the apple tree orchard and scanned the branches, searching for the last few apples. "I see a few."

"Up!" Daisy shouted, dropping the pail to the ground.

Sara hoisted her to where she could reach all but the highest ones. If Hunter had been with her, he would've been able to raise Daisy high enough to let her pick those, too. No one would suspect how good he could be with children, particularly when engaged in a project or experiment. It seemed a shame that he didn't have his own, even if he didn't realize it. "I'll get those last three."

"Okay." Daisy began methodically filling the bucket with the apples she'd picked.

Sara stole another glance at Lisa's funky tiny home. "Do you like having Aunt Lisa live so close?"

Daisy's nonchalant shrug suggested Lisa didn't exactly relish her nieces. "Lucas is fun."

Sara smiled, doubting Lisa would be happy to learn that her dog outranked her.

"When we were little girls, your aunt Lisa used to love to finger-paint. She painted everything. One time when no one was paying much attention, she painted Grandpa's car!"

Daisy giggled. "I want to paint a car."

"No, no!" Too soon she realized her mistake. She'd have to warn Mimi. "Stick to paper, sweetie."

Daisy scrunched up her tiny face and held up the bucket for the rest of the apples. "Okay."

"Aunt Lisa used to like to cook, too. Does she help your mommy with dinner?"

Daisy shook her head. "No, silly. But sometimes she comes and eats with us and takes our cookies."

"Well, I suppose I can't blame her for stealing your mom's yummy cookies." She tapped Daisy's nose, but was surprised to learn that Lisa wasn't spending more time with Mimi or helping with the kids.

When they returned to the house, Sara asked Mimi about it.

Mimi laughed. "We're talking about Lisa, right?"

"I know she's not the most proactive person, but when you ask, she'll usually help out."

"The way I see it, when you love someone, you should look for ways to help without the prompt. Especially if they're letting you squat on their property for free." Mimi shook her head as she measured the flour. "I'm tired of having to ask. She's old enough to be able to anticipate—to know what I need and do it, you know?"

Sara conceded. She thought of how often she'd stopped in to visit her mother-in-law, kept the pantry stocked with Hunter's favorites, bought birthday presents for in-laws without reminders, and tended to Jed when he got sick. "I know exactly what you mean."

After rinsing the apples, Sara began peeling and chopping while her sister started making the pie dough. Daisy's attention span didn't last. Sara smiled, watching her wander into the living room to play.

"I see that look on your face, and I worry," Mimi said.

"Worry?"

"I can't imagine how it feels to face the challenges and losses you've suffered to try to have kids." Mimi hesitated, and Sara could tell from her expression that she didn't know how to finish her thought. "But is it possible that some of the trouble in your marriage has more to do with your emotional landscape than with Hunter's behavior?"

"You think it's *my* fault?" She set the knife down.

"It's no one's *fault*, Sara." Mimi's face shone with empathy. "For two years you've given everything you have to one goal, and now your tank is empty. The fact that you and Hunter are dealing with that loss so differently causes tension, which is made worse because you've got nothing in your tank."

Mimi then walked over and slung an arm around Sara's shoulder. "Could Hunter be more attentive? Sure. But isn't it also up to you to refill your own tank? You could try grief counseling. Just a suggestion. Bottom line, if you love him and he loves you, there are other solutions you might try before calling it quits."

Sara eased away, picked up the knife again, and peeled the apples with a little more force. They worked side by side in silence for a few minutes.

While her sister rolled out the crust, Sara's phone buzzed. She wanted to ignore it but couldn't. Not when her whole world had flipped on its head. Resigned, she pulled it from her pocket. Gentry's name appeared on the screen.

She set the knife down again and froze. An image of Gentry sitting on the floor at Jed's feet flashed, bringing up the pain Sara had been sitting on. She almost didn't answer the call but then worried that something had happened to Jed, or Hunter.

She turned away from Mimi. "Hello."

"Sara, gosh, I expected your voice mail. I mean, I'm glad you answered, but I assumed you wouldn't want to talk to me."

Sara didn't have the strength to converse with Gentry about anything other than an emergency. "Is everything okay with your dad?"

"Yes . . . well, I mean, he's basically the same. More upset today because of what Hunter pulled, but that's not why I'm calling."

What had Hunter pulled? She almost asked but then remembered she didn't want to talk to Gentry. A conundrum, now that she wanted to know about Hunter.

"Colby says you left town. Is it true? Did you leave because of me?" Gentry's voice cracked. "I told you I'm sorry. I never thought I'd get attached to my baby. I swear, Sara. I never meant to hurt you or Hunter. Now you've left, and he's gone crazy."

She couldn't picture Hunter—the sanest, most controlled person she'd ever known—out of control. "What did he do?"

"Went all legal on Dad. Basically, kicked him out as CEO and took over. Something about bylaws and Dad being incapacitated—I don't really understand. My mom's furious, and Dad's pretty unhappy, too."

Hunter hated losing command of anything, yet he'd lost control of the adoption and of her. No wonder he needed to seize CTC. Even so, he'd regret humbling his father this way. Maybe not today or tomorrow, but one day.

He might be spiteful now, but Hunter loved his dad. He'd spent his whole life in service to Jed. The irony was that, as much as her husband probably believed he'd gained control of the situation, he didn't see how he'd lost control of himself.

Sara pressed her thumb and middle finger against her temples.

"Sara, are you still there?"

"Yes." She wanted to hang up, but something stopped her.

"Do you hate me?"

Her body flashed hot and cold. Only Gentry would put her on the spot that way. "Hate" was a strong word. One she never particularly understood. Betrayed, hurt, angered, sure . . . but not hatred. "No."

"Thank you." Gentry sniffled. "I know I've screwed up and hurt you, which is the worst, because, of everyone in my ridiculous family, you've consistently been the nicest to me. Will you ever forgive me?"

"Does it matter? I'm here, you're there." She projected ahead, picturing a future without Hunter, Colby, Leslie, and the rest. Wondering if they'd mend fences. Imagining not seeing Gentry's child born or raised, and not being involved in Colby's wedding one day, whenever that happened. Could she really live the rest of her life without seeing Hunter or his smile? Without knowing how he was doing or, eventually, whom he was seeing?

That last thought reached through her chest and gripped her heart.

"I thought you just needed to clear your head, not that you'd actually stay in California. Holy shit, Hunter will lose his mind if you divorce him. He'll *never* forgive me." Those last words came out as a frightened whisper.

Sara thought about what Mimi had said about Hunter's relationship to CTC.

Even if her marriage ended, she didn't want to see him destroyed. She didn't even want to see him hurt. She loved him, after all.

As much as she'd been urging him to let go of the company, now she knew it would be wrong for him. Colby would vote with him, but he'd need Gentry's vote to win. "He might forgive you if you don't vote to sell. He's given everything to CTC, Gentry. I understand how you've grown attached to your child. It's your right to keep your baby, but don't take Hunter's baby from him, too. Trust him to make it flourish."

"But my mom and dad—"

"Your parents have everything they could ever need, and so do you. Hunter will have nothing left if the company is sold." Her throat ached. "I hope you'll think about that, but I've got to go."

"Okay."

"Goodbye, Gentry." Sara hit "End" before Gentry could say anything more. Her throat felt raw. She set the phone down and stared at it, forgetting that she wasn't alone.

"You okay?" Mimi finished the latticework on the pie, carefully avoiding eye contact.

"I don't know." It hurt to learn Hunter was so distraught that he'd usurped his own father.

She had her family for support, but Hunter wouldn't turn to anyone. Colby would reach out, but he'd shut her out, too, unable to see how self-destructive his actions were until it was too late.

"Sara?"

Then something she'd never considered dawned on her. Maybe he'd shove all his sorrow down so deep the only thing left would be a hollow shell. A visage of Hunter staring at her with absolutely no feeling in his eyes made her knees weak. She sank onto a kitchen chair. "I honestly don't know."

Chapter Twenty-One

It'd been five days since Sara had left him. Ignoring his mom's advice, he'd been convinced that Sara would regret her rash move and return to work things out, so he hadn't groveled. In fact, they'd only spoken the day after she'd left.

"I'm sorry I left the way I did, but I felt like I had no choice."

"You had a choice." They both had choices in this marriage, and if she planned to cast up his shitty decisions, he'd call hers out, too.

"I guess I made it, then."

He'd worn his heart on his sleeve long enough; now he'd hide it until the bruising healed. "I guess you did."

In the silence that followed, his heartbeat intensified until it seemed to be pulsating in his throat. He waited for some glimmer of hope—an opening that would signal a desire to come home. He'd take any crumb she offered, but he wouldn't make the first move. Not when she'd been the one to tear it all apart.

She finally spoke . . . more of a whisper, really. "I don't want to argue anymore. We both deserve better. We deserve to be happy."

"Are you happy now?"

"Not yet."

Just like that, hope died. "Sounds like you've made up your mind, so I won't fight you. You want to separate? I'll pack your things and send them to you. You want a divorce? I'll give you whatever you need to be 'happy.'"

"Hunter . . ."

"What? Is that wrong, too? Am I not giving you what you asked for? Sorry I'm not perfect. Sorry I can't read your mind. Sorry that the ways that I've loved you haven't been the exact ways that you've needed. But as insensitive as you think I've been this past year, at least I didn't quit on us." He hung up, unwilling to prolong the painful confrontation.

Unable to process the reality of his crumbling marriage.

Unprepared to face a future without Sara.

With each passing day, the truth sank in. Sara meant every word in that note, and she probably wasn't coming back. The pain of that reality had carved near-permanent frown lines around his mouth and eyes. If his marriage were his only personal relationship in crisis, he might be able to eat or sleep.

Unfortunately, it had also been five days since he'd ousted his father as CEO. The initial thrill of one-upmanship had faded. He couldn't put a name to the mash of emotions that hijacked his soul. The only good outcome of what he'd done was the fact that Jenna steered clear of him.

His power play had shifted the mood of the office, provoking whispers among the employees. Now that he had Pure Food's formal letter of intent in hand, he'd be derelict if he sat on it. Besides, holding off on a board vote would only tighten the knot in his stomach.

"Are you sure you want to do this today?" Bethany handed him the stack of bound pro formas he'd requested. "You're in control now. Why not stall until you have deal terms from King Cola?"

"I have to do right by the company, the employees, and the shareholders. If I can't do that, I don't deserve the title." He didn't look forward to facing his father today, whom he hadn't seen since the blowup with Gentry. Colby had kept him apprised of his dad's condition, which had neither improved nor deteriorated. Hunter had expected a call after the argument with Jenna, but his dad had gone underground. "I'll round back with you after the meeting."

"Good luck. I'm pulling for you. I'm sorry Sara isn't here for support, but if things don't go well, and you need a shoulder—"

He raised his hand. "I'll be fine."

A lie, but in this instance, it worked. No need for her to think he couldn't handle himself, or to give her false hope that Sara's absence left an opening for something more personal than their collegial rapport, if that's even what she wanted.

He raised the stack of materials. "Here goes nothing."

"I have faith, Hunter. CTC has to remain a Cabot family business."

He nodded, hoping her faith would be satisfied.

Haru knocked on the doorframe. "Excuse me. Everyone's in the conference room when you're ready."

He nodded sharply, then forced his feet to move. Along the way to the conference room, people watched and whispered. His father's arrival had heralded a lot of speculation. Hunter wasn't ashamed of the decision he'd made regarding the bylaws, only of the way he'd gone about it. He should've talked to his father first—another mistake to add to a growing list.

His father caught his eye through the glass wall before Hunter entered the room. He'd taken his normal seat at one end of the table, flanked by Jenna and Gentry. Hunter almost stumbled, having forgotten that he'd also be dealing with his sister today. He wondered if she even cared about the damage she'd left in her wake.

Stay calm.

"Dad," he said upon entering the room. Standing a short distance from him, he asked, "How are you?"

"I've been better." His father laid his hands flat on the table, staring at him with no small amount of resentment. "I'm surprised you invited us here so quickly after hearing from Pure."

"Are you? And here I thought *my* loyalty to the family and company had been proven year after year after year." His snappish tone could be blamed equally on his sleepless week and his own hurt feelings. He couldn't bring himself to acknowledge Gentry or Jenna.

At least he had Colby on his side. She and Alec had been checking in on him daily, quietly reminding him he wasn't *completely* alone. He kissed her hello and took the seat at the opposite end of the table, facing his father.

"Let's just vote so we can leave," Jenna said.

"Hold up." He kept his gaze on his dad. "There's more to examine than just looking at Pure's offer."

"Is there?" His dad sat back and crossed his arms. "I'm almost afraid to learn what else you've been up to this week."

Hunter met his father's leery gaze.

"As you know, I've no interest in selling. I believe in this company and its future." He took a breath, looking at Colby because he needed to see a friendly face.

"We've *all* heard this song and dance," Jenna said, but his dad covered her hand with his to back her down.

"Last year I'd brought up the idea of ready-made tea, but you put me off. For the past several few weeks, I've done additional research and had some off-book discussions with King Cola. I haven't had enough time to nail down specifics, but KC is exploring the possibility of a partnership of its bottling division with CTC to produce ready-to-drink iced tea."

His dad waved him off. "Hunter, a whole new product line is a monumental undertaking."

"It would be if we were going it alone, but pairing up with a bottler and its distribution infrastructure makes it less risky. The compounded annual growth rate of this billion-dollar market in the past five years was sixteen percent. In North America, eighty percent of tea drinkers drink iced tea. This continent is also the fastest-growing region for ready-to-drink tea. Doing this will not only diversify CTC's revenue stream but also give us a big boost in a high-growth market."

"Why would King Cola be interested?" Jenna asked.

"The soda market is losing ground due to increased health concerns and shifts in consumer habits. Noncarbonated drinks, like water and sports drinks, are gaining market share. King Cola doesn't have a tea product or expertise, while we have a nationally recognized name and beloved flavors. It's a perfect marriage." Not long ago he believed himself an expert on perfect marriages, he thought dimly.

"It's still risky. The Pure deal is money in our pockets today." His dad leaned forward. "As you've made abundantly clear, I'm not in a position to lead this company, am I? So why should I care about this idea?"

"Everyone, including me, hopes you'll be back here soon." That was an undeniable fact. "If you don't want to come back in a full-time capacity, I'm ready to lead, Dad. Let me take us to the next level."

Jenna rolled her eyes.

"That's unnecessary, Jenna." Colby leaned forward. "Hunter's dedicated himself to this place and its future. We owe it to him to consider his plan without dismissive eye rolls and pouting."

"Thank you." Hunter squeezed her hand. "After Pure's due diligence review—"

"Which you sabotaged," Jenna interrupted.

He ignored her, keeping his gaze on his father. "Pure has revised its offer down to one hundred twenty million. You said at the outset that, if they materially changed the initial offer of one hundred forty, it wouldn't be a slam dunk. And now, if we hold on to the company and make a deal with King Cola, the value of the company should increase by twenty percent in a few years, maybe more. Why let Pure buy us cheap and waltz off with that value?" He passed out the projections and analyses he and Bethany had put together, which included a side-by-side comparison with the Pure deal. "Take a few minutes and look at these numbers."

He noticed Gentry eyeing him, but she didn't flip through the spreadsheets. She wouldn't be able to read them, anyway, so he supposed it didn't matter.

He met her gaze and held it, hiding any emotion. He hated the fact that he needed her today, but she was the tiebreaker. He wanted this so badly he was tempted to kiss her ass. Then he thought of Sara's pain—of his failed marriage—and he couldn't do it.

"I think this is an exciting idea." Colby closed the binder. "I also have complete faith that Hunter can run the company."

"I don't." Jenna's nostrils flared. "This stunt he pulled this week shows a certain immaturity, don't you think?"

"It could've been handled with more sensitivity, but his rationale wasn't flawed. If I were general counsel and unconcerned with familial relationships, I'd have advised that he follow the bylaws." Colby grimaced. "Sorry, Dad. But the company needs a leader, and you aren't well enough now."

His father nodded at Colby, then sighed and looked at Hunter. "Let's be truthful. Our family has had a rough time lately. I've been sick, Gentry's decisions have had some harsh consequences, and now your marriage is in trouble. I'd like to think that we'll work through these issues, heal, and move on at some point—sooner rather than later. But right now, the wounds are fresh. Given what's going on with Sara and you, I'm not so sure you're in the right frame of mind to lead the business, let alone lead it through a major overhaul like this King Cola deal would require. And that's the other thing. This isn't a done deal. They're interested, but there will be due diligence and other negotiations that need to fall into place. If we pass on Pure and the KC deal falls through, then what?"

"I'm not just saying this because it's what I want, but I really don't think the deal will fall through. King's highly interested, but it's a huge company, and just like with Pure, things can't move at lightning speed. Even if it does fall apart, there are other soda companies and bottlers out there. It's a solid idea, and we're in a perfect position to pitch it," Hunter responded.

The room fell silent for what felt like a year. His father's gaze wandered out the window. Jenna impatiently tapped a pencil eraser against the tabletop. Gentry's head bowed, but her forehead wrinkled as if she was concentrating. Colby's wan smile indicated she was bracing for his inevitable disappointment.

He dad heaved a long sigh, then met Hunter's gaze. "I've always been proud of you and your work. Of your commitment here and elsewhere in your life. I know I've made you promises, and that I've let you down. I'm sorry about that . . ." For a moment, elation filled Hunter's lungs; then he saw his father rub his forehead. "But at the end of the day, I still think the safest move is to sell. Who the hell knows where the economy will be in a year or three? Right now we can all walk away with the money to do whatever we want. You can start something of your own, Hunter. Build your own legacy."

"So that's it." He couldn't feel his body. "You're voting to sell?"

"I'm sorry, but yes. I'm voting to sell." His father's gaze dropped to the table.

"I vote to keep the company." Colby pressed her lips together.

Jenna looked right at him. "Sell."

So this was it. Just as he'd thought when he first walked through the doors. All the work he'd done meant nothing. The sacrifices he'd made, and their costs, for nothing. Unexpectedly, he chuckled.

"What's so funny?" Jenna asked.

He lifted his pro forma. "This is probably the biggest and most complex business decision we've ever had to make as a group, and the deciding vote goes to the person in the room least qualified to analyze the options. The one person without a full-time job, who now, because she's about to be a mom, has a very personal motivation for wanting a windfall of cash." He let the binder fall before he stood and paced in a tight circle. "How does that make sense? In what kind of crazy universe should all my hard work and talent and knowledge count for nothing more than Gentry's opinion?"

"She owns as much stock as you do," Jenna snapped.

"I don't have an issue with that, but at least admit that she's the least qualified person in the room to make this decision."

"Stop it, Hunter." His dad coughed, and everyone turned to him. "We're not going to continue to tear into each other. I've always taught you that fair doesn't mean equal. I understand your frustration, and obviously you are one of the most qualified people in this room when it comes to understanding this industry and our company. But both your sisters will be affected by the outcome, and they both get a say. We've heard from Colby. Now it's time for Gentry to make a decision."

Gentry visibly shrank in her seat. He had to admit her lack of attitude today surprised him. He held his breath, waiting for the ax to fall.

"If we don't sell, I still get dividends like always, right?" Gentry asked their dad.

"Of course."

She looked at Hunter. "And those payments should go up if you're able to branch out into the iced tea business?"

"Yes." He stood completely still, every hair on his body vibrating in anticipation of her decision.

"You and Colby both have said that you think I'm good at PR, and launching a new product line would require a lot of marketing and PR, right?"

He rocked back on his heels, surprised. "Yes."

"Would you consider giving me a full-time job in the marketing department?" She sat up a bit, not looking at her mother, whose eyes had gone as wide as sand dollars.

"Would you be willing to start at the bottom—part-time, until you finish your degree—like I did?" Hunter folded his arms, unsure of whether he really wanted her here every day. He was still angry, and now he'd have to watch her belly grow with the child who was supposed to be his and Sara's. But she did own part of the company, and it might be a small price to pay to keep it in the family.

"As long as you don't plan to shove me in a storage closet." Her customary smirk popped into place for a second, but then she must've thought better of it.

"You'd start in a workstation in the marketing department, just like your mom did." He remembered Jenna from way back then, when he'd been a kid playing on the floor by his dad's desk, pretending to be a businessman.

"Then I vote for your plan." She looked at her shell-shocked parents. "Sorry."

No one spoke for a moment.

He ran his hands through his hair because he didn't know what else to do. "Thank you."

Colby grinned. Jenna shook her head. But most puzzling was the way his dad looked at Gentry with a proud smile.

"Well, well. I didn't expect this. Who knew you could negotiate?" His father patted Gentry's hand before looking at Hunter with a shrug. "I guess you have your answer."

He felt disembodied, because deep down he'd been expecting the worst despite believing with every fiber of his being that this was the right call.

"Dad, I truly hope that you'll be back, so together we can take this company ahead like we'd always planned."

His dad pushed himself up, wincing and rubbing his knee. "We'll see. We'll see."

Jenna sat still, as if paralyzed by her disappointment. His dad tapped her shoulder. "Come on, don't look like that. Maybe you should thank Hunter for the fact that he's created an opportunity for you to work with your daughter."

"I can't believe this." She looked at her husband with dismay and displeasure. It would take her a while to process the loss.

"Gentry, I'll let Ross Hardy in HR know to expect you tomorrow morning. Jenna, why don't you think about where Gentry should start, and get together with Ross to discuss it."

She managed a cordial tone. "I'll call him later, after I get your father home and settled."

Hunter walked around the table and extended his hand to his dad. "I know this isn't what you wanted, but I promise I won't fail. I'll make you happy that it turned out this way."

"I hope so, Hunter." His dad pulled him into a hug. "Maybe this will be a first step towards bringing the family back together."

Hunter patted his dad's back, still not quite reconciled with forgiving Gentry, and unconvinced that he and Jenna could ever be completely civil.

Colby gave him a big hug on her way out the door. "I'm so happy for you."

"Me too." He hugged her. "Should we celebrate at Gab-n-Eat?"

"I wish, but I have to get to the restaurant now. I'll talk to you later." She waved and followed their dad and Jenna into the hall.

Gentry stood a distance from him. "Just so you know, I didn't do this so you'd forgive me. I know you're pissed, and maybe you'll never be able to look at me without being mad, but I won't keep defending myself. I voted like I did for myself, and also because I think Sara was right when she said this place is your baby. It is, and you deserve to keep it, just like I deserve to keep mine."

In typical fashion, she breezed past him, leaving him standing there with his mouth hanging open.

When had Sara said that? Probably while complaining about his schedule while Gentry was living with them.

He strolled back to his office, his mind racing with thoughts about his victory, his sister, his wife. He should be popping champagne instead of sitting alone at his desk staring at his fish. He stroked the wood desktop with his palms and glanced around his office. His second home.

He'd always liked it here, but today, at the pinnacle of his career, it just felt big and empty.

He picked up the phone and called Sara, but it went to voice mail. He hung up without leaving a message. She'd hardly be pleased to learn about what'd he'd done this week. She hated his commitment to CTC and might even take his news as some kind of snub.

◆ ◆ ◆

Sara rolled up her yoga mat and wiped her neck with a towel. "That felt great. I'm glad I came."

"Me too." Lisa nodded, tossing her towel in the wire basket in the corner of the locker room before taking hold of Sara's hand and dragging her to the fitness center's café. "It's great having you around. Not as lonely."

"Lonely? You always act like you're having the time of your life."

"'Fake it till you make it,' sis." She paused to order two peach-oat smoothies, then resumed the conversation. "Oh, don't look at me with cow eyes. I'm fine. I mean, I live in a house that's smaller than your closet, and I haven't had sex in three months, but I'm fine. I like my freedom. I can pick up and go wherever I want, whenever I want. Maybe you should get a tricked-out tiny home and we could travel together!"

Sara laughed. "No, thanks. I don't need much, but unlike you, I'm not a nomad. I like a home. A place. If I stay, I'll need to start thinking about that, and about going back to work."

Lisa smirked, shaking her head. "I thought you'd finally seen the light and ditched the nine-to-five life."

"I don't like having too much free time on my hands." She thought about Colby's foundation and the Angel House. Leaving without warning or goodbyes hadn't been her finest hour. Ty's face flickered painfully. She sipped the smoothie, determined to focus on the present, and remembered her mom's plea. "Maybe *you* should consider getting a second job. It's a great way to meet new people. As for me, it'd be an important step in starting over."

She said those words but couldn't imagine a life, or family, that didn't include Hunter. Each day they'd been apart, seconds took hours to pass. He'd been so angry when they'd spoken on Friday. Almost taunting her with her hasty decision . . . not that he'd been completely wrong.

She'd thought to call since then, but each time she'd chickened out. Had she secretly hoped he'd miss her so much he'd come down here to drag her back and promise to find balance? Just like her sister, Sara was faking it, too.

"Yoo-hoo . . ." Lisa snapped her fingers in front of Sara's face. "Where'd you go?"

"Nowhere." She shook her head to clear the fog. "Let's get back to you. How can you be lonely with Mom, Dad, Mimi, and her kids nearby? Daisy and Betsy are the most adorable things ever."

"Mom and Dad lecture—you know, they talk about something like they're having a discussion, but really it's all about trying to make a point. Usually a point about something I'm doing wrong." Lisa pulled a lemon face. "I thought living at Mimi's would be fun, but she's never up for anything, always complaining about money or tied up with the kids."

Sara swiveled her stool and shot her sister a wry look. "Maybe you shouldn't complain about Mimi while you're parked on her property."

"I'm not freeloading. I babysit for her sometimes, and I've bought the girls some stuff, too. I'm just as hard up for money as she is, though, but I have a better attitude." She then waved Sara off. "You can't relate because you're rolling in money."

"Not really." Sara would trade that wealth for a family in a heartbeat. "Hunter's the one with money."

"You don't have a prenup. You could walk away with half of everything. How awesome is that? You'd be a super-rich divorcee."

Blood money. She had no interest in making off with the profits from the very entity that had caused so many fights with her husband. "No. I'd just take my own 401(k)."

Lisa's jaw dropped. "That's ridiculous. You were with the guy for fourteen years. You moved away from home, took care of him and his family, waited to have kids, et cetera, all because of him. He owes you."

"He doesn't owe me. We made those choices together. We were young and wanted to enjoy our marriage before bringing kids into it. We didn't know we'd miss our chance. Trust me, I wanted to marry him. I loved him, and I'm not out to hurt him."

"And to think you were always the genius of the family," Lisa teased. She slurped the bottom of her smoothie cup. "You know, if you ditch him, you'll be better off. I never liked him."

"What?" Sara's brows pinched.

Lisa held up her hands. "Okay, okay. That's a bit overstated. I thought he was bossy and arrogant."

"He's not *bossy*." She pushed her half-empty cup away. "He's assertive and confident."

"A know-it-all." Lisa shrugged one shoulder.

"Informed," Sara insisted.

"A geek with those retro specs." Lisa put her thumbs and index fingers together and peered through the circles like they were eyeglasses.

"He's gorgeous, and he rocks those vintage glasses." No one—*no one*—would look at Hunter and see anything less than sheer beauty. Was her sister blind?

"Huh." Lisa licked her straw to get the last drop of smoothie. "Well, if he's so great, then what the hell are you doing here?"

Sara met Lisa's wry gaze before glancing at the ground. "I'm not sure."

Lisa tossed her cup in the trash and gestured toward the door. On their way to the car, she said, "Before you go starting a new life thinking it's going to be so much better, maybe you ought to make sure you're really done with the one you're leaving behind. If you're gung ho about going back to the nine-to-five life, why not work for Cabot Tea? At least that way you'd see Hunter more and be helping him build the legacy."

Sara hadn't considered working at CTC since college. When Hunter had convinced her to move to Portland after graduation, his family had offered her a job. She'd turned it down because, although she'd been qualified, it felt like nepotism. She'd needed to prove—to herself and them—that she could get a great job without the Cabots' help.

As the years had worn on, she'd been thankful for that decision. Had she worked in marketing for Jenna, she'd have been in the middle of turf battles between her boss and her husband.

Now her marriage hung in the balance, and if working at CTC might help her and Hunter reconnect, maybe it was worth consideration—assuming Hunter was able to stop the sale, of course. And assuming that he'd welcome her back.

Did she want to go back?

When they got in the car, Sara pulled her phone out of the glove box and noticed a missed call. Hunter. He hadn't left a message. Still, he'd called. Her leg bounced nervously the whole drive home. When Lisa dropped her off, she ran into the house, grateful that her parents were still at work.

She went to her room and sat, cross-legged, on the rosebud quilt and stared at the phone. Two yoga breaths later, she dialed her husband.

"Is everything all right?" His familiar husky voice sounded so wonderful that her eyes started to sting.

"Yes. I just . . . I saw that you called."

"Oh, that." There was some kind of shuffling on the other end of the line. "It's nothing."

"A pocket dial?" Her shoulders slumped and she frowned.

"No. I just, well . . . I did it. CTC won't be sold, and I have a great plan for expansion."

She smiled, surprised by her own elation. As much as she'd resented his obsession with it all, she was glad he hadn't failed. "Congratulations.

I'm not completely surprised. There's never been any goal you've set that you haven't achieved."

He didn't respond immediately, then said, "We both know that's not true."

She supposed he meant the marriage, or possibly the adoption, but was too afraid to ask. She wished she could see his face. "Well, I know you might not believe this, but I'm glad for you. How will you celebrate?"

No doubt Bethany would be full of praise and eager to "celebrate." Would he turn to her, now that Sara had gone? The thought wrought another frown.

"Funny thing about that. I don't feel much like celebrating by myself. Besides, I had to make a deal with the devil, so it's not all cupcakes and confetti."

"Oh? What did you promise Jenna?"

"Not Jenna." He cleared his throat. "Her spawn."

"Your sister?"

"Yes, my sister, who surprised everyone by negotiating her vote in exchange for a PR job."

"Wow!" Sara wondered if her plea had swayed Gentry's vote. She hoped so. She'd like to think that, in some way, she'd ultimately supported Hunter even though he might never know it.

"Even Jenna was speechless." He chuckled. "That was priceless."

"How's your dad? I heard you removed him as CEO."

"Temporarily." She heard the defensiveness in his voice. "I stepped up while he's unable to do his job."

"I can't imagine he sees it that way."

"Listen, let's not bicker about the company." He paused. "Can we talk about us?"

"Of course."

He cleared his throat, then fell silent. "Actually, it's been a week. I'd rather talk in person. I know you're hurt and angry, and I get that you needed space, but let's not end everything with a quick note and a long-distance phone call. Let's really talk. Can you come home?"

Home. Hearing that word roll off his tongue sent longing tumbling through her. She fingered the pendant around her neck, the engraved coordinates beneath her thumb beckoning.

"Sara?"

If she wanted to end the marriage, she should stay put and send for her things. "I'm here."

"Is that a no?"

Would he be open to counseling? Might working together help? "I'll come home . . . to talk."

"Great. That's great. I'll get you a plane ticket so you don't have to drive."

"No, that's okay. I'll drive." She'd need her car to gather her things in the event she ended up leaving for good. She didn't say that, though. Maybe it wouldn't come to that, after all. Maybe this time apart had hit a reset button.

"Tomorrow?"

"Tomorrow's a weekday. You have to work."

"It's a long drive. I'll be home before you get there, I promise."

She smiled. "Okay. I'll leave around eight, so I'll be there around five or so."

"I'll be waiting."

Chapter Twenty-Two

Hunter knocked on Ross Hardy's door around eleven thirty. "Hey, Ross. Just checking to make sure things went smoothly this morning with Jenna and my sister."

"So far, so good. Jenna just took Gentry to get her set up at a workstation." Ross stood and extended his hand. "I meant to stop by yesterday to congratulate you. Great job. I'm glad we won't be absorbed by Pure. Let me know when you want to talk about hiring needs if this thing with King Cola happens."

"It might be good to get together sooner than later. The head of KC's business development is coming here next week to negotiate preliminary terms and partnership ideas for the venture. I'm guessing they'd handle all the manufacturing and distribution, but we'd need to staff the executives, especially marketing and brand-development folks. Why don't you and Bethany get together with Haru and block out some time on my calendar on Monday?"

"Will do."

Hunter nodded and then left, pausing at the stairwell between their offices that led downstairs to where the marketing team worked. He knew, for the sake of his family, he'd have to find a way to get over his bitterness toward Gentry.

She'd meant well when she'd proposed the adoption. She hadn't set out to devastate him and Sara. It was her baby, and he'd always known she might change her mind. It had to have been painful for her to wrestle with her doubts. To face him and Sara and rob them of the hope she'd initially given them. Logically he knew this, but his heart couldn't quite catch up to his brain.

He needed to stop viewing her as a mini Jenna. To see her as his sister, just as much as Colby, and to build a relationship with her that counted.

He trotted down the stairs and found her seated at a workstation near Jenna's office, slurping a large glass of OJ. "Hey."

Gentry looked up from the paperwork she was filling out. He saw his own discomfort reflected in her face. "Am I in trouble already?"

"No." He glanced around, all too aware of others' eyes and ears. "Walk with me for a second."

"You're the boss." She stood. In heels, she was only a couple of inches shorter than he was. He wondered if she'd be able to stroll around in that kind of footwear once her belly started getting big.

If Sara did come back to stay, it would be hard for her to watch. His heart ached for his wife every time he acknowledged that she'd never experience pregnancy. And he wondered how he'd feel when his niece or nephew was born, knowing that it might've become his son or daughter.

Shaking off those thoughts, he led Gentry to a small conference room and then sat back against the table and crossed his arms and legs. "I want to thank you again for voting with me. I also want to warn you that you'll have a hard time winning over your coworkers. Given your lack of degree and experience, many will resent you. Even if you had those things, some would still say you only got this job because of your last name."

"Gee, great pep talk, bro." She gave him a little "Go get 'em" punch.

"I'm being serious, Gentry. I'm trying to help you, so drop the act and listen. If you want to succeed, make friends, and win respect, you'll have to come in early, stay late, and solve your problems without leaning on your mom. I'd suggest you try to get Becky Miller to mentor you. She's got a few years' experience on you, so it'd be a good fit. If you can find ways to make her job easier for her, you'll become invaluable. Understand?"

"Are you sure you're trying to help me?" She crossed her arms. "'Cause it sounds like you're trying to scare me into quitting."

"I'm being as helpful and honest and *brotherly* as I know how. You're going to have to work twice as hard to prove yourself. I know, because I've been in your shoes. I worked my ass off, and it still took time before people believed I'd earned those promotions."

"Okay. I'll prove myself to everyone, including you. I know you don't trust me much, and I guess I can't blame you." She met his gaze, which had to be hard.

He gripped the table at his hips. "Let's not talk about the adoption. It is what it is, and I'll eventually be happy for you and your baby. I just need more time."

"I *am* sorry that I hurt you and Sara and caused her to take off."

"Much as I'd love to blame you, I can't. Sara and I have stuff to work out that has nothing to do with you." Having said more about his marriage than he'd intended, he pushed away from the table and dismissed his sister. "Now get on back and finish up whatever I interrupted."

She turned to go, then whirled around and hugged him—a quick, silent hug, except for the jangling from her multitude of bangle bracelets. After flashing a lopsided grin, she ducked out of the conference room.

Extending an olive branch of sorts hadn't been as hard as he'd thought. It had been the right thing to do . . .

In fact, for his dad's sake, he needed to go one step further. Inhaling, he girded himself before going to Jenna's office.

"What?" She glanced up from her computer screen.

He closed the door and took a seat. "We need a truce."

She blinked. "How generous, now that you've won."

"I'm serious, Jenna. We don't have to pretend to understand or even like each other, but we have to stop picking fights. For Dad and for Gentry."

Jenna sat back, her gaze glued to his. "Why now?"

"Dad's sick. Gentry's pregnant. I'm tired." He leaned forward. "Aren't you tired?"

"You've been at me for at least a decade. Sorry if I have a hard time trusting this about-face."

"Jenna, let's be completely honest. I'll admit that I've been a bastard at times, but you admit you haven't been the warmest stepmom. When Colby and I were children, you never even embraced us for Gentry's sake. I've always assumed you just wanted my dad for yourself. Maybe I'm right, maybe I'm wrong, but it doesn't matter. The bottom line is, like it or not, we're a family . . . a screwed-up one, but still a family. It's done neither or us, nor the people we love, any good to be at each other's throats, so let's lay down our swords."

Jenna stared at him for a minute. "I'll make an effort if you do."

"Okay. I'll let you give my dad the good news." He almost made a quip about her probably taking credit for the détente, but then reminded himself of the promise he'd just made.

"Thank you." She stood when he did.

He saw no reason to hug. Maybe one day this truce would lead to actual warmth, but he couldn't fake something he didn't feel. He simply nodded and headed back toward his office.

He planned to work through lunch today so that he could leave early, pick up flowers and dinner, and be home before Sara arrived.

On his way back up to his office, he considered the compromises he could offer Sara to convince her to give them another chance. The King Cola deal would be critical to his success, and starting up a new venture meant a lot of work. Right now he was juggling the CEO and CFO jobs. If his dad couldn't come back soon, Hunter would need Ross to search for a new CFO. In the interim, he'd have to delegate more to Bethany and Jenna, God help him.

But he would do all that and make better use of his time at home. Maybe Sara would bike with him and Alec. He'd ban working on

Sundays as much as possible and let her set the agenda. He'd even squeeze in time at the Angel House with her once a month, if possible.

He'd go back to the beginning and woo her all over again.

He was passing Haru on his way into his office when she stopped him. "I have someone from Trident Realty on hold."

It took him a minute to recall that name. The apartment he'd rented for Pam and Ty. This couldn't be good news. "I'll take it."

He went to his desk and picked up the line. "Hello, this is Hunter Cabot."

"Mr. Cabot, this is Bill Hitson, the building manager at Bridgetown Gardens. I'm sorry to call, but your name is on the lease for unit one seventeen, and your business card was also on the refrigerator."

"Is there a problem?" Of all days to be thrown a curveball by Pam, for Pete's sake.

"I don't know how to tell you this, but your friend is dead, and your son is here alone." The man's accusatorial tone galled Hunter.

"He's not my son. They were just people we were helping." He waited for an apology that never came.

"Well, I've called the coroner." Skepticism lingered in his voice. "Based on the paraphernalia, it looks like a possible overdose. I need to know what to do with the boy. The cops will probably have questions about the drugs, too."

Holy hell. He racked his mind for any information Sara had given about Ty and Pam but came up empty. He'd have to contact the Angel House. "I'm not familiar with her family situation or her drug dealer, but perhaps someone at the shelter where she'd been staying previously would know. Any idea how long she's been dead?"

"Can't be sure. It probably happened through the night. I let myself in because the neighbors were complaining about the kid crying all morning."

Sara would be beside herself when she learned of Ty's trauma. "I'll be right there. Don't let them take the child."

"I can't make promises."

"Understood." Hunter hung up and headed out the door. "Haru, I won't be back today. Cancel all my calls and meetings. Make my apologies. There's an emergency I need to take care of. I'll call later."

His mind and heart were speeding at a hundred miles per hour, thinking about the child who'd been sitting alone with his dead mother, confused and afraid. About how life could cruelly change without warning. How, despite Sara's urging, he'd been more or less blind to the hopelessness—the powerlessness—that people like Pam must feel to do drugs, or those like his brother-in-law had when taking their lives.

He'd been blind to his sister's marital problems. Blind to Mark's depression. Blind to Gentry's loneliness. Christ, he'd been blind to the significance of his own wife's needs.

And now a defenseless little boy's future was at stake. A future Hunter could shape if he chose to get involved. Hope he could restore—security he could provide—for one person. A purpose loftier than any of the goals he had for CTC. He nearly pulled over to handle the wash of emotion that poured over him, his body trembling from the onslaught.

By the time he arrived at the apartment complex, the police and members of the coroner's office were there. Hunter entered the apartment, searching for Ty, but a portly female officer blocked him just inside the entry. "Can I help you?"

"I'm looking for Ty, the little boy. Is he still here?" He looked over the officer's shoulder into the small living room.

"DHS took him."

"Dammit."

She raised an eyebrow. "They thought it best to get him out of this environment as fast as possible."

Made sense, but it didn't help Hunter's immediate dilemma. He turned to go, thinking about whom to contact at DHS to get information, but the cop stopped him again. "Hold up, sir. We have some questions."

"Get in line." When she pulled a sour face, he peered at her name tag. "Officer Folino," he began, putting a hand to his chest, "I don't have answers."

Her gaze narrowed. "Let's start with your name."

Shit. "Hunter Cabot."

"How well did you know the victim"—she briefly looked at her clipboard—"Pam Wendell?"

"Not well at all. My wife volunteered at a local shelter, the Angel House, which is where she met Pam and Ty. We decided to help them until Pam could save some money from her new waitressing job. I briefly spoke with Gloria, the director at the Angel House, but she couldn't provide any detailed family history. She said Pam cut ties with her family some time ago and didn't give Gloria further details."

"So you don't know where she got the heroin?" The officer made a note on her clipboard.

"No idea. Again, I was told she was clean and sober. I haven't been here since the day I dropped her off." He crossed his arms, his patience beginning to fray. "Now, may I please go and find out where they've taken the boy? My wife will be worried about him."

Officer Folino glanced toward the other officer, who was speaking with the coroner in the apartment. "We may have more questions for you."

"Fine. Here's my card. Call or come by anytime."

She eyed the card. "Okay, go. But don't leave town."

"I'm not going anywhere." Hunter jogged back to his car and scrolled through his contacts, looking for the number of Joyce Douglas, the woman who had come to do the SAFE home inspection. He got her voice mail. "Ms. Douglas, this is Hunter Cabot. You met my wife, Sara, and me several weeks ago when you came to our home in Lake Sandy to do an inspection as part of our application to be foster parents. I'm sorry to trouble you today, but I've got an urgent request and don't know who else to call.

"DHS just picked up a toddler in Clackamas named Tyrell Wendell because his mom OD'd. My wife has a relationship with that child from when she volunteered at a local shelter where he and his mom had lived for a time. I'd like to get some information about where he is now. We'd finished our classes, and I think we're certified to be temporary custodians, which is what I'd like to do. Can you please call me back?"

He sat in his car, staring at his phone, willing it to ring. Goddamn it, he hated waiting on others. He pressed his hands to his thighs to stop his knees from bouncing.

Hunter had to get Ty placed with them. He stared at his phone. Apparently, Ms. Douglas didn't check her messages regularly. He might as well do something productive while waiting for her call.

An hour later, he walked out of Target with a car seat, toddler clothes, and some books and toys. He'd finished wrangling the seat into his car when his phone rang.

"Hello?"

"Mr. Cabot? This is Joyce Douglas returning your call."

"Thanks for getting back to me." Never one to let niceties impede expediency, he asked, "Did you locate the child?"

"Yes. He's at the North Clackamas branch with a social worker named Ruth Matthews. They're trying to determine whether he has any relatives in the area."

"I'm of the understanding that he doesn't have family, which is how he and his mom ended up in a shelter. In that case, my wife and I would be happy to foster-parent him." Sara might not even want to stay married to him, but time was of the essence, so Hunter needed to play a bit of chess.

"I'll make a note of that and let Ms. Matthews know."

Not good enough. "Will she call me today?"

"It may take a little longer, but we will be in touch."

Still not good enough. "Today? Because you have all of our information. Wouldn't the child's best interests be served by placing him with someone familiar after this trauma?"

"Of course, but we need to verify certain things first."

Bureaucracy. "Of course. I'll wait to hear from you. Please call me on this number as soon as you know more."

He sat in the parking lot for a few minutes, watching moms and kids load in and out of cars. Because he rarely left the office during the week, it surprised him to see so much life going on all around him in the middle of a weekday afternoon.

One young mother hauled an irate toddler out of a shopping cart while she struggled to open the side door of her minivan. The boy's little legs kicked her, but she barely reacted, looking like she'd done that a thousand times or more.

How would Ty respond to life with him and Sara? The poor kid had been born with an addiction, suffered from a speech delay, and now had lost the only parent he'd probably ever known. What kind of start was that? Would he ever accept Hunter and Sara as parents?

Of all his goals and accomplishments, this would surely be the biggest and most important challenge he'd ever taken on. And the only one that he'd ever felt unqualified to handle.

Sara, on the other hand, was eminently qualified. She deserved to raise this little boy. She'd done research to help him with his speech. She'd spent weeks trying to get close to him. No other foster parent would have that bond.

Hell, he hated red tape, and he was done sitting around waiting for what he wanted.

Thirty minutes later, he sat in an uncomfortable metal chair while his nerves crawled under his skin. Government offices always had the same look and smell: stark, a bit dingy, not nearly enough natural light.

"He didn't seem to recognize you, Mr. Cabot." Ms. Matthews was searching for his and Sara's DHS application file. She wasn't rude, but she didn't move fast enough for him.

"I already told you his relationship is with my wife, not me. But our application is complete and approved. Ms. Douglas was supposed to call you. We're qualified to be foster parents. There's no reason for Ty to end up with strangers when there's another option."

"I appreciate your feelings, but we're still trying to verify that he doesn't have other family." Another firm reply. He wasn't going to get around her.

He edged to the front of his chair. "How long will that take?"

"I don't know." She set her hands on the desk. "Where's your wife?"

"On her way back from Sacramento." The less said about that trip the better. "She's been visiting family, but I expect her home for dinner."

"Well, it's nearly dinnertime now. Why don't you go home and I'll contact you once we've done our job. If everything checks out, we can bring him over tonight or tomorrow."

"If Ms. Wendell and Ty had other family, wouldn't the Angel House or other hospitals or something have that information? Both have intake procedures with emergency contact info."

"I promise I'll work on it as fast as I can." She studied the screen. "I see that your paperwork just came through. Listen, I know you're anxious, but I can't rush the process. We have guidelines in place to ensure that the children are protected. I have your card and your address. I'll update you as soon as possible."

He stood, recognizing defeat. "I'll be waiting. Thanks."

It was almost five. He was going to be late for Sara, and he'd have to give her the bad news about Pam without the promise of good news.

◆ ◆ ◆

Sara pulled into the garage at four thirty, having left Sacramento before eight because she'd awakened early. Hunter hadn't expected her until five, but she'd hoped he'd be here waiting for her like he'd promised. She told herself not to be disappointed that, yet again, he'd lost track of time at work.

She took her suitcase out of the car and let herself into the house. Having been away for a week, the familiar scent of home caught her off guard. Its smell—indescribable except for the hint of lavender cleaning products—was a weird but comforting scent. Definitely better than the wet dog odor in Lisa's tiny house and the cooking oil aroma of Mimi's.

Sara left her bag in the mudroom and walked into the kitchen. No dishes in the sink. No grime on the stove. He'd probably eaten every meal out. Or not at all. Unlike her, he'd never been a stress eater.

Launching a new division without his dad's help would mean he'd be busier than ever before. If she asked him to give that all up for her, he'd only resent her later. Besides, loving him should mean supporting his goals. Mimi had been right about a few things, including the fact that Sara had to take some responsibility for her own happiness instead of expecting Hunter to sacrifice his dreams just because her biggest one didn't come true.

She stood at the sink, staring into the gloaming at the moss-colored lake below. Leafless branches crisscrossed one another, obscuring some of the view. Crisp, dry leaves gathered in the corners of the stone retaining walls that stopped things from sliding down the cliff, and some made a nest in the fire pit. It had been months since they'd lit that up and sat beneath the stars.

She found a lighter and went through the glass doors to the patio, collected twigs and other kindling to add to the dry leaves, threw two logs on top, and lit it up. The crackling sound and smoky air immediately unwound her. Wine would help, too, so she went inside to see what they had. She'd just crouched to open the wine refrigerator when Hunter came through the garage door.

He stopped, his face lit with relief. Softly, he said, "Hey."

She stood with the refrigerator door open, feeling as awkward as someone on a blind date. "Hi."

"You beat me."

"Not by much." She gestured toward the patio. "I started a fire."

He took two steps, halted, then came forward with his arms extended to envelop her in his tight embrace. "I missed you."

She hugged him, inhaling his scent, luxuriating in the familiar warmth and strength of his body. They clung to each other in silence, almost as if either was afraid to speak. She had so much to say yet didn't know where to begin. Before she had the chance, he started.

"I have a lot to tell you about what's gone on, what's going on, and what might be happening in the near future. I know I'm not perfect—I'll never be perfect—but I can do better. I hope . . ."

"Slow down." She cupped his cheek. "How about we pour some wine and sit outside while we talk. I actually have some things I want to say first, if that's okay."

He glanced at the clock, then said, "Whatever you want."

He chose a red without looking, pulled the cork, and poured them each a glass, then followed her to the patio.

Above the trees, the first stars of the evening twinkled in the sky, offering her the chance to make a secret wish for a new start. They sat side by side in the Adirondack chairs. He swirled his wine round and round, taut face straining to smile, which wasn't a surprise. He had no idea what she wanted to say.

She gulped some wine, took a deep breath, and waded in. "First, I want to apologize for the way that I left."

"Sara—"

"No, wait. No matter how upset and hurt I felt that morning, taking off was hardly helpful. I could blame you, Gentry, and God, but I'm responsible for my own actions, and I'm sorry."

"Forgiven." He leaned forward, elbows on his knees, glass still in hand. "My turn?"

"Not yet." She rubbed her hands along the chair's arms. "Despite the way I left, the trip did me some good. I needed time with my family, my sisters. You know I love being with Daisy and Betsy, but more importantly, my sisters and I talked a lot about life, marriage, kids—everything."

"They think you should leave me." He stated it as fact instead of a question.

"Actually, no. They made me take a hard look at myself and the fact that I wasn't taking any blame for our problems." When he raised his eyebrows, she continued. "So while I still want you to invest more time in our marriage and to share more with me, I think maybe I've been expecting you to do the impossible. You can't take away my grief over the way my body has failed me and us and our dreams for children, yet somehow I wanted you to put everything on hold and solve that for me.

"I'm the only one who can come to terms with my limitations and accept that the future will be different than I'd thought. Maybe counseling will get me over the hump. In the meantime, I need to go back to working full-time so I feel useful and productive. On that note, I thought maybe you'd hire me at CTC now that you need to market a whole new line of products." She smiled, deciding a little joke might be needed. "I have it on good authority that I'm a wiz at brand management."

He sat back, wide-eyed. "I didn't expect that."

"I'm sure you didn't."

"My turn?" When she nodded, he set his glass on the ground and bore that beautiful gaze of his into hers. "I always suspected I'd be a mess without you, and now I know it's true. I don't want a future that you aren't part of. No matter what your family said, you were right about a lot of things. As much as I've always loved you, I've taken you for granted in lots of little ways.

"I've always known what mattered most to you was family—yours, mine, ours. Yet my behavior toward Jenna hasn't done the family any good. My ambitions have pulled me away from the people I love, especially you. I can do better. I want to do better—for you and everyone else. I'll delegate more so I can set aside my weekends for us. Once I get a new team up and running, I'll keep better work hours during the week, too."

"If I'm part of that new team, we'd be working together, like your dad and Jenna." Sara smiled, imagining working side by side with him to launch a new product line. Working toward a common goal would signal a new chapter in their lives.

"A week ago I'd have loved that idea, but now I don't think it'll work. That's got nothing to do with you. It's just—"

Her heart sank a little. "That's okay. You don't need to make excuses. I know marketing is Jenna's area, and you just hired Gentry. Too much family. Too many unresolved feelings."

"That's not it." He scooted forward and held her hand. "How about you let me finish? I promise—"

Then his phone rang.

"Please don't get that." She bit her lip.

"I have to, but I swear you'll forgive me when you find out why." He stood and turned away, mumbling into the phone for a few minutes. His voice sounded animated and light when he said, "That's great. Yes. Yes, we'll be here. Thank you."

When he faced her, he had a peculiar smile on his face.

"What?"

He knelt before her, clasped her hands again, and kissed them. "Babe, I have some sad news, but there's a silver lining."

"Is your dad okay?" Gosh, she hadn't even thought about Jed, let alone asked about him.

"He's about the same, maybe slightly better." Hunter inhaled deeply. "This is actually about Ty."

"Ty?" She recoiled, unprepared to handle bad news about that little love. Hunter's suddenly grave expression didn't ease her worry.

"I got a call from the apartment super this morning." He tightened his grip on her hands. "Pam OD'd sometime in the last twenty-four hours."

"Oh no, Hunter! That poor little baby lost his mother." Her troubles scattered as her thoughts all ran to wondering what would happen to Ty.

"I know." He stroked her hair. "I spent all afternoon tracking him down. I requested that DHS place him with us. I didn't mean to assume you'd give us another chance, but I couldn't risk waiting . . ."

She went still, blinking at Hunter, who remained kneeling before her. "You tracked him down?"

"That's why I wasn't here before you arrived. I'd hoped they'd let me bring him home, but they were still running down leads on any natural family and doing a boatload of paperwork. That was the social worker who's got Ty. She'll be bringing him here this evening for the time being.

"They still need more time to search for family, but if that fails, and we want to make it permanent, there will be lots of paperwork, inspections, and court dates. At least, for now, he'll be safe here with you. So you see, now might not be the best time for you to go back to work full-time."

She launched from her chair and against his chest, kissing his face and hugging him. "I take back all my complaints about your grand gestures, Hunter Cabot."

He kept her locked against his rib cage. "I'll be honest . . . I'm a little nervous. Can you handle it if we can't keep him forever?"

He eased her away so he could look in her eyes. That unpleasant possibility would be at least as painful as losing the chance to raise Gentry's baby. Yet she'd survived that blow and the failed IVFs. With help and support, and with Hunter's unconditional love, she could probably survive anything.

"Yes, because I know we'll have done our best and made a difference in his life for however long we have him." She kissed her husband for the first time in a week. He tasted like wine, hope, and hunger. "Thank you for not letting him be handed off to strangers."

"So you're staying. You aren't going back to California?"

"Yes, but not because of Ty. I'm here because I love you and you love me. With work and compromise, we can turn this marriage around and fall even more in love."

He held her close, swayed side to side. "Not possible for me to be *more* in love, babe. Since the day I met you, you owned every square inch of my heart."

Epilogue

"Don't panic. The ambulance is on its way." Sara handed Gentry a bottle of water as she forced her to lie back in the front seat of her car.

"It's too soon." Gentry's eyes widened with fear.

"Gentry, look at me. It's only three and a half weeks early. Everything will be okay. The ambulance will take you, and as soon as Hunter arrives, we'll follow behind."

"But your car."

"I'll deal with it later. We can leave it here and get it towed." Sara took deep breaths to calm herself now that the Saturday-morning shopping spree had turned into a birthing. Unfortunately, Sara had inadvertently run over a nail when parking the car and now had a flat tire and no spare. A hundred yards away, inside Posh Baby, there were several moms buying things for their kids. If push came to shove, surely one of them would know how to help Gentry.

"Oh God, Sara. I'm scared. I'm not ready. I'm really not ready." Gentry's face turned red as she clamped down against another cramp. "And I've messed up your seat."

Gentry's water had broken on the sidewalk, but now her wet backside was leaving an imprint on the leather.

Tears—frightened tears—leaked from Gentry's eyes.

"It's fine, and you *are* ready. Stop worrying. Focus on your breathing. Focus on happy thoughts." She stroked Gentry's hair. "You're going to be a mom today."

Sara's heart was full enough that she could say those words without pain or envy. The past six months she'd been Ty's mother. At first it had been rough. His trauma—his loss and confusion—made him withdraw and then act out. She and Hunter had hired psychological and occupational therapists to work with him. This past spring, he'd finally started to open up to them little by little.

Sara had recently talked Hunter and Jenna into letting her work part-time on the launch of the new product line, too. Between counseling, parenting, and starting to work together, her marriage had gotten stronger.

Pretty soon they'd go to court to finalize the adoption, and no family or other obstacle stood in their way. She could not be more in love with any child than she was with her little tiger.

Minutes ago, she'd strapped Ty into the car seat and thrown a bag of Cheerios and a banana at him to keep him occupied while they waited for an ambulance. He was kicking his legs and crunching away, blissfully unaware of what was happening in the front seat.

"Ty, you're going to have a cousin!" Sara was so pleased that the family was expanding and Ty would have one more person to love, and to be loved by.

He returned her smile, although she knew he had no idea what that really meant. In the distance, she heard a siren.

Gentry looked up, her eyes alert. "Oh, thank God. I know you're great and all, but I really didn't want to have this baby in your car with only you for help."

Sara chuckled. "Me neither, Gentry."

The ambulance pulled up beside them, and the EMTs soon approached. It took her a second, but then she placed the tall one with wavy brown hair and haunting green eyes. "Ian? Ian Crawford?"

He looked at her, perplexed. "Yes?"

"Sorry. We met at the Angel House months ago. You were just back from Guatemala and came to visit your mom. I'd been injured." She extended her hand. "Sara Cabot."

"Oh yeah. Good memory."

"Sara, enough with the reunion. This baby's going to come out while you're yammering." Gentry scowled.

"Oh, sorry. Oh! Ian, this is my sister-in-law, Gentry." She grinned, having always wanted Gentry to meet a nice man like him. "She's in labor."

He smiled at them. "I see that. Why don't you let me in there?"

Sara stepped aside, embarrassed. "Of course."

While the EMTs were transferring Gentry to the ambulance, Hunter arrived. He stopped to say something to his sister, then came around to Sara and Ty. "Not Gentry's typical shopping spree."

Laughing, she hugged him. "No. And now my car needs a new tire. I didn't want to wait for roadside assistance in case Gentry needed me to go with her."

"You go. I'll stay with Ty and get the car towed. We'll come join everyone at the hospital after." He leaned down and tugged on Ty's foot. "You ready for an adventure with Daddy?"

Ty nodded and smashed more banana in his mouth. The sound of Gentry shouting made them all turn and look.

"I'd better go keep her calm. See you later." Sara kissed both her boys goodbye and then went to the ambulance.

◆ ◆ ◆

Six hours later, the family gathered in Gentry's room to meet the newest member of the family, Colton Cabot—Colt, for short. He had a mop of black hair and deep-blue eyes, although she knew those eyes might change color within the coming days. His coloring was more olive toned than Gentry's, so he must look like the elusive Smith.

On some level, it saddened Sara to know that Gentry's child would never know his father, and that Smith had no idea he had a son. And although the tiniest pang of regret tightened her chest when she thought about how Colt might have been hers to raise, it vanished when she saw the glow in Gentry's green eyes as she held her son.

"He's beautiful, Gentry," Sara said, her vision blurred from tears. She clutched Hunter's belt. "Beautiful."

Hunter had Ty on his hip. He leaned down to kiss his sister's head and let Ty get a closer look at his cousin. "Ty, meet Aunt Gentry's son, Colt. You'll teach him how to play with blocks one day."

"Bocks," Ty repeated, and Hunter buried his nose in his son's cheek.

Colby elbowed her way to the bed and sat beside her sister to look at her newest nephew, her new engagement ring sparkling in the sunlight heralding Colt's birth. Alec stood at her side, hand on her shoulder, as she cried and hugged her sister.

Jed and Jenna were arm in arm, proud grandparents. He'd been doing better, although he still had occasional bad days and periodic checkups. He'd returned to work in a part-time capacity to oversee the launch of the new venture with King Cola, which was on the horizon. So far, Hunter's predictions and efforts were on track to pay off as he'd promised.

Even Jenna and Hunter's truce had held since the big vote. No one would ever accuse them of being close, but the bickering had subsided, which made it easier for the rest of the family to relax at gatherings.

"We did it," Sara whispered to Hunter.

He wrapped his free arm around her shoulder and raised a questioning brow. "Did what, babe?"

"We made a happy family."

ACKNOWLEDGMENTS

I have many people to thank for helping me bring this book to all of you, not the least of which are my family and friends for their continued love, encouragement, and support.

Thanks, also, to my agent, Jill Marsal; as well as to my patient editors, Chris Werner, Megan Mulder, and Krista Stroever; and the entire Montlake family for believing in me and working so hard on my behalf. I've been eager to stretch into new territory, so I'm grateful that they've all given me permission to write these Cabot stories.

A special thanks to Liz Keogh, Katy Lee, and Jen Moncuse, who educated me about IVFs, foster care, and adoption, and helped me make Sara's journey authentic.

My MTBs, who help me plot, and my Beta Babes (Katherine, Suzanne, and Tami) are the best, having provided invaluable input on various drafts of this manuscript. Also, thank you to Laura Moore and Lisa Creane for your thoughtful feedback and insight into what wasn't working with the early drafts.

And I can't leave out the wonderful members of my CTRWA chapter, especially my MTBs. Year after year, all the CTRWA members provide endless hours of support, feedback, and guidance. I love and thank them for that.

Finally, and most important, thank you, readers, for making my work worthwhile. Considering all your options, I'm honored by your choice to spend your time with me.

SNEAK PEEK

When You Knew
(The Cabots, Book 3)

We know what we are, but know not what we may be.

—*Shakespeare*

Chapter One

Gentry's Wordplay

Colic:

According to *Merriam-Webster*—a condition marked by recurrent episodes of prolonged and uncontrollable crying and irritability in an otherwise healthy infant that is of unknown cause and usually subsides after three to four months of age

According to me—karmic payback for reneging on my offer to let Hunter and Sara adopt my baby

Colt had been screaming all evening, as usual. Colic, they said, although labeling it did nothing at all to help Gentry's infant son or her to live with the never-ending fussing. No amount of soothing, bouncing, rocking, or walking quieted him if his eyes were open.

She was alone and on the verge of a nervous breakdown, her thoughts as slippery as quicksilver, fueling the stress headache pulsing behind her eyes. Her son's screeching response to the doorbell, which echoed off the vaulted ceiling and plate glass windows, didn't help.

With her unhappy child bristling in her arms, Gentry raced across the living room—sidestepping a growing stack of unread parenting magazines—to reach the door before the visitor rang again. If she'd actually succeeded in getting Colt to sleep this evening, she might've shot the fool on the other side of her door for risking waking him. In fact, she might shoot him, anyway, just because it had been that kind of day, and her frustration needed a target.

She flung her door open, baby pressed to her chest, and gawked at her half brother, Hunter. "You?"

Hunter and his wife, Sara, stood in the dusky summer sunset. Wide eyes and slack jaws contrasted with their elegant Saturday-night attire. Were they stunned by her impolite greeting or by her shabby appearance? Probably both, she conceded.

Seconds ticked by before Hunter found his voice. "You're alive."

"Depends on your definition." Gentry retreated into the house, knowing they'd follow even though she hadn't invited them to visit. She couldn't shoo them away, but she didn't want them to see her strung out, either.

Expecting Gentry to fail was something of a Cabot family tradition. For most of her life, she'd been happy to live "down" to their expectations. In rare moments of self-honesty, she could admit that, at times, she'd even turned it into a game. An immature dynamic, for sure, but one that hurt a lot less than being ignored or than trying and failing. She didn't, however, want to be seen as a failure of a mother.

Colton was the only perfect, innocent, precious thing she'd ever produced in her entire life. The problem? She had no idea how to be a mom, let alone be a good one. Hadn't exactly had a great role model.

"We just left A CertainTea." Sara held up a to-go bag that smelled like curried seafood. Her signature smile returned, which complimented her simple summer sheath and shiny hair. Gentry smoothed the loose hairs that had pulled free from the ponytail, unable to recall the last time *she* had looked as sharp. "No one has seen or heard from you in almost three days. We thought we'd check on you on our way home and drop off some food."

Hunter and Sara lived about a half mile up the road. Their proximity had been one of the reasons Gentry had picked this unit. Its oversize deck and lake views didn't hurt, either. The only flaw was the cliff of a backyard, which descended to more than one hundred feet to Lake Sandy. Not the *best* play space, but that view! She figured the flat front yard and nearby park would suffice.

Sara set the bag on the entry table, her gaze homing in on Colt. Gentry almost wished Sara had held a grudge against her for keeping Colt, because Sara's graciousness inflicted far worse guilt. The look of love her sister-in-law gave Colt only made it harder.

"Thanks." Gentry's stomach gurgled at the whiff of real food. Getting to the grocery store had become harder than climbing Mount Everest, so she'd been making due with Ritz crackers, oatmeal, and eggs. A fact underscored by the empty red-and-yellow box tipped over on the coffee table.

Hunter stood, legs apart, hands on his hips. His owlish gaze roamed the living room, taking inventory of the remnants of what had once been a lovely, contemporary condominium.

Baby blankets lay strewn on several surfaces. The outrageously pricey Roche Bobois sofa cushions were askew. Two half-empty baby bottles sat on various tabletops sans coasters, and brightly colored baby play gyms, bouncy seats, and other necessities ate up a majority of the floor space. The pièce de résistance? The hideous white plastic sculpture—otherwise known as the Diaper Genie—looming in one corner.

If Gentry didn't already know that her brother's house never looked like it had been ravished by a monsoon despite them chasing after their foster son, Ty, the look on Hunter's face confirmed it. "What the hell happened?"

"Nothing." Gentry rhythmically jostled Colt, but he fussed and cried, heedless of how much she wished he'd stop just long enough to convince Hunter and Sara that she knew what she was doing. His tiny head bobbled against her collarbone.

She tucked her nose against Colt's cheek to smell his sweet skin and then looked into those inky-blue eyes—the color of a moonless night sky—and swore she'd do right by him. Somehow she'd learn, on her own, to be what he needed and give him everything he deserved.

Someday. As soon as his constant crying ended and her mental fog lifted. *Then* she'd finally experience the bliss reflected in every other young mother's face. Tonight, however, there'd be no bliss. At the moment, she'd settle for thirty minutes of peace and quiet.

Sara reached both hands toward Colt, soft smile on display. "Can I hold the little pumpkin while you eat?"

"And shower," Hunter muttered, earning himself a sharp look of disapproval from Sara. He raised his hands in surrender.

Hunter and Sara probably thought they'd make better parents for Colt than Gentry did. As much as she wanted to prove them wrong, right now she wanted that curry shrimp more. "Sure."

Gentry handed her son to Sara, whose entire face lit with adoration. Would there come a day when wondering if Sara coveted him a bit would no longer be the first thought Gentry had whenever she saw her son with his aunt? The thought wasn't charitable or fair of Gentry, considering how quickly Sara had forgiven her.

Forcing her uneasiness aside, Gentry retrieved the to-go bag from the entry table. Anything from their sister Colby's restaurant qualified as the best food in the Greater Portland area. Colby's boyfriend, Alec, was A CertainTea's chef and had spent years training in Mougins, France.

Gentry practically skipped to the kitchen, clutching the bag with greedy hands. Her brother followed her and waited while she reheated the food in the microwave—the one appliance her mom had taught her how to use.

"Gentry." He then waved his hand up and down, obviously unimpressed by her formula-stained robe, old lady slippers, and ponytail. "Are you okay? You seem a little . . . overwhelmed."

"You just caught me at a bad moment." She turned away, pretending to study the plate spinning in the microwave. He didn't need to know that the so-called bad moment repeated over and over, minute by minute, day by day, like a hellish version of *Groundhog Day*.

He tipped his head, eyes filled with doubt. "Will we see you back at work starting Monday? I hate to pressure you, but the ready-made tea launch is just around the corner. We need all hands on deck in the marketing department."

The family business, Cabot Tea Company, had entered into a joint venture with King Cola to produce and distribute ready-to-drink iced tea. Hunter had pretty much gambled the family fortune on the new product launch. He'd been growing more intense by the day in an effort to ensure the launch went off well.

"I thought the launch wasn't until October," she deadpanned.

His brows rode up on his forehead. "What?"

"Oh, for God's sake, Hunter. I'm joking." She snatched the plate from the microwave and grabbed a fork. He was lucky she was starving, or he'd have gotten an earful. "I know the schedule. I've been on some calls with my mom and the team."

Just not FaceTime or Skype—*God forbid!*

The first too-hot bite burned the roof of her mouth, but hunger kept her chewing. She heard herself purring the kinds of sounds that, in another context, might come from the bedroom—not that she could remember *that* feeling much these days. "Alec's the best chef *ev-ah*."

"Colby would agree." Hunter smiled for the first time since he'd arrived.

Gentry had taken her third bite when Sara came into the kitchen with Colt, forehead creased with concern. "I think he's a little warm. And this cough. Have you been to the doctor?"

Gentry loved Sara, but her worrywart reflex and preference to parent "by the book" added unnecessary stress to motherhood. If Ty's adoption went through, no doubt the poor tyke's childhood would be a series of very well-intentioned and warmly enforced rules and expectations, tutors, and lessons. Sara probably googled every little boo-boo, too.

Gentry didn't believe in raising kids that way. She wanted Colt to be a free spirit. To explore without limitations so he'd become a confident, interesting, outside-the-box kind of man.

"I don't need a doctor. Colt's warm because he's been crying all evening. That takes a lot of exertion." She chomped another shrimp. Honestly, it tasted orgasmically good. Was that a word? Well, it should be. *Note to self—check* Merriam-Webster.

"His cough sounds wet, but I can't tell if he's wheezing. You know, preemies are more susceptible to illnesses like RSV. Maybe you should have him checked just to be sure." Sara patted Colt while swaying with him, cuddling him like a beloved, if screechy, teddy bear.

"At eight thirty on a Friday night?" Gentry made a face. "The pediatrician's office is closed, Sara."

"What about urgent care?" Sara suggested with a hopeful smile.

"This isn't urgent. And look at me. I'm in no state to leave the house." Gentry ate the last shrimp with a bit of despair now that the plate was empty. If Hunter and Sara would look away for three seconds, she could lick the plate. "Besides, the people in that waiting room are *really* sick. Why expose Colt to those germs when it isn't necessary?"

"Good point." Hunter's surprised expression irked Gentry. As if her common sense was as rare as snow in Florida.

"What if I call Ian?" Sara's pleading eyes were hard to ignore. "He's in town . . . at a motel, actually. He can listen to Colt's lungs and make sure there isn't a problem."

Ian, the humanitarian EMT Sara had wanted to fix Gentry up with many moons ago, before Gentry decided to keep her baby. The same EMT who'd arrived on the scene downtown when Gentry's water had broken unexpectedly and Sara's flat tire prevented them from heading to the hospital right away. How fitting that her second run-in with him might be as humiliating as the first.

"Why's he at a motel?" Gentry wondered aloud. She recalled thinking him handsome, which said a lot considering the Freddy Krueger–caliber labor pains stabbing her when they'd met. Not that it mattered. Handsome men weren't a priority. The last time she'd dived into that pool—her one-night stand in Napa with a gorgeous man she knew only as "Smith"—she ended up with Colt. Now she hadn't the interest or time for men or, sadly, sex.

"I'm not exactly sure, but Gloria said something about his girlfriend kicking him out when he returned from Haiti." Sara had met Ian's mother, Gloria, because that woman ran the Angel House, a homeless shelter for women and children where Sara volunteered. "It's possible he doesn't have the security deposit to rent someplace new."

"What's he even doing in the country?" Gentry asked.

"Maybe he hoped to save his relationship." Sara kissed Colt and stroked his fuzzy hair, clearly less interested in Ian's story than *she* was. "Let's see if he'll come take a listen."

Gentry shot Hunter a look. He shrugged, which meant he knew that Sara wouldn't let up, and he wasn't going to argue.

"You're totally overreacting." Gentry placed the back of her hand on Colt's forehead, which did feel a little warm. Not scary hot or anything. She rummaged through the kitchen drawer stuffed with 1,001 infant gizmos. When she located the baby thermometer, she held it up and almost cried "Eureka!" Instead, she stuck it in Colt's ear until it beeped. "Ninety-nine point six. Nothing a little baby Tylenol can't handle."

"That won't help his lungs. Wouldn't you rather be safe than sorry?" Sara shrugged a shoulder to emphasize her point.

A quiet stare-down ensued for four seconds, maybe five. *Fiddle-flippin'-sticks.*

"Fine. Call Ian." Hopefully, the guy would laugh, and Sara would back down. Gentry reached for her son. Once she had him in her arms, she said, "Excuse me."

While Sara called Ian and conferred with Hunter, Gentry took Colt to the bathroom and dabbed a cool washcloth across his forehead. She checked his writhing body for a rash but found none. His nose was runny but not totally full of gunk.

Sara's concern niggled, even though Gentry seriously doubted the need to call in reinforcements. While she changed his diaper, she was struck by his absolute dependence on her judgment. His utter trust. *In her.*

Her poor son.

If he could speak, she'd know what he needed. Instead, she remained stymied, trying to decipher one cry from another. Trying to determine if his head, ears, or belly caused the ache that kept him crying. What? What? *What?*

She lifted him and swayed, humming softly in an attempt to comfort him and herself. In all honesty, at any second she could fall apart or asleep—a real toss-up. In the privacy of the bathroom, she blinked a couple of times to hold back the tears pricking her eyes, clinging to her child. *It's us against the world, baby.*

Either God took pity on her or Colt had finally worn himself out, because his crying subsided to a dull kind of whine. Gentry took a deep breath and rolled her shoulders back. By the time she returned to the living room, Ian was knocking on the door.

An inadvertent glance in the mirror set off a new shock wave of horror. No wonder Hunter and Sara had been stunned into silence when they'd first arrived.

She closed her eyes, momentarily imagining herself in her normal clothes: Gaultier, perhaps? Trendy high-heeled shoes that drew attention to her long legs and ankle tattoo. A multitude of bracelets on her arm. Her auburn hair artfully woven in a waterfall braid. The image of her old self enabled her to tip up her chin and pretend her robe wasn't covered in spit-up.

She opened her eyes just as Sara escorted Ian inside. At least her messy apartment would still look like a palace compared with the disaster zones he'd navigated.

◆ ◆ ◆

Ian hadn't known what to make of Sara's call. They'd spoken only on a few brief occasions, but his mother held her in high regard. He remembered their first encounter, when she'd been hurt by someone's abusive husband who'd barged into the shelter. Once he'd made sure she wasn't hurt, she'd shifted to the role of matchmaker, bringing up the very sister-in-law who now stood before him. The one he'd later met when she had unexpectedly gone into labor.

Hopefully, no part of Sara's agenda tonight involved playing Cupid.

He stepped inside the ostentatious, newly constructed unit, with its picture-perfect views framed by massive plate glass windows. This joint probably cost upwards of a million bucks. Like a reflex, his mind immediately calculated other uses for that kind of money: medicine, water, clothes . . . food. Or a donation to the EMT training facility he wanted to build in Haiti in his father's name.

"Ian, thank you for coming out of your way tonight." Sara led him into the living room. She gestured to the imposing man on her left. "This is my husband, Hunter, and his sister, Gentry, whom you might remember. And that little bundle is Colt."

Ian shook Hunter's hand, reminding himself not to nitpick these people. Sara volunteered at the shelter, and the Cabot family had started a foundation that supported a number of community-outreach programs. If they also thought monogrammed dress shirts and expensive watches were important, who was he to judge? "Nice to meet you."

He then turned to Gentry, who didn't look particularly grateful to see him despite the polite smile on her face. She sure hadn't primped for his arrival, he thought, holding back a wry smile. Clearly, she was no more interested in Sara's matchmaking than he was. *Good.*

Ian had zero interest in being fixed up with any woman. Especially not now, after being booted from his apartment by his ex, Farrah. His disinterest in women went doubly so with respect to an heiress to the Cabot Tea fortune, who'd likely drive him up the wall with her First World complaints and oblivious privilege.

"Sorry. I asked Sara not to bother you." Gentry's smoky voice could make another kind of guy a little dizzy.

If he *had* been in the market for a woman, she might tempt him. Despite the circles under her eyes, the ratty ponytail, and bathrobe in need of a serious washing, Gentry Cabot was a head turner. She was tall and proud, with striking green eyes and curves the robe didn't hide, and his body reacted like any hot-blooded man's should have. Luckily, his brain put on the brakes.

ABOUT THE AUTHOR

Photo © 2016 Lorah Haskins

National bestselling author Jamie Beck's realistic and heartwarming stories have sold more than one million copies. In addition to being named a 2017 Booksellers' Best Award finalist, her books have also hit Heavy.com's Top 10 Romance Novels of 2015 and been selected as a Woman's World Book Club pick. Critics at *Kirkus*, *Publishers Weekly* (including a starred review), and *Booklist* have alternatively called her work "smart," "uplifting," and "entertaining." In addition to writing novels, she enjoys dancing around the kitchen while cooking, and hitting the slopes in Vermont and Utah. Above all, she is a grateful wife and mother to a very patient, supportive family.

Fans can sign up for her newsletter at www.jamiebeck.com, which includes a fun extras page with photos, videos, and playlists. She also loves interacting with everyone on Facebook (www.facebook.com/JamieBeckBooks).